PRAISE FOR JEAN
AND THE SONS OF DE

"Jean Johnson's writing is fabulously fre   wildly entertaining. Terrific—fast, sexy,   , and utterly engaging. I loved it!"   —Jayne Ann Krentz, *New York Times* bestselling author

"Cursed brothers, fated mates, prophecies, yum! A fresh new voice in fantasy romance, Jean Johnson spins an intriguing tale of destiny and magic."   —Robin D. Owens, RITA Award–winning author

"What a debut! I have to say it is a must-read for those who enjoy fantasy and romance . . . Jean Johnson can't write them fast enough for me!"   —*The Best Reviews*

"A paranormal adventure series that will appeal to fantasy and historical fans, plus time-travel lovers as well . . . It's like *Alice in Wonderland* meets the Knights of the Round Table and you're never quite sure what's going to happen next. Delightful entertainment."

—*Romance Junkies*

"An intriguing new fantasy romance series . . . A welcome addition to the genre. Cunning . . . Creative . . . Lovers of magic and fantasy will enjoy this fun, fresh, and very romantic offering."

—*Time Travel Romance Writers*

"A must-read."   —*Romance Reviews Today*

"An intriguing world . . . An enjoyable showcase for an inventive new author. Jean Johnson brings a welcome voice to the romance genre."

—*The Romance Reader*

"An intriguing and entertaining tale of another dimension . . . Quite entertaining."   —*Fresh Fiction*

Titles by Jean Johnson

SHIFTING PLAINS
BEDTIME STORIES
FINDING DESTINY
THE SHIFTER

The Sons of Destiny
THE SWORD
THE WOLF
THE MASTER
THE SONG
THE CAT
THE STORM
THE FLAME
THE MAGE

The Guardians of Destiny
THE TOWER
THE GROVE

Theirs Not to Reason Why
A SOLDIER'S DUTY
AN OFFICER'S DUTY
HELLFIRE

The GROVE

JEAN JOHNSON

BERKLEY SENSATION, NEW YORK

THE BERKLEY PUBLISHING GROUP
Published by the Penguin Group
Penguin Group (USA) LLC
375 Hudson Street, New York, New York 10014

USA • Canada • UK • Ireland • Australia • New Zealand • India • South Africa • China

penguin.com

A Penguin Random House Company

This book is an original publication of The Berkley Publishing Group.

Berkley Sensation Books are published by The Berkley Publishing Group.
BERKLEY SENSATION® is a registered trademark of Penguin Group (USA) LLC.
The "B" design is a trademark of Penguin Group (USA) LLC.

Library of Congress Cataloging-in-Publication Data

Johnson, Jean, 1972–
The grove / Jean Johnson.
pages cm—(Guardians of destiny ; 2)
ISBN 978-0-425-26224-5 (pbk.)
1. Witches—Fiction. I. Title.
PS3610.O355G86 2013
813'.6—dc23   2013032752

PUBLISHING HISTORY
Berkley Sensation trade paperback edition / December 2013

PRINTED IN THE UNITED STATES OF AMERICA

10 9 8 7 6 5 4 3 2 1

Cover art by Don Sipley.
Cover design by George Long.

ACKNOWLEDGMENTS

I know that when the Sons of Destiny series ended, a lot of readers requested more of the Corvis brothers. More stories, more appearances, just plain more. And I said, "No." Mostly, I said "No" because I was not planning on writing any more stories wherein the eight brothers and their wives were central characters, the heroes and heroines of the stories. Then I snuck in a cameo of Koranen and Danau, and even of Morganen, into my anthology of erotically revised fairy tales, *Bedtime Stories*—specifically into "Snow White and the Seven Dwarves"—but they weren't the main characters there, either.

That's pretty much how this series will go. We'll see old familiar faces, or for those of you new to both series, hopefully they'll be intriguing people whose backstories you'll want to know. But they're not the main characters, and I know that may disappoint some readers. From my perspective, everyone has a story to tell. Sometimes it'll be an utterly fascinating, gripping tale. Sometimes it'll be a bit more plebian, or even downright boring. Hopefully, these new heroes and heroines will entertain you somewhere between the first two, at the very least.

Anyway, my thanks to my beta ladies on this, and to you, my readers, for being willing to try a new series. There are so many stories I want to tell, so many new and interesting people to meet and places to explore, I cannot always come back to familiar faces or stick around in favorite territories. But I'll always try to produce a really good story nonetheless.

Jean

ONE

Calm the magics caught in thrall:
Put your faith in strangers' pleas,
Keeper, Witch, and treasure trove;
Ride the wave to calm the trees,
Servant saves the sacred Grove.

WESTERN KATAN

Aradin Teral eyed the priest tottering with uneven steps from altar to altar in the Westraven Chapel, located in the heart of the Katan continent. Prelate Tomaso was ninety if he was a day, with hair not only white but wispy and thinned with age, a face with more seams than a student tailor's practice piece, and two canes to hold himself upright. Still, the man was revered by the locals, some of whom stood in the center of the eight altars. The rest, including Aradin, stood or sat on the benches placed outside the eight altars and watched while the new father toted his infant daughter from altar to altar in the priest's wobbling wake.

In accordance with local customs, the newborn was to be blessed by both the God Jinga and His Wife Kata at each pair of

Their four altars, representing the four seasons, four aspects, four this, and four that. It was an interesting religion, one of the older ones around, and apparently a conglomeration of two individual sets of worship combined many centuries ago into a single faith to unify two nations into one. Enough time had passed that the two different styles of worship for the local God and Goddess had been successfully and smoothly blended. Normally, Aradin would enjoy it, as he enjoyed learning about any manner of new culture or faith in his travels.

This time, however, he wasn't traveling abroad for the usual reasons. If he had been, Aradin would not have been in a large chapel like this, watching a newborn receive an elaborate set of blessings. The Darkhanan sighed under his breath, wondering how long this service would take. At the moment, the most elaborately decorated, flower-wreathed altars were the ones for summer, given the actual time of year down here below the Sun's Belt. Unfortunately, the age-stooped priest was only just now moving on to the blessings for autumn. Those would be followed by the rites for winter, and then spring, before closing the "year" with one last rite at the summer altar.

(*This won't do at all,*) Aradin thought. Not to himself alone, but to the Guide he bore inside the Doorway of his soul. (*He's kind and thoughtful and everyone respects him . . . but I seriously doubt Prelate Tomaso could survive a trip through the Dark. He'd be liable to die physically in there from the shock of it. That's never a good idea.*)

Teral shrugged mentally. It was all the older male could do, since Aradin was the one in command of their shared body. (*So we look at the next on our list. Or better yet, ask him who he thinks would be a good representative before their local Gods. Just don't mention politics.*)

(*I have to. We almost picked Priestess Tenathe. If we hadn't been there the day word of the Corvis brothers' claim for independence reached her ears, we would've picked a woman enraged enough to sabotage every-thing,*) Aradin reminded his Guide.

(*Yes, yes, I know,*) Teral dismissed, clasping a mental hand on his Host's mental shoulder. (*The Seers have predicted this Nightfall place will be the focus for the new Convocation of the Gods, if all goes well, and it is vitally important that Orana Niel speaks before the reconvened Con-vocation. But it's hardly our fault the Katani government cannot stand these Nightfallers.*)

(*Only the politically active ones,*) Aradin thought back, snorting softly under his breath. (*I don't envy Cassua, having to deal with the Mendhites. They've been seeking a Living Host since before the Aian Con-vocation fell.*)

(*Heh, feel sorry for our Brothers and Sisters who have to pick out a Mekhanan priest,*) Teral joked back, though it wasn't much of a joke. Official Katani policy might have been anti-Nightfall, but at least this was a civilized and polite land. The kingdom of Mekhana was not. Or rather, its government was not.

The priest's voice, wavering but rich with belief, rose and fell in cadences that were familiar, even if the rituals themselves were not. Both males could understand the words being said; Aradin wore a translation pendant, which allowed him to read, write, hear, and speak in a specific language—in this case, Katani. But while the actual words of the blessings and aspects being invoked were unfa-miliar, there was something soothing about being in a fellow priest's presence.

Then again, after having spent almost four months roaming this land, Aradin and his Guide, Teral, were becoming increas-ingly familiar with the Katani way of life.

Like Darkhana, Katan had a God and a Goddess. The priest-hoods of both lands accepted both males and females, mages and non-mages. Then again, both lands had a fairly even ratio of one mage born for every fifty without any added powers, their numbers more or less evenly divided among males and females alike. Of course, the Katani religion was a bit more lighthearted about some things, following in the wake of their so-called Boisterous God Jinga, who served as counterpart and foil for the more Serene Goddess Kata.

Back home, their God was Darkhan, the slain deity who had formerly been the Elder Brother Moon. Millennia ago, His highest priestess, Dark Ana, had bound her very life to His out of love and worship. When the third and farthest moon had been destroyed by demonic efforts, shattering His original power base, she had managed to salvage the God of their ancient people. Now, He served as the God of the Dead, He Who Guides Lost Souls to the Afterlife.

The high priestess' sacrifice had directly aided the world's effort to thwart an invasion attempt by the denizens of the Netherhells, and the upwelling of faith and gratitude had elevated her to Goddess level, forever bound to the Dead God. A new faith had been born, rising out of the ashes of the old, and the people of Darkhana had moved on. That background and its resulting mythos didn't exactly lend itself to an overly cheerful or buoyant religion, though the Darkhanan faith wasn't completely somber.

Since all lives, all souls around the world went through the cycle of being born, eventually dying, and of traveling through the Dark on their way to the Afterlife, home of the Gods, Darkhanan Witches didn't think of themselves as being the one true religion, or the only faith worth following. Their entire philosophy when traveling abroad was based around being an adjunct to whatever beliefs a person might hold while they were alive, and an advocate for that person when they were sent to the Gods for judgment on how they had lived their lives, whether that judgment would end in a punishment or a reward.

(*We celebrate life, and we do not fear death,*) Teral murmured, following his Host's sub-thoughts. The newborn squirmed a little in her father's arms, emitting a *mehhh meh* sound that said she would need nursing soon, but otherwise cooperated. (*So while this ceremony is going on a bit long compared to some we've seen . . . it's an auspicious day whenever we can celebrate life, even if it's in a foreign way.*)

(*Dark Ana, you're feeling preachy today,*) Aradin groaned. He stifled another sigh, since he didn't want to seem impatient or bored with the proceedings.

(*I'm feeling my mortality, such as it is,*) Teral admitted. (*Which is odd, because I died in my fifties, and not my nineties—as you well know— but I suppose it's just a touch of envy, seeing this aged gentleman still getting around, doing what he was ordained to do.*)

(*I should be so lucky, living to be so old,*) Aradin replied, irritation fading as quickly as it had risen. It had to fade; if it didn't, their shared life would have quickly become unbearable. Both men had lived together, two spirits in the younger man's body, for well over a decade now. Learning tolerance was one of the key requirements for being a Darkhanan Witch, if an unspoken one.

(*Well, you won't be* that *much older in a few moments,*) Teral pointed out, looking through Aradin's hazel eyes, (*because it looks like the ceremony is coming to an end.*)

Sure enough, as the priest's voice wavered and rose in a final benediction, the gathered worshippers chanted a mass, ". . . *Witnessed!*" that rang off the vaulted ceiling. Naturally, it startled the infant, who immediately began squalling. The father brought her over to the mother, who had been placed in a cushioned seat of honor at the center of the eight altars. While the new parents fussed gently over the infant, the deacon, a sort of junior assistant-priestess, urged all the witnesses to head for the tables laden with food around the outer edge of the church, food which everyone else had brought as an offering to the Gods and to the new child.

Not hungry, Aradin watched the locals mingle and gossip. He smiled and dipped his head in a friendly way when people came near, but otherwise dismissed his presence as being ". . . just here to chat with Prelate Tomaso" and "I'm in no hurry; I'll get to my business once you're all done celebrating this new life."

One of the older women sat down next to him after a while and proceeded to talk Aradin's ear off about this, that, the other, all of it local gossip about the family with the newborn, their family members, the history of the village . . . all things which Aradin had no clue about. Patience was another trait favored by Darkhanan Witches, as was politeness. Though he hadn't originally intended to become a Witch-priest, he had learned how to be patient, polite, and kind. Which meant listening to the elderly woman prattle on until her middle-aged daughter came to collect her when the post-blessing party began to wind down.

(*I'll be happy when we can get back to trading and talking herbs again,*) Aradin thought, smiling politely in farewell as the village gossip moved off with her family. (*Searching for holy representatives is rather tedious. Though I did like her story about her nephew and the pig down the well.*)

(*Only because we didn't have to help rescue it,*) Teral agreed, chuckling. (*Ah, I see through the corner of your eye that the priest approaches.*)

Sure enough, when Aradin glanced to his right, he saw Prelate Tomaso hobbling their way, using his two canes for balance and a touch of support. A quick glance around the chapel hall showed it was now nearly empty, and that the assistant-priestess had grabbed a mop and rag to start cleaning off the now emptied tables. Without fanfare or fuss, the locals had gathered up their food and their belongings and taken themselves out, leaving only a bit of scrubbing and sweeping to be handled by the local church staff.

The elderly man smiled a semi-toothy smile—several were missing from old age—and wobbled over to a spot on the bench next to the foreigner. With a few audible creaks from his joints, he sat down, sighed in relief, then turned toward Aradin.

"Well, well, young man! To what do I owe this honor? It isn't every day a priest of distant Darkhana comes to visit our far-flung land," Tomaso stated without preamble. His voice was light and strong with energy, despite his deep age.

Aradin raised his brows in surprise. He spoke quietly, not wanting his deep voice to echo off the walls now that there weren't any other noises to muffle and mask it. "I wasn't aware anyone in this region was familiar with my Order. Katan is very far from my home."

"*I* and not *We*?" the local chief priest asked, in turn surprised. He poked an arthritic, age-spotted hand at the broad-sleeved robe Aradin wore. On the outside, the robe looked to be a plain, sturdy, travel-worn shade of tan linen. The inside, however, was lined with a very tightly woven, stark shade of black. "Is this not the robe of a Darkhanan Witch-priest? The lining, I mean? It may have been sixty or so years, but I do distinctly remember meeting with one of your Order."

Aradin smiled wryly. "Forgive me. Yes, it would be *we*; and *our* home. I speak in the singular out of habit so as not to confuse the people in the far-flung lands where we travel. I am Witch Aradin Teral, a procurer of priestly paraphernalia and magical mundanities for the Church of Darkhana, and thus something of an emissary in foreign lands." He offered his hand, palm up and mindful of the older male's swollen joints. "You are Prelate Tomaso of the Holy House of Kata and Jinga, correct?"

"That is correct," the elderly priest agreed. He rested his fingers on Aradin's palm for a moment, then squeezed with a bit of strength. "And a pleasure it is to meet with you. The last—and only other—one of your kind I met was a Witch named . . . Ora Niel?"

"High Witch-priestess Orana Niel, yes; Ora is her nickname . . . and now that you mention her, I am not surprised you would remember her and her Guide after all these years," Aradin chuckled wryly. He gestured at the study around them, and the land beyond. "I am actually in Katan on her behalf."

"Oh, indeed? How fares the young lady?" Tomaso asked.

Considering the "young" lady in question was technically older than both of them combined, Aradin grinned ruefully at the label. "Still more than a match for any man or woman alive, and still as young-looking and lovely as ever. That is, the last I saw her, which was . . . two full turns of Brother Moon ago, if I remember right. As for the reason why I am here, I was—sorry, *we*—were wondering if you could help us with a little quest we're on?"

"Well, that would depend upon the nature of the request, of course," the Prelate cautioned. He patted Aradin on the knee. "But I'm sure it will be something manageable, or at least not too unreasonable. What is your quest, young man?"

Aradin cleared his throat, consulting silently with Teral on a good way to word their request. Finally, he sighed. "Well, we need to find a priest or priestess who would be the best possible emissary between your Gods and your people . . . *without* politics getting involved. Someone who has the holiness to speak with blessed Kata and Jinga on your people's behalf," he stated, nodding at the eight altars, "but also some level of authority with which to bring back the words of the Gods to your people, and have them be heeded. But again, without politics muddying the issues. The perspective of a . . . to put it politely, a bureaucrat, would only make the situation difficult to manage properly, and possibly make it prone to failure."

Tomaso wrinkled his brow in thought. He had plenty to spare, and the pouty look of his half-scowl was almost cute in a way. Brows working, he mulled it over, then asked, "Perhaps what you need is a Seer, not a priest?"

"That would be more of a one-way form of communication,

from the minds of the Gods to the mouth of Their chosen vessel, to the ears of us mere mortals," Aradin corrected gently. "That is also a matter of simple warnings of the future. What we seek is a two-way communicator who can work with those things we mortals already know about. An arbiter and an advocate. Someone who is used to speaking with your God and Goddess, bringing the concerns of your people to Them, and bringing back whatever rulings or prayer-effects They may choose for Their replies."

"Well, I don't know about rulings, exactly," Tomaso mused, scratching at his wrinkled, stubbled chin, "but if there's any priest or priestess in the Empire who speaks with the Gods on a daily basis about the concerns of their parishioners, and manages the sheer power of prayers on a daily basis, all without dabbling in politics . . . then it would be the Grove Keeper. That's about as far as you'll get from politics for a holy intermediary who also possesses a distinct level of authority."

"The Grove Keeper?" Aradin asked. He could feel Teral's confusion and curiosity alongside his own. "I don't think either of us have heard of that position before. At least, not outside of the land of Arbra, where their deity is the Goddess of Forests . . . and I'm not sure if that is one of the titles or not. What do they do?"

"He . . . actually, I think it's a *she* right now," the elderly priest corrected himself. "She is the Guardian of the Grove, a place which used to be the Holy Gardens where Blessed Kata and Jinga were wed, uniting the two main kingdoms of this continent into a single empire ages ago. Unfortunately, when the Convocation of the Gods destroyed the Aian Empire two hundred years ago, give or take . . . the Grove became a place of untamed, uncontrolled magics. Energies too powerful to allow pilgrims to visit or betrotheds to wed."

"That sounds like yet another location in need of healing," Aradin muttered dryly. (*Which means it is all the more imperative*

Orana Niel speaks at the Convocation of Gods,) he added silently to his Guide.

Tomaso continued, patting Aradin's knee. "If there is anyone who is an expert on judging the merits and turning the petitions of the people into the quite literal power of prayer, it would be the current Grove Keeper. If you will indulge an old priest in the lengthy process of rising and retiring to my study, I will see if I can find a map showing you how to get to the Grove. That is, if you are prepared to travel that far, and to face the dangers which make it an ill-advised place to visit for the unprepared, never mind the unwary."

"I am a well-trained mage, and a cautious man by nature," Aradin comforted him, clasping the older priest by the shoulder. Rising, he turned and offered his hand to assist the elderly clergyman to his feet. "And my Guide is even more careful than I. If it is not forbidden for a foreigner to visit such a holy place, then we will go."

"Forbidden? No, not at all," Prelate Tomaso dismissed. "But difficult? Yes," he grunted, struggling to his feet. "It is no longer the garden of delights it once was—one more tug, young man! Ahhh, there we go. This way . . ." Canes in his hands, the priest headed for one of the doors leading into the wings of the church. "My body may be getting old, but the Gods have given me a still-sharp mind. I remember your fellow Witch's visit. She brought the most lovely, delicate tea from some place in Aiar. A mountainous land . . . Cor-something . . ."

Aradin perked up at that. "Oh, yes, I've had a variety of Aian teas in our travels. And other things. Studying plants is one of my specialties. I'm always eager to find out what plants are being harvested and used in various ways locally for magical, medicinal, and culinary uses wherever I go."

"Heh! You'll find the Grove a terrifying place, then," Tomaso chuckled. "But before you go, I think I can find a tin of spell-preserved tea somewhere. Will you stay and have a cup, while I dig for those maps? And perhaps—could I have a chance to meet your, erm, Host? No, sorry, your Guide, was it? You would be the Host, yes?"

"Yes, and we'd be delighted," Aradin agreed, following him through the door. Privately, he wondered what the elderly priest meant by that quip about the Grove, but knew he'd either learn it in conversation or learn it when he got there. The polite thing was to let his host dictate their conversation. "Teral would be happy to meet you in person as well, so to speak. At least with you, we won't have to explain what to expect first."

Chuckling, the Prelate continued to lead the way, his pace slow but otherwise steady. "I suspect you'll have to explain it to the Grove Keeper, if she has the time to meet with you to discuss your request. They're usually wonderful people, the Grove Keepers, very trustworthy, but they're often far too busy with their duties to bother with learning about foreign lands and exotic oddities."

Aradin smiled wryly. "That actually fits in with what we're looking for. I can only hope she'll suit our needs."

Saleria, Guardian of the Grove, did not want to get up. In fact, a part of her was afraid to get up. To get up, face the unending labor and the burden of her day.

Earlier, she had woken under a nightmare of being bound in chains to forever wander the paths of an increasingly menacing, overgrown garden, one filled with shadows that moved and hissed in unnatural ways. The plants themselves seemed to have taken on a demonic twist, with the glowing red eyes, fangs, and claws of beasts from a Netherhell. As things stood right now, the Grove wasn't that far off from the dream. Not yet fully malevolent, but . . . unsettling.

She had finally relaxed after waking, taking stock of her normal surroundings, and had gradually drifted back to sleep, but now that it was daylight, she knew she had to get up. Duty demanded that she get up. She just didn't want to comply.

Her bed was soft, comfortable, and at this time of year kept cool by spell. The birds were chirping noisily outside the diamond-paned windows of her bedchamber, the morning light was bright and cheerful, and she could hear the faint creak of the plants growing fat on magic, warm sunshine, and yesterday's brief but thorough rainfall. But mostly she heard the birds twittering cheerfully. Noisily.

Groaning, she dragged the spare pillow over and plopped it on top of her head. That cut out the bright light and muffled the bird-twitterings, but did not disguise the sound of the door opening. Nor did it shield her from her housekeeper's cheerful greeting.

"Good morning, Keeper! It's time for your breakfast."

The pillows sandwiching her head did muffle her impolite reply, but didn't stop Nannan from tugging at the one atop her head. Saleria tugged back, clutching it in place. She got the covers ruthlessly stripped away instead. That let a bit of the early morning warmth wash over her lightly clothed body, a warning that the day would soon grow hot.

"Oh come now, Your Holiness," Nannan scolded, lightly swatting Saleria on the rump. The younger woman yelped, but the matron ignored it. "Time to get up and get to work. Those prayers aren't going anywhere without you, you know . . . but those plants might!"

Just once, Saleria thought grumpily. *Just once I'd like to see her be silent when she comes into my bedchamber . . . or not come in at all. Unfortunately, she is right about the damned plants.*

Disgruntled, she allowed the housekeeper to drag her out of bed and into a lounging robe so she would be decent at the breakfasting table. The food was hot and filling, vegetables and meat with a bit of cheese-toasted bread. Saleria did appreciate that she didn't have to cook it. She also liked how the bath was already drawn for her by the time she was done eating, and that she had a fresh set of clothes to slip into once she was dry—clothes which, like her bedding, were enspelled to keep her cool in the face of the day's rising heat.

It all made for a very nice change from her early days as an acolyte, and later an assistant, when all junior priests and priestesses had to do every little chore around a temple or a chapel.

Of course, such luxuries freed her up for greater responsibilities. She didn't have a traditional parish, nor a traditional congregation. So instead of heading to a chapel hall to begin the morning rituals—there were priests who handled that for her here at Groveham, on the edge of the Grove—she headed out the back door of her home, which abutted the wall guarding the sacred garden. Opening the tool shed, she grabbed one of the crystal-tipped cutting staves stored inside and surveyed the great wall ringing the Grove. Today, she chose to turn right.

Originally, there had been a magnificent entry gate, opened every morning by the Grove Keeper for pilgrims and petitioners. The Grove had been quite popular with visitors, particularly those who wished to be wed on such hallowed ground. Now, however, the gates were shut, with enspelled chains fixing them in place. There were other modest entrances into the Grove, but only this one was used consistently, and the others could only be unsealed with permission from the Grove Keeper.

Groveham itself handled the pilgrims who still came ". . . to at least be near the Grove" when seeking the blessings of Jinga and Kata. It stretched out to the west, down to the lake and the major trade river that permitted easy travel between the northern and southern halves of the land. The Grove occupied the center of a modest valley ringed by a wall made of costly imported stone, since the local hills were made of soil, not rock.

Almost every building was made of wood and plaster, save for the building housing the city guard, with its barracks for the men, a courtroom for formal judgments, and the prison cells for the infrequent misbehavior of the town's inhabitants and visitors. Even the Keeper's House was wood, save for the wall it shared with the Grove.

The Grove rated the same level of care as the Guard Hall; the original wall had first been a wooden fence, erected and carved with warding spells in an attempt to control the comings and goings of pilgrims. Prior Keepers had struggled to keep them out to be sure they didn't denude the local plant life just to "bring home something touched by the Gods." But wooden structures were easily destroyed, and that had made the Keepers import stone for a more stout barrier.

That had happened around three hundred years ago, and a good thing, too. These days, the mortared stone barrier and its plethora of embedded warding crystals were kept well-maintained to make sure the plants didn't go anywhere. Not because of pilgrims, which were not allowed in the Grove anymore, but because they might try to go somewhere else of their own volition.

It looks like the blackberry vines are getting out of hand today, Saleria thought, tightening her grip on the pruning staff. Imbued at one end with a collecting crystal, and the other end with razor-sharp, heat-treated spells, it was designed to slice through and cauterize anything it touched when held and activated. Mostly it was the plants that were warped by the wild magics streaming out of the three rifts, but sometimes the small animals, insects and birds and such, were mutated, too.

Extra-long, wickedly curved thorns flexed and curled as she approached, reminding her of her dream of clawed animal paws on the plants. One of the vines whipped away from its attempt to climb the wall, lashing at her. Saleria jumped out of the way and slashed when she landed. A second vine flailed between her legs, missing her ankle by an inch. She was grateful she wasn't wearing a skirt, and that her knee-high boots were crafted from sturdy leather.

Her clothes weren't standard priestly wear. Most of the priests and priestesses across the empire wore long flowing robes or gowns in white, edged with swirling curls of whatever the current seasonal colors might be. In summer, those edging colors were often pink and purple, hues meant to represent flowers. Their shoes were low-cut, suitable for temple grounds where everything was tamed and tidy, and they rarely wielded weapons.

Saleria's clothes were white with pink and purple trim, yes, but she wore a set of tightly woven trousers, a tunic, stout leather boots, matching gloves that covered her to mid-forearm, and a sashed jacket. The jacket was cut to resemble the robes her contemporaries wore, but it only fell to mid-thigh, not to her ankles. Each item was embroidered or carved with protective runes, most to protect her from attack, others to keep her warm in winter and cool in summer.

They could protect against, but not prevent, those attacks. She whirled and lashed again with the staff. A third vine lopped off with a sizzle of scorched vegetation, and a fourth fell as well. The rest of the vines quivered and backed off a little, cowed by her forceful attack. She marched forward, slashing at a few more that dared to reach for the outer wall.

Once they were cowed, she swung the staff around and touched the fallen vines with the crystal-knobbed end, siphoning off the extra energies. If she didn't do that, the severed plants could very well use their excess energies to set down roots and grow more of their kind.

Her job was part warrior, part groundskeeper, and part mage-priest. Not exactly something one trained for under the usual circumstances. Saleria was lucky; her father had served as a lieutenant in the Imperial Army as a young man. He had trained all three of his children to fight physically as well as magically. In contrast, her mother was a modestly powered mage who served the road-and-sewer crews for their home city to the south. Her sister served as an architect's assistant, a fellow construction-mage like their mother, and their brother had gone into the army in their father's footsteps.

Saleria herself had felt the call to be a priestess in her mid-teens, a decision she had never regretted. Her family hadn't, either; since she had chosen the priesthood, her magical education had been paid for by tithes and taxes, rather than out of their own pockets. Her deep belief in the God and Goddess had driven her to study hard, to ensure she would be a truly worthy holy servant. Of course, she had never quite outgrown the urge to stay in bed and sleep late in the mornings, but once she did get up, she did her job well.

A good thing, too. The blackberry vines weren't the only plants trying to escape the confines of the Grove walls. The marigolds were on the move. Rolling her eyes, she waded forward, swinging her staff with the enchanted end set to thump, not cut. Each over-sized plant came up to just above her waist, with a blossom as broad as her torso and leafy limbs that didn't do more than bruise individually. As a mass, though, they could batter cracks into the wall if she let them stray close.

The trick was to get them separated and herded away from the wall. Thankfully, they weren't intelligent; once pointed in a particular direction, they just shuffled that way until nightfall. They did, however, have to be kept away from the sunflowers. Saleria didn't know why the two flower species couldn't get along. She wasn't an herbalist, wasn't a gardener, and frankly wasn't certain if anyone would ever know enough about the oddities here in the Grove to control them. As it was, for two hundred years, the Grove Keepers had been forced to focus on the simple containment and magic-draining of the many plants and the sources of their warping.

Once the mobile marigolds were pointed away from the wall, Saleria continued on her way. Every morning and evening, just after sunrise and just before sunset, she patrolled the walls. The brisk walk did her good, keeping her fit and healthy, and so long as she kept up with the chore, it wasn't too onerous. Except she couldn't quite shake the unsettled feeling that lingered in the wake of her nightmare. It left her feeling dissatisfied. Disaffected.

Grumpy.

She didn't let those emotions out, however. No mage of her great power level dared work their will from unchecked, unfiltered emotions. Certainly not near such a great source of power as what was contained within the Grove walls. At three points in each day, Saleria had to attend one of the three locus trees, giant growths which had been grown in an attempt to contain the magics spilling out of the three hair-thin rifts in the Veil between Life and the Dark. Dragged into the Dark by the deaths of people and animals, excess magic flowed back out through those rifts.

Unchecked, unfiltered, and most importantly, *unpurposed*, that magic warped whatever it touched in ways a little too close to random for comfort. Unfettered emotions would only make everything worse. The north tree she attended after her first round with the walls. The south tree, just before her last round. The east tree she handled either right before or right after lunch, depending on how many duties she had around that point in the day.

Each trip took about an hour to tend the garden and siphon off the excess energy, and up to two hours to focus it and the energies collected by her staff crystal into prayers. Any modestly powered, competently educated mage trained in combat or at least self-defense could handle trimming the path along the inside of the wall and—on a good day—handle collecting the energies off the locus trees. But focusing it into fueling prayers in ways that were precise, controlled, and effective without unwanted side effects required a powerful priest-mage.

"You don't need an assistant to do your morning rounds for you," Saleria mock-recited from her last attempt at getting one out of the High Prelate for her district, Nestine. She kept her magic tightly under wraps, but her words echoed off the wall to her right, pitched nasally high in echo of her superior priestess, a thin, pinch-faced woman who had wielded her political power perhaps a little too long. *"Your duties are light, you have the time, and anything less than your best effort would be an indulgence!"*

She swiped hard at a branch in her way. *Never mind that most Grove Keepers last only ten or fifteen years before exhausting themselves to the point where they have to retire, and that an assistant would lighten the strain immensely . . .*

She slashed at a fern growing near the waterfall cascading down through a specially built channel in the wall, forcing it back. It shrank in on itself with an almost shy level of swiftness, making her feel sorry for taking out her irritation on the poor thing. Personalizing the plants could be dangerous. Here in a place where magic literally was a work of random will, a stray thought could twist things toward a particular idea, even make them real. Breathing deeply, she relaxed as best she could, clearing her mind, and continued across the little crescent-moon bridge fording the stream.

From up here, at the highest, easternmost end of the Grove, she had a good view of all three towering locus trees. Dark brown–barked and gnarled in their limbs, coated with leaves and moss tufts of a hundred different shades, they moved in subtle ways that had nothing to do with the wind, and everything to do with the power they struggled to contain. This close to the eastern locus, the creaking was quite audible. Loud enough that it almost hid the rustling approach of something through the ferns and bluebells of the underbrush.

Wary, Saleria waited. A minute or so after she stopped moving, something slightly larger than the size of her head cautiously poked its wiggling snout out from under the bushes. She held herself still, until the animal revealed itself one paw-step at a time. It took her a few moments to identify it, not as a rat but rather as a shrew. A very, very overgrown shrew. A creature known for eating three times its weight on a daily basis in its thumb-length size. This one was as long as her forearm, which meant it could very well be interested in eating all of her.

It leaped, jaws gaping in anticipation of a meaty bite. Her staff slashed down, cutting the creature in half. Side-stepping the fallen bits, she pinned the front half to the ground with the point of the business end, grimacing at the blood now staining the mossy ground. This part of her job, she didn't like, but she liked the thought of being bitten even less.

She didn't tap the creature's remains with the crystal end of the staff; that was blood-magic, and forbidden. Killing an animal for food was acceptable, even necessary for good health. Plants alone did not provide all the nutrition a human needed to survive on this world, after all. But to steal their life-energies for magical purposes, that was what demons did, not good people. It was one of the oldest of the Laws of Gods and Man, that animal sacrifice—humans included—was anathema.

Whatever scraps of life-energy that weren't drawn along with the animal's spirit into the Dark, on its way to the Afterlife, were reserved for the plants to absorb. The cycle had to be preserved. Plants gave life-energy, the power behind all magic, to all the animals, and that energy was returned when their bodies returned to the earth at the end of life. Stealing life-energy for magic weakened mages, tainting them with the demonic touch of the Netherhells. Only in very special circumstances would a mage—a good mage— ever spill blood, and usually only their own.

Once, early in her apprenticeship to Grove Keeper Mardos, Saleria asked him what would happen to the magics spilled when these warped animals were slain. His reply had been vague. Sometimes it seemed like the energies just returned to the plants in the usual, normal, perfectly sane way. Sometimes, though, it seemed to quicken the mutation of the nearest plants.

Yet another patch of Grove ground I'll have to watch for abnormalities. If I had an apprentice or an assistant, I could spend my time in trance, examining what happens to the flow of powers. But no, I'm not allowed to bring along anyone to watch my back.

Grimacing, she muttered under her breath another odious quote, mincing the words half through her nose, until she sounded almost like a buzzing wasp. *"Most powerful mages aren't interested in living a priestly life, and so all of our powerful priest-mages are needed exactly where they already are, with none to spare."*

Bollocks to that.

The moss didn't seem to be wiggling or growing or changing in any way. At least, not right away. Content for now that the body was truly dead, she nudged both halves a little farther away from the wall-edged trail so the remnants of the shrew-thing could decompose, returning its physical nutrients as well as its energies to the soil. Stepping carefully around the stained patch, she continued on her morning rounds.

Taking life-energy from the plants was normal and natural, a part of the cycle of magic. It could be used without harm or taint. But she didn't take it from every plant she met, just the ones that were threatening the wall or the path. Taking all the plant life forces would have been just as bad as taking the life of an animal, a needless waste.

Not that she had to take many, for nothing else challenged her authority. Even the southern locus tree more or less behaved itself, allowing her to drain the magic with her crystal-tipped staff. No lashings, no writhing vines or thorns, no limbs trying to pick her up. Just a quiet draining with barely even a gnat to buzz by and threaten her nose with a tickling as it passed.

Wary, staff crystal glowing like a reddish, cabbage-sized sun, Saleria retreated back to her home. A relatively calm start to her day wasn't the usual way things ran at the Grove. Still, it was with relief that she hung the staff with its now brightly glowing gem in the tool shed for the moment and retired to her study on the ground floor of her home.

Daranen, her appointed scribe, got to have the luxury of sleeping in an extra hour, compared to her. Sometimes he joined her at breakfast, but not today. That did not mean he had a light workload, though; the middle-aged man often stayed up later than her, reading the day's mail. But he was always up and ready to work when she got back from her first set of rounds.

In the last three years, Saleria had grown to expect him sitting in his favorite green tunic and trews at his desk when she returned from the Grove. It was a nice desk, set at an angle to hers so that both could enjoy the view through the bay window at the front of the cottage. She could almost envy him getting to sit in such a comfortable, padded leather chair, too. She certainly didn't sit all that much throughout her day.

This morning, Daranen was there as expected, clad in one of his many green outfits, but he was not seated at his desk. Instead, he had taken one of the cushioned chairs opposite it and was chatting companionably with a strange man. Their backs were to Saleria when she entered, but when Daranen heard her, he finished whatever he was saying in a murmur and politely stood, giving her a bow. "Good morning, Keeper Saleria."

"Good morning, Daranen," Saleria returned. Her gaze flicked between the middle-aged, brown-haired man and the younger, blond-haired male rising from the other chair. He, too, turned to bow to her. "And good morning to you, milord."

"Keeper, this is the Witch-priest Aradin Teral of far-distant Darkhana, which is a land placed far to the north and east of the Sun's Belt," Daranen introduced. "Witch-priest, this is High Priestess Saleria, Guardian of the Grove and Keeper of the Holiest Garden of Katan."

"Holiness," the stranger murmured, bowing a little deeper in politeness at her rank. He was clad in a fine-spun brown tunic and trews cut along Katani lines, and a pair of sturdy walking boots that looked like they had seen some wear. But he also wore an open, floor-length, deep-sleeved, deep-hooded robe that was a light shade of brown on the outside, but lined with a linen so black, it made his lean-muscled frame stand out all the more whenever he moved.

"Holy Brother," she replied politely, hoping that was the correct form of address for a foreign priest—it was for a fellow Katani priest, at any rate. It seemed to be acceptable, for the fellow nodded his head politely.

Saleria assessed him as her father had taught her, by seeking out the subtle clues to the man's profession. Aradin seemed a rather handsome fellow, in a lean sort of way. He wasn't nearly as thin or pale as the new Groveham Deacon, a young man by the name of Shanno, but he wasn't at all pudgy, like the older Daranen was starting to turn. Then again, a man who traveled was generally a man who stayed fit. Still, he did more than just walk; his wrists were lean, the tendons well-defined, and there was no spare fat about his face; she guessed he was familiar with some form of self-defense, though she could see no blade or staff about him. Of course, Saleria had a similar level of fitness, and her staff had been left in the shed just inside the garden. *His may have been left at one of the inns here in Groveham.*

He did have a certain calmness, an aura of peace about him of a kind that few warriors held, but which was common in a priest-hood. It was not completely unheard-of for foreign clergy to travel to far-flung lands, nor for them to want to visit a place where two Gods had been joined in marriage before Their chosen peoples, uniting their kingdoms as one, but it was not a common occur-rence. Saleria couldn't remember if she'd heard of a kingdom called Darkhana before, but it sounded like Daranen had a clear idea of where that was, and might even know if this fellow was a legitimate holy man. The Grove had its share of rare foreign priests, but it also bore the occasional visit from false would-be Seers and the like. Thank Kata and Jinga, not that often.

"Have you come hoping to see the Grove?" she asked their visi-tor, curious. For all that the Grove was the center of her world these days, she wasn't so naive as to believe other lands would have heard of its troubles, even after two hundred years had passed. Some for-eign visitors—priestly or otherwise—came simply because they had seen it mentioned in an old book and were curious. Those were the ones she had to forewarn with the truth. Not often, but once or twice a year. "If so, I'm afraid it's a bit too dangerous for casual viewing these days."

"Not exactly, though I do have a personal interest in magically enhanced gardening," Priest Aradin said. At Saleria's bemused look, the blond man waved it off with a graceful flick of his hand. "Mostly, I am here to discuss a potential need which I am hoping you, in your office as a formal go-between for your people and your Gods, would be interested in fulfilling. Do you have time for a discussion today?"

Saleria lifted her brows, then turned to Daranen. "Well? Do I?"

"Ah, yes, just a moment." Hurrying over to his desk, her scribe picked up a book-sized chalkboard and a stack of folded parchments. "Fifty-three petitions for rain in the northlands interspersed with the usual requests for good sunlight in the southern regions listed on this slate, reworded in the usual way into the standard prayers to avoid both flooding and drought. They all vary in the original request, but that's what it all boils down to in the end, and is an ideal mass prayer for today's needs. The rest are minor requests for things like finding lost pet dogs and such, which can be put off for later in the day."

"Drought prayers only take half an hour or so," Saleria murmured, recalling similar requests. "So . . . yes, milord, I do have time to chat with you. Though I should get those drought prayers out of the way first."

He nodded politely, a lock of his blond hair slipping forward. It was darker than her own, more of a sandy color, and rather thick. It was also long, following the current trend in Katani fashion. If his eyes had been a bit more slanted and his outer robe set aside, he might have been able to pass for a native, but there was just enough of an exotic air to the man to make him look intriguing.

His voice, a deep, smooth bass, pulled her attention back from her musings. It came with an odd shift in the way he stood and studied her, tipping and twisting his head slightly to the side before he straightened it and spoke. "I realize my next request may be a bit unusual, being a holy man of a completely different nation . . . but may I observe your prayer rituals? I ask in respect for your Order's traditions," Aradin added, an oddly mature look in his hazel eyes. "One of my jobs as I travel is to observe the rituals and rites of other faiths."

That puzzled her. Saleria frowned in her confusion. "Why would a priest from another faith be *ordered* to observe foreign religious rites?"

"In Darkhana, we have our own customs for daily life," Aradin told her, gesturing at himself with both hands, then held one out toward her as well, "but in one thing, all lands are the same. We are born, we live, and we die. Your God and Goddess oversee the four seasons of life, from infancy through youth, maturity, and on into the elderly stages. Our God and Goddess oversee the transitions from Life to the Afterlife, and all that lies between.

"Although I am from Darkhana, which lies a very long distance from here, all cultures must deal with death and its transitions. All deaths, in all lands, go through the same stages: The deceased must make the passage through the Dark to the Afterlife where they will be judged and assigned their just punishments, rewards, and perhaps reincarnation chances by the Gods . . . and the living must be comforted and counseled through their grief.

"In that regard, our faith is a . . . a supplement to your own, in a way. We specialize in such things. Wherever we go, we need to be prepared to handle bereavement, to ensure souls are not lost as they make the journey toward the Afterlife. Yet we cannot really stand ready to help others in this, our holy task, without understanding the local system of faith," he concluded, clasping his hands lightly in front of his torso. A light shrug accompanied his words. "One of the best ways to achieve understanding is to observe the local religion in action, which we would like to do. With your permission, and with great respect on our part."

Saleria blinked at him. "'We'?" she finally asked. "'Our'? Who is this *we* you reference? Is there more than one of you in your delegation?"

"In a way, yes. In a way, no—one moment," he added. Again, he closed his eyes and tipped his head, as if stretching a muscle in his neck. Blinking, he opened his eyes again. Giving her a rueful smile, the foreign priest spread his hands slightly. "*We* are a Dark-hanan Witch. This body—my body—belongs to myself, the man named Aradin. I was raised an herbalist and a mage until my late teens, when I was sent to an academy with the intent to study more of the ways of Hortimancy—plant magics—than my family alone could teach me. In the middle of my trip, I was asked to go to the aid of a Witch-priest who had been caught under a storm-felled tree."

"I don't understand," Saleria interjected, frowning. "What has this to do with using the plural for yourself?"

"It has everything to do with it," Aradin told her. "Darkhanan Witches are twofold. Like our Goddess and God, there are a Host and a Guide. The Host is the living person. The Guide is a deceased former Witch, whose spirit is bound into the Host so that they may literally help guide the person hosting their soul. In this way, their lifetime of accumulated experience and wisdom can be preserved and passed down. Teral—the Witch pinned under the tree—was dying, and I was asked to become his Host, so that I could continue to preserve his experiences, and the memories he had from his Guide, Alaya . . . and when she was a Host, that of her Guide, and of his, and of his, stretching back for over a thousand years.

"The person who spoke just now, with the request to watch you pray? That was Teral, my Guide," Aradin explained. "He and I can share control of my body, whenever I will it. We can also do more—if I may demonstrate?"

Bemused, she glanced at Daranen, who looked equally intrigued. She gestured with a hand for the foreign priest to proceed. "Provided it harms none, you may."

He smiled wryly at her as he lifted the deep hood of his robe up over his head. Dropping it down past even his chin, he pulled the front edges closed, then tucked his hands up the opposite sleeves, and bowed slightly. A strange ripple passed through the flesh hidden beneath the beige folds, then he straightened up. Only . . . it wasn't the lean, blond priest anymore.

The now slightly taller, broad-shouldered figure lifted his hands to the hood, shifting it back out of the way. The face he revealed was older, with a dark, neatly trimmed, gray-streaked beard. His hair, also dark brown with faint threads of silver, fell to mid-chest, the same as Aradin's, but that chest was broad and strong . . . and the tunic and trousers he wore were of a slightly different cut, dyed a somewhat faded forest green.

"As you can see," the new figure in the Witch-robes stated, his voice a smooth baritone instead of a deeper bass, "I have the ability to appear as myself, whenever my Host wills it." One hand on his chest, the other sweeping to the side, he bowed to her. "Teral Aradin at your service, Holy Sister."

"Teral Aradin?" Daranen asked, brows lifting. "Not Aradin Teral? So . . . whoever holds the current appearance puts his name first?"

"That is correct," the new foreigner stated.

Saleria blinked, trying to regather her wits. She was sensitive to the flow and twists of magic; it was part of her job as Guardian and Keeper of the Grove to be aware of such energies. Yet she had felt nothing. Frowning softly, she tried to make sense of it. "How is this trick managed? I sensed no spell at work. I can see no aura or hint of an illusion, either."

"It is holy magics. The robe is a part of it, though any sufficient amount of darkness will suffice," Teral stated. He lifted a hand, rubbing at his bearded chin for a moment, then shrugged. "I suppose a dark enough shadow might do as well, provided no eyes lay upon the Witch making the transition. As for it being an illusion, this body is still physically that of my Host, though it is currently shaped like my own. When I was still alive and Host to Witch-priestess Alaya, she could take on her feminine form whenever I willed it as well, and be accounted in all ways a female, save that it was still my body at the end of the day."

Daranen let his jaw drop for a moment, then shut it, swallowed, and glanced at Saleria. "Begging pardon . . . and no insult meant, milord, but . . . I'm not sure I could agree to that, myself. Being turned into a woman? Thank you, but *no*."

Teral smirked at the younger man. "I found it to be an advantage in understanding the other gender. I have passed along some of that understanding to my Host, Aradin, as well. Our Order finds it very useful to have both genders understand the ways and thoughts of the other. Of course, it also depends on who is available to take up being the next Host when a previous Witch dies. But still, it is useful."

"I am sure it is," Saleria murmured, at a loss for anything else to say. She shook her head to clear it. "As fascinating as this is, I am not sure it would be wise to allow you into the Grove. Not for fear of your bringing insult or disrespect," she added quickly, firmly, as the older priest drew breath to speak, "but because the Grove is simply too dangerous for the unwary.

"You are, however, most welcome to visit the Groveham Chapel," Saleria allowed. "Prelate Lanneraun is elderly, but well-versed in tending the needs of both the local congregation and those Katani who travel here on pilgrimage for one reason or another." She paused, eyed him warily, then added, "Erm . . . if you would kindly switch back, so that I could tell your, ah, Host of this?"

Teral held up a hand in a gentle, graceful motion. "There is no need for that, Holy Sister. Unless one of us steps into the Dark to consult with the Knowing, or to help escort a soul to the gates of the Afterlife, we are always here, and always aware of what our other half experiences."

She didn't quite believe him, but she didn't quite disbelieve him, either. It was all rather . . . fantastical, that was the word for it. Like some storyteller's tale. "Well, erm . . . gentlemen," Saleria managed politely, giving the foreigner a slight bow, "if you will excuse us, my scribe and I need to consult on the prayers at hand. Since it seems to be a lovely day budding outside, perhaps we could meet in the square up the lane from here? By the fountain with the entwined fishes? I shouldn't be more than an hour at most, if not less."

"As you wish, Holiness. We look forward to speaking with you in a little while." Bowing, Witch Teral pulled his hood back up over his head, tucked his hands up his sleeves, and . . . shrank slightly. Straightening, Witch Aradin revealed his face, bowed a second time to her, and allowed Daranen to escort him—them?—to the front door.

Bemused, Saleria moved over to her desk and dropped onto her padded leather chair, utterly at a loss on how to handle the weirdness of this foreigner. *Two men in one body . . . one technically dead, but able to "live" again in his own form, thanks to the other? And they travel the world, studying other lands? How very bizarre . . .*

The twittering of a bird outside reminded her that time would not stand still while she tried to make sense of outkingdom ways. Sitting up with a grunt, she sorted through the neat stacks of correspondence Daranen had placed on her desk and started reading the letters with the requests for drought management. Saleria pushed thoughts of Aradin-and-Teral out of her mind.

Strange two-in-one foreigners would have to wait while the Keeper of the Grove attended to her daily work.

TWO

Aradin fingered one of his translation pendants, his mind not really on the Aian book in his other hand. The pendant, a silver-wrapped stone strung on a long braided leather cord, was one of many he had made in his travels. When worn, it permitted him to read, write, hear, and speak in whatever language it was enchanted to translate.

The polished, flat disc of agate felt comfortable under his thumb, warmed where he had rubbed it, cooler where he hadn't touched it all that much. He stroked its smooth surface, then rubbed his thumb over the little beads decorating the bezel, but his mind was more on the Keeper of the Grove than on the book of mirror-based magics he had fetched from his bags to kill time while they waited.

(*You're thinking of her again,*) Teral observed lightly. (*I think that's the third time you've tried to read that paragraph.*)

(*Well, she is worth thinking about. Intelligent, a little innocent, strong-willed, and beautiful,*) Aradin admitted. (*Eyes that shift between blue and gray, depending on how the light reaches them . . . lovely blonde curls . . . rose lips . . .*)

(*Are you turning poet on me?*) Teral asked, mock-suspicion in his mind-voice.

(*Well, how else would you describe her?*) Aradin retorted, snorting softly out loud. He tried to settle a little more comfortably onto the bench near the fountain for a fourth read, but gave up. (*And those curves . . . !*)

(*Technically, she doesn't have overly lush ones,*) Teral observed lightly.

(*No, but what she has, she carries with confidence, and that makes her all the more appealing,*) his Host countered. (*Are you going to try to lie and say you do not find her attractive yourself?*)

(*I didn't say that,*) the Guide snorted. (*Were I still the Host and our mission not a concern, I'd have flirted quite shamelessly with her. I was considered quite the catch even up to the day of my death, you know.*)

(*Catch-and-release, though,*) Aradin sighed. (*Hosts and Guides of the same gender have a hard enough time finding anyone to accept our dual lives. I cannot imagine many who would accept an opposite-gendered pair for long.*)

(*It is very rare,*) Teral agreed, sighing mentally as well. (*Still, no one makes love quite like a Witch. Or are you forgetting the fun we had with that Arbran sea-merchant two years ago?*)

(*What, the one we met on the Isle of Storms? Oh, she was quite the opportunist,*) Aradin thought, chuckling. ("*I've never made love with two men before,*") he thought in a mental falsetto. ("*Or should this only count as one and a half?*")

Teral chuckled as well. Then cleared his throat. (*Blonde approaching to your left. I believe from the curls and white clothes it is our fellow priestess.*)

Tucking the book's attached ribbon between the pages, Aradin slipped it into one of his deep sleeves, letting Teral take the tome and stash it under the cover of the spell-enforced darkness deep inside his robe. Rising to his feet, he bowed to the Keeper as she approached.

She nodded, her eyes sweeping down over Aradin's body. It was a look more assessing than appreciative, though he thought he saw a slight spark of the latter. He didn't ask why she studied him. There was just something about the way the Witch-robes hung on his body that made him look deceptively frail. Until one took a second, deeper look. Teral, on the other hand, looked beefy upon first glance, like he should have been a blacksmith instead of a priest.

He had the strength for it, too; if the tree that had fallen on him had not pierced his chest and crushed his hips, he would have been fully capable of moving it aside. With effort, and perhaps a touch of magic, but still mostly by muscle. By comparison, Aradin's slender frame and loose clothes hid lean muscles and whiplike reflexes. One did not travel the world without being proficient in self-defense, and both versions of Aradin Teral were capable men . . . but most underestimated the Host, based on superficial appearance alone. Still, some women liked the lean sort more than the muscular. Or at least Aradin could always hope they did.

"Holiness, it is a pleasure to see you again. I trust all went well?" he greeted her politely.

"Relatively well. There's a spot of wild magic running around the Grove I cannot quite track down. It's affecting the animals," she added in an aside, frowning off into the distance. Shaking it off, she gave him a smile. Once again, Aradin was struck by how lovely she was. "But things are under control for the moment, Kata and Jinga willing."

"Naturally," he agreed. "Would you care to retire once more to your office?" Aradin offered, gesturing back at the large, two-story house at the end of the lane. "The things I would ask you are not the sort meant for open gossip and rampant speculation, though they aren't a terrible secret."

She eyed him again, then gestured gracefully back up the lane. "To my study, then. If you don't mind my scribe listening in, that is."

"I think that would be fine. He strikes me as a competent, trustworthy man," Aradin said, falling into step at her side. She was a little taller than average for a Katani woman, if still shorter than him by about a finger-length. Their strides matched fairly well, something which pleased him. From the gossip he had gleaned by listening in the dining hall of the inn last night, the Keeper of the Grove did a lot of walking each day. So did he, since it was sometimes awkward for a Witch to have and keep track of a mount. More convenient to simply travel on foot, or hire some means of faster travel when needed.

"I, for one, am rather glad he is so competent," Saleria admitted as they walked. A child skipped past, the young girl waving to Saleria before continuing on her way, an empty basket dangling from her other hand. On her way to market, no doubt. "I inherited him when I took over the position of Grove Keeper, and he has done an excellent job of managing my clerical needs."

Her word choice made Aradin smile. At a curious glance from her, he explained. "The holy priests and priestesses of Mendhi, far to the west and north of here, are called *clerics*. That is where the word *clerical* comes from—and it is pronounced almost exactly the same in Darkhanan as it is in Mendhite and Katani. Then again, their Goddess is the Goddess of Writing, so it only makes sense for Her servants to be both scribe and priest."

"I see. I did not know the word was from Mendhi," Saleria confessed. She blushed slightly and shrugged, gesturing at the street while they walked. "But then I honestly don't know much about the world beyond the boundaries of Katan. I think it's one of the advantages of living in an empire which spans an entire continent. You never have to worry about anyone else causing problems along your borders—that is, not to sound callous," she added quickly, and gestured at the Grove beyond her home, "but I have enough to worry about."

"Are things really that bad in the Grove?" Aradin asked her, following her into her home.

Saleria gestured for him to shut the front door behind them. Once it was closed, Saleria glanced out the window set next to the door. No one had been near enough to hear his question, not even the little girl who had gone off on her errand. She nodded, looking at Aradin. He had a face . . . *they* had faces which inspired confidence, since the older, bearded version had looked equally trustworthy. And it wasn't a secret, exactly, but she didn't want stray gossip spreading through the town, raising everyone's fears needlessly.

"Things are bad enough, yes," she told him. "I keep asking the Arch Priest's staff for an assistant, but they keep saying I'm doing fine. *Yes*, I'm doing fine, if all I'm supposed to do is *contain* the problem. But what I'd really like to do is figure out a way to *solve* the problem so that the Grove can be safe for visitors once more. That takes help. One to continue to contain everything while the other studies what's wrong."

(*Oh dear,*) Teral murmured. (*She's not going to like our request, then. Or be able to fulfill it when the time comes.*)

(*Unless we can get her an assistant, which might just as well be me.*) The more tantalizing wisps of information he heard about the Grove behind this house, the more Aradin felt intrigued by what was really happening inside. (*Everything we've heard so far suggests too much magic is warping the plants and animals in there. I may not be an expert on animals, but I do know how to control and manage the effects of magic on and in plants.*)

(*What do you . . . ? Oh! I see your point,*) Teral said, following

Aradin's thoughts. The long-standing prohibition of one living being reading another living being's thoughts did not apply to him, as Teral was technically dead. After several years of living within the younger man's Doorway, Teral could follow his sub-thoughts with some ease. (*Yes, that could work. If you* can *actually prove your worth in such a task.*)

Aradin didn't reply; Saleria had ushered him into her office and was gesturing at the seat he had occupied earlier. The green-clad cleric, Daranen, looked up briefly from his correspondence, but otherwise didn't comment. Taking the seat across from Aradin, Saleria settled into the padded chair.

"Now, I believe you were going to ask me some questions?" she prompted Aradin.

"Yes . . . First, I should like to explain how I came to be here, why I am on this quest. It may help you to make up your mind," Aradin told her. At her nod, he began. "Darkhanan Witches have a . . . hidden advantage over most priesthoods. As you may know, theologically, all religions agree that once a soul reaches the Afterlife, all questions shall be answered. Our greatest Witch calls it the 'full knowing' and says it occurs in an instantaneous flash of comprehension and understanding."

"Which who?" Saleria asked, distracted by the odd aside.

"Forgive me. Not *which* as in to choose, but *Witch* as in a specific type of Darkhanan mage priest or priestess," Aradin clarified, giving her a rueful, apologetic smile. "I wear a translation pendant which tells me what to say, but does not guarantee that I say it correctly. In your language, the word *which*," he enunciated carefully, "is very similar to our word *Witch*. Forgive me for speaking sloppily."

"I don't know anything about translation spells, I'm afraid," Saleria confessed, wrinkling her own nose. "The more I speak with you, the more I feel my training is inadequate. I'm beginning to feel distinctly ignorant about a lot of things."

"Hardly that, I'm sure," Aradin dismissed. "You've simply focused on different things. I myself would be hard-pressed to carry out a Darkhanan wedding ceremony, if Teral hadn't conducted several dozen in his life, and it's been a few years even for him. I certainly haven't conducted any myself beyond a few practice attempts while I was being trained. We all flounder in certain neglected areas of our life; that doesn't make us any less wise in others."

That brought out a relieved smile on her face. *Yes, he's definitely a smart fellow. And a wise one*, Saleria thought. *Maybe there's something to this legacy of accumulating wisdom through extended lifespans. Of a sort.* She offered a bit of her own history, warming up to him. "Well, I have conducted a handful of marriage rites. Not in the last few years, either, so we have that much in common. You were saying something about a 'knowing' or whatever?"

"Full knowing," Aradin corrected. "Such a thing is only accessible to those who have achieved the Afterlife. The regular 'knowing,' of the sort which most Darkhanan Witch-priests have access to, comes from the Dark."

"The place between Life and the Afterlife?" Saleria asked, puzzled. "I thought there was nothing there but ghosts wandering through the darkness, seeking the Light of the Afterlife. That, and excess magic."

"I see you know your energy cycles," he praised. "What most people outside of Darkhana do not know is that while the Dark does not contain the full knowing of the Afterlife, a properly trained Witch can go into the Dark, ask it simple yes-no questions, and receive a response. Or rather, a response of yes, no, or some degree of ambiguity."

That shocked her. Saleria stared at the handsome blond foreigner. "That's . . . that's the power of a Seer! The Gods separated Seers from mages, because the powers they deal with, the things they touch . . . !"

Aradin shook his head quickly. Teral whispered snippets of half-forgotten information in the back of his mind as he explained things a Darkhanan took for granted. "No, nothing that strong. The questions can only be asked of what is happening right now, or what has happened in the past. All questions of the future by an ordinary Witch are given the ambiguous answer. All questions must also be asked in as simple yet exact a manner as we can manage, or it invokes ambiguity as well.

"We also do not like wandering the Dark for very long, because even for a trained soul, it is very draining and potentially dangerous, so we don't ask of it as many questions as you'd think. It is a very taxing process for all who try. But . . . there are Seers in Darkhana. They work in conjunction with our Witches," he told her.

"There are?" Saleria asked. Then shook her head, impatient with herself. "Of course there are. There are Seers in every land. Even I know that much."

"Yes, and they See glimpses of the future in snatches of rhyme, or visions, or words on a page. Once they See, *we* go into the Dark to ask clarifying questions. It doesn't always work, of course . . . but we can get clear answers from time to time about certain things, particularly once the prophecies start coming true," he allowed. "And one of those things is the fact that the Convocation of Gods and Man, which ended roughly two hundred years ago, is going to be reconvened soon. In order for that to happen successfully, each kingdom must have a holy representative of their local Gods—a priest or priestess—who can speak on behalf of his or her people."

Sitting there under those watchful hazel eyes, it took Saleria a few moments to realize what he was implying. She frowned at him. "You mean . . . me?" At his nod, she shook her head. "No. No, surely there are more appropriate priests—what about the Patriarch? Surely *he* would count first and foremost, as the Arch Priest?"

"The holy advocate must be an advocate for the *faith* of their

people, not for their politics," Aradin told her. He paused, cleared
his throat delicately, and added in that deep, soothing voice of his,
"All signs, milady, point to the Convocation being reconvened by
a *rival* of the Katani Empire. The current political clash between
your homeland and this other land make it too risky to involve
anyone in the uppermost positions in your hierarchy. Such rival-
ries could lead to sabotage at the Convocation . . . which in turn
could lead to a second Shattering."

She winced at that. She could easily envision his words. "That
would be bad. We haven't the Portals to cause dangers, like what
happened here . . . but that would still be bad."

"Yes, I was told it was the far-ranging damage of the previous
Shattering that destroyed the Portals you had opened to Aiar, and
rendered your Grove inhospitable. I'm sure you can see my concerns about not wanting to involve your Patriarch, who is of a similar mindset to your king, politically," he added. "That sort of
damage, and its underlying conflicts, must not happen again."

Grimacing, Saleria nodded reluctantly. "This was once a beautiful garden, open to all, and safe for all, with normal plants and
normal animals within its sacred walls. The physical ability to
cross from here to the heart of Aiar was shut down, yes . . . but the
Keeper of the day still chose to show images from the Convocation
while it was happening, and the Portal frames imploded. My pre-
decessor thought we were lucky to have no physical damage, but
what did happen was worse in its own way."

"My condolences, but you can see our concern. Your people's
holy advocate must be someone who focuses on the true needs of
your people, and who will not be swayed or led astray into conflict
by political ambitions," he said. "We have asked many Katani citizens in the last two weeks who they thought would be a true representative and advocate. By all accounts, your very job is to focus
your holy efforts and energies upon the needs of your people, and

you have done it well. Your lack of knowledge about other lands speaks highly of your lack of interest in interkingdom politics—an asset in this case, and not a detriment," Aradin pointed out. "I am therefore here to ask you if you would be willing to represent the people of Katan at the next Convocation, when Kata and Jinga are Named and made manifest along with all the other Goddesses and Gods of the world."

"I . . ." The very idea was absurd, impossible . . . yet very much in line with what she normally did. On the one hand, it was flattering to know she held the apparent trust of her people, to have sent this man her way. On the other hand, any rival kingdom would be located somewhere away from the continent, and that would mean weeks, maybe months of travel. Therein lay the stumbling block to accepting his request, however enticing the thought of standing before her God and Goddess in person might be. "I'm sorry, but I couldn't possibly leave the Grove unattended for a single day, let alone the months such a trip would surely entail. Even to travel to Aiar, which is due north, requires a calm summer voyage of two weeks, since one has to navigate the Sun's Belt reefs . . ."

Aradin held up his hand. "The journey would not take nearly so long as you'd think. My fellow Witches and I are under orders to cooperate fully with escorting all carefully selected advocates from their homelands to the site of the Convocation. We have a way to make the trip almost as short as a trip through one of the ancient Portals . . . though it is not one we commonly use, nor do we normally speak of it, because it is not a pleasant method of travel."

"But if it is like the old Portals, surely that's worth any discomfort?" Saleria asked. She might have been ignorant of far-distant lands, but she wasn't ignorant of the implications. "If you Witchpriests can make such travel possible, you could each make a fortune serving to assist in worldwide commerce and travel!"

"Aside from the fact that it would force most of my Brother and

Sister Priests to abandon their normal works in tending to our people . . . Teral tells me the transition feels very much like dying," Aradin confessed. He knew such a thing might put her off, but he wasn't going to lie about it. "I'll remind you he *is* deceased. He knows well of what he speaks."

"That doesn't sound pleasant, no," Saleria admitted, wincing a little at Aradin's warning. "But the old records spoke of the Convocation taking weeks, even a month. I still couldn't spare that much time from my duties."

"Not unless you had an assistant," Aradin pointed out. "If you did, then they could stay to tend the Grove, and you could go to present the needs of your people. Do you not already deal every day in petitions from your people on the things they wish your Patron Deities to handle? The more I learn of your position and what it entails, the more well-suited you seem for this task."

She shook her head. "The higher-ups won't send anyone to me, and if I insisted vehemently that I needed one, all those politics you want to avoid would undoubtedly get involved. I can see why you'd want to pick me, and I am flattered, as I neither know nor care about any rivals to the Empire. That's for King and Council to worry about. But I will not abandon my post."

"What if I *could* get you an adequate assistant?" Aradin asked her. "All you'd need is someone who can contain the plants and animals of the Grove until your return, correct?"

"It's more complex than that," Saleria dismissed. Rising, she paced a little. "Every hour of every day, great magics flood the Grove. They must be contained, drained away from the plants and animals, given a purpose, and sent out to do good in the world, instead of being allowed to sit here, stagnate, and warp everything within reach. It is a daily task. I can only rest for a few hours here and there in the daylight, but never for a full day, as it takes everything I have to wrestle all those powers into something beneficial."

She stopped, flushed a little, and glanced back at him, abashed by her own words. "Which means . . . I need an assistant. And I come full circle with my own argument." Turning to face him fully, Saleria clasped her hands lightly together. "The question is, Witch-priest of Darkhana, *can* you find me an adequate replacement? Do not think to look within the priesthood here in Groveham," she added in warning. "Prelate Lanneraun is physically old and frail, and Deacon Shanno is too young, impetuous, and barely powered as a mage. Neither would survive a walk around the wall, let alone the rest of it."

"I would first offer myself, actually," Aradin stated. At her frown, he quickly held up a hand. "Yes, I know I come from a different kingdom, and thus a different faith. But what Teral said earlier this morning is true; we Witches believe we are an adjunct to all faiths. We stand ready to assist in the local customs and beliefs wherever we may roam. With the approval of our own God and Goddess, no less, and no record of an objection anywhere in the records of the old Convocations of God and Man."

"But if you are to provide some sort of Portal-like escort to the new Convocation, how can you remain behind at the same time?" Saleria asked. "Or are you referring to yourself as Portal-like in the sense that you will be unable to move from this location?"

He smiled wryly. "Well, yes, I would have to remain behind. Certainly I would have to remain here in order for you to be returned in the same manner, if you felt you could survive the trip a second time. As for whether or not I am strong enough, I was not a weak mage to begin with, but now I have the added benefit of Teral's power to back my own."

"His what?" Daranen asked, lifting his head once more from

his correspondence. He blushed at Saleria's sharp, questioning look, but set down his pen for the moment. "Forgive the interruption, but you yourself said your Guide is dead and has no body of his own. How could his powers as a mage be added to yours?"

Aradin tipped his head. Saleria realized that meant he was handing his body over to his Guide to speak. Though the voice was the younger man's deep rumble, the inflections turned into those of an older man. "That is what makes our holy Witches so different. Anyone with an understanding of death and how to bind spirits could replicate part of what we can do . . . and such attempts are often twisted perversions wrought by servants of the Netherhells. They can only force open the Doorway in the back of a person's soul to thrust in another spirit for a form of possession, or even to rip open a Doorway into a recently deceased corpse to reanimate it in a grotesque parody of life. What *we* do is holy, with the blessings of the God of the Dead Himself.

"Unlike the abominations of those who practice unholy necromancy, our actions are undertaken with free-willed consent from all parties. With the will of the Gods to back our efforts, we are able to restore almost all the benefits of life to our Guides. They—we—can take on our original appearances, at whatever age we still feel ourselves to be. We can remember everything we ever did, said, or observed while we lived. We can access almost all of our original magical strengths, and spells . . . and we can share most of those energies with our Hosts. Not quite all of it, for some of it must remain a part of what binds us to our Hosts, but most of it.

"This is why a Witch must be a mage as well as a priest or priestess," Teral added, shrugging the younger man's shoulders. "We have non-mage members of the priesthood back in Darkhana, and we have non-priest mages who attend to various secular spellcrafting needs, the same as in any other kingdom. That is what my Host, Aradin, originally intended himself to be, a simple, if strong, mage. But together, we are more than either of us could have been alone . . . and I assure you, neither of us was weak to begin with."

Seeing him stand differently, and speak slightly differently, but while wearing the body of Aradin, was a bit confusing. Saleria struggled to accept it, as she strove to accept his explanations. "Well . . . under normal circumstances, there's nothing wrong with being a weak mage. It's simply how the Gods have made you, and a weak but well-trained and inventive mage is certainly far more useful than a strong but undisciplined or poorly educated mage," Saleria stated. She returned to her seat and braced her elbow on the armrest, rubbing at her forehead. "The Grove, however, is not for the weak, body or mind—did you know I'm the twenty-ninth Keeper of the Grove since the Shattering of Aiar?"

The Witch tipped his head, blinked, then shook it. When he spoke, she could tell it was Aradin back in control once more. His voice might have been deeper in this body, but his tone was lighter, less matured. "No, I did not."

"I think the longest a mage-priest ever held this job was fifteen years. The shortest, just over two months . . . though that was mainly due to an unexpected death. Most of the rest of us last around ten years . . . and then . . . we're done." She flicked her fingers again in a dismissive gesture. "Exhausted, injured, stressed . . . At most, the Keepers who are so spent find their magics reduced and are forced to send for a replacement. I took on this position knowing full well the most I'd be able to do for years afterward would be to teach holy magic. I'd barely have enough to contain a single pupil's mistakes, never mind enough for complex craftings and castings.

"I *would* take on an assistant, were I permitted one, but who could be as strong, as cautious, and as conscientious? Who would want to put up with . . . with rampaging marigolds, and giant rabid shrews? *That* was just this morning. Plus there are all the religious aspects, the duties and expectations, the obligations . . ." Saleria shook her head. "Then there is the responsibility of ensuring all the energies involved are kept safe, and not stolen, or warped, or used for untoward ends." She looked at the man across from her, with his unshaven face and blond hair hiding that second, darker, bearded visage. "How could I trust a stranger?"

Her words were pointed, but Aradin had a counter for them. He braced one elbow on the arm of his chair, fingers laced together, and leaned forward. "Perhaps by taking the time to get to know the person who just might be able to help you? Then you—we—wouldn't be strangers, now would we?"

A faint *snerk* sound snapped Saleria's head to the side. She stared at her scribe, who sat with shoulders hunched and his teeth sunk into his bottom lip. At her dark look, Daranen shrugged and smiled. "He has you, there, Saleria. That *would* end the label of 'stranger' rather neatly."

"Yes, but he implies that *he* would make me an adequate assistant. A foreign priest of a foreign God and Goddess, with unknown strengths and weaknesses, in the Sacred Grove of Jinga and Kata?" Saleria challenged her scribe. Challenged both of them, for she turned back to Aradin Teral and addressed him as well. "I'll grant you that I am not one bound to secular politics, and that because of my office, I always have the needs of the Katani people held first and foremost in my mind and heart when I work, but *I* hold those needs in mind and heart. You do not. What sincere, deep-rooted interest in the welfare of the Katani people could you possibly hold?"

"We are pledged—Teral and I—to give aid and succor to *all* mortals everywhere, as Witch-priests. This includes the citizens of the Katani Empire, since from what I understand, none of your people are immortal," Aradin stated dryly. "Bring out a Truth Wand, if you do not believe me. Pluck and knot a hair from my head. Should you prove to be the right holiness for the job, and we prove to be the right assistant to help manage things while you attended to the needs of your people at the Convocation, we would even bind ourselves in a carefully stated, mutually agreed upon mage-oath.

"We have already bound ourselves in other oaths to this task. The resurrection of the Convocation of Gods and Man is too important not to take every precaution and make every effort to ensure its success," he told her. She made a soft, scoffing sound, not quite a snort. Aradin pulled out his biggest weapon. "It has already been prophesied, Holy Sister. It *will* happen. It is up to us mortals to ensure it happens in the best way possible for all who are involved . . . and as it is the Convocation, that means *all* the world's people, Katan included."

"By a foreign Seer, no doubt. One whom I have never heard about, so naturally I must take your word for it," Saleria scorned.

"By a Katani Seer." Aradin tucked his hands deep into his sleeves, rummaging in the Dark with Teral's help. *Where is it . . . where . . . ? (Teral, isn't it among the loose scrolls in the leather sack?)*

(No, I don't think it's in the sack. I think it's in the brown chest with the roses carved on the lid,) Teral finally said. *(It's not one we've consulted recently, that's for certain.)*

Grimacing, Aradin stood and pulled his witchrobe around his body, moving two paces from the chair. "One more moment . . ."

As she watched, frowning in confusion, he tugged the deep hood of his robe down over his face and throat. Cut off from daylight by the spells woven into the holy cloth, he was free to reach into the Dark directly. With both his and Teral's will focused on finding exactly what they wanted, it did not take long.

The first few times Aradin had been exposed to this little perk of Witch-craft, he had been amazed and flabbergasted; Teral had been forced to manage the trick for both of them, since it required a very keen, firm will to make it work. But work it did, and was part and parcel of how their entire Order communicated over long distances, assisted others in traveling when there was dire need for it, and "carried" their belongings with them, without actually having to physically carry a thing. After a full decade of practice, Aradin could manage this quite well on his own, though his Guide didn't hesitate to help.

As soon as they both had their hands on what they wanted, setting it at their feet, Aradin stepped back into his robe-shrouded body and spun away. The folds of his cloak parted around the object, leaving a chest as broad as any pillow and as tall as any footstool on the floor of the Grove Keeper's study. Saleria sat up, eyes widening as she stared at the bronze-bound, carved mahogany chest. There was no way he could have smuggled that thing into her study under his robes, and no hint of magic, no cry of empowered words to suggest the use of a Gate of some kind.

"How did you . . . ?"

Shifting the hood of his cloak back from his head, Aradin knelt in front of the chest. He worked on the clasp while he spoke; the metal was cold and stiff from its time in storage. "The Dark, as you know, exists between Life and the Afterlife. But what most people forget is that it touches all corners of existence. All at once. It is the realm of spirits and magic, the souls of the departed and the life-energies that get sucked into the Dark in their wake.

"These spirits snap free of their physical bodies and head toward the home of the Gods—all the Gods," he added, wanting to remind her that Darkhanan priests were not exclusive in their services and beliefs. "They can do so from any point in the world, and still wind up in the same place, if they will it." The latch was stubborn, but it did move, squeaking a bit as metal rubbed on metal. "But that is the point, isn't it? It is the will of a person that dictates how swiftly they head toward the Light of the Afterlife.

"Or they—injuries or illnesses permitting—can turn around and resume occupying the shells of their bodies. And for those who are trained in the holy secrets . . ." a few more tugs pulled it free as he spoke, ". . . one can will the existence of storage space in the Dark—*ungh*! There we go." Lifting the lid up and back, he riffled through the scrolls and papers nested inside. "Burgundy ribbon, if I remember right . . . burgundy . . . no, that's too scarlet . . . ah! Here it is."

Pulling out the scroll, he untied the ribbon holding it shut. Unrolling the beige parchment, Aradin showed it to her, but given the first half was written in Darkhanan, her blank look was understandable. He recited the preamble for her.

"A prophecy of the Duchess Haupanea of the Duchy of Nightfall, Empire of Katan, penned by Chaiden, night-scribe to Her Holiness, tentatively entitled 'The Synod Gone.'" He tilted the sheet toward Saleria as she shifted off her chair to kneel at his side, wanting a better look.

This close, he could smell a subtle hint of a flower—possibly honeysuckle—soap, and a bit of spice. Striving to be subtle, he leaned a little closer and inhaled. Definitely honeysuckle, and a touch of something else. Some sort of sweet spice from the local markets. *An intriguing combination. I wonder who makes her soaps?*

She was waiting for more information. Focusing his thoughts, Aradin continued. "According to the Department of Prophecies here in your own empire, Duchess Haupanea lived during the time of the last Convocation. She left behind a number of prophecies that suggested she would have shaped up to be quite powerful as a Seer.

"Unfortunately, she perished at a young age during a side effect of the Shattering, but this information comes from a copy extracted from the imperial archives from . . . seventy-five or so years after the Shattering? Obviously I wasn't around then," he dismissed, "but a previous Darkhanan Witch uncovered this information with the assistance of your Department of Prophecies. The actual prophecy comes from about a year or so before the Shattering. It's written in the original Katani at the bottom."

Taking the scroll from him, Saleria unrolled it further, reading the doggerel written on the page. Some Seers spoke in poetry, some in impassioned rants, and some penned their visions, hand moving across page without the owner's volition. This was one of the first kind, obviously.

Gone, all gone, the synod gone, destroyed by arrogant might,
But not forgotten, not abandoned, not lost into the night.
Old and new, Mankind and Gods, again they both shall speak;
Names be named, lands confirmed, repentances two seek.

Eight and mates shall pave the way, shall build the holy hall.
Eight more and mates shall guard the world, to save or ruin all.
By eight who are kin, by six familiar, one runaway, one unknown,
By mates and friends, by guides and aides, by outworlder on throne.

Gone, all gone, the synod gone, brought back by exiled might;
By second try, the fiends must die, uncovered by the blight.
In dark and day shall living and dead assemble each worthy soul,
For each represents, to beg and assert, the world then remade whole.

Through dark and life, by ship and spell, by first, then second light.
Destroy the false, which spurs the lie, but for this world shall fight.
By one who will stay, and one to betray, and third who shall turn away;
Gone, all gone, but synod's pawns shall come again one day.

With the last line recited, Saleria sat back on her heels, brow creased in puzzlement. She looked at the Darkhanan kneeling across from her on the other side of the open chest. "This thing speaks of the Convocation of the Gods? Are you sure of that?"

"Yes," Aradin said. Reaching over the chest, he tapped the parchment "There are several lines that confirm it. 'Synod' is an ancient Fortunai word for when all the clergy, all the priests and Holy Orders, get together to discuss holy writ and holy law. Such things are—or were—done at the Convocations. The third line of the first verse speaks of Gods and Man both speaking, again an image of the Convocation. There is a 'holy hall' in the first line of the second verse, and an assembly of worthy souls in the third line of the third verse, both of which are signature elements of a Convocation, plus a true representative of each nation's religious needs . . . which is covered in the second line of the second verse.

"We can tell that Darkhanan Witch-craft is involved, because it speaks of 'dark and day' and 'living and dead' which we interpret to mean the Hosts and Guides who navigate the Dark, the means by which we will assist the true representatives of each nation to attend the Convocation when it is time for it to begin. Plus one or two other signs we already knew about," he added dismissively. "Or at least have had time to question the Dark about."

"Question the Dark," she repeated, skeptical.

"Yes. Remember, we can only ask questions and receive a true answer for things that are happening, or have already happened. Our best Witch has been questioning the Dark about this and other prophecies for a very long time. The 'exiled might' and the 'eight who are kin' have finally come into play, which usually means the rest of the prophecy is also due to come true," Aradin told her. "You have no idea just how long our Order has been working on getting the Convocation of Gods and Man reinstated. Generations' worth—basically since right after the Shattering ended the last one. We are *very* committed to seeing that all aspects of its reinstatement go smoothly."

He didn't say more than that. It was enough that he could tell from her softened frown that she was considering the truth of his words, paired with the truth of the scroll. Well, their words, technically. It was actually Teral who had worked the hardest on paying attention to this task, not him, but then Teral had heard about it long before his death by fallen tree. Aradin himself hadn't cared, and would have continued not caring, if he hadn't met the subjects of the "repentances two seek" part. Meeting a pair in as desperate straits as those two could change anyone's mind.

(*Best not to talk about it, though,*) Teral murmured, following his Host's thoughts. (*Most people just don't understand, and it takes too long to explain.*)

(*Why do you think I'm leaving it out?*) Aradin shot back.

Lowering the scroll to her lap, Saleria shook her head, blonde curls sliding over her white-clad shoulders. "It's rather strange . . ."

"What is?" Aradin asked. Since she seemed done with the scroll, he reached across the chest to take it.

She handed it back with a shrug. "When I was in my teens, I had a . . . a revelation that I was meant to serve the Gods. Life-changing. But if this scroll of yours is a true prophecy, and you think I am destined to be a 'worthy soul' sent to represent my people at the next Convocation . . . I'd think I should feel like I was part of a prophecy. But it's a different feeling from my moment of revelation. This does feel important, like there is something there, but . . . it's not life-changing."

That made him smile wryly. "Not all revelations are life-changing. And not all life-changes are revelations." Closing the lid, Aradin caught her hand and gently squeezed it. "Now I'm not saying you are the absolute perfect choice for being the Katani representative at the next Convocation of the Gods . . . mainly because neither I nor Teral have asked the Dark yet if you will be . . . but from everything we've heard about you on our way here, and after speaking with you, I'd like to think you have that potential.

"I'd also like to get to know you better," Aradin stated. It was the truth. Saleria was not a conventional priestess, even for a cleric of a foreign land. She fascinated him, with her mix of wisdom and naivety . . . but to be honest, so did the little snippets he kept hearing about what was wrong with her Grove. He focused on luring her with that as well. "Plus, I think I may have enough knowledge about the many interactions between plants and magic to be able to help you with your difficulties.

"If so, that would solve *both* our problems. I could stay and tend the needs of the Grove while you go to the Convocation to tend the needs of your people . . . and as a mage-priest, I would be willing to swear before both your Gods and mine to take every bit as much care with the tending of the Sacred Grove as you yourself would take. An oath-binding, even." He gently stroked the backs of her fingers with his thumb.

Feeling his warm, lightly callused skin caressing hers, Saleria blushed. She wasn't accustomed to anyone holding her hand. At least, not like this, not in a courtly way. Now that she was the Keeper, her time had been deemed too dedicated to the needs of the Grove to receive petitions in person, so she no longer even prayed in the presence of others, let alone clasped hands with them for a joint prayer. His scent reminded her of that exotic perfume, sandalwood, with a hint of musk. His eyes were a mix of wood brown and leaf green, reminding her of a garden. Of what the Grove should be.

She knew she was woolgathering, but then Aradin—the younger of the two—was attractive. Part of her mind strayed from the subject at hand, wondering what strictures or rules Darkhanan priests and priestesses had on their courtship practices. Part of her mind wondered why she was even thinking such an absurd, abstract thought, and another, third part wondered how she would even begin to find out the answers to such personal questions.

Not like I could bring it up in polite conversation. At least, not right away. It would take several conversations to find out what else he might want from me . . . or with me . . . but the only way that would ever happen is . . .

Behind her, Daranen coughed discreetly. "Shouldn't you be getting ready for your midday path-walk and tree-draining, Holiness?"

"Oh, right." Tugging her fingers free was easy; he didn't clutch at them or resist, just let them slide from his grasp as if in one last caress. She could still feel the lingering warmth of his skin on hers, and wished she could just take his hand and not have to think about being the Keeper of the Grove for a while. Blushing, Saleria rose to her feet.

So did Aradin Teral. He smiled at her, tugged his hood up into place, swooped the folds of his voluminous robes around both his body and the chest, turned completely around in a swirl of tan-and-black hemline, and faced her again. The chest had vanished somewhere in that spin, and again she could detect no magic in the act.

"How . . . ?" she asked, distracted by its disappearance. "I sensed no magic whatsoever, yet it had to be by magic. So how did you do that?"

"I'd tell you, but most people outside our Order don't like hearing the answer," he told her, pushing the hood off his head one more time. It was still the younger, blond-haired Aradin, or at least his body. And he stood and talked like the younger man did. "So, since there's nothing more to discuss while you think about it, should I accompany you on your walk today?"

"But I do want to know," Saleria protested, clinging to her curiosity. She stepped forward as she spoke, one hand coming up to touch his tan-robed arm. Her eyes searched his, and she felt odd, as if she were . . . flirting with him. . . . *I'm flirting with him? I guess I am.* "Please? It'll plague me all day if I don't know, and then I'll be distracted, and get mauled by a . . . a stray, ambulatory fern bush or something."

Just a little bit taller than her, he had an excellent view of her eyes from this close. They looked a bit more gray than blue here in the indirect daylight that illuminated her study. They also looked sincerely interested in his answer, wide, framed with short but thick golden lashes. A straight nose lay between them, and her rose-pink lips rested below, slightly parted as she awaited his answer.

What he *wanted* to do was kiss her. What he had to do was answer her question. Shrugging, Aradin spread his hands, then clasped them. "As you may know, death draws magic into the Darkness. Additionally, you may know that certain weak points in the Veil between Life and Death allow some of that magic to rush back into the world again, yes?"

"Yes, I know all that. I deal with it on a daily basis," she dismissed impatiently. "Particularly the spewing back out into the living world part."

"Well, if you know how to open a doorway into the Dark . . . a one-way opening *into* the realm of the wandering dead, rather than a Fountain being a doorway flowing *from* there to here . . . then your magic gets sucked *into* the Dark, does it not?" His smile didn't falter, though he did watch her pupils expand in shock, along with a shiver that rippled over her frame. He softened his smile, taking pity on her. "We of Darkhana are not afraid of *any* aspect of death, Holy Sister. It is simply a transition between states of existence. A transition which many of us have learned to master . . . and no, I do not refer to immortality."

"Oh, you don't?" Saleria asked, dropping her hand so she could fold her arms across her chest.

Tipping his head, Aradin let Teral answer for both of them. "There is nothing that a mortal being can do to completely stop the advancing of age in a human's body, young lady," the older Witch stated. "Slow it, yes, but there is nothing we *should* do to stop its advancement, beyond taking care for our good health. We can slow it through exercise and good food, and even a few spells, but aging is part of the experience of being human, of being mortal.

"Without physical signs of the passage of time, then time itself becomes meaningless. Weeks and months and years all slide past. Reference points are lost. Confusion sets in, and the lessons we strive to learn are washed away in the flood of same-again same-again, day after day. We start to lose the urgency of life, and with it, the compassion for our fellow beings." He gave her a gentle smile. "We give power and compassion to our Gods *because* we know we are mortal, fragile, and somewhat short on time."

"Yet don't you Guides have a sort of immortality of your own?" she asked, shifting her palms to her hips. She . . . didn't feel like flirting with him as much, when it was Teral, for all that she liked the look of Aradin's body. Saleria kept that point of awkwardness to herself, though, pursuing instead her curiosity. "What's to stop you from binding yourself to the next priest, and the next?"

"The bond can only be set once for a spirit whose body has died," he stated, shaking his head. "When Aradin dies and his body decays, I will be released into the Light, because I can only be bound once, and I chose to be bound to the Doorway found in his body, with his permission. It is my physical anchor, just as my body was the physical anchor for my own soul when I was alive, and the anchor for my own Guide, Alaya. And some day, should Aradin choose to become a Guide, he will have one choice and one alone, with no taking it back and no changing his mind—changing his soul—for another's Door," Teral revealed. He paused, then tipped his head, Aradin's head, handing back control of their shared body.

Once again, it was Aradin who spoke. ". . . I did not make the choice to be his Host lightly. I would not ask anyone else so lightly, and I shall hope I won't ever have to make it as abruptly, either. Normally, one or more acolytes are chosen and trained in the last few years of a Witch's life, serving alongside the person who is expected to become their Guide. That helps ensure the personalities hopefully match. If not . . . it can be a rough transition period while the two get to know and learn tolerance for each other."

"As your experience was?" Saleria asked, guessing shrewdly from the slight hesitancies in his words.

Aradin dipped his head in a brief but telling nod. "It could have been considerably worse, but we're both honest enough to admit the first few months were . . . awkward. Becoming a Witch-priest was not on my original list of things to do with my life. But we have managed to strike a very reasonable compromise. We get along as well as any two close friends, now."

Saleria studied him a long moment, then shook her head. All this swapping back and forth was confusing, the differences subtle and hard to catch. "If it's all the same, if you turn out to be suitable for helping me . . . I'd rather only one of you spoke from, well, one body at a time. Each your own body. It gets confusing otherwise. Just pass along what the other one wants to say, if you don't actually switch, please?"

In the back of Aradin's mind, his Guide sighed. (*Typical . . . but understandable. Since your points are valid on each of our suitability for the problems at hand, please let her know that I agree to her terms.*)

(*Not like I have much of a choice, either. We are under orders to cooperate wherever it is in the best interests for all. And if nothing else, we can at least try to be more discreet when switching control. Though to be honest, I think it'll remind me of our earliest days,*) Aradin agreed, a faint smile twisting his mouth. Reviving the Convocation was their goal, and that had to come first. Shrugging, he spread his hands. "Teral agrees to your terms, and I shall do my best to comply as well."

"Good," she said. "No insult to your Guide or anything, but I prefer to *see* the person speaking with me. It's one thing when you're around a corner, but another thing entirely when you're using someone else's lips. It's very disorienting."

Aradin nodded, a lock of his blond hair sliding free of his robe. "That is quite understandable. Even a few people within our homeland's borders still find it awkward to speak to one while seeing another. We have grown . . . lax . . . in our protocols, and both of us apologize."

The bow he gave her was as graceful as it was sincere. Saleria couldn't find fault with his—their—politeness. *And that's enough of that line of thought,* she decided silently. *Or my head will end up aching abominably from trying to keep track of it all.*

Another soft, semi-discreet cough from her scribe reminded her of her sense of duty. Sighing, she headed for the door. Then stopped and turned back to face the strange two-in-one priest. She made another decision, a split-second decision, and spoke with it firmly in her mind.

"Boasting or truthful, you have claimed you understand the interactions between plants and magic, and claimed you are a strong mage—singly or together makes no matter," she dismissed that part. "If you think you can help assist me, then come now, and prove it. You may take a few moments to visit a refreshing room, which is just two doors down on the left. I will fetch waterskins and a spare pruning staff. Do understand that, should you choose to accompany me, you will do as I say, when I say it, and otherwise not interfere."

"Of course," Aradin agreed quickly, bowing again. Not as

deeply as before, but with similar sincerity. "I will be as a mere apprentice, and you my teacher."

Nodding, she led the way out of her office. It was time to go on her next set of rounds. *Apprentice. Teacher. Right. He's too smooth, too experienced, to hold such a subservient role for long, I'd think. Well, we'll see how well he does when he meets up with his first carnivorous vine.*

THREE

Aradin stared in awe at the mutated tangle of plant life that blocked their path, shades of dark green vines, medium green leaves, and bright, white, trumpet-shaped flowers striped faintly with faded gold. "*Magnificent . . .*"

Saleria raised her brows at that. She didn't quite look at Aradin, mainly because she wasn't about to take her attention away from the mutated cross between morning glory and thettis-vine, with the conical blossoms paired with wicked, toxic thorns at the base of each bud. She did, however, speak in a very dry tone. "More like a nightmare made manifest. The toxin on those thorns will slow our reflexes. The leaves are spongy, designed to absorb our blood for nutrients. Our drained corpses will be wrapped in root vines to decompose and feed the whole plant more directly.

"But the flowers are very pretty, I'll grant you that. Possibly magnificent, if one ignores all the rest. Alas, I cannot," she finished, gaze roving over the tangle of vines that blocked their path.

Today's tangle was thicker than yesterday's, though by squinting and shifting a little, she could see it was not as deep. "It also has a rudimentary sense of cunning."

"Cunning?" Aradin asked her. He, too, did not lift his gaze from the dense layers of vines mounded over the flagstone-lined path. At the edges of his vision, he could see the great, bramble-like branches of one of the nearby locus trees, and of course a pro-fusion of foliage ranging from tiny little mint plants carpeting the edges of the flagstone-lined path to great towering palms with fernlike fronds swaying softly in the breeze overhead. Insects buzzed, birds twittered, leaves rustled gently. It looked like a pas-toral setting, save for the fact that this strange, not-quite-morning-glory thicket was blocking their path.

"It constantly tests me, trying to catch me by one means or another. Except it really doesn't know much, other than to grow thin and stretched out, or to grow dense in a short patch of the path. Dense is easier to clear quickly in just a few strokes, though there is more of a chance that several of those thorns will scratch me and inject their venom," she said, pointing at the long, straight, gleaming spikes at the base of each flower-bell. "Spread out more linearly over the path, they have more room to flail and it takes longer to clear, but fewer thorns will strike me in a single blow, and I have fewer vines to dodge, so I'm more likely to cut each one that attacks."

"I see now, and I must agree. Cunning, yes; smarts, no," Aradin agreed, following along. "It seems to have the aspects of two dif-ferent plants. The base is clearly one of your morning glory plants, a tenacious vine but one lacking thorns. The other . . . The shape of it reminds me of a plant I saw illustrated in a book from the seas to the north and west, I think."

"*Thettis*. It's an ornamental thorn-vine which sprouts tasty ber-ries that can be distilled into a soporific for healing and pain-management medicines—an appropriate gift for the original

Grove," Saleria stated. "I cannot be completely sure, but round about this area was where the original gift from the Althinac ambassador was planted. The morning glory . . . could have come from anywhere. A stray seed eaten and then defecated onto the thettis by a local bird, perhaps. But the thettis bush was a gift, of that, I am sure."

"A recent acquisition?" Aradin asked, and received a shake of her head, her blonde curls bouncing over her shoulders with the quick, sharp move.

"No. From at least four hundred years ago. There are records of all such plants gifted to the Empire, which were naturally brought here to the Grove, making it a showcase of foreign plants as well as native ones. A true garden of the Gods, since it is said that every earthly delight can be found in the Afterlife. The Grove was supposed to be an echo of such a place, with every ornamental or useful herb, bush, and tree gathered into one place."

"Only now it's gone wrong. Those who caused the Shattering have much to answer for," Aradin murmured. He narrowed his eyes. "Did one of those vines just move a little?"

"It did." Hefting her pruning staff, Saleria prepared herself for the assault. "Stay back. Remember, the spells on the flat end will cut us as well as our attackers, if you aren't careful. Using a staff for walking is not the same as using a staff for fighting."

He lifted his own in a two-handed stance, ready to wield it. "Our foremost Witch believes that everyone in our Order should be schooled in non-magical self-defense as well as magical. We are each required to learn at least four close-fighting styles and one ranged skill before being allowed to leave the training cloisters. Teral and I both learned combat with knife, short staff, and Arbran-style wrestling, involving holds and escapes as well as blows and blocks. He also learned sword and bow. I learned mace and sling."

"Sling?" Saleria asked, distracted by that. "Isn't that a child's toy?"

"It's more versatile than you'd think. I am an herbalist. I can craft potions, put them into carefully cleaned and wax-sealed eggshells, or thin-baked pottery balls, and hurl them at my enemies. If I have the time to prepare them," he amended, tipping his head ruefully. He didn't mention that he had several such missiles already prepared, labeled, and stored within the infinite, close space of the Dark. Instead, he lifted the staff she had loaned him. "This pole is a little bit longer than I'm used to wielding, but I think I can compensate. But as it is your Grove, you may certainly lead the way. I'll just watch your back."

Saleria nodded and shifted her weight to move forward, but curiosity held her back. Unable to help herself, she asked, "Why magnificent? Of all the words one could choose, about a plant like *this* . . . ?"

"It's the blending of the features. I can tell three things went into its making," he told her, "and it's all very well done. A master Hortimancer couldn't have done better. An insane master, to create an ambulatory monstrosity like this, but still, well done."

"What—*three*?" Saleria asked, so surprised that she turned to look at him. As her booted feet scraped on the gritty flagstones, the vines moved, whipping outward in an attack meant to bind. She yelped in shock, but reacted on reflex, whipping her staff up and around. The spell cut through most of the tendrils, but some were longer than expected, rising up out of the bushes on the side of the path to try to curl around her legs.

Aradin's staff whistled through the air, whipping the enspelled end through the impertinent vegetation. Severed bits of limbs skidded across the path, while the main plant shuddered and rustled, retracting itself. It still lurked close to their route, but didn't try a second attack, and didn't loom over the path.

Saleria nodded her thanks, and lifted her chin at the flowered mass. "Cunning, and for the next hour or so, it will remember and avoid a second attack. But by tomorrow, it will have forgotten and will try to attack again. Sometimes, if an animal goes astray nearby and has to be put down, I'll drag its corpse here to dispose of the body faster than letting it rot . . . but I don't *really* want to feed it."

"I probably wouldn't feed it, either," Aradin agreed.

"So, we have morning glory and thettis. What's the third plant?" she asked, touching the crystal end of her staff to the fallen, dying vines. The ones still attached twitched a little, but did not move in their direction.

"It's not a plant," Aradin corrected, his gaze still on the bundle of vines.

That started her again, though this time she didn't shift her stance. It might seem subdued, but there was no point in taking a chance. "It's not?"

"See those tiny hairs along the vines? And the round little lumps that gleam like dark pearls?" he asked, pointing over her shoulder so she could sight along his arm. At her nod, Aradin explained. "Those are cilia and ommatidia. The little hair-structures, the cilia, detect vibrations, like odd sorts of ears. I think they 'hear' only at certain pitches, since it isn't reacting to our voices, but it did react to the scrape of your foot on the ground. The ommatidia . . . are insect eyes. Insects aren't as good at seeing as humans are, and nowhere near as good as an eagle or a hawk, but they are watching us for movement and proximity.

"As I said, this is as good as the work of any mad master Hortimancer . . . since only an insane person would try to blend animal and vegetable like this," he finished.

Saleria stared at the vines in horror. Before, she had simply, if grimly, disliked the thing, dealt with it whenever it grew large enough to menace her, and moved on to the next overgrown whatever. But combined with bits from a bug? *Creepy.* In a tight, clipped voice, fingers white-knuckled on her staff, she stated, "I am now *very* uncomfortable, knowing that."

"The more I think about it, the more I believe the previous abominations we've met on just this one walk through the Grove may have had a blend of three characteristics as well. Not the quieter, less aggressive blends," he murmured, "but the ones that have tried to attack us, yes. You were talking about the three, ah, locus trees each producing magic, and needing to be drained on a rotating schedule? I suspect that, if there are ever hours where you have to skip a round, or are too sick to go out at all that day, the excess magics spill over and warp through each other, surging and eddying and crossing like little whirlwinds of power."

"That would make some sense," Saleria admitted. "The few times I have been ill with a cold or fever, the Grove has usually been wilder a week or so later. Uncontrolled, unpurposed magic may be strong, but without a concrete purpose behind it, driving it with the will of the mage, no magic can create whole beasts or bushes in a single day."

"But it can begin the warping process," Aradin said. Lifting his staff, he tipped it at the vines. "Shall we prune this bush-beast back a little further and continue on our way, then?"

Nodding, Saleria eyed the vines, then lunged a little, slashing in a sudden attack. More bits of warped plant limbs dropped to the path. She did it again, and a third time. Once it was trimmed back to her satisfaction, she started to tap the vines with the crystal end of her staff, then stopped. Eyes wide, she glanced at Aradin.

"Wait . . . if these are part *animal*, then . . . then isn't this blood-magic?"

"They are far more plant than animal, so I think it shouldn't matter as much as you'd think. Besides, you have been doing this for many years, you and your predecessors, yes? And you are obviously not corrupted by the madness of the Netherhells whispering in your ears?" he added. At her hesitant nod, he shrugged. "Then the Gods have already accepted it as beneficial. I wouldn't drain that shrew-thing you mentioned, but something that is two parts plant and one part tiny insect shouldn't be a problem."

"Right." She hesitated a moment more, then touched the cuttings, draining the magic still trying to make them twitch. Unlike animals, plant bits did not die within a minute of being severed from the bulk of the original plant; in fact, if conditions were right, they could take in water, grow new roots, and become a new problem. It was therefore best to ensure they shriveled and died completely. "Not to mention the use to which it is purposed does nothing for me personally, but is instead purposed specifically to help others. So . . . it is not evil. So long as I take great care to *ensure* the energies are not used for evil ends."

"That is the way magic works in all lands, yes," Aradin murmured, following her. His staff had a crystal, too, but he intended to let her gather the majority of energies. He didn't want her having even the slightest suspicion that he was interested in such things for his own ends. He honestly wasn't—neither of them were, Host or Guide—but it was still wise to conduct themselves circumspectly.

That, and her rump presses rather magnificently against the folds of her trousers and jacket, whenever she bends over a little bit, just like that . . .

(*A magnificent rump, indeed,*) Teral agreed, following his line of thought with equal masculine appreciation. (*But don't speak aloud the same word for her backside that you used to describe a monstrous amalgamation of plants and insect.*)

(*My dear Guide, I am not that stupid,*) Aradin retorted, watching her stretch out the staff again. Though he did continue to enjoy the view as she drained the last few severed tendrils.

* * *

Saleria snuck yet another glance at her companion. So far, Witch Aradin Teral had proved as good as his word. Their word? His, theirs, it mattered not. He had let her take the lead—a thing not all men were inclined to do—and had done nothing more than support and defend her movements when the magic-warped inhabitants of the Grove had proven a bit too bothersome. But now, after visiting the eight altar-stones arrayed along the major inner paths and trimming back the excess growths, it was time to visit the Bower.

She knew from her conversations with other Guardians scattered around the world that the Bower corresponded to a Fountain Hall, the chamber holding the energies from a singularity-point, spewing magic much like the rifts from the shattered Portals did. Of course, a Fountain Hall had its rift in the center of its chamber; the Bower was instead located in the center of the triangle formed by the three locus trees. But there were similarities . . . including the vast amount of somewhat tamed magical power available in the Bower.

No one in Katan would dare try to wrest away control of the Grove's magic from the Grove Keeper. It would be considered tantamount to slapping Kata on the rump and yanking up the back of Jinga's trousers. Not a good idea. As much as the belief and faith of the people as a whole created a kingdom's Patron Deity or Deities, and gave Them the power to enact miracles great and small, the Gods did have minds of Their own sometimes. They would probably not react with benevolence or forgiveness to such an act of hubris, either the slapping-and-yanking, or the theft of the Grove's power.

But Aradin Teral was an outlander, an outkingdom foreigner, a stranger from a far-distant land. . . .

"Teral says he has noticed how you keep glancing at me in the last few moments, and would like to know why," Aradin stated, catching her off guard. "I find myself curious as well."

Saleria blinked, then cleared her throat. "I . . . er . . . How?" she finally asked. "You didn't once look at me."

In fact, he wasn't looking at her now, but Aradin didn't have to. He tapped the edge of his face next to his eye. "Any Guide can shift his attention to see things in the Host's peripheral vision. There's a small learning curve, but it's been quite handy so far, particularly in potentially dangerous situations. Or ones where I need to be socially aware." Now he glanced her way, giving her a smile. "So you might as well ask what you wanted to ask. Whatever it is, we won't be offended, I assure you."

Stopping on the path, she planted her free hand on her hip, the other keeping her staff carefully upright so it wouldn't bump into either of them. "Even if I ask something obnoxious, like 'Which do you prefer to eat, feces or rotting corpses for breakfast?'"

Caught off guard, Aradin choked on a laugh. He swung around to face her, his staff equally upright, but with his hand over his mouth. Snickering a bit, he coughed, cleared his throat, and addressed her question. "Oh, I hardly think you're the sort to ask something truly obnoxious. You've been more than gracious all this while, and I don't see that ending any time soon. But you do have an important question you wish to ask . . . so, why not ask it?"

"Alright. While it would be unthinkable for a Katani to try to wrest control of all the magic available in the Grove, for fear of incurring the wrath of our God and Goddess," Saleria explained, "you, on the other hand, are a foreigner. More than that, you are a foreign priest, to foreign Gods. You care not a whit for our Patron Deities. How do I know you will not try to wrest control of the Grove from me, or steal its powers, or . . . ?"

He held up his hand. "I, Aradin of Darkhana, bind unto my

powers this vow: I promise I have no intention of stealing the powers of the sacred matrimonial Grove of Holy Kata and Jinga, nor of
using those stolen powers in ways which would bring grave harm
to yourself, the people of Katan, your Patron Deities, or the rest of
the world, save only whatever may be needful in the name of self-
defense or the defense of others. So swear I, Aradin of Darkhana."

Bands of silver light edged with dark blue shimmered over his
body, sweeping him from the crown of his blond head to the soles
of his brown-booted feet. Saleria blinked. She hadn't expected
that. Not a mage-oath, binding Aradin to the exact wording of his
vow via his own powers. It was deeply satisfactory, however. And a
neatly spoken piece of law-speaker's cleverness. He could not *steal*
the powers . . . but he could still be free to borrow them, by request
or by gift.

"You surprised me," she admitted. "But . . . it is well-spoken. If
craftily." She started to move forward, then checked herself after two
steps and faced him again. "Now, what about *Teral* making that vow?"

A grin cracked his lips, showing his mostly straight white teeth;
one of his canines sat just a little bit crooked. But that grin confused her, at least until he spoke. Lifting his finger, Aradin waggled
it at her. "You are very, very clever to have spotted a potential loophole like that, milady. Well done! Here, hold my staff while we
trade places."

Taking it from him, Saleria watched as he pulled his hood over
his head and down to his throat, then tucked his hands into the
robe's sleeves. As the heat of the day had increased, he had pulled
the robe shut around his body, no doubt keeping it cool via temperature charms. Now his frame shifted, he straightened, and the
taller, broader-shouldered, older figure of Teral pushed the hood
back. Giving her a slight bow, he spoke in his smooth, cultured
baritone.

"I, Teral of Darkhana, bind unto my powers this vow: I promise

I have no intention of stealing the powers of the sacred matrimonial Grove of Holy Kata and Jinga, nor of using those stolen powers in ways which would bring grave harm to yourself, the people of Katan, your Patron Deities, or the rest of the world, save only whatever may be needful in the name of self-defense or the defense of others.

"So swear I, Teral of Darkhana." This time, the bands of dark blue light were stronger than the silver, though the latter still sizzled from graying brown head to beige-clad toe. Bowing, he straightened and raised one eyebrow. "I trust that will suffice as to *both* our intentions, Holy Sister?"

She smiled wryly and dipped her head in return. "It will suffice, Holy Brother." He started to shift the hood forward, no doubt to switch bodies again. Saleria quickly held out his borrowed staff, forestalling him. "Please, stay for a little bit, and walk with me. I am curious about you as well."

(*Go ahead,*) Aradin encouraged him. (*You're due some time in your own body.*)

(*Only because she swears this "Bower" place isn't dangerous. I'd rather you did all the ducking and dodging,*) Teral joked silently. Nodding his head, he accepted the staff and gestured for Saleria to take the lead. "As you wish, milady."

Now that she had his—their—acquiescence, Saleria wasn't quite sure where to begin. She started walking again, letting Teral follow a few paces behind. Aradin's comment about obnoxious questions did raise a point, so she started with that. "I am not at all familiar with the, ah, ways of your kind. If any question I ask *is* obnoxious, please forgive me in advance, and just let me know it isn't something you care to answer."

"Such courtesy is appreciated." Watching the younger woman's hips sway with each step, Teral could not only see what Aradin had seen; he could feel their shared body responding to it. (*I do believe there are some serious drawbacks to being flesh and blood. At least, where my dignity is concerned.*)

(*Feels good, doesn't it?*) Aradin teased. It was still his body, and he could still feel the blood pooling at the sway of those hips, but it felt distanced, almost numb, since he wasn't the one in control.

(*Indeed.*) Teral smiled pleasantly when the blonde priestess glanced back at them. Her almond-shaped eyes and high cheekbones made her look very different from Darkhanan women. The differences were exotic and alluring, making both men aware of her unpretentious beauty. (*No hints of painting or primping, no subtle tricks or artifice, just natural, beautiful woman, as her Gods clearly made her to be. Oh, to be alive again . . .*)

(*Albeit with your Alaya's permission,*) Aradin chuckled in the back of Teral's mind. (*These days, you'd need mine.*)

The view he had was much like peering at a bright window or a scrying mirror over Teral's shoulder from a hushed, darkened room. The perspective was a little off, too, since his Host's version of the body stood just a little bit taller. But he was used to it by now. Everything behind and around him was dark, save for what Teral saw, quiet save for what Teral heard . . . and the whispers of what Teral thought. The stronger the thought, the louder the whisper. The thought prompting his quip hadn't been loud, but it was one he himself had been thinking.

(*Then again, Teral, I'm not sure if this Katani woman would care to have either of us as a lover. You're technically a dead man in a borrowed body, and neither of us is alone, unless one of us steps into the Dark.*) Aradin started to say more, then hushed. Priestess Saleria had finally found a question she wanted to ask.

"So . . . how did you become a Guide?" she asked.

"A tree fell on me, and Aradin was the nearest willing mage I could ask to be bound to before I died." At her flustered look, Teral smiled. "Or did you mean what made me choose to become a Witch in the first place?"

"Yes, that," she corrected herself. A swipe of her staff severed a tree limb bending their way. She paused to drain it into the glowing crystal at the other end of her staff. "I meant . . . I had a revelation, a moment of divine inspiration, I suppose you could say. I was in a youth choir, organized by the cathedral in my city—my father is an instructor for the Imperial Army, and my mother serves as a road crew mage, so it wasn't a case of following in either's footsteps.

"Anyway, we were singing a hymn to the seasons, to the four faces of our Gods . . . and it was so sublime, every note blended in purity and harmony . . . perfect. Just perfect. I knew then that I was being called to serve my Goddess and God." Smiling softly, ruefully, she continued toward a structure of intertwined branches forming a lacework dome. "It sounds silly to say that a 'mere song' inspired me to become a priestess, but over a decade later, I can still remember how perfect everything was in that moment. How holy and pure.

"I could have become a secular sort of mage, but I felt my powers would be better used to serve everyone, not just those who could afford my services," she concluded. "I know what made Aradin a Witch-priest—proximity to you and your tree," Saleria dared to tease lightly, since neither man seemed to treat it like a huge tragedy, for all that it had been. "But what made *you* choose to be a Witch-priest, instead of a normal priest, or a normal mage, or . . . or a bookbinder or something?"

"An excess of mouths to feed. My mother would get pregnant at the drop of her nightshift," Teral stated bluntly, though with humor in his tone as she gaped at him. "That, milady, was how *she* put it. I was seventh in a family of thirteen children."

"Goodness!" Saleria exclaimed softly, impressed by that. "Um . . . not to be rude, but . . . ?"

Teral knew what she was trying to ask delicately. "There was just something about Mother's energies that, ah, prevented contraceptive amulets and potions from working for her . . . and she did enjoy being mother to a huge brood of little ones. Ours was the house where the neighborhood children would congregate to play, and study, and be accepted, thanks to her. Father worked as a glass-maker, but the trade in our city could only support so many apprentices, and his wages only so many mouths to feed. Particularly when we became teenagers, with the huge appetites to match.

"I was very good at the scholarly arts, so the high priest of our cathedral was willing to sponsor an apprenticeship for me to become a member of the clergy, a clerical sort of priest. But then puberty struck, my magic started coming out, and he had me transferred to Witch-craft training. I had some aptitude for trading and negotiating, so eventually I was apprenticed to this rather elderly woman named Alaya Vondren. Her Guide was male, you see, and they thought that with so many sisters in my family background, I could handle being paired with a female when it was Alaya's turn to pass on and become a Guide," Teral stated. "They already knew she could handle being paired with a male."

They were almost to the Bower, following the path as it switched back and forth at a gentle slope down into the bowl-like vale at the heart of the Grove. Saleria kept an eye out for warped plants and animals, but her curiosity was strong. "You've mentioned you have a God and Goddess . . ."

"Yes, the Dual One. Darkhan, the Dead God, formerly the God of Elder Brother Moon before its destruction thousands of years ago," Teral said, "and His Host, Dark Ana, formerly the mortal Arch Priestess Ana."

"Well . . . I can understand why it would be more *comfortable* to be paired with someone of the same gender constantly sharing your life," Saleria stated, "but from a theological standpoint, wouldn't it make more sense for all of you to swap genders every generation, so to speak?"

He chuckled, his voice deepening almost to Aradin's bass. Grinning, he rubbed at his neatly trimmed beard. "You've hit the nail on the head with your hammer, there. Yes, it would make more sense. But to serve as a Witch, one must be *willing* to do so. Growing up with as many sisters as brothers, older and younger and all learning how to get along with each other, I was . . . comfortable, I suppose you could say, around the fairer sex. From listening to my sisters' plaints, I could understand some of how they thought. Then again, I wasn't completely sure I'd want to share my life with Alaya once she'd passed on from Host to Guide . . . until I got to know her."

"Oh? A charming, sweet lady?" Saleria asked.

"Sweet? No. Charming? Yes," the older priest agreed. "She was sharp but fair, clever without needing to resort to cunning, and wouldn't put up with nonsense from a young man. Or anyone else, really. And in time, I grew to love her as a close friend and confidant, both before and after we joined as Host and Guide. Vondren, I respected and trusted, and missed him once he was gone . . . but part of him lived on in Alaya's memories, and in Alaya's work. She had traveled a lot as a purchasing agent for the Church, as had he before her. I learned the craft of negotiation and diplomacy from her, and Aradin has learned it from me."

"Yes, I've noticed how charming and diplomatic he can be," Saleria observed dryly, motioning for Teral to stop. They had reached the edge of the Bower. Here, there were magics woven into the giant, gazebo-like structure that would keep out anything hostile, hungry, or hurtful. But sometimes creatures liked to lurk in the bushes just to either side of the intertwined structure. It wasn't as if she could alter her daily routine to avoid being seen.

Nothing seemed amiss, so she nodded and moved inside. A rustling noise was her only warning. Spinning, she brought up her staff, but Teral had already moved, warned by both noise and Aradin's sharp gaze catching the movement at the corner of their shared eyesight. Swinging his staff, the middle-aged priest *whack*ed it into the overgrown, rabbity thing that leaped out of the bushes on too many legs, jaws agape and tail trailing . . . a rope of spider-silk?

It did not matter, save that the line of silk showed where the body of the beast was flung by his soundly struck blow. The thing smashed into the bushes halfway up the hill and tumbled down through the foliage. It came to a rest under a fernlike bush, just barely visible, and still breathing but otherwise not moving. Teral grimaced. "Sorry. Meant to hit it with the cutting end, not the crystal."

"Still, a well-struck blow," Saleria praised, grateful the older man hadn't been harmed. She moved up beside him, both of them warily watching the rabbit-spider-thing for signs of further aggression. "And I thought Aradin said *he* was the one with mace-wielding skill."

"Oh, it bleeds over," Teral admitted. "I can wield a sling well enough to bring down supper, if need be. After a few tries, but still, only a few. And he can shoot a deer at fifty paces with bow and arrow, if he's really hungry. Should we be going after that thing?"

"It's in a patch of peaceferns. Unless it's really hungry, the mutant should go to sleep for several hours, then wander off. I'd rather not try to get to that spider-thing myself, since I'd come under the soporific effects of the plant's perfume," she said.

"That thing has flowers?" Teral asked, squinting at the fern. Aradin focused, too, and whispered into his mind. "Ahhh, I see— or rather, Aradin sees. Tiny little knobby things that look more like miniature fiddleheads than flowers, the same shade of green as the rest of the plant, save for tiny paler green speckles . . . Have you tried an air-cleansing spell, to filter out the perfume?"

"Well . . . no, but it would have to be paired with a body-cleansing charm, to remove the pollen," she said.

"Mm. Well, if you'll permit it, this is more Aradin's area of expertise than mine. He'd be willing to climb up there and dispatch the creature, if you like," Teral offered. "Though I suspect it's as much to get a closer look at the plant-life as anything."

"I'm torn," she murmured. "That creature is large enough to be a menace, and should be removed, but I shouldn't like to endanger your Host. I appreciate the offer, but . . ."

Teral placed his hand on her shoulder, turning just enough to face her without ruining Aradin's edge-of-the-eye view of the downed brown rabbit-spider thing. "Please, Priestess; we are here to help, and are fully prepared to help. You should not be the only person to face all these dangers, and the Gods know this. In fact, I suspect the hand of Threefold Fate in arranging for my Host in specific to be the one assigned to this continent. He is a formally trained Hortimancer, and he has been sent here to find you, a woman who cares for her people but naught for politics, all while tending an overgrown nightmare of a garden that should be restored and remade safe and sane.

"The three hardest things to say in the world are 'I love you,' 'I'm sorry,' and 'I need help,'" Teral continued. "You are clearly a strong woman, for you are set in circumstances which would clearly require at least three people to manage easily. The latter-most statement should not be a problem for you, nor should it be *made* a problem by those around you," he added softly, gently. "Is it not one of the Laws of God and Man, 'Ask and you may receive; stay silent, and you will not' . . . ? Ask, Holy Sister, and you shall receive our help; this, I pledge to you."

It was a supreme irony that this strange, two-in-one outlander was so willing to help her tend to the holiest place in the entire Empire of Katan where her own Order was not. . . . *Bollocks to them!* Saleria thought, frowning at the idea of being offered help but having to refuse it for . . . for whatever internal, priestly-political reason her superiors may have. "Alright. Witch Teral Aradin . . . or Aradin Teral, whatever . . . would you be so kind as to very carefully get up there and dispatch that poor rabbit-spider-thing, so that it doesn't attack us or escape the Grove at some point?"

"As milady commands," Teral murmured. Handing over the staff for a moment, he swept the hood up over his head, tucked his arms in his sleeves, and bowed politely under its dark embrace.

Bodies once again swapped, Aradin pushed the hood back. He frowned in thought a few moments, accepted the gardening staff from Saleria once more, and began murmuring spells in his deep voice. Magic rose from his body like a mist, weaving its way around his leaner frame until it flashed and faded into a rippling aura that could be seen more from the way it made the eye twitch than from any distinct visual effect.

A second murmur thickened several patches of air into misty, flat-topped clouds. They formed a stairwell and footpath just above the plants. As soon as the last one was laid, he swiftly mounted the makeshift steps and hurried toward the twitching animal. Impressed, Saleria wondered if he would be willing to teach it to her. Such a thing would make her own daily routine that much easier, if she could just walk *over* minor mutated plants which weren't troublesome in order to get at the heavily mutated animals and plants that were.

Of course, it would be far better if I didn't have to deal with mutated plants and animals at all . . . Recent conversations with Guardian Kerric, up north in Aiar, suggested there were other things she could be doing with the magic of her not-quite-Fountains, things to drain and use the excess energies. Ways to permanently do so, without the need for a living mage to constantly pray every day. *Perhaps not automatic prayers; those need to be guided by a willing spirit. But . . . little things, perhaps creating and maintaining aqueducts of water for the dry northlands, though that might prove to be too far away for the magic to reach. Or some system of heating and cooling for the local houses, or . . .*

She watched as Aradin studied the creature a long moment, then slashed in three strokes. It squealed and thrashed on the first, thrashed again on the second, and twitched on the third. Its movements slowed, then stopped. Aradin bowed his head, murmured something with a hand stretched out over the creature's body, then turned and made his way back at a more leisurely pace. A few murmurs shed the cocoon of shimmering air from his body. Saleria caught a whiff of perfume-laced pollen, but only a whiff before the soft breeze wending its way through the Grove carried the soporific stuff away.

"Three parts animal," he stated, dismissing the puff-clouds with a gesture once he reached the flagstone path. "Rabbit, jumping-spider, and mouse or shrew. Milady, as one mage to another, I say to you this place *needs* to be brought under control. In my oath, I swore I would not use the powers of this place to cause harm, but I am not the one you should be worried about. There is so much magic steeped into everything living within the garden's walls . . ."

Breaking off, he shook his head, looking past her into the Bower, though with the kind of faraway gaze that said he wasn't really seeing it.

". . . Such negligence makes me wonder why your hierarchy would be so blind to the needs of this place. Unless, of course, absolutely none of your priesthood has ever studied the interactions of magic, animals, and plants," he concluded, focusing on her again. "Otherwise, they are willfully allowing massive mutations to occur, and for no good reason that I can see."

"I *think* there may be a prophecy involved, based on something Jonder, the previous Keeper, said about the mess I was inheriting from him," Saleria murmured. She looked at the Bower and shrugged. "I suppose I could contact the Department of Prophecies to see if there is. Who knows? Maybe that prophecy you showed me—which I should check up on, to verify—has a corresponding one that is also going to come true about this place, and I can finally get more than myself working on this place.

"I may not know much about foreign lands, but I do know prophecies tend to . . . to go off in clusters, like flocks of geese taking to flight." She paused, debated whether or not to say her next thought, then shrugged mentally and said it anyway. "Which is rather apropos, since geese taking off tend to defecate on everything, and that's often how a flock of prophecies going off tends to feel, from what I've heard."

Aradin smiled wryly at her simile, but otherwise said nothing to that. Particularly since he'd heard similar things, too. He didn't know if there were any other prophecies dealing specifically with this place or not, just the ones dealing with his assigned task. Instead, the Witch gestured wordlessly at the upside-down basket of brown-barked, interwoven boles stretching a good sixty feet wide and roughly sixty feet high at its center.

Nodding, Saleria led him into the moss-floored heart of the Grove. Beyond the woven woodworks and mossy ground was another odd sight. Leafless vines dangled down from overhead; each one dripped a thick, colorful liquid like sun-warmed honey, but in shades of blue and pink and green as well as amber. Each slow dribble collected in a small, moss-edged basin. Aradin eyed those little pools of pastel liquid warily.

Thankfully, there were plenty of mossy paths between the vines, marked by dark and light, tough strains of moss, or at least something mosslike, thick and cushiony underfoot. He followed her down to a stone slab that served as her altar, wondering what the purpose was for the sap. It wasn't until he squinted, invoking his ability to see the flow of magical energies, that he gasped and stumbled, overwhelmed by what he Saw.

Saleria, hearing his sharp intake of breath, turned to see what was wrong. She barely managed to get him braced as he lost his footing on the mossy path. Steadying the foreign priest, she waited for him to recover his senses. He did so with a sharp little shake of his head and a rapid double-blink.

"I . . . That stuff is . . . is pure concentrated magic." He pointed at the saplike substance and gave her a wide-eyed look. "In liquid form!"

"Yes," she admitted, since anyone with the ability to see the flow of energies through the aether could have told that much. "I only gather the excess energies directly in my patrols. The locus trees themselves focus most of it into these collection basins."

"Collection . . ." His wits were still a little scattered, as were Teral's. Both Host and Guide squinted again, focusing on trying to See where the energies went once gathered. "I don't . . . Grove Keeper," he finally asked formally, "*where* do these concentrated energies go, once they gather in the basins?"

"They return to the land, of course," Saleria stated matter-of-factly. It was quite obvious to her way of thinking; the earth beneath their feet was a great grounding source. It quelled and calmed lightning, and it shunted energies off of mages' shields while dueling, so it made sense to her that the sap should drain into the land. That was how magic should be returned to the plants.

Except he was gaping at her with a mixture of shock, disbelief, and even a touch of horror.

". . . What?" Saleria finally asked, wanting him to explain his reaction. "Magic *should* go back into the land, to feed the plants and make them grow. That *is* the cycle of magic, you know."

"Not *this* much magic!" Aradin protested. "That would be like . . . like stuffing a baby full of fatty, super-sweet foods, and then not realizing why your infant looks like a padding-stuffed footstool two breaths from a heart attack! I apologize for the crudeness of my analogy," he added as she recoiled a little, "but plants should *not* be force-fed vast amounts of magic. From the thickness of the ground cover within the walls of this Grove, I would not be surprised to learn that that sap is being shared among all the various root systems. And because it is mixed into the groundwater, it is no doubt the *cause* of all these plants being mutated. Or at least, the main cause, augmented by eddies of overflowing magic from the . . . what was it you said? The locus trees?"

She touched her hand to the base of her throat, horrified herself by the idea. *All this time . . . ?* "Surely . . . surely you exaggerate?"

"I wish I could—here, let me fetch out a seedling," he stated. Resting his borrowed staff against the edge of the altar, he reached into the sleeves of his robe. Teral silently passed him a stalk of sugar cane from its storage spot in the Dark. Pulling it out of his sleeve, the younger Witch showed his hostess the finger-long stalk of greenery and its little burlap-bound ball of earth-encased roots. "This is one of a hundred samples of sugarcane from your northern coast which I picked up for trade with my people. I haven't been able to pass them to my fellow Witches in Darkhana just yet because it is summer here, which means winter back home, above the Sun's Belt and the seasonal divide—they're safer being stored in the stasis of the Dark for now, since nothing ages in its embrace.

"But watch what happens if I imbue it with some of my magic. *Pure* magic," he stated in clarification. Balancing the root-ball on his left hand, he held up his right and focused his will. With a whisper of breath, greenish light streamed out of his palm and his fingertips and soaked into the cane stalk. It stood there for several long moments, then trembled slightly . . . then quivered and flexed, growing in both length and size.

The crackling, creaking sound it made as the elongated leaf-stalk grew from one finger-length to three and spilled out a couple extra leaves was clearly audible. Eerily familiar, in fact. Saleria paled, realizing that this was some of the same sort of rustling noises that had serenaded her all day and all night for each of the three years she had served as Keeper and Guardian of the Grove.

He speaks the truth . . . Sweet Jinga, this is the truth! Swallowing, she looked at the mage-priest, who ended the demonstration with a dismissive flick of his fingers. The cane-plant continued to grow another finger-length even though the flow of energy had ended, turning it into a stalk as long as his forearm. But it did eventually stop.

"See what I mean?" Aradin asked her. "But this magic differs from your 'pure sap' over there by one very important factor. The only thing I was focusing on was growing a large, healthy plant . . . but I was still *focusing* the magic." His free hand pointed off to the side at the dripping vines. "*That* stuff is not being focused, other than that I believe it may have been separated from mixed kinds into purified types of magical energies. Copper for communication, silver for scrying, grass green for healing and growth, light purple for transport, pale blue for weather control, or who knows what the colors mean . . . but if all it's doing is seeping back into the ground and isn't being used properly . . . ?"

"The . . . the result would be . . . madness," Saleria murmured, the horror of it shocking her senses. She turned in a slow circle, looking out beyond the sheltering wickerwork of the Bower dome. At the madness beyond their enspelled shelter.

"Exactly. Madness. A monstrous amalgamation of intents and

purposes blended together by random chance, rather than by a guiding hand," he stated flatly. Lifting the sugar cane stalk one last time in poignant reference, he carefully tucked it root-ball first up his sleeve, returning it to its place in the Dark. "In fact, I would think the very soil of the Grove is super-saturated with pure magic-sap, if it's been dripping and dispersing through the ground for roughly two hundred years. No *wonder* this place is a mess!"

His words made her feel ashamed for never having realized it. For never having questioned it . . . since his words did make a horrible sort of sense. Saleria rested her staff next to his and folded her arms defensively across her chest. "Well, pardon me for not being a fancy *Hortimancer.* I am a mage-priestess of Kata and Jinga, and my lessons revolved around imbuing prayers with magic, not the imbuing of magic into plants!"

(*Gently,*) Teral cautioned his young Host. (*She's about to resist any idea you'd offer her, because your words sound like accusations of incompetence and idiocy.*)

Aradin knew his Guide was right. It wasn't how he wanted her to feel, either. Quickly switching to diplomacy, he held up his hands in a placating gesture. "I know that, and the fault *isn't* yours, Saleria. It isn't even likely to be that of your superiors; they, too, would be far more focused upon the spiritual needs of your people—too busy looking at prayers for the health of the forest, and not paying any attention to the needs of each individual bush and tree. Literally.

"The fault, if there is one, lies with whoever *created* this system and then did *not* explain it properly to their successors. You have been left a horrible mess through no fault of your own, you and your immediate predecessors," he told her, sympathy in his gaze, "and you have been forced to deal with it for the last two hundred years with no instructions or clues about what is really happening.

"In fact, you are to be commended for managing it as well as you have, with all the knowledge of a priest plopped into a garden mangled by generations of ignorant management. *But*, ignorance can be enlightened with knowledge," Aradin reminded her, raising a finger in caution as she drew in a breath to speak. "Whoever left your predecessors with no understanding of what should be done, *that* person was negligent, leaving their successors in ignorance. Ignorance can be turned into a chance for education and exploration, so there *is* a great deal of hope for both the safe managing and the eventual restoration of the Grove as a place where people can walk safely, without needing the disciplined will of a highly trained mage."

Somewhat mollified, Saleria still tipped her head in puzzlement, then lifted her brows. "Ah. Because their *thoughts* could inadvertently focus the magic, literally soaking the ground underfoot. In fact, those thoughts have probably been wafting over the walls and their wardings for all I know. Even those with the least affinity for magic can still cast a potent curse if they put every ounce of thought and will and emotion behind it, and this place is saturated, so even a casual unshielded thought could cause problems. I suspect the wardings on the walls of the Grove hold out such things from the townsfolk as well as strive to contain the mutations living within . . . but no wall or ward is perfect."

"Exactly. I came in here with my thoughts and my energies carefully shielded, as all trained mages do when traveling in unfamiliar or potentially dangerous territory. As you yourself naturally do, when walking its paths," he pointed out. "But the average Katani? Chaos, the moment they step inside. Or perhaps off the flagstone paths, since I can feel a subtle warding spell upon them as well as on the outer wall. I suspect the lack of flagstones underfoot here in the Bower means that whatever prayers you send out from here are amplified by that more direct level of contact with the sap-soaked ground."

She nodded. "It has always been more effective if I send out the empowered prayers from here, though the moss has always felt mostly dry to me, and has never left undue stains. And the basins . . . the liquid in the basins does go down visibly after each round of prayers," she murmured, glancing at the nearest pool, a slowly dripping vine of lavender-hued goo. Saleria looked back at Aradin. "But what can we do about the sap? I know how to channel the energy in the containment crystals into prayers, but the sap?"

"My alchemical skills are a little rusty," Aradin admitted, turning to look at the vines all around them, "but I would think such a liquid, purified and filtered into clean types of fluid magic, would make for absolutely astounding bases for potions. Those green ones . . . Wait, let's experiment with another cane stalk. May I?"

Bemused, but following his train of thought, Saleria nodded and gestured for him to proceed. Fetching another finger-length seedling from the depths of his sleeve, Aradin crossed to one of the green-dripping vines and carefully guided the stalk under one of the slow-forming droplets. With the clothbound root-ball in his fingers, he let just one drop splat onto the stalk. It oozed along the leaves as he tilted it first down, then up . . . whereupon the seedling grew with a similar creaking rapidity after a similar pause. Just one drop was enough to make the plant swell to the length of his full, out-stretched arm.

"Unguided, unfocused . . . My aura-sight says it's perfectly safe to eat, but I find myself leery to try," Aradin stated quietly, showing her the stalk. "I don't know what a travel-refined sap might do . . . Perhaps make it become ambulatory, able to uproot itself and walk about? Or an elemental fire; would that make it resistant to being burned, or make it spontaneously combust?"

"I . . . I don't know," Saleria whispered, thoughts whirling with the implications. Abruptly, she turned and tipped her head back, surveying all of the vines. "So much sap . . . so many different kinds . . . All this time, we should have known. We *would* have known, if *tradition* could have allowed more than one Keeper to tend the Grove at a time!"

"Your people could make a fortune selling liquefied magic," Aradin murmured, distracting her from what looked like an impending tirade. He didn't want her upset here in the heart of the magic; her shields were probably adequate, but he didn't want her testing that theory. "In fact, I'd be willing to pay for the chance to experiment, to see if it *could* be used as the base for various potions." At her sharp look, he shrugged. "I've been dealing more with the buying of herbs than the making of unguents in the last few years, but I did pass my alchemical classes with fairly high marks."

A frown creased her brow. "That doesn't seem right. *Selling* the liquid doesn't seem right," Saleria clarified, catching sight of his puzzled look. She spread her hands. "This is the Sacred Grove. All holiness, and by extent, all prayers, and thus all magic emanating from this place, is to be put to use for the betterment of all of Katan. I could no more sell a bottle of sap than I could sell a prayer!"

"I cannot fault that kind of reasoning, as one priest to another," Aradin allowed. "But it is of limited supply, and if it can be bottled and used in brews, then your government—secular or religious—will want to seek some sort of recompense for its existence, and to regulate who receives some, and who does not . . . and most likely they will wish to see a profit from its sale, rather than have it be handed away for free. After all, they have to feed and clothe and house *you*, do they not? And feed and clothe and house your scribe? Such things cost money."

"Yes, and Nannan, my housekeeper, and all the paper and ink that Daranen has had to buy," Saleria murmured, following his line of thought. She winced at that, and at the thought of her own which followed it. "*Bollocks* to bureaucracy! If I told any of the higher-ups about how this sap *might* be useful in potions, they *will* try to regulate it. Stranglehold it, in fact. But it should be preserved for holy uses!"

(*Convocation?*) Teral suggested, along with an undercurrent of thought that whispered in several layers through the back of Aradin's mind.

"Ah—Teral just offered a possible solution to the dilemma," he stated, holding up his hand to forestall more swearing from her. Not that either he or his Guide could be offended by her brief invective; the members of the priesthood on the Isle of Storms were much more vulgar when they wanted to be, and Teral still remembered that trip all too clearly from his own lifetime. Aradin focused on the needs of the present, explaining what his Guide was thinking. "One of the rights of the advocate at the Convocation of Gods and Man is to make petitions to their Patron Deity or Deities."

"And that means . . . ?" Saleria asked.

"For the time being, you and I could work to contain the overflowing magic. I could do a little experimentation with potions-crafting, and working on undoing the warped amalgamations of plants and animals in the Grove. Once we know what the possibilities are, *you* could present our findings to Blessed Kata and Jinga. At that point, you could ask *Them* if it would be permissible to use the liquid magics in potions, and whether or not it should be sold, or regulated, or handed away for free," Aradin said. "You could even ask Them to fix the Grove so that it no longer spews wild magics into the world, and thus return it to a natural sort of garden, however holy."

"That would be a very wise and balanced solution to the problem," Saleria agreed, thinking over the possibilities. "Not even the Arch Priest would go against the word of Kata and Jinga Themselves, and the King certainly wouldn't dare. Our God and Goddess have been known to manifest in person and depose an unworthy mage-king or -queen where needed. They have done so at least a full dozen times over the course of our long history . . . I think."

A sly smile curved the corner of his mouth. Daringly, Aradin teased her lightly, "Let me guess, history lessons were lumped into the same category as outkingdom lands when you were learning how to be a priestess?"

She lifted her chin a little as she replied, but wasn't too offended. "I've always been far more concerned about the current needs of my fellow citizens of Katan, and not what our ancestors needed. There's nothing I can do about the needs of the past."

"A good point," he conceded, dipping his head in a slight bow. "Now, since it is always wise to have clear thoughts and clear options when going before the Gods . . . may I have your permission to set up an herbalist's table here in the Bower and conduct a few experiments?"

"What, right here?" she asked, looking around at the moss tiers of ground and half-tangled wickerwork dome surrounding them.

"It would be best done right here, because you yourself already ensure that no one else reaches this spot without your permission and your escort," Aradin reminded her. "That makes it the safest place to avoid our experiments being detected by bureaucratic minds. It also ensures that I work under your supervision, and only with your permission, and that no one else can meddle with or imbibe my experiments unwittingly."

"I don't know about supervision, exactly," Saleria murmured, eyeing him. "Usually when I'm here, I'm concentrating on focusing gathered magics into prayer-spells. Or conversing with my fellow Guardians from other points around the world."

"You converse with others from here?" Aradin asked. "How, if I may ask?"

She nodded at one of the copper-hued puddles near the altar at the center of the moss-lined hollow. Its vine almost touched the surface. "Some of these basins serve a clear purpose. That one there permits voice-based communication with other Guardians who govern unwieldy pools or focal points of magic. All it requires is a touch of the liquid . . . though I am told that if I ever bring a mirror in here, Guardian Kerric can link a simple visual scrying surface between his power-source and mine. I have considered it, particularly in light of the troubles he's been seeing over the last few months, but, well . . ."

"You don't want anyone peering into the heart of the Grove and possibly trying to wrest away control of it?" Aradin guessed shrewdly.

She blinked in surprise and shook her head. "No, the power of my God and Goddess would prevent that. No, I'm more worried about leaving a mirror out in the open, where the rain could fall on it, the temperatures could shift and crack it with too much cold or too much heat, or even a bird could fly past and drop its liquid chalk on the surface just at the wrong moment in time," she muttered bluntly. "The point is, the Bower keeps some things out, yes, particularly hostile plants or hungry creatures, but not *all* things are kept outside the gazebo's weave. This *is* a garden, not a stronghold."

"That makes sense," he allowed. "Though with a properly enspelled frame, such things won't matter. In fact, I was just reading a book about that sort of thing, written by an Aian mage, Kerric Vo Mos. It had some clear instructions on how to enchant a protective frame for an outdoor mirror."

"Kerric Vo Mos, you said?" Saleria repeated, brows lifting.

"Yes. I could show you the book if you like," he told her, gesturing at the wide cuff of his sleeve.

"No, that won't be necessary. You see, Kerric Vo Mos is the same Guardian I just mentioned," she told him, mouth curving up in humor.

His brows rose. "*Oh.* I did not know that. But that means you should already know the man knows mirror-based magics like no other," Aradin said, eyeing her. "Not that I'm advocating a mirror must be placed in here; just that it can be done safely, with the right precautions and protective spells. The decision is yours."

Saleria nodded, then frowned softly in thought. Finally, she sighed and threw up her hands, letting them drop at her sides. "Fine! Educate me in all the finer points of all the bits of the world I've been missing ever since I chose to become a priestess. But it'll have to be done piecemeal, since there's only so much time I can allot out of each of my days for education. I still have to walk the paths, drain the plants and the trees, and convert it all into prayer-energies."

The smile he gave her was a ruefully amused one. "If I were to spend all our spare time—widespread and scattered though it may be—in teaching you such things . . . then I would have to stay here for the rest of my natural life. Are you prepared to host me that long, Holy Sister? The Convocation may happen a few days from now or a few months, but what you propose would require a much, much lengthier association."

He looked rather appealing when he smiled like that. *Of course, he looks rather appealing any time he smiles, period,* Saleria acknowledged, studying him. *So why does it annoy me all of a sudden to be called his Sister, even if it's only by vocation?* Sighing, she let it go for the moment. Sort of. "I'm prepared to do whatever it takes to get this Grove under better control, so that it no longer poses a danger to pilgrims who come here seeking to be closer to our God and Goddess. If that means asking for your help, then I shall ask for it . . . within the strictures of my office and the guidelines as I understand them.

"And I'd like you to call me Saleria," she said, prompted by that inner, annoyed thought. "That is, if I may call you Aradin or Teral as appropriate? If we are to work together on the problems of this place, I'd say that strict formality is a thing for chapels and cathedrals, not for a pair of gardeners trying to tame the Grove. So we don't really need to keep calling each other Priest or Witch or Holy Sibling, yes?"

His smile widened. "I quite agree. Saleria."

"Thank you, Aradin." *There, that feels a lot better. A silly little thing, setting aside an otherwise appropriate label, but it feels right*, she decided, smiling back. Turning her thoughts to what lay ahead, she said, "I'm not sure of what your experiments would require, but if you're willing to assist me on morning and evening rounds, it would free up the time to bring in whatever might be needed—and *bollocks* to the Prelate who says I cannot have an assistant," Saleria added firmly. "*I* am the Keeper of the Grove. *I* shall be the one to decide how best to Keep it."

Aradin grinned behind her back, enjoying her burst of assertiveness. (*I do believe we're a good influence on the lady.*)

(*I doubt her superiors would say that*,) Teral observed dryly, but not without humor. (*But yes, I do believe we are. As she says, it's* her *job, not theirs.*)

FOUR

Seated in her study, Saleria did not have to wait long to speak with Councillor Thannig, the Councillor for the Department of Prophecies. As Keeper of the Grove, she had a scrying glass that connected directly to one of the many mirrors in the Hall of Mirrors at the capital. All she had to do was catch the attention of a page, who sent off for the Councillor requested, and wait. It seemed he wasn't far from the Hall, though, for he came into view within just a minute or so, his teeth gleaming white in his brown, northern-born face.

"Keeper Saleria, how lovely to hear from you. I am flattered that Your Holiness requests my aid," Councillor Thannig praised her, smiling in warm welcome. "In fact, I just received a report that mentions you . . . or at least, your office. How can the Department of Prophecies assist you today?"

Surprised by his words, Saleria lifted her brows. "Ah . . . what sort of report regarding me?"

His smile faded, replaced by an expression more rueful and somber. "We have been digging up old prophecies regarding those meddlesome fools on the Isle of Nightfall, off the east coast of Katan, and their attempts to reconvene the Convocation of Gods and Man. We haven't had any truly strong Seers in several hundred years, but a few of the lesser ones in the interim have given missives which we're beginning to see come true. One of the ones we unearthed in the process, the Song of the Guardians, specifically mentions the Grove. If you like, I can have a copy of it made and sent your way."

"Was one of them by the last Duchess of Nightfall, the Seer Haupanea?" Saleria asked.

He frowned for a moment in thought. "I . . . hmm. I think so. At least, I think some of hers are in the mix. She didn't make that many," Councillor Thannig dismissed. "Now, what else can the Department do for you?"

"Actually, that is exactly why I called," Saleria admitted. "I'd like to know all the prophecies related to the Grove . . . and out of curiosity, any involving this Convocation of Gods and Man. If Kata and Jinga are going to be summoned in some impending Convocation soon, I should like to petition Them for Their aid in fixing the many problems with the Grove."

"Well, we haven't selected an appropriate representative yet," Thannig hedged. "The Arch Priest would like to have that honor, but so would Lady Apista, Councillor for the Temples . . . though considering she gave those exiled fools on Nightfall a sacred bell to ring, summoning an incipient crown, she's not in high favor in the Council's eyes at the moment. I honestly don't know why she did so. She's ruined her ranking in the budget debates for Temple repairs and constructions."

Someone called out something to him from beyond the edge of the mirror's reach. Leaning out of the frame, he stroked the edge to give himself a moment of aural privacy while he conversed. It gave her time for her rather troubled thoughts.

Politics? They're all worried about politics *in the face of the Convocation being restored? When having it* be *restored—by whomever—would give us far greater wonders and glories than mere* politics? *Jinga's Bollocks! Aradin warned me, but I didn't actually believe it until now.*

Here was the exact reason why Aradin had avoided the Council of Mages and the Arch Priest in his search for an appropriate representative. Saleria knew what "ringing a sacred bell" meant, since it was part and parcel of the duties of all priests to know what that meant. If any portion of Katan wished to secede and demanded a sacred bell so they could summon a manifestation of a new God and/or Goddess, the priesthood was *required* by law to present the petitioners with one.

The ugly implication behind this careless revelation is that these bureaucrats would not *have given the exiles a sacred, blessed bell to Ring the Bell to declare their independence from Katan. I know why she did it, because the Councillor for the Temples would not care to break the covenant of her vows with Kata and Jinga . . . but these . . . these politicians don't see the whole, and thus holier, picture at hand.*

Well, bollocks *to that,* she thought firmly. *They shall not get a single word otherwise out of me . . . and I shall figure out a way to be the representative of our* people, *not our political ambitions.*

Thannig shifted back fully into view and stroked the edge of the mirror, restoring sound. "Sorry about that. Where were we?"

Keeping her expression calm, if solemn, she merely said aloud, "Something about politics, milord. You may concentrate on that however you wish, Councillor, since the ways of government have little to do with the ways of prayer . . . but there are signs that the Grove will soon be free to change to something calmer. If this Convocation is the means, then so be it. If not, there are still things I can do, and should be doing, as Keeper of the Grove and Guardian of its magics. Which means I really do need to know what prophecies might be associated with it, so I know what to look for in the coming days."

"Of course, of course. I'll have them copied and sent by messenger to you," Councillor Thannig promised. "Is there anything else the Department of Prophecies can do for you, Keeper?"

"Thank you, but no, that should be plenty," Saleria demurred, not sure she wanted to deal with any politicians right now. "Forewarned is forearmed, and that's all I should need. You have my gratitude for your willingness to assist me in my search . . . and I shall say a prayer for you and the Council," she added on impulse. *A prayer to hopefully bring you all to your good senses.* "Kata and Jinga bless you, Councillor Thannig."

He gave her a slight bow, one dark-skinned hand splayed across his blue-clad chest. "We on the Council live to serve . . . or at least, that's what we're supposed to do. Have a good day, Keeper Saleria. May Kata and Jinga bless you, too."

A gesture from his hand ended the connection, leaving her with a blue glow for a moment before the mirror returned to being a normal reflective surface. Reaching up, she pulled the curtain back in place over the mirror, which was mounted behind her desk. The addition of the curtain had been one of her requests to Nannan upon taking up the guardianship of this place. The thought of someone staring at the back of her neck unnerved the young priestess. She had enough trouble with her danger instincts being roused and sharpened daily by her walks through the Grove; she didn't need to worry about that as well.

As if conjured by thought, Nannan bustled into the study, her hands damp and clean, but her apron dusted with flour and bits of dough. "Daranen suggested there might be more than three for the evening meal. Who would the fourth one be?"

"A foreign priest who is something of an expert in magics,

plants, and herbalism. He will be working with me for a while," Saleria informed her housekeeper. *I don't think the messes in the Grove can be untangled in just a few days, though.* She didn't say that out loud yet, because she didn't know what Aradin's long-term plans were. "Easily several weeks, I should think. Probably longer."

"He's not to be staying *here*, is he?" Nannan asked her in a disapproving tone. The plump, matronly woman might be ruthlessly cheerful in the morning, but she didn't approve of priests or priestesses getting up to "shenanigans." Which meant she did not like Shanno, the young Deacon of Groveham, who in the half-year since his arrival had flirted shamelessly with whichever young lady might smile his way. Saleria couldn't object to Nannan's distaste; there was something about the younger priest that irked her, too, though she couldn't put a finger on it. But this was another matter, one not related to the young, brash deacon.

Dismissing thoughts of Shanno, she instead considered her housekeeper's words. Sitting back in her chair, Saleria tapped her lips gently with both forefingers, then pointed at Nannan. "That actually isn't a bad idea. Though I suppose I should see first if his ideas will work and his presence will be helpful before offering him one of the guest rooms here."

"You cannot be serious!" Nannan protested, rearing up to her full, if modest, height so that she could look down her nose at Saleria.

It was rather like being stared down by an affronted hen. Biting her inner cheek for a moment to quell the urge to smile, Saleria sat up again, giving the older woman a calm look. "I am quite serious. There are seven bedchambers in this house. I have one, you have one, and Daranen has one. That leaves four to spare. Since your husband has long passed, your children are grown and gone, Daranen is a confirmed bachelor—"

Nannan snorted at that. Saleria knew it was because the widow fancied him a little, but let it pass, continuing smoothly.

"—and my family lives a month's ride to the south, there is no reason to hold all four of those rooms ready for unexpected guests. Or rather, any further unexpected guests," she amended. "I highly doubt an entire troupe of foreign dignitaries is about to descend upon the Keeper's house, demanding lodgings. I will give it another day or two to observe Aradin Teral's progress on his efforts, and if they prove viable, I shall invite him to stay here, where it will be more convenient. As he will be *assisting* me in my many duties with the Grove, the budget for the Keeper of the Grove can very well pay for his food, as well as giving him free lodging."

"But, Your Holiness, to have a strange man in the house!" Nannan protested. "What of your sanctity? What if he has designs on your position, and its power? He could seek to wrest away your control of the Grove!"

"Bollocks to that," Saleria snorted, making her housekeeper blush at the vulgarity. She didn't let Nannan's stare stop her from continuing briskly, "Boisterous Jinga would thump him on the head with His own holy fist, I am quite sure of it."

Nannan shifted her hands to her flour-dusted hips. "Well, what if he has designs on your *person*, hmm?"

That wrested a soft laugh from her. Smirking, Saleria leaned back in her seat again. Her thoughts had strayed a couple of times in that direction already, so she wasn't offended by the possibility. *Not when they're both handsome men . . . though I'd far rather court the living half. Not sure I'm comfortable with the thought of being intimate with a technically dead man . . . Oh, but that Aradin . . .* "And what if he should?"

Nannan gave her an affronted look . . . then gasped, her eyes widening in realization. "Oh! Then *Kata* would thump him with Her fist, of course. Well, I suppose it would be okay in that case . . ."

And that wasn't the conclusion I myself had drawn. Mainly because Saleria highly doubted it. For one, neither Aradin nor Teral struck her as the sort of man who would push himself on a woman. For another, much was made of the northern God's exuberance and passion for life versus the southern Goddess' calmer temperament, but it was well-known among the priesthood that Kata was no shy, shrinking flower when it came to Her Heavenly marital duties.

Indeed, it was said that She was the one who had given the sacred knowledge of how to make contraceptive amulets to Her people so that they could enjoy such pleasures without the worry of unexpected, unplanned-for children. Not Jinga, as one would have expected, though there was a male equivalent to the female version.

She didn't disabuse Nannan of her notion, however; instead, Saleria let the housekeeper leave with a flick of her hand, muttering something about attending to the day's baking. Something else made Saleria think it wasn't likely either man would seek to dally with her, however attractive she might find him. Yes, Aradin was quite handsome; in his own way, so was Teral. However, the two men moved and operated in one body as if never out of the other's sight.

Or the other's mind, whatever . . . I can only imagine that would be a detriment to lovemaking. No doubt their whole priesthood is sworn to celibacy, poor things. Maybe a little flirting is allowed, since the way Aradin looked at me, and touched me—that was flirting. But full-on intimacy?

Some among the Katani clergy swore themselves to vows of chastity, to take no lovers until marriage. Others swore their passions to their Patron Deity, seeing it as a sacred duty to love vigorously and well . . . provided no promises were broken. She didn't know of a single priest or priestess in the empire who had sworn vows of celibacy, however. They did take vows to break no oaths, cross no marital boundaries, and respect the rights of all to say "no" whenever they wished to say it, at whatever point in the proceedings—but not true celibacy.

No priest or priestess in Katan would swear to take no lovers at all, nor any vows to avoid marriage, should they be interested in it. Such a thing would go against the very underpinnings of their faith, for Kata and Jinga Themselves had willingly wed, and Their marital efforts had made the entire continent quite fruitful for a full year afterward, despite a terrible drought plaguing its northern half at the time.

No, They were Maiden and Lover, the romantic aspects of Spring, plus They were Father and Mother, the nurturing aspects of Autumn. And the Lord and the Lady might be the protective aspects of Summer, but They did not shy from adult activities . . . and it was believed that even the wisest aspects of Winter, the Crone and the Guide, were still capable of being loving toward each other, and thus lovers, despite the frailties and difficulties of old age.

So my God and Goddess would not object if I could dally with one of the two . . . but I think I'd balk at both at once. It is written that Kata and Jinga insist that pairings of two males or two females is not anathema, though male-and-female is more normal. Two of whatever is normal . . . but to put three into a relationship? Saleria shook her head and sighed.

Daranen came back into the study at that moment. He had a fresh satchel of letters posted to the Grove Keeper from all over the empire balanced on his shoulder. Sidling behind his desk, he glanced her way. "Such a heavy sigh. Care to share?"

She opened her mouth to refuse, then changed her mind. *He, at least, is easier to talk to than Nannan about certain things.* "I'm thinking of allowing Aradin Teral to reside here in the Keeper's house with us. Would that bother you?"

"Not really. You told me when you came in earlier that he freely oathbound his powers against stealing the might of the Grove out from under us, and against using its powers to cause serious, willful

harm," her scribe reminded her. "And he does seem sincerely interested in helping us—oh, speaking of the Darkhanan Witch, I saw
him in the market, bartering with the mercantile shopkeeper for a
series of glass flasks. Master Denisor looked rather taken aback at
having the quality of his wares questioned so thoroughly." Daranen
chuckled at the memory.

"Aradin . . . no, sorry, Teral did say his own father was a glass-
maker," Saleria pointed out, getting the two men straight. "And
Aradin has apparently been trained in apothecary-style herbalism,
as in the brewing of potions, powders, unguents, and salves. No
doubt he's trying to find suitable containers for his impending
experiments."

"Experiments?" Daranen asked, raising one eyebrow at her.

She envied his ability to do that; Saleria could raise or lower
both simultaneously, but had yet to figure out how to arch just one.
"Yes, experiments—I told you about the oath, but I forgot to mention the rest of it, sorry. Aradin is going to help me see if any of the
magic-warped plants in the Grove have useful properties which
can be extracted and preserved. If not . . . we're going to figure out
a way to remove them from existence."

Now he raised both brows. "No more attacks on the village
from ambulatory masses of roses and marigolds?"

"Nor from walking gladiolas, or flying bluebells," she promised. "And no calf-sized foxes with seven tails and fish fins on their
backs, either. If he can make progress on helping me unravel the
troubles in the Grove, that is."

"Shall I just nip out and see if he needs help carrying any of his
belongings over from the inn, then, to make sure he doesn't waste
any time walking every day from there to here and back?" Daranen
asked, half-rising from his desk. He grinned and sat back down
again, clearly only half joking. But still, somewhat serious about
welcoming the other man. ". . . Right, then. If there's anything I

can do, ask me and I'll try my best. But most of what I do best is
sort correspondence and compose the exact wordings for prayers."

"And that is a task you do exceedingly well. I've never been a
great speech-writer, but you know how to turn a phrase just right—
I'm still surprised you haven't taken up the priestly vows, you're so
good at it," Saleria admitted, nodding her head at the mail satchel,
fully as long as Daranen's arm and as big around as either of them
could clasp the cylindrical sack. Some days, the sack wasn't quite so
full, but other days, he brought in a sack and a half of letters and
scrolls filled with petitions, requests, pleas, and prayers. "Have you
the evening's prayer list drawn up?"

Daranen shook his head. "Almost. I had to rewrite the 'lost
pets' prayer list a little bit. I'll have the scroll ready to go by your
evening walk. And I'm not taking holy vows. I much prefer my
secular freedoms, thank you."

Nodding, Saleria lifted her chin at the bay window. "Then I'll
go visit the market. Do you need anything?"

He smirked. "No, I've done my shopping, but you can say hi to
the man when you see him."

She started to protest that the Witch wasn't her reason for
going, then sighed and let it go. She *was* curious about Aradin
Teral, and what he was purchasing. Leaving the study, she headed
out the front door.

This section of Groveham featured walled residences with garden spaces. Not because the owners were wealthy and exclusive
about whom they allowed into the privacy of their homes, but
because they were located near enough to the Grove wall that an
additional wall was considered helpful in slowing anything that
escaped from the Grove. She could hear children shouting and
playing some sort of chasing game in one garden, though the gate
was closed. A trio of boys was drawing chalk designs on the cobblestones in front of another gate; happy domestic sights and sounds.

Once children turned six, they were given basic education in reading and writing during the morning hours, but were often let go at midday so they could play in the afternoons. At twelve, they were often apprenticed into a craft, or if their parents or a sponsor could afford it, granted a higher level of education. Her parents had enrolled her in a higher school in their city, since she hadn't made up her mind yet at the age of twelve if she wanted to be a mage-warrior in the Imperial Army, following more or less in her non-mage father's footsteps, or a mage-for-hire like her mother technically was, or . . . well, at fifteen, she had felt called to serve the God and Goddess, and that was that. *No time for play after that, when I had to catch up with all the acolytes who had been apprenticed three years earlier than me.*

The shrieks and the laughter were good sounds, though. They also sent a brief pulse of pity through her. *At least Katani priests can marry and have children. I can't imagine what Darkhanan Witch-priests could do, living their dual lives. Who'd want two men for their mate, and one of them dead at that?*

Or worse, she wondered as the thought occurred to her, *what if a woman was married to one Witch-priest, only he died and ended up Guide to another man. Would her husband, now a Guide, expect to continue their marriage? Would she even want to, given it's technically the body and life of another man? And the children—surely they'd be of the Host's body and seed, not her late husband's. I can't imagine the kinds of headaches that must cause. Or . . . or if he ended up Guide to a female Host, or . . .*

A new thought crossed her mind. *What would the children think, to find their mother or father suddenly dead, and yet not really dead? What would that do to a culture? Do those whose parents aren't chosen to be Guides grieve all the harder for not seeing their parents again, even if it's only secondhand?*

She didn't know. She didn't even know if these Witches were

permitted children. Deep in thought, she navigated between the various townsfolk and visitors as she reached the edge of the market, until a familiar tenor broke through her thoughts.

"Your Holiness! How nice to see you outside the Sacred Grove," Deacon Shanno called out. "And such good timing, for there are many people here in town to see you."

Heads turned her way, most of them belonging to visitors. Several of them started toward her, while behind them, she could make out the pale, smirking face of Shanno, his blond hair pulled back into a braid and his brow banded by a polished copper circlet. A bit pretentious of him to wear a circlet when he wasn't a nobleman, but it was copper, and it was unadorned with either design or gems.

Annoyed, Saleria kept her expression calm and bland. "You know very well that all petitions must be presented in writing, and not in person, Deacon Shanno. I *am* to be allowed a normal life outside of my duties, which includes the politeness of not being pestered by unending petitions in person. Thus said Holy Kata and Holy Jinga."

A few hesitated. A few more of the men and women who had come to Groveham to be near the Sacred Grove pressed closer, drawing in breaths and opening their lips to speak. She cut them off, her gaze still on the apprentice priest.

"I am in some ways considered Their closest servant next to the Arch Priest, but even so, *I* would not go against the will of the Gods," Saleria added dryly. Expressions fell. She hadn't meant to disappoint so many, but the deacon riled her with his assumptions and airs. Focusing her words on the men and women before her, she added politely, "Every petition is important, no matter what the request. If a person takes the time to organize their thoughts and put their wishes onto paper, then their request is made all the more clear. Every single letter and scroll *is* read, I assure you . . . and there are free writing supplies available at the Groveham cathedral, and a box which is cleared twice daily, with all petitions brought to me in an orderly fashion.

"Being a mere mortal, I cannot guarantee what answers They might give," she added, lifting her palms and her eyes upward to the sky, "but it is my sacred duty to read and pray on your behalf when I am in the Grove. When I am here in the market, however . . . I am merely looking for food."

Most of the visitors to the town sighed and nodded and turned away; some headed for the cathedral, with its eight walls and high dome. One couple lingered, a pair with the medium brown skins of northern Katan. Holding hands, they approached Saleria. The young woman glanced at her swain, blushed, and gave the Grove Keeper a hopeful look. "Your Holiness . . . could we have your blessing on our impending wedding?"

"And any advice you could give?" her betrothed added. They had good-quality clothes, the sort merchants might wear, and obviously had enough money and time to make the journey here, but they looked young to her. Young, and impressionable.

Saleria composed her reply carefully, giving them a smile. "My blessing you may have: May you each know a long and good life filled with many more moments of happiness than sorrow. And the blessing of Sweet Kata and Joyful Jinga you shall have as well, when Prelate Lanneraun witnesses and blesses your walking of the eight altars. As for marital advice . . . I have not been married, myself. I am therefore not qualified to lend you any, other than that marriage between mortals is never perfect.

"There will be times when you merely disagree, and times when you fight," Saleria warned them gently. Sometimes young couples like this rushed into marriage, though there was hope they were wise despite their tender years. "The important thing is to remember that you *choose* to love each other. Every single day, when you wake up and face the new day, you have a choice. You can choose to love, and forgive, and seek to compromise and take turns. To share the day's tasks, triumphs, and tragedies, to support each other through the difficult times and to help make your good times even better. You can choose to understand, to forgive, to set aside or peacefully discuss and listen to each other's worries, needs, and requests . . . or you can choose differently, to tread some path other than love.

"Each and every day, you can make that choice, and you make it every single time you interact with each other, in how you interact. I hope both of you choose wisely, and follow through on your decisions to the betterment of both yourself and your partner," she finished. "That is the *only* advice I am qualified to give."

"Your words are most wise, Holy Keeper," the young man stated, giving her a formal bow. "We will keep your advice in mind."

"Yes, we will," his betrothed agreed, smiling warmly as she curtsied to Saleria. "May the Gods bless you with the kind of love we know, Your Holiness. The Keeper of the Sacred Marriage Grove should know a long and happy marriage, herself."

Saleria chuckled and blushed, and gave them a brief bow in return, since she still wore her mostly white Keeper's trousers and jacket; curtsying was for skirts or long robes. "Thank you for your kind thoughts and blessings. I am obliged to remind you that the Grove is closed to visitors, but our Prelate is skilled in marital ceremonies, and the town itself is more than ready to assist you with any other of your needs. May the Gods bless you, and may you enjoy your stay in Groveham."

"And you," they offered in parting.

Saleria moved past them, angling toward the slender blond man with the copper band girding his forehead. She drew near just in time to hear him loftily proclaim, ". . . keep my doors open to all who come, should *I* ever become the Keeper of the Grove."

"*Deacon* Shanno," Saleria stated, letting her tone in the use of his minor title show her reproof, "you have *actual* duties to attend to at the cathedral, do you not? Perhaps these kind people will allow you to do so." Mindful of the watching eyes of visitors and townsfolk alike, she waited until most had drifted away, then spoke quietly, though kept her expression pleasant. "Shanno, why do you keep doing that?"

"Doing what?" he asked innocently. Or rather, mock-innocently. She wasn't fooled. Tossing his head, his golden, chest-length locks sliding over his white priest-robes, he shrugged. "I'd think you'd be happy to garner the attention of your fellow Katani. After all, they *should* have the right to bring their petitions to you directly, as the one priest in all of Katan who can speak directly to the Gods and be assured They will listen."

"It is forbidden because there are too many people who want to touch the divine. *I* am mortal, not divine, but if I do not keep that distinction clear, they could run the risk of worshipping *me*." She watched him roll his eyes, and sighed impatiently. "Did not your instructors at the temple schools teach you *anything* about what happened to Keepers who were mobbed by crowds of pilgrims?" she asked him. "Keeper Bareias, whose ribs were broken? Keeper Shantan, whose knee was ruined so badly, even the best of Healers had trouble putting it to rights? And the post-Shattering panics that lead to the *death* of Keeper Patia?"

The young deacon snorted and looked away. Saleria stared at him. This was why she didn't like him, or at least part of it. *Too young, too arrogant, too self-convinced he knows everything and everyone else knows nothing. Kata, Jinga, I hope You give him a solid lesson in wisdom and humility someday . . .*

"When she died, Shanno, there wasn't anyone on hand to contain the mutations in the Grove for weeks, and *that* led to the Vegetable Riots. Half the town wiped out because the crowds could not control themselves in their rush to 'garner the attention' of the Keeper!" Saleria asserted, lifting her hands toward him. "*Think*, Deacon, before you speak. There is no one here in Groveham, nor for a hundred miles around, who is strong enough to take care of the Grove should something happen to me." *Yet another reason why I keep asking for an assistant . . .*

"I could," the young man boasted.

She gave him a pitying look. "No, Shanno, you could not, or you would have been selected to be on the list of potential Keepers already. I have seen that list, and your name is *not* marked upon it. It took a manifestation of the Gods Themselves to get people to leave my predecessors alone. Please do not try to change the way things are. You have not that power, and you never will."

"Well, maybe that's because I'm not fully into my powers yet," he countered, chin still lifted in his arrogance.

That wasn't how she meant that last version of *power*, but she knew he wasn't going to listen. For such a youthful stick, he was as stubborn and unyielding as steel sometimes. The deacon— appointed a bit too early to the rank, in her opinion—looked like a stiff breeze could knock him over, and Saleria couldn't help but wonder if a bit of wind might catch the underside of his jaw like the sails on a fishing boat when he lifted it like that. If will alone were enough to manipulate magic, perhaps he could have been a possible candidate . . . but not before having that self-importance lurking in those blue eyes knocked out of him somehow.

At her rough, weary sigh, Shanno continued stubbornly. "Every- one knows that a male mage's strength in magics continues to bloom well into his early twenties, and I am just now twenty, as of last turn- ing of Sister Moon. I could turn out to be even more powerful than *you*, Jinga willing."

Not knowing how to refute that politely—because it *would* take a miracle from Jinga, who might have the sense of humor for it, to give a weak mage like Shanno the sheer strength of both body and mind to withstand the needs of the Grove—Saleria gave up trying. Shanno was too young to believe anything she'd say about his physical and magical strength not being up to the task.

At twenty-six, she wasn't that much older than him, but she, at least, had the sense to know her limitations. She also had the benefit of early combat training, thanks first to her warrior father, and then later to her combat-mage teachers. Shanno . . . she didn't think he'd be able to win a wrestling match more than half the time with a non-ambulatory marigold, let alone a thettis/morning glory/bug vine.

"Just . . . please refrain from trying to draw attention to me again like that, Shanno. Be respectful of your rank as a deacon, which includes the responsibilities it entails, which means toward your fellow priests as well as to your parishioners. Have a good day," she finished politely, before moving on, deeper into the Groveham marketplace.

Pushing him from her mind, Saleria moved toward one of the dairy farmer's stalls. Maryam, the seller, offered her a sample from a platter of little brown-veined cubes, murmuring that they had been made with a locally brewed stout for extra flavor. Nibbling on the first piece, Saleria slowly nodded; the stout lent a nutty, sharp tang to the cheese. She reached for a second piece, debating how much to buy from the older woman . . . and heard a hushed exchange behind her.

"The Holy Keeper likes that cheese!"

"We should probably get some—the Gods must've blessed it!"

Closing her eyes, she sent up a brief prayer for patience, then managed a smile and turned, eyes seeking out the pair of speakers. It wasn't the young couple who had approached her for a blessing and some advice, but it was a pair of visitors from among those who had thought to approach her after Shanno revealed her identity. Clearing her throat, Saleria spoke.

"I choose this cheese simply because I like the way Maryam, the maker, flavors it with stout. Other than that, it is just cheese—and like any other cheese, either you will like it, or you will not. There is nothing holy about it," Saleria finished dryly.

Behind her, Maryam chuckled. "Not the stout-soaked, no, it's quite solid . . . but the *emmentha* cheese has lots of holes in it!"

Caught off guard, Saleria broke down into a laugh. Catching her breath after a few moments, she grinned over her shoulder at the older woman. "That's not quite the same sort of 'holy' . . . but you're quite right, there are a lot of holes in that one. Tasty holes, too." Looking back at the middle-aged couple, she addressed the visitors again. "I swear to you, at this moment I am just another woman enjoying the marketplace, the same as you, or her, or that elderly lady over there."

The man merely frowned at her, but the woman craned her neck to look in the directions Saleria pointed. He persisted. "We came here to see the Sacred Grove. But everyone says we cannot go into the Grove, and that we must be content with being near it. If you are its Keeper, then you are Sacred as well. Why should we not worship you as the next-nearest thing?"

Saleria shook her head and tried not to damn the young deacon in her thoughts for this trouble. "I am just one servant in a long line of servants; my job is to tend the unruly plants within the Grove, and to pray on behalf of all the written petitions I receive, *not* to be worshipped. Worship Kata. Worship Jinga. They are worthy of your admiration, your faith, and your love for Them. You can go to the cathedral and go up to the viewing balcony, if you wish to see the Grove. But ever since the Shattering of Aiar, which warped the aethers and ruined the great Portals, the Grove has been too dangerous even for a moderately powered mage to enter, never mind gentle souls such as yourselves.

"Dealing with it is my task, and my holiness begins and ends within the walls of the Grove. Out here, I am simply another priestess, for all my fancy titles. Now, if you will excuse me, this perfectly ordinary priestess is hungry for perfectly ordinary cheese—"

"Oy!" Maryam protested, scowling at her. "It is *not* ordinary cheese! It is very *fine* cheese."

Saleria smiled and rolled her eyes. "—and I am going to purchase her *fine* but otherwise perfectly ordinary cheese in order to sate a perfectly ordinary, normal sense of hunger. May the God and Goddess bless you, and I hope you enjoy your stay in Groveham."

They continued to watch her as she turned back to the dairy farmer. Saleria purchased a small wheel of it, tucked it into the string bag she had brought, and moved on to the next stall. Thankfully, that last couple didn't follow her. Saleria made a few more purchases, wandered the market stalls and the shops that ringed the square, then finally found her erstwhile new assistant still haggling over several vials in the glazier's shop. Both he and the glass merchant, Denisor, glanced up at her arrival.

Denisor smiled and waved briefly, Aradin lifted his chin in greeting, and the two men concluded their bartering. The last of the vials went into the straw-padded crate on the counter, more straw was piled on top, and a lid was settled overall. Sealing it with a spell, Aradin lifted the crate to the ground and swept the folds of his Witchcloak around it, making the crate vanish in that odd, seemingly magicless way of his. The glass merchant blinked, then shook it off and looked at her.

"And what can I do for you, Your Holiness? A bit of glass for your home?" Denisor asked her.

"I'm here to see him, actually," Saleria said, nodding at the foreigner. "Have you everything you need, Aradin?"

"I could use a few more things, but I have enough to start," he told her. He nodded at the merchant and held open the front door for Saleria. "I can come back for the rest tomorrow. You said earlier that you attend to the last tree right before your evening walk?"

"Yes. I use the energies siphoned from it to strengthen the wardings on the Grove wall, so that hopefully nothing can escape while I rest overnight," she said. "You are welcome to join me in my evening rounds, since you've behaved well so far."

"I would like that. Will we be visiting the Bower?" Aradin asked her, taking no offense at her words. He knew they stemmed from the protective nature of her job.

She nodded. "We can, if we go now."

"Then let's do that," he agreed, smiling at her.

Unaccountably, Saleria felt her cheeks heat. There shouldn't be any reason for her to blush just because a man smiled at her, but he did smile at her, and she did blush. Swallowing, she turned away, hoping he hadn't noticed.

(*Adorable,*) Teral observed. (*Did you see how her cheeks turned pink?*)

He wasn't the only one. Aradin kept smiling as he followed the Guardian of the Grove. (*Indeed. Do you think it'd be wrong to mix our quest with some pleasure, now that it looks like we'll be working with her on more than just the Convocation problem?*)

(*From the way Priestess Tenathe tried to get me into bed with her, at least some of their priesthood doesn't have any issues with chastity or celibacy,*) Teral pointed out. (*But a single blush does not make a fully welcomed attraction, either.*)

(*I'm just glad you didn't take Tenathe up on that offer,*) Aradin muttered mentally. (*Older women are fine, but when she went on that rant against the people of Nightfall, that would've been awkward, trying to extract either of us from her affections as well as denying her the position of representing Katan.*)

(*Affections had nothing to do with it,*) Teral chuckled. (*More like plain old lust, if you ask me.*)

(*So to speak,*) Aradin amended dryly. (*I do want to ask her, but I'm not sure what the right timing of it should be.*)

(*Opportunities can present themselves, but sometimes a man has to simply seize a good enough moment and make a gentle inquiry. I suggest in private, though,*) Teral cautioned him.

(*Private-private, or will you be around?*) Aradin joked lightly. He had to dodge around a clutch of elderly women coming from a side street, which forced him to hurry to catch up with their hostess.

(*Well, I'd like to know the results,*) Teral said, his mental tone the equivalent of a wry shrug. (*But if you want me to leave, I can. I believe it should be nighttime in Darkhana by now, so I could always go meet up with the others in the Dark.*)

(*I don't mean to kick you out,*) Aradin said, mindful of his Guide's rights and needs.

(*I know, but we can report that we finally have a potential priestess to represent the Katani people. Or rather, I can first query the Dark on my way to the gathering to see if she* is *the best match, now that we have a candidate again,*) his Guide offered. (*With the previous potential candidate, Tenathe didn't know about the people of Nightfall and the Katani king's opposition to their efforts when I first asked if she thought she could be a representative of her people to the Gods, but the moment she threw her fit, that parameter changed everything. This one does know . . . more or less.*)

(*Let me ask her formally before you go,*) Aradin said. Clearing his throat, he spoke quietly, pitching his voice for Saleria's ears as they turned the corner toward her home. "Saleria . . . the country which has the potential for the thing I mentioned . . . they are considered a foe by your nation's king. Would that make you hesitate to represent your people, if in doing so your very presence *helped* them succeed in their task?"

"What, the Convocation?" she asked, not catching on that he wanted to speak about the subject obliquely in public.

"Shh," he said. "But yes."

"Why should I want to stop it?" she asked, giving him a puzzled look. "Such a thing should be celebrated, encouraged, and assisted back into being."

(*Promising . . . Go on,*) Teral nudged him.

"Well, your king wishes it to be done by his own people, rather than outlanders," he confessed.

Frowning softly at that, Saleria considered his words. She considered them all the way into the Keeper's house, and beyond. Only when she had shut the Grove door did she respond, by asking a question. "Who has the better chance of pulling it off the soonest? Katan, or this other land?"

"Nightfall. Technically, it is a part of Katan that has rebelled and broken away from your Empire, and they are determined to prove their independence by hosting the Convocation, with all the Gods and Goddesses of the world as their Patrons," Aradin told her, and braced himself for her reaction.

"You sound very confident about that," Saleria stated. Her tone was merely thoughtful.

"They have the cooperation of the Witches in gathering the Names of all the Gods and Goddesses."

Folding her arms, Saleria studied him thoughtfully. She did have the gossip Councillor Thannig had given her, but she wasn't going to blindly trust Aradin . . . or Teral . . . on what the dual Witch knew. "How do you know all this? As far as I know, the only Nightfall I've heard of is a small island on the eastern side of the continent—a continent which is the entire Empire of Katan—and if it is some *other* Nightfall, then it would be much farther away. So. How can you know all this? How do *you* know they're trying to resurrect the Convocation?"

(*That's not so promising,*) Teral observed, (*but go on.*)

Aradin suppressed the urge to roll his eyes at his Guide. Teral wasn't the person standing in front of him, after all. "One of our fellow Witches ended up in the city of Menomon, which lies well outside the bounds of your empire. While there, they heard of a request for the Scroll of Living Glory by the people of Nightfall, which contains details on how to re-invoke the Convocation of the Gods. They—the Witch pairing—asked questions of the Dark, and determined that the people of Nightfall, which is indeed the former Katani island in question, have the best chance at succeeding. Not the only chance, but the best, as circumstances currently stand.

"The people on Nightfall do seem to be in a state of rebellion against your empire," he continued. "I don't know all the details, but it seems they have Rung the Bell in proper ritual form to make themselves a new, independent kingdom, have been answered with a holy crown . . . and apparently intend to manifest *all* the Gods and Goddesses as their official Patron Deities."

She knew about a city of Menomon, though thanks to Guardian Sheren's misfortunes a little while ago, the Fountainways between there and here had been closed while the older mage recovered. Aradin's words only confirmed what Saleria knew. What little she knew, technically, since until now her world had revolved predominantly around the Grove, the village, and all the petitions received. *But now we have a piece of Katan breaking away and trying to restart the Convocation.* "How ambitious of them."

Aradin shrugged and clasped his hands lightly together. "There is enough ambiguity in the Dark's reply to put the end result in some small shadow of doubt, but less so than for any other nation about which we have queried. At the moment, they have the best chance . . . if perhaps not the only chance. So. What is your opinion of that?"

Saleria knew what he was really trying to ask. He wanted to know if she would try to sabotage their efforts—an absurdity from this far away—or try to wrest control, or stop it from happening, or whatever. She didn't care for any of those things, however. "I guess I'd say good luck to them, and may Kata and Jinga bless their attempt."

He frowned, taken aback by her light reply. "You honestly don't object?"

"It occurred to me, as we were walking through the house just now, that if *my* king wanted to do it, he'd probably want to invoke the Convocation *here*." Spreading her hands, she indicated the carefully spell-warded patch of flagstones that kept the Grove-warped plants away from the entrance to her home. "This is the holiest spot in all of Katan, and it is *utterly* unsuited for a meeting of Gods and Mankind. Even if you *can* wrest a miracle antidote from your dripping magic-sap experiments and somehow leech the excess spell-saps from the soil of the Grove, it will still take far too much time. *Years'* worth of time.

"I may not be a Hortimancer, but even *I* can guess that much," Saleria told him. "If these Nightfallers have Rung the Bell to demand Divine Patronage, and if they seek to reconvene the Convocation of Gods and Man . . . then the two events are probably tied together, which means they have less than a year and a day to do so," she added. "That is far sooner than anything this Empire could put together, I am sure."

"Possibly yes, possibly no . . . since with enough magic and effort, just about anything is possible . . . but probably they couldn't," Aradin agreed.

"Probably not, no. It would be far better for the whole world to have the Convocation of Gods and Man restored and resumed, regardless of who hosts it, than to let the world continue to suffer from its lack. And . . ." She hesitated, bit her bottom lip, then confessed with a touch of distress, "And my *own* prayers to Kata and Jinga about healing the Grove have gone unanswered all this time . . .

"Maybe, just maybe, if They appear in person at the Convocation, and if *I* can represent our people before Them, then *maybe* I can get a straight answer out of Them as to why they've let this place . . . fester!" Sweeping her arm out, she indicated the wilderness within the encircling walls. "That is far more important than *who* hosts the return of the Gods. All kingdoms will be welcome once it resumes, and that is all that matters."

(*I think now is not the time to point out that those kingdoms who misbehave toward the host kingdom can be excluded from the next one,*) Teral murmured quietly.

(*Ah, but not from the first one,*) Aradin countered. (*They all have to be represented at the first one, all the active kingdoms with duly manifested Patron Deities. I remember reading that in one of your scrolls on the matter, and it's the reason why we have Witches lurking within reasonable snatching range of Mekhanan priests. . . . I do think she's the one, Teral. Or an incredibly good actress, but I'll bet it's the former, not the latter.*)

(*I'll verify it with the Dark, but I don't believe she's acting, either,*) his Guide murmured. (*Be careful with yourself while I'm gone. You won't have me watching out of the corners of your eyes.*)

"Right," Aradin murmured, answering both his Guide and his hostess.

The feeling of Teral slipping out of his Doorway and into the Dark that lay behind it was like a cold winter draft in a fire-warmed room. He was used to the sensation, the way it prickled across his skin, but it always helped to have a distraction until the goose bumps went away. He gestured at the tool shed that contained her assortment of pruning and collecting staves.

"Shall we each grab a staff and head for the Bower, then? The sooner I learn how you tend the Grove, the sooner I can learn how to substitute for you when you go off to represent the people of Katan."

Saleria nodded and opened the stout, weathered door.

FIVE

In reverse order of her morning treks, which usually ended with a visit to the northern tree, Saleria's first destination at the end of her day was the southern locus. Today also involved a nasty mass of spiderwebs apparently grown by cloverleaf-covered . . . things . . . which scuttled this way and that, avoiding the slashings of their staves. Forced to use spell-summoned fire to bring the confrontation to an end, Saleria stared grimly at the charred section of wild-grown garden. It wasn't large, not more than a couple strides in diameter, but it did make a black and ugly stain on an otherwise verdant view.

"I hate this part of my job," she muttered quietly. Not with any force behind it, magical or emotional, but simply as an unpleasant fact. One which she was resigned to by now.

Aradin did not like the sound of that. He thought about it for a moment, then the blond priest-mage asked, "May I say something which could be construed as potentially sacrilegious? No offense is meant, of course, but as an outlander . . . sometimes we can see things more clearly. From a certain point of view."

Saleria shrugged, her gaze still on the patch of scorched plants and earth. "Say what you will."

Gently, Aradin asked her, ". . . Wouldn't it be easier to burn all of it down and replant from scratch? Save the locus trees, of course. I mean, the *land* is what is holy, where your God and Goddess were wed. Somehow, I don't think these unnatural amalgamations of plant and animal were what They intended for Their Keepers to maintain. Or for that sap to literally soak uncontrolled magics deep into the ground."

He was right. His words *were* a sacrilege. Except Saleria could see his point all too well. "I would not advise suggesting that to anyone else, Witch-priest, or you would find yourself cursed and reviled. But . . . it isn't something I haven't already considered myself. That's why I hate this part of my job. It *would* be easier just to remove all of this through scorching and burning and starting anew . . . though I hadn't realized the magical sap was the source of the energies seeping into the land. But we'd just have the same problems in a few months or a few years."

Her gaze shifted beyond the blackened ground to a delicate little ground-plant with doubled, conjoined blossoms that together looked like a heart shape, with a little extra bit dangling below. It was called bleeding heart, and while the normal plant filled the forest floors to the south with subtle perfumes, dark leaves, and shades of pink for blooms, the version that now existed here in the Grove had become something more.

"But there *are* useful plants here," she stated. Stepping over the burnt bits, she muttered a skin-warding charm and plucked a trio of stems, each of a different hue. Carrying them back to him, she held one of them up, careful to not breathe too deeply. "This one, the peachy-yellow . . . here, inhale its scent."

Wary, but willing to trust her, Aradin leaned close to the half-dozen flowers dangling from the stem, and inhaled. The first impression of his cautious whiff was the typical flowery scent. In the next moment, however, a grin curved his lips, and a ticklish sensation bubbled up from his lungs. It emerged as a spill of laughter, a slightly giddy sense of chuckling happiness. Except there was no reason for him to laugh like that. Blinking, Aradin stared at her. "What the . . . ?"

"This is what we call *bleeding heart*, for its shape," she said, turning the stem so he could clearly see the heart-shaped bells with their little conjoined pendulum-petals curling from the middle of the two blossoms. "Two flowers grown conjoined so that they form a little heart with a droplet-like bit at the bottom. Elsewhere, they're just flowers, pretty to look at, but little more. But here in the Grove, they have mutated. This peachy-yellow one causes feelings of laughter and merriment. This dark brown one . . . here, have a sniff," she urged.

Again, he hesitated, but again he complied. Again, the flower-scent, and again, an emotion. This one drew his brows down. Aradin started to turn away, but stopped himself. *Analyze the emotion, Host,* he chided himself. *These plants clearly change emotions. Don't just be affected by it;* think *about it.* Holding himself still, he concentrated on identifying the urge to, well, pout. "I feel . . . petulant. Or perhaps . . . disappointed?"

"Disappointment," Saleria agreed. She dropped the brown one to the ground and held out the last one. "Try this pale blue one."

This time, he didn't hesitate, though he was wary of a plant that could make him *feel* things. Sniffing at it . . . he relaxed, sniffed again, and analyzed. ". . . Contentment?"

"Peace, but close enough. There's a pale bluish-purple that gives true feelings of contentment, though not necessarily of peace—oh, avoid the orange-red ones, the color of a glowing coal in a dying fire," Saleria warned him, following his gaze to the rainbow of blossom hues available. "Those evoke feelings of hatred with distinct overtones of violence."

"Amazing," the Witch murmured. He almost asked what use the flowers could possibly be . . . but then his thoughts spun them into several alchemical possibilities. Plants had always been quite useful for augmenting magic in various ways. This, however, was a leap forward. In the hands of someone good, and combined with the concentrated sap energies, the power of the potions involved would be quite staggering. In the hands of someone evil, devastating would be a very mild word for it. That made him frown. "I am in two minds about preserving such plants."

"Oh?" Saleria asked, lifting her brows.

"The possibility to calm agitated souls would be a huge benefit, but . . . to *force* someone to laugh? These things could be all too easily abused, milady," Aradin warned her. "By unscrupulous Alchemists, and enspelled perfume makers, and who knows who else."

"True," she acknowledged. "But the scents fade quickly once plucked. I don't even know if they can be distilled and preserved or not. But then I'm just the Keeper, a one-woman tender of this magic-warped garden with no time on my hands to experiment." She started to say more, then paused, frowned, and considered her own words. Looking up at him, Saleria asked, half to him, half to herself, "Or is that the *reason* why only one Keeper has ever been allowed to tend the Grove since the Shattering? To give us little to no time to experiment with such things?"

"I don't know," he admitted quietly. "But as you are the Keeper of the Grove, it is your choice to allow others to know about this particular plant's existence, let alone to allow them to experiment upon it or not. Or upon any of the others."

His words settled her thoughts. Squaring her shoulders, Saleria nodded. "True. Very true. And at the moment, I am inclined to let you experiment . . . carefully, and cautiously . . . with some of what the Grove can do. Or rather, what it has already done. There's no point in thinking ahead to new possibilities when we have so much to learn about that *is* out there," she added, gesturing at their overgrown, terraced surroundings. "The first task is to clean up two hundred years of warped magics. *Then* we can discuss experimentation."

That made him choke on a laugh, and not because she was gesturing with the hand still holding the peach-hued spray of flowers. "You don't ask for much, do you?" Aradin asked, clearing his throat. "I suspect you're going to need to hire a few more mages if you want all of it done within your own lifetime. Oathbound mages, so that they cannot abscond with any plants or concoct anything without your permission. But still, if your own Order will not supply you with what is needed, then you do have the right to go looking outside the holy ranks."

"True," she agreed. "My scribe isn't a priest, but his work is needed for the Grove. Same with my housekeeper, so I don't have to exhaust myself cooking and cleaning, or living in a mess and eating at the nearest inn." Lifting the pale blue blossom to her nose, she sniffed for a moment, enjoying the aura of calmness the flower imbued, then dropped both it and the other stem onto the ground. Turning her staff around, she touched them with the crystal end, absorbing a tiny bit of energy from each plant as it withered. "Let's get to the southern locus and get the wall recharging over with. Sunset is drawing near."

Nodding, Aradin started to follow her past the scorched spot when a tiny, crawling something at the corner of his eye caught his attention. It was enough to prompt his muscles; he slashed out and down, searing a last clover-leaf spider-thing. A long, careful look showed no others moving about. Hurrying forward, he caught up to the athletic Keeper after several long strides.

Once he was within comfortable chatting distance, he asked, "I get the impression you don't like being in the Grove at night. Most plants require daylight. I wouldn't think they'd be active at night."

"Most are quiet, yes . . . but some still move around, and . . . well, so are animals. Active at night, I mean. Which probably explains why more of the Grove plants *are* active at night," she added soberly, remembering the bug-eyes on that vine earlier in the day. "If they're amalgamations of both plant and animal, the animal half would permit them extra mobility when the sun is not feeding them energy. It's not the fact that some are still active that prompts me to move, however. It's that I don't have good night vision, and cannot always see the dangers before they're upon me."

"Ah. That makes sense. I have a few spells in one of my grimoires that might help with that, with ways to enhance one's vision magically," he offered. "But I can understand wanting to—"

Something bushy leaped out at them. It wrapped its branches around Saleria's body from knees to shoulders and dragged her off the path. Startled, Aradin bolted after her, staff whirling. He slashed behind her back, cutting through a thick branch with a *thump*-and-*sizzle* of burning plant. The bush-thing shrieked and rustled, tightening its grip on the grimly chanting priestess. Her clothes started to glow with a golden light. A second aura sprung up, one with a fiery orange hue to it. Quickly putting up a personal shield of his own, Aradin flinched as the bush-thing burst into flames a second later.

Coughing a little on the smoke, Aradin looked around to make sure nothing else was going to attack while Saleria patiently, grimly waited for enough of the bush-beast to char and die so she could escape. She looked like she was holding her breath, and when she broke free, lurching back onto the path, she did gasp for air. None of her clothes were singed when she cancelled the shield-spell, though some of the bush-beast's soot soiled her white outer jacket.

Saleria wrinkled her nose and dusted it off with her free hand. Or tried to; the dark speckles merely smeared. Giving up, she resumed heading up the path to the southern locus tree. "I love reading the prayer petitions and knowing I can do something about them. I *don't* love the rest of this job."

"I don't blame you," Aradin murmured.

They moved up the path, both keeping an eye out for more attacks or interruptions. The closer they got to a locus tree, the more its towering spray of branches shaded the overgrown garden around them. Moving up and down along the winding path, they approached the southernmost tree. The Bower was a broad structure, big enough to dwarf the Keeper's home, but so was the base of each locus tree.

Aradin had seen and studied a wide array of plants in his travels, but even for him, it was difficult to discern exactly what kind of tree the locus had originally been. The closer he got to this one, his second chance to study one, the more he realized it wasn't what *kind* of tree . . . but rather, what *kinds. That's a bit of birch, there . . . and pine . . . cedar . . . oak . . . is that maple? Some of these branches have needles, some have leaves—is that a spray of willow leaves?*

It made sense, in a twisted sort of way, that the locus trees might be amalgamations of several species as well. The whole of the garden was filled with such things. Following in her wake, Aradin watched as Saleria touched a rune near the cutting tip of her staff. A golden glowing line swung out at an angle, allowing her to lower it to the moss-edged stones of the path. Scorching as she scraped, she shoved back the encroaching growths, and occasionally swiped the searing-hot spell up and around in an arc, clearing the undergrowth that led to the base of the tree.

Or rather, to the hollow at the base of the tree. The last time, Saleria had asked him to wait outside. This time, Aradin slipped in behind her, walking as softly and quietly as he could, in case she had simply forgotten he was there. The flagstones seemed to lead a winding course between the almost wall-like rise of the smaller roots, but that was a misperception, he realized; the cracks between flagstones were straight and square-cornered, not angled or curved as they were on other winding points in the Grove.

Which means this was *once a straight path . . . and here's a different sort of stone. Yes, strong, pinkish granite . . . and a line of black basalt*, he identified, staring at the ground. *Here's where the original Portal stood.* Reflexively, he glanced up, but there wasn't a rectangular archway overhead. Just a mixture of intergrown trees.

The space under the heart of the locus tree was not dome-shaped so much as it was cone-shaped. Besides themselves, the paving stones underfoot, a shimmering, pale gray light overhead, and the roots and trunk of the great tree all around, there was only one other object: a four-stepped footstool, placed in the center of the floor.

The dark rectangle of rock it rested upon looked very much like similar thresholds he had seen on a trip to the Empire of Fortuna, which still had functional Portals, if only within its own boundaries. The Portal gates had been massive rectangular doorways, broad enough for two carts to have driven through side by side. Here, the basalt of the threshold looked like it ended at the base of the upswept inner roots, and thus was indeed wide enough for two carts, but from the way the interior wall of the tree swept up and in, there wasn't really that much room available when one was upright; more like barely a cart's width.

Lifting his gaze to the peak of the conical space, he squinted against the light. It wasn't as bright as sunshine, but it was bright enough. No bigger than a modest-sized worm, a finger-length piece of yarn cut from pure daylight, the rift hung at the very peak of the space. It did so in a hazy cloud of mistlike energies. Some swirled up into the tree trunk like upward-trickling beads of moisture.

Some dripped downward like falling sparks from a blue white fire, only to evaporate before reaching the floor.

His hostess did something to kill the cutting spells on her staff, then inverted it. Stepping up onto the footstool, she gripped her staff by the deactivated end and stretched up onto her toes to get the crystal orb to touch that rift. Seeing her sway, Aradin set his staff on the ground and moved up behind her. He was taller than her in either form, but he didn't take the staff from her. Instead, he grasped her by the ribs under her arms and lifted her up off her feet with a grunt.

Saleria gasped and swayed a little, but quickly resumed the chore of sucking the spare energies into the faceted egg on the end of her staff. She hadn't expected the lift, though it did make gathering the upper energies a little easier. The trick was making sure the crystal never actually touched the rift for more than a fraction of a heartbeat. Overloading the crystal with too many energies might make it explode, and that would be bad.

He was remarkably strong for having such a relatively lean body; she didn't feel his arms start to tremble until the last few seconds or so. Lowering her staff in a decisive motion got her lowered as well, until her boots touched the top level of the step stool. "Thank you," she stated, turning to face him. Only to find he was right there, facing her from the next level down. That meant his head was just a little bit lower than hers. That those intriguing hazel eyes were close enough for her to see little flecks of blue and green among the streaks of brown and green.

"Have you . . . ?" Aradin hesitated, and licked his lips.

Saleria followed the flick of his tongue. The glide made her aware of how nice his mouth was, of the faint hints of a blond beard striving to grow on his shaved chin. Aware of the heat of his strong frame, a kind of heat that had nothing to do with temperature runes controlling her comfort on such a warm day, and everything to do with the masculine scent of him. She blinked and looked into his eyes again. "Have I . . . what?"

"Have you, ah, taken any oaths of chastity? Celibacy? Abstention from . . . romantic congress?" he asked her. His cheeks picked up a faint pink glow.

"I . . . well, no. Of course not," she repeated, bemused by this turn of the conversation. "You couldn't get anyone into the priesthood with a mandatory vow of celibacy, not when we have a married God and Goddess. But . . . uh . . . surely your own Order . . . ?"

He smiled and slid his hands around her waist. A subtle pressure on the small of her back swayed their bodies together. "For the same reason, we don't have any."

"But—what about Teral?" Saleria asked, feeling a little awkward at the thought that the older Witch might be studying her behind those hazel eyes.

Aradin shook his head in brief dismissal. He liked the feel of her leaning against him, the warmth of her in his arms. His Witchcloak had kept him cool in spite of the day's heat, but it was open along the front, letting their bodies touch. Letting their bodies stir a different sort of warmth in his flesh. "He's gone into the Dark to ask it a few questions, and to seek out a friend. He won't be back for a while."

"Oh." She mulled that over. "But . . . what about when he comes back? Isn't that awkward for . . . ah . . . relationships? Always having that other person there, or at least almost? Watching both of you, whatever you do?"

Sighing, Aradin loosened his hold on her waist. He didn't release her or step down, but he did ease his grip in case she wanted to move away. "It can get awkward, but only if we *let* it get awkward. And it's far less so for a fellow Darkhanan than an outlander such as yourself. But it doesn't have to be awkward. At the end of the day, this is still *my* life, and my choice. Teral . . . approves. Tentatively," he amended, tipping his head in acknowledgment of his Guide's reservations. "We don't know everything about your culture, though we did know that casual . . . entanglements . . . are not frowned upon, with the right precautions."

A soft frown pinched her brow. Saleria considered his words, and their implications. Particularly the unspoken ones. "But what about long-term entanglements? Is that the price your priesthood pays, never being able to know and hold on to a lasting love?"

The *snork* sound that escaped him broke the somber mood instilled by her words. Biting his lip, trying not to let his shoulders shake too much, Aradin shifted his hands to her face. Gently cupping it, he mastered his mirth. "No, it *doesn't* cost us the price of never being able to have a permanent love. It does make it a little rarer, since many people don't care to share their beloveds with more than one person at a time. But, I'll ask you this:

"What would you expect would happen if you fell for a man who had a son from a previous love? Someone whom he was responsible for? Someone he *couldn't* set aside on a whim and ignore?" Gently, he tipped her face so that their foreheads touched. "Would that stop either of you from knowing love and happiness, always having that boy constantly around, watching and listening, and demanding attention?"

"Well . . . no," she allowed. Her training had included how to counsel widows and widowers with children on the risks of new romantic relationships. "But Teral isn't your son," she pointed out. "He's older than you."

"And if I came with an aging father or grandfather who depended upon me for care, would you automatically cast all of us aside as not worthy of your time or your affection?" he asked her next. At her wry look, he smiled wryly and released her cheeks. Sliding his hands down her arms, he laced his fingers with hers. "It is true that some people cannot manage it. They have neither the patience nor the energy to deal with children, or parents, or whatever. But many more do. Teral likes what he sees so far in you. I like it, too. If either of us should fall in love with you . . . since our tastes in women are similar, you'd more than likely just have *two* men falling in love with you."

She didn't untwine their fingers, but neither did she let the subject go. "What if Teral is the one who falls for me, and . . . and I for him? But not you? What would you do? What if you fell for someone else at the same time? Or . . . or you and I for each other, and Teral for, oh, my housekeeper, Nannan? How would you explain *that* love-tangle?"

Wincing a little, he dipped his head. "That does start to complicate things, yes. But I as the Host would have the highest priority, and control of the situation. If it were just you and Teral . . . and I had no others in my life . . . I would consider giving the two of you time to share and grow your love. If it were all four of us— and as I have yet to meet your housekeeper, I have no idea how she'd react to such a thing—then my life, wants, and wishes would still have priority. If all four of us were amenable to sharing, then it might be very possible . . . But in most cases, it would simply devolve to you and me, and Teral would have to content himself with warmer memories from his own life, and mild displays of affection."

"I'm . . . not sure I could handle that. Teral and some other woman, I mean . . . if you and I were involved," Saleria clarified. She laughed a little. "Actually, the four of us I *know* I couldn't handle. I rely upon my housekeeper for managing my home, but I know I wouldn't be able to share more than that with her. Our personalities clash a little too much for such . . . emotional intimacy."

She looked down at the last two words, a little embarrassed to be discussing them so soon or so freely. That only focused her gaze on the bit of sternum showing at the neckline of his plain green tunic. A corner of her mind wondered if he had any chest hair.

Freeing one hand, Aradin lifted it to her chin, nudging her head and her gaze back up to his. "I was promised by Alaya, Teral's own Guide, that I would eventually find great happiness when I took her Host as my Guide. That *I* would find happiness—not both of us, as in Aradin-and-Teral. Now, I have no idea if you are going to be involved in that happiness, but I do know I'd like to at least test the possibilities of it. If you're interested. I find you smart, amusing, and admirable in your dedication to your work. The rest will take effort, open-mindedness, and time."

His words made her blink. "Dedication. Work. Right. We need to get moving. I don't want to have to ward the last bit of the wall in the dark."

Nodding, he started to move aside, then shifted back in front of her. "One moment; we forgot one little thing . . ."

"Oh?" Saleria asked, lifting her brows. Only to find his mouth brushing lightly against hers. *Ah. A kiss. Yes, we shouldn't forget a kiss . . .*

Lightly wasn't enough, though. Swaying into him, she returned the touch of his lips. Most of her felt grateful he wasn't celibate by vows, and clearly not by inclination, though Saleria still wasn't sure about this life-sharing business. But this—this was just a kiss. A wonderful, sensual, delicious kiss. Hints of stubble rasped against her chin and cheek when he tipped his head, deepening their connection, their taste.

A kiss that ended in a sudden intake of his breath. Pulling back, Aradin blinked, cleared his throat, and told her, "Ah. Teral is back. He's asking if you want him to step out again for a bit?"

Conflicting emotions tumbled through her, like tart currants and bitter nuts poured into some sort of sweet batter. Part of her just wanted to keep kissing him, regardless of who watched. Part of her wanted to send Teral away before she even tried. Part of her was thrown off the thought of more kissing by this reminder that, no matter where the Guide was, she was technically kissing two men at once. The rest of her . . . knew what her duty was.

Regret dipped her gaze to the hands that had risen to his chest at some point in their kiss. She wanted to explore the warmth of his skin, but sighed instead, and gently removed her touch. "I really do have to set the wards, now. That must come first, before all else."

"Of course." Backing down the remaining two steps, Aradin offered her his hand for stability. He felt better about the implicit rejection in her choice when she accepted his help without hesitation, though. *Of course, a little distraction might help her get over the weirdness she's no doubt feeling.* "Are all the locus trees shaped like this one on their insides? I stayed out of the eastern one, last time."

"As you should've stayed out of this one," Saleria reminded him, activating the cutting end of her staff as they exited the living cave. "But it's alright. Even without your mage-oath, I believe you'd be trustworthy. And yes, they're all shaped like that, as if several trees around the clearing had been drawn in and up, twisting together to form a protective shelter. Keeper Patia was the one who conceived of the way to contain the rifts, who grew these trees . . . but she was killed shortly after starting the process. She may have been a Hortimancer, and had a plan in her mind, but I don't know.

"I do know they all have step stools in them, though I really should get that particular one replaced with something a little taller . . . which I keep saying every few days or so," she muttered wryly. "It gets the job done, but . . ."

"Let me guess: You forget about it the moment you get home again?" Aradin asked her, eyes flicking around the Grove as they emerged from the twisting path tucked between the roots of the trees.

"Pretty much. When I get back to the house, I just want to relax, forget about all the hard work I've done, eat a nice meal, attend to evening prayers—simple ones, with no force of will or magic poured into them—and rest." She wanted to roll her eyes and sigh, but while the air did escape her lungs a little roughly, her eyes flicked in wary little glances all around. "Having to constantly be alert is exhausting for both mind and body."

Aradin murmured a sympathetic sound, following her back to their starting point. As she fell silent, her concentration on the potential dangers of the Grove, Teral spoke in his mind. (*Looks like the two of you are getting along nicely.*)

(*Yes, though she's uncertain about getting involved with two men in one body,*) the younger Witch sighed mentally. He, too, kept a sharp eye out for other surprises, but spared half his attention for his partner. (*What did the Dark tell you about her?*)

(*Provided nothing changes drastically, she'll make a very strongly affirmative representative at the Convocation,*) his Guide murmured. (*Rather surprisingly strong a "yes," in fact, far better than the last one.*)

(*Did you meet with the others?*) Aradin asked next.

(*I found Niel and Tastra at the Meeting Tree, along with a few others. Niel said to tell you thank you. He also said that makes fifteen left for the others to find, plus capturing a suitable Mekhanan priest without in turn being caught,*) Teral relayed. (*I am very glad we were already out and about in the far direction from that blighted land when the call went out to start choosing representatives.*)

(*As am I. Has he had any indication the Convocation will be in the next few days?*)

(*No, but he has started issuing orders that travel packs be made ready. He did hint that he and his Host will be leaving their current location soon. Within a turning of Brother Moon, from the sound of it,*) Teral added. (*Mind that branch; I think there's something on it.*)

Aradin glanced to his right, but whatever it was, the branch stopped swaying after just a moment, and nothing else moved but himself, Saleria, and a bit of early evening wind in the highest branches of the locus trees. They passed the burned spot where the spider-leaf-things had been. Teral viewed these things through the edges of Aradin's vision, and offered a comment.

(*Looks like you had an interesting time without me.*)

(*This place is insane . . . and I want to stay and fix it, if I can. This goes beyond the reason why we're here, studying Saleria for the Convocation of the Gods,*) he warned his Guide. Mentally, he slashed a hand outward, indicating the overgrown garden, though physically he moved with the same fluid caution as ever, hands cradling his borrowed staff. (*This place is a mess, and it has been* badly *mismanaged ever since the last Convocation. Barely managed, with only one magepriest to tend the whole place. And it's not Saleria's fault.*)

(*Is it not?*) Teral asked, his tone pointed. Aradin drew in a breath to argue with himself, but his Guide gently cut him off. (*If she is named the Keeper of this place, then it should be* her *decision how to manage it. Which includes pulling in extra staff as needed. The sergeant overlooking the actual battlefield sees so much more than the general studying the terrain maps back home.*)

(*True,*) Aradin conceded. (*She* is *taking charge of her battlefield now. I know I've helped goad her into making that decision. But how can I look at this place and* not *feel offended by its mismanagement? As a Hortimancer, it is my duty to coax the* best *in magical effects from the plants that I grow and tend, for the betterment of all. Except I don't have any to grow and tend, and have just been seeking and buying new ones for the gardens back in Darkhana.* This *place, however . . .*)

(*Yes, I know,*) Teral soothed as they reached the back entrance to the Keeper's house and turned left to start following the outer wall. (*But it is* not *your* God and Goddess' *holy garden. It is hers. If you*

want to stay and help, you will have to prove it to both *sets of Patrons—
you can start by asking if she'd be willing to carry a petition on your behalf
regarding the proper, better management of this place. Once you have
more of her respect and trust, of course . . . and locking her in an embrace
doesn't count.*)

(*I'm not a callow youth,*) Aradin reminded his Guide. The distance from the locus tree to the Wall wasn't all that far, thankfully,
which meant they were finally near enough to see it without
obstructing foliage. (*I know quite well that sex does not equal trust.*)

(*True . . . What is she doing now?*) Teral asked, peering through
Aradin's eyes. The combination of the brilliant blue white glow of
the crystal and the golden sunlight slanting in from the west made
it hard to be sure, until Saleria moved into a patch of shadow. Then
it became more clear.

She reached up to tap the crystal end of her staff to a dull orb
set in the middle of one of the crenel-like peaks along the Grove
wall. As the two males watched, a tiny bit of the bright energy
gleaming in the egg-shaped sphere bled into the dull round orb,
until it glowed with a steady, mild, bluish light. Tiny little gems
dotted along the top and the base of the wall started glowing as
well. When they reached back to the last set of tiny, lit dots, and
halfway to the next darkened orb, she moved to it and touched the
charged crystal to it as well.

(*She's a glorified lamplighter,*) Teral thought in disgust. Aradin
would have protested, except he could sense his Guide's sub-
thoughts even before he expressed them. (*She has so much more power
in her, and there are ways to extend the locus powers directly to these wardings, yet they have her wasting her time recharging them manually? Gods
Above! There had better be a damned good reason for this horrible mess,
prophecy or no, or I'll have to go find and slap some sense into the spirit
that left this place in such a mismanaged mess!*)

(*I'm sure they've long since moved on to the Light of the Afterlife, and maybe even been reassigned by now,*) his Host thought dryly. (*But if they're still in the Dark, give them a second slap from me.*)

(*I'll do that,*) Teral promised. (*Now, if you're going to follow through on staying here and helping out, why don't you ask her what's happening?*)

Nodding, Aradin moved up to join Saleria, rather than hanging back. "I think I know what you're doing, but I'd like to make sure I have it right. You're emptying a bit of the gathered energies into those ward-crystals, right?"

"Yes. It's just a simple mnemonic spell—I don't even have to chant it verbally anymore—and it's very much like opening a spout to add a dribble of cream to a cup of Aian tea. It can take seven or eight seconds to fill the main orb, then a single second more for each pip-crystal on the wall," Saleria told him. "So a total of twenty seconds per orb . . . thirty seconds total, to get from one to the next," she added, lifting the crystal away from the orb and taking several swift strides forward. "It takes longer to do evening rounds than morning, and I—"

She stopped mid-sentence, hearing a chime in her ear.

Aradin peered at her in concern. "And you . . . what? Is something wrong?"

"Bollocks!" she cursed, frowning in the direction of the Bower. "That's the communications chime. But *who* would be calling me in the middle of evening rounds?" Torn, she glanced at the wall with the unlit orb just beyond the brightly glowing crystal on her staff, and the sunset-silhouetted wickerwork of the Bower in the distance. If she hurried, she'd get there within a few minutes, but the outer wards would never get done before the sun set at this rate. "*Bollocks!* Why do they have to call *now?*"

Aradin made up her mind for her. Holding out his staff, he waited until she absently clasped it, then grasped the brightly lit one in her other hand. "What are the mnemonic words to open the flow of energies?"

She blinked at him. For a moment, they stood there, each with a hand on a staff. For a moment, the dutiful side of her brain argued in a tantrumlike way that this was *her* job, and not the responsibility of some foreign priest-mage. But that part of her brain sounded an awful lot like High Prelate Nestine, high-pitched, nasally, whiny, and obstructive. *Bollocks to that!* she thought, and mentally shoved her instinctive, internal objections aside.

"The mnemonic is *joula-joula-drip-drop-dribble.*" She blushed a little as she recited it, and added quickly, "*I* didn't come up with it. The previous Keeper, Jonder, didn't, either, nor did he know who had. It's just been that way for a very long time, is all. *Joula-joula-drip-drop-dribble*, and you picture it acting like a teapot spout in a thin stream, with your thumb on a reverse plunger style stopper."

Taking the staff, he lifted it to the orb and concentrated on the visualization, reciting the words. He could *feel* the press of the energy, and wrapped his mind carefully, cautiously around the orb as an extra safety measure. "*Joula-joula-drip-drop-dribble . . .*"

Light spooled from the faceted crystal to the polished orb in a misty stream. It soaked in, taking about ten or so heartbeats under the extra restriction, then slowly started spreading to the smaller gems embedded in the wall. Saleria watched anxiously, still hearing the chime of the communications stream in the distance. When the last needed gem was filled, he stopped murmuring the chant and pulled the staff away.

"I do this, and I keep an eye out for anything that might attack, yes?" he asked her. "I think I can manage it from here."

She nodded. "Yes, exactly. Well done—thank you! I'll be back before you know it!"

Nodding in return, he watched her turn and sprint back the way they had come, seeking the best path back to the Bower. (*I hope she'll be alright.*)

(*She should be. Mind on your work,*) Teral advised him. (*You've a job to do.*)

"I know what I've promised to do," he murmured out loud, and crossed to the next orb. "Keep your share of our eyes and ears open while I get this spell just right."

SIX

Breathless from her run, Saleria dropped to her knees by the northeastern of the copper-hued pools, set her Keeper's staff onto the moss next to it, and swirled her hand over the rippling liquid. A column of mist rose up, pulsing with energies. She touched it with one finger. *"This is Guardian Saleria. Who is this?"*

"Guardian Kerric, of the Tower. I need to ask a huge favor of you, Guardian of the Grove."

It sounded like Kerric, but he sounded . . . stressed. Unhappy. Frowning, Saleria asked, *"What's the favor?"*

"I have a problem which I need to show you, along with several other Guardians, because it is both alarming and frustrating me to no end. I'm sending you a mirror and a scroll with instructions on how to link it to the Fountainways for communications—I pledge to you, as a fellow Guardian, these are mirrors set to receive and send images and sounds only, no spells or methods of controlling anything you guard."

"*Alarming?*" she repeated, seizing on that word out of all the rest. She didn't like the sound of that.

"*Remember that discussion we had a few months back, when I mentioned an invasion by the Netherhells?*" he asked.

"*Yes, I remember it,*" Saleria said, trying to remember exactly what he had said back then.

"*Well, it's back, it's fluctuating, it's affecting several points around the world, and I cannot pinpoint what causes it nor what stops it because I am not there, in the regions being affected. But you and the other Guardians are there. And while I can talk your ears off about what I've been seeing in my scrying mirrors, it's never going to be as effective as showing you the images I've been recording. So may I please have your permission to link you to the Tower's scrycasting network? I promise that in several hundred years, the Tower has never once used its mirrors to subvert other mages' homes, energies, or territories.*"

"*You sound like you've been reciting those words a little too much,*" Saleria observed, hearing the weariness in his voice.

"*I have. I finally convinced Guardians Tipa'thia and Dominor to join the network. I've also got the Guardian of Althinac, and the Guardian of the Vortex . . . Would you please join us in a conference scrycast, Guardian Saleria? The more strong mages we have working on this, the more likely we are to find a solution, because Guardians are the* last *sort of people to help* cause *a demonic invasion, which means we're first and foremost in the responsibility of stopping one. We certainly have the power for it, once we find it.*"

She knew what her duty was—to keep the Grove safe and pure from outsiders—and her duty spoke in that same nasal voice as a certain superior, assistant-denying priestess in her life. Paired with her nightmare of demonic bushes and beasts, the combination sent a prickle of warning up her spine. Scrubbing at the nape of her neck, Saleria thought carefully about it.

She didn't hesitate long. Something about Aradin's presence had awakened a streak of rebelliousness in the priestess. *Bollocks to that. I'm going to trust Aradin Teral—I am trusting him . . . er, them— and I am going to trust Guardian Kerric, and the rest. This is my Grove to tend and keep, with all the powers and responsibilities that entails . . . and I am sick and tired of obeying rules and orders which mismanage this place, and all the true responsibilities I have regarding the powers I Keep.*

"Send your scroll and mirror—ah, wait, is the mirror delicate, or can it be left outside?" she asked, aware of the scant shelter given by the lacework tangle of the Bower dome.

"*They're enspelled to be nigh indestructible in most circumstances. Certainly you can't crack the frame while they're being used as a mirror-Gate, because they* cannot *be used as a mirror-Gate. Unless you deliberately throw it back into the heat of a glass forge, it should be fine, rain, snow, or sun.*"

"Then send it through," Saleria told him. "*I'll get ready to catch it and the scroll.*"

"*Thank you.*"

Rising, she braced herself, closed her eyes, and reached into the energies woven into the roof of the Bower dome. Sending and receiving things via the riftways was not quite as smooth as what she had heard from the other Guardians regarding their Fountain-ways. For one, it was often pure luck as to which rift an object might come from. For another, she was *here*, not beneath the base of any of the three locus trees.

Still, however incomplete the design of the post-Shattering Grove seemed to be, the riftways had been rerouted to come here. It was the conversion from magical tunnel to enspelled root-based tunnel, to the air over her head that was rough. Sinking mental fingers into the network, she shaped her magic into a cushioned lining for the passages.

It was a good thing, too; the mirror thumped and tumbled three times in the transition. Even with Guardian Kerric's promises that it was nigh indestructible, her heart still missed a few beats in the mental scramble to soften the blows. A bright swirl of light opened up over her head, and the mirror descended, slowing as her magic shifted with a murmur into a netlike shape. The scroll wasn't quite so worrisome; it did bang about a bit as well, but it arrived intact, landing in a second, smaller weaving.

She did heed the instinct to check them for possible magical traps, but the scroll was simply a scroll, and the mirror was exactly what it was supposed to be: polished, silvered glass in a metal frame, both carefully enchanted for transmitting visual and audible scryings in both directions upon command, and only upon command, but otherwise unsuitable for use as a mirror-Gate or a spying device. There were too many subtle flaws in the glass, physically preventing such a use; plus the spells involved against scrycasting and anti-scrying were far more refined than what she had seen before. But not to the point of being completely unfamiliar.

Since she didn't exactly have a place to set the mirror, she leaned it against a mossy boulder, tucked the scroll into her belt, and approached the northeast communications pool. Swirling the mist up out of the surface, she attempted to contact the Tower. "*Guardian Kerric, are you there?*"

It took him a long moment to answer. "*Yes, I'm here; sorry, several conversations at once. Did you get the mirror and the scroll?*"

"*Yes,*" she confirmed.

"*. . . And have you enchanted it yet with the spell to connect it to the Fountainways?*" he prompted her.

"*Oh. Right. I'll, um, be back shortly.*" Grateful he couldn't see her blush, Saleria canceled the mist-spell and went looking for the scroll over by the mirror. It took her a few moments to realize it was tucked into her belt. Blushing harder, grateful no one could see her acting like a fool, she pulled it out and worked loose the red ribbon binding the spindles together.

The instructions were thankfully written in Katani, though the script was a bit archaic in style. Puzzling through them took her several minutes, and practicing the spell—without magic empowering it—took long enough to be aware of just how golden-red the sunlight had turned. A glance to the west showed the sun just beginning to touch the top of the Grove wall, which meant sunset was a very short time away indeed.

As much as she wanted to run through the complex mix of verbal and gestural components a few more times to be sure of the images meant to be held in her thoughts while shaping the energies at hand, she didn't have much time left. Drawing a deep breath, she squared her shoulders, rested the unrolled scroll on the boulder, and started chanting, fingers, wrists, and elbows moving in graceful, precise angles, helping her to shape the intent of her magic with body as well as mind.

The glass of the mirror flared when she released the last bit of magic, fingers flicking upward. The light slowly faded, turning the surface a soothing shade of sky-blue. A few seconds later, the mirror chimed and the blue started to pulse and ripple in shades both lighter and darker. It was, Saleria realized, very much like the "hold" pattern used by the Council of Mages on the few occasions she had needed to contact them.

The last time she had seen it had been while waiting to speak with Councillor Thannig, in charge of the Department of Prophecies. Stooping, she tapped the mirror and stated her activation word, pushing a bit of will and magic behind it. *"Baol."*

The blue field shifted immediately to an image of a curly-haired man in a brown tunic that fastened down the middle of his chest with odd, ribbon-knotted buttons. Behind him, she could see a book-lined wall, but the lighting that fell on his face didn't quite match the lighting on the books. *Some sort of privacy illusion masking the real background*, she realized. *Like the blue backgrounds some of the Councillors use.*

"Greetings! You must be Guardian Saleria," the man on the other end stated, flashing her a brief smile. It lit up his gray eyes, giving him a charming air. His voice, no longer distorted by the echoing effects of the Fountainways, was as familiar as his face was not.

"And you are Guardian Kerric," she guessed, and received a nod in return.

"Correct." Again, he smiled, then sighed and rolled his eyes a little. "If you will kindly wait a few moments, I'm still trying to get Guardian Koro through the steps of connecting his mirror to the Fountainways. There is a privacy screening spell imbued in the mirror that blanks out anything beyond four yards—roughly two body-lengths—from the surface of the mirror. You can choose a plain blue background, a library like mine, or from among a few other choices, though it's currently set to blue if you don't want to do anything.

"Otherwise, you could perhaps spend the time while you wait hanging your mirror upright, instead leaving it at this awkward angle you have it at," he added, peering at her. "But do leave the link open; the moment everyone is connected, we will begin. Oh— hang the mirror sideways; it will help with what I'm going to be showing everyone. It's been strung on the back for both vertical and horizontal. If you'll excuse me, I need to put your link on hold . . ."

"Right," she murmured, as he shifted his arm below her field of view and made the screen turn a rippling blue again. Straightening, she blinked, then turned in a circle, peering around the sunset-gilded Bower, her mind finally processing his last suggestion. ". . . Hang it from *what*?"

Somehow, Saleria didn't think hanging it from the sap-dripping vines would be a good idea. Lacking anything else, she gave up and dug in her pouch. Grease pencil in hand—no mage went anywhere without some means of scribing power-focusing runes, and chalk was too easily dissolved in the open-to-the-weather Grove—she scribbled a line of markings along the upper edge of the mirror. Investing energy with a snap of her fingers and a lift of her other palm, Saleria floated the mirror up off the moss-cushioned ground. Then winced. It was the wrong orientation for Guardian Kerric's request.

"*Bollocks*," she muttered, and quickly scribbled a second set of runes along one of the long edges. A twist of her hand shifted the orientation of the rectangular frame from vertical to horizontal. It continued to pulse blue for a while more, long enough for the golden light of the setting sun to retreat up to the top of the Bower . . . which was when Saleria noticed something odd.

What she had thought were budlike, waxy nodules on the underside of the Bower weavings were now starting to glow. The light was soft and pastel, and would not be noticeable from a distance, but it was very similar to the pale blue glow of the warding stones set in the Grove wall. The nodules also came in more colors than blue. Soft pink, pale green, watery yellow, faint amber, dim lilac . . .

As the sun finished setting and dusk closed in, the different colors combined into a soft glow about as strong as the light from both Brother and Sister Moons when they were full. Saleria glanced up at the sky to make sure it wasn't actually moonlight allowing her to see. Sister Moon was up in the east, slowly waxing toward the full of the coming summer solstice, but the larger curve of Brother Moon had already gone down, and had been a sliver, nowhere near full. Not for over two more weeks. The light cast from those nodes along the underside of the Bower was brighter than what the smaller of the two moons could cast, though not by much.

I suspect there is some long-forgotten way to make them glow brighter, too, Saleria decided, turning in a slow circle so she could peer at the fist-sized bumps. *But I've always completed my rounds quickly, then tried to put the Grove out of my mind . . . and the few times trouble has stirred, I always patrolled the wall paths, not the interior.* Her next thought annoyed her, furrowing her brow with a frown. *What else do I not know about my own Guardianship, thanks to having had to waste the last three years of my life just trying to keep up with plant containment and prayer management?*

Her annoyance was strong enough to thoroughly squash that inner voice, the nasally one that sounded like High Prelate Nestine. *Bollocks to the lot of them! I am in charge, and I will decide what to do with this place. Somehow. With Aradin's help, and maybe a few others' . . .*

The mirror chimed again, rippling into the image of Guardian Kerric. "There we go. Now that everyone is on the scrycasting together . . . allow me to make all the introductions." His hands lifted in odd poking and snatching gestures, and small rectangles started to appear down either side of his centrally aligned image. "Starting with your top leftmost corners and going down each column, we have . . . Saleria of the Grove, Dominor of Nightfall . . . Migel of Althinac . . . Keleseth of Senod-Gra, Pelai of the Painted Temple . . ."

Saleria didn't see her own image in the top left corner, but she did see a man with long, dark brown hair and the slightly slanted eyes of a fellow Katani, followed by a man with a more rugged face, round eyes, and shorter, darker hair. Both were clad in dark tunics, though they were cut differently. Following him were two women, one elderly, with a tanned, wrinkled face and gray-streaked white hair that fell in waves to her red-clad shoulders. The other had a very round face by comparison, with high cheekbones and almond eyes, though the most eye-catching things about her were the subtle markings drawn on her skin. Some continued all the way down onto her shoulders, visible beneath the straps of a sleeveless black vest. It was a garment that was far too daring for most Katani to have worn but which looked oddly right against her inked flesh.

One of the two dark-haired men introduced interrupted Kerric. Saleria belatedly identified him as the one named Migel. "Wait, please—I thought Guardian Tipa'thia was in charge of the Painted Temple. Who is this Pelai? How do we know she isn't a usurper?"

"She's not a usurper," the elderly woman, Keleseth, retorted tartly. "She's a duly appointed apprentice to Tipa'thia. I've already worked with young Pelai on several occasions, at Tipa'thia's request. The girl is trustworthy, and has my respect."

The woman they were talking about, the round-faced, tanned woman with strange markings inked in lines both subtle and bold on her face, throat, and what could be seen of her shoulders, shook her head. "It is right to doubt me; I am only an apprentice. But Tipa'thia . . . Guardian Tipa'thia is suffering from an ailment of the heart, and cannot withstand the rigors of her Guardianship at this time. The Healers reassure me she will recover within the week, but it is not the first time, and so I have been set to watch in her place. I am not sure of what help I can be, since I am not fully attuned. But what help I can give, I will."

"You can be helpful, Pelai, because you are *there* in Mendhi where some of these invasions may take place," Kerric asserted. "Back to the introductions, if we don't mind?"

Saleria nodded, glad to get things back on track. With eighteen Guardians to keep track of—counting herself, which she could not see, as well as Kerric's larger-than-the-rest image in the center of the mirror—that was still a lot of people.

"After Pelai is Kelezam of Charong, Mother Naima of Koraltai—whom several of you know was a past Guardian and is standing in for the current Guardian Serina in the final weeks of her pregnancy—plus Ilaiea of the Moonlands, and Koro of the Scales . . ."

Kelezam . . . could have been either male or female. The eyes were brown, the brows dark, the skin lightly tanned, but the hair and the face from nose down were covered in a dark blue cloth that had been wrapped to conceal the Guardian's identity. Mother Naima also had her hair covered, but only in a white wimple and head-veil, leaving her squarish, middle-aged face exposed. She had a kind smile and hazel eyes, and reminded Saleria of one of her early teachers in the Katani Church.

The woman after Naima was also clad in white, but Ilaiea had no head covering; instead, she had long, straight hair so pale, it looked cream, with odd, pale gold eyes. It took Saleria a moment to realize the woman's pupils weren't completely round, but were instead shaped more vertically, almost like a cat's. Only the light golden tan to her skin kept her from looking like an odd albino. Guardian Koro, on the other hand, had darker tanned skin, jet-black brows, and strange, round viewing lenses perched on his nose. The large crystals were tinted a rich cerulean, deep enough that the exact color of his eyes remained hidden behind them, and his hair—undoubtedly black—was more or less hidden by a deep, dark brown cloak draped over his head and shoulders.

It was clear that not every Guardian wanted their physical identity known to the rest. Saleria herself had no reason to hide, but then this wasn't a group of petitioners crowding around her in a marketplace. She shook off the thought of her earlier encounter as the Guardian of the Tower continued.

"And on the right, top to bottom, nearest column first . . . we have Daemon of Pasha, Alonnen of the Vortex . . . Marton of Fortune's Hall, and Suela of Fortune's Nave," Kerric introduced, nodding to the scrying windows set to his immediate right, in between glancing downward, no doubt at whatever out-of-sight notes he had taken on who was who. Saleria couldn't blame him; there were a lot of Guardians in this meeting.

The first, Daemon, was a man in his prime somewhere between Aradin's and Teral's ages, with short blond hair, blue eyes, and light skin. The second male was a more ruddy-faced man who wore green-tinted viewing lenses much like Guardian Koro's, a soft woolen cap much like the head of a medium gray mushroom to conceal most of his hair, and a mouth-muffling scarf knitted from darker shades of gray. His nose was a bit sharp, sticking out above the muffler almost like a raptor's beak, and his eyebrows an indeterminate shade of brown.

On the other hand, Guardian Marton had brown, curly hair and hazel eyes, his somewhat overweight face—unusual in a mage, where expending magic meant expending life-energy—looking a bit older than Daemon's, unconcealed by anything that could impede identification. The woman in the image below his had sun-streaked light brown hair and light brown eyes, with similar facial features, sort of ovalish heads with pointed chins, high hairlines, and high cheekbones. They didn't exactly look like siblings, but they did seem to be from the same nation, probably Fortuna, from what their titles suggested.

". . . And in the final, far right row, we have Tuassan of Amaz, Shon Tastra of Darkhana, Sir Vedell of Arbra, and Callaia, newly appointed Guardian of Freedom's Thought," Kerric finished.

Saleria nodded at Tuassan; his skin was a rich dark brown, the hue of someone who lived close to the Sun's Belt, much as those who lived in the far north of Katan could boast. She knew Amaz was a kingdom along the southern coast of Aiar, just to the north of the Belt. Tuassan was one of the four she had worked with before, and it was good to actually see his face for once.

Shon Tastra of Darkhana . . . she belatedly realized was a Darkhanan Witch. He also looked older than Teral, with greenish eyes, long, light brown hair streaked heavily with gray, narrower shoulders, and the same ubiquitous black-lined, sleeve-bearing cloak that Aradin Teral wore, visible when he lifted a hand in greeting. The outer layer of his robe, however, was a shade of blue just a little bit darker than the masking background the mirrors provided. When he held himself still, only his head, throat, and a stripe of dark green tunic down the middle of his chest could be easily seen.

Sir Vedell was also older than average, with a gray-streaked beard, short-cropped brown hair, fair skin, and brown eyes. A scar marred one cheek, but otherwise he looked like any confident man just past his prime. Callaia, the last of the women and the last Guardian to be introduced, looked rather young. She also looked rather sober; either that, or possibly annoyed by this meeting.

Her viewing lenses were grayish and small, unlike Koro's or Alonnen's; the wire frame perched on the end of her nose, allowing her blue gray eyes to look out over their tops. Of all of them, her hair was the curliest, framing her face in thick ringlets. For a brief moment, Saleria wished she had hair that luxuriously curly, instead of merely wavy. *But then it's probably a pain to comb out and keep tangle-free . . .*

Having given everyone a chance to examine their counterparts, Kerric cleared his throat and resumed speaking. "Unfortunately, while there are a lot of you attending this call, you are the only Guardians I could get to cooperate with this endeavor. Nor are all of you going to be affected directly by what the problem is, unless circumstances keep changing randomly . . . which they have been, so there are no guarantees. But the more minds we bend to this problem, the greater the hope is that some of us will have clues to what is going on, and that all of us will be able to think of a solution."

"What *is* the problem, Guardian Kerric?" the last woman to be introduced, the curly-haired blonde named Callaia, asked him tersely, almost tartly. "Forgive my impatience, but it is early morning here, and I have much to do today."

"I may know something of what is wrong already, but it is sunset here, and I would like to retire for the night at a reasonable hour," Saleria added. "Can you summarize it for the others?"

Kerric quickly lifted both hands, cutting off the further comments that started to emerge from the scryings of the men and women in their little mirrors-within-a-mirror windows. "Please, milords, miladies, fellow Guardians. I will explain if you'll let me. As you may know, one of my specialties is mirror-based magics. A few years back, with the blessings of several pertinent Patron Deities from around Aiar, or at least their clergy, I was able to craft a special mirror that could peer one year into the future . . . and just a few months ago, I saw the mighty Empire of Fortuna being overrun by what looked like a massive demonic army from a Netherhell."

Shocked silence reigned for a moment, then several of the others started to raise their voices in protests, questions, and denials. Saleria kept silent, but only because the news wasn't a shock to her. Nor was it to the dark-haired Dominor of Nightfall, whose blue eyes had narrowed in a thoughtful frown. Guardians Marton and Suela looked and sounded the most offended, asserting firmly and loudly that such a thing could never happen in *their* homeland. Guardian Kerric raised his hands again.

"Please! Some of you already know of this, and the mirror *has* been tested for the accuracy of its foreseeings. If things *do not change*, then these invasions will happen . . . but that is the key, isn't it? Things can and may change . . . which means for the worse, or for the better. The first image happened shortly after the disaster with Guardian Sheren's Fountain, which has since been shut down for the interim, which is why she hasn't been included in this conference. Hopefully, she will finish recovering and get her Fountain reconnected to the rest of us so that she can join these discussions, but as Menomon is one of the few places I have *not* seen under attack, same as with Althinac and a few other rare places, we can use those lands as a . . . a controlled test subject, where we know nothing they do out of the normal will alter anything in the years ahead.

"The *important* news, good gentles, is that after figuring out how to refocus my future-scrying mirror, I have been able to project it anywhere from one year up to five years into the future . . . and I have repeatedly seen hints and images of demonic invasions from the Netherhells. Some days they go away, other days they come back. As I said, these images *change* from hour to hour, day to day, based upon tiny actions and influences that seemingly have no connecting threads.

"In fact," Kerric added dryly, "the very first image came when I was debating whether to exile a group of invasive traitors either to Darkhana or to Arbra. When I chose Darkhana, the visions came back, but choosing Arbra negated the visions of Fortuna being invaded within a year. I have since kept an eye upon the exiles with the help of Guardian Sir Vedell and most recently Guardian Alonnen. Some of their actions may or may not cause the demonic invasion . . . but some seemingly have *nothing* to do with it, as one of the visions shifted in the middle of the night, when all involved were sleeping innocently. Or as innocently as power-hungry thieves might get."

The Guardian of the Vortex spoke up. Aside from that rather hawkish nose and those green lenses, there wasn't much to be seen of his cap-and-scarf-covered head. His voice was a mild, low tenor, proving he was at least as male as his looks suggested. "I can corroborate their activities, as they have come within the far edges of my scrying range. In the last three weeks, they have hired themselves out as an extremely effective mercenary group to various holdings along the Mekhanan-Arbran border, and have been able to disarm or disable any number of Mekhanan engineering items."

"Skills they no doubt picked up while running the gauntlets of the Tower," Kerric apologized. "Let's hope they continue to fight for a righteous cause, though I apologize in advance if they turn to the other side."

Alonnen shrugged. "The Arbrans aren't too sorry at the moment, since it's been wreaking havoc against their long-standing enemy. I also heard a rumor just before this meeting that the current bounty on their heads on the Mekhanan side of the border is rather substantial, since one of them is a fairly powerful mage . . . and powerful mages usually attract very unwanted attention within that land."

Kerric nodded and picked up the thread of the discussion. "As you can see, one group of people can have a huge impact on the world. We think they are only a small part of the Netherhell problem, however. In over half of the images so far, the worst of it starts within Mekhana's unpleasant borders within half a year or so, *except* when something happens to the priesthood within Mekhana. *Then* the invasions start in other lands. But we don't know what happens to cause the collapse of their priesthood."

"A collapse of their priesthood would be a good thing," Sir Vedell stated dryly. "But that would only happen if their thrice-blighted God went away."

"You said it moves to other lands. What lands would those be?" Keleseth of Senod-Gra asked, her tone clipped, her age-lined face stern with impatience. She repeated herself as Kerric glanced down, checking his notes. "You said Menomon and Althinac and Senod-Gra are not involved, but which ones are?"

"Actually, Senod-Gra *is*, in some of those visions, and Althinac is one of your nearest neighbors, of this gathering," Kerric told her. He lifted a clear pane of crystal into view and tapped on it with his fingers, summoning up glowing writing. "So far, my analysis has identified the following locations as potential starting points, with anywhere from just one vision through to many repeating incidents: Mekhana has the most, followed by the Jenodan Isles, Charong, Mendhi, Senod-Gra, the Draconan Empire, three kingdoms in Aiar—including Pasha, Amaz, and Garama—plus Fortuna at least twice, and Nightfall Isle just the once, with no repeats since . . . but with no guarantee it couldn't come back around to starting there, either. Or that it couldn't start in Katan, or Aurul . . . or worse, a land we have no way to easily watch over."

"Such as Garama?" Tuassan of Amaz repeated, his tone skeptical. "I think my Fountain is connected to every single Fountainway on Aiar—and I know yours is, Guardian Kerric—but I've never heard of any such Guardianship in the land of Garama."

The Guardian of the Tower grimaced. "Unfortunately, there *used* to be a Fountain and Guardian in the Garama region of the old Aian Empire . . . but it was lost when the Empire Shattered, and there's no powerful school of mages nearby I could contact as a substitute for examining whatever events might trigger a demonic emergence there, of all places. I'm hoping to arrange an expedition to Garama to look for its remnants, to see if the Fountain has been sealed somehow, or if it is still there. I will select a trustworthy mage from among my own staff and oath-bind them to manage the Fountain if it still exists and is unguarded . . . but I won't hold my breath."

"Well, don't look for much help from Pasha for the time being," Guardian Daemon stated. He rubbed his short-trimmed, sandy blond goatee, cropped as closely as the matching blond hair on his head, then flicked his hand out expressively. "On the bright side, I doubt any of the king's sons would dare go so far as to dabble in demonic pacts in order to gain the throne. But we *are* embroiled in a nasty civil war at the moment. I have my hands full protecting my Fountain and trying to keep the worst of the magics being flung about from wrecking too much of the land, for the non-mages' sakes."

Saleria blinked, frowned, and turned away from the mirror, trying to think. "What was that . . . What was it that he showed me . . . ?"

"Guardian Saleria?" Kerric asked. "You have something to say?"

Turning back to the mirror, she nodded. "Yes, prophecies. I have a guest from Darkhana who is helping me with something—helping a lot of us, around the whole world—with something found in a set of prophecies. Guardian Daemon's comment about people trying to claim the throne made me think of one of its lines . . . hold on . . ." Wracking her memory, she dredged up the line. "Something something . . . ah! *By mates and friends, by guides and aides, by outworlder on throne.* That was it. Perhaps you should be looking for your solution outkingdom, instead of from within, if the prophecy speaks of the need for a leader on a throne?"

One of the other Guardians coughed. Dominor lifted his fist to his mouth for a moment, clearing his throat. "I am fairly certain that one is referring to *our* 'outworlder on throne' . . . which has yet to fully happen, but which will happen soon. At least, she's the only outworlder I know of, and she's already here, working on turning Nightfall into a kingdom with herself as our queen."

"There was something about *fiends* in the prophecy I read as well," Saleria said, peering at his face in its rectangle in the uppermost left corner of the mirror. "And 'fiends' is commonly used as a nickname for Netherhell demons. Which is why I thought it might apply."

Pelai spoke, catching their attention. "The Guardian of the Grove is correct about one thing. Prophecy may very well have something to do with all of this. I will request the librarians in the Great Library to look for records of unfulfilled prophecies involving the Netherhells, demons, fiends, wars, and invasions."

"We have a fairly extensive library here as well, which I could have the nuns search." The offer came from the white-wimpled, middle-aged woman named Mother Naima.

Guardian Dominor groaned and covered his face with a hand. "For the love of the Gods, Naima, *don't* tell Serina what you're up to. She's fretting enough over her pregnancy."

Mother Naima snorted. "As if I would! By the way, you *should* be coming over soon, yes?"

"Yes, but not until this meeting is done," he dismissed. "And I'll not be upsetting my brothers or sister-in-law just yet over speculations on something that might *not* happen, and so far probably won't begin on Nightfall itself . . . though I will give this problem my attention. Once my wife finishes giving birth, that is."

Kerric, Saleria noted with a bit of sympathetic amusement, looked like he was striving his best not to be impatient at all the sidetracked conversations. He cleared his throat after a moment. "*Ahem*. As I was saying, we *all* have things to contribute in this discussion. Since we have at least a few months before we'd probably *have* to act in some fashion, I would like to send each of you the sets of recordings I have made so far from the future-scrying mirror, and my notes on locations and possible triggering events. Not that I have many of the lattermost, but at least it's a start.

"Each of you know your own regions far better than I ever will," he added pointedly. "I am setting aside a portion of the Tower's scrycasting abilities and powers to work as a routing matrix; these mirrors we're using all link to here and thus to each other, so please feel free to use them to talk to each other. And though some of us have more direct and immediate problems in our own lands to contend with, we are *all* Guardians of this world, defenders and protectors of its most precious resources. This includes our neighbors both distant and near, as well as ourselves, our families, and close friends. The Netherhells are therefore *all* our problem."

"What sized crystal will we need to store the scrycast recordings in?" the gold-eyed, middle-aged Ilaiea asked. She sounded rather autocratic, as if she were more accustomed to being in charge than most Guardians in Saleria's admittedly limited experience. Still, the odd, golden-eyed woman had a practical question.

Saleria didn't have a crystal, though. Technically the crystal at the end of the staff lying on the ground a few steps away was more than large enough, but it was bound with spells for empowering the cutting and scorching end of the staff, and meant mostly for storing and releasing energy in a controlled flow. "I don't have any crystals around for storage, myself."

Kerric held up his hand as a few of the others started to explain whether or not they did as well. "It's alright if you don't. I know Keleseth, Tuassan, Daemon, and a few of the others have the capacity to store and manipulate scrycast recordings, but it won't be necessary. I have prepared enough scrycasting Artifacts for everyone. I'll send them through, one at a time, in a moment. They'll come in pre-spelled cages, which can be used to project the captured images onto a flat, whitewashed wall—and yes, I'll send them with instruction scrolls. They're common among some of our clients, but only a few of you may have seen them before.

"Brother Moon will be at new-dark in four more days," he continued. "Let's have our next mass scrycast meeting at that point in time . . . and I'll continue to experiment with the forescrying mirror and see what new information I can turn up. Please write down your observations and ideas, however wild. At this point, I'm willing to consider anything. Can everyone agree to meet again in four days? You're free to contact each other between now and then; just activate your mirrors in the usual ways and state the name of the Guardian and/or their location to make the connections. Or call for 'the Tower' to reach one of my assistants, who can help connect you if you've forgotten a particular name, since there are quite a lot of us at this meeting. In four days, then? At the same time? We can arrange for other, better times at that meeting, once we all know our schedules and can correlate them to one anothers'."

A few murmured agreements, and a few nodded their heads, including Saleria, but no disagreements met his proposal. Kerric nodded and started naming Guardians, distributing the crystals with half-seen flicks of his hands. Watching him, Saleria almost missed when it was her own turn to catch the incoming Artifact and scroll. Mostly because she was envious that he clearly knew exactly how to manipulate the powers of his own Fountain, and could do it so well.

Catching the cage and scroll as she had the mirror and its scroll, she cradled them in her hands and nodded a farewell to the others. The mirror flared blue for a moment, terminated at Kerric's end, then became a simple reflective surface, showing her the dimly lit environment of the Bower. Without the other Guardians to focus on, she could hear the *plop* of an occasional droplet of sap hitting its designated pool. She could also hear the evening breeze rustling through the leaves beyond the protective cage of the Bower, and the faint buzz of insects.

Insects which could very well be morphing into part-plant hybrids . . . An unsettling thought. Hoping it wasn't so, Saleria debated what to do. She had the caged crystal, with its gem-strung wire box, and a scroll on what to do with it, but barely sufficient light to read the instructions, and no white wall to play the captured images against once she did. She had the pruning staff, which she picked up . . . but she had no portable light source other than its faint, low-charged glow to lead her on the paths out of here.

She also had a fellow mage somewhere out there, one who had only experienced a small taste of the Grove's weirdnesses and dangers. Reworking her clothes, she belted her overjacket so that she could tuck the caged crystal and the scroll into it. That left her hands free to wield her staff. Charging the end with enough personal power to make it glow, she headed out of the Bower.

The mirror chimed, startling her. Returning to the patiently hovering frame, she held her crystal-topped staff off to one side to keep it from blinding either her or her unexpected caller, and activated the mirror with her free hand. "*Baol.*"

To her surprise, it was Guardian Shon Tastra . . . though she didn't know why she should be surprised. The older gentleman smiled and dipped his head politely. "Guardian Saleria . . . we are given to understand you are hosting a Darkhanan Witch, is this correct?"

"Yes, a man . . . a pair of men," she corrected herself, "by the names Aradin and Teral."

"Just Aradin Teral, no 'and,'" the Guardian Witch corrected gently. "But yes, I understand what you meant. In fact, my Guide, Tastra, spoke with Teral just a little while before Guardian Kerric's scrycast. Based on some of her conversation with him, I wanted to reassure you personally that we—the Church of Darkhanan Witches—did indeed assign him to the Empire of Katan to look for a suitable representative of your people before the Convocation of Gods and Man, and that Tastra has verified Teral's queries of the Dark regarding your suitability."

That was the first Saleria had heard of it, but then again, her thoughts right after Teral's return had first focused on the awkwardness of her kissing two men in one body, then on the tasks of the Keeper, re-energizing the wards that kept the weirdnesses of the Grove confined as much as possible within its walls.

"And the answer to that query would be . . . ?" she probed delicately.

"That you are eminently suitable. As a fellow priest, I thank you for your willingness to represent the best interests of your people," Guardian Shon stated, giving her a slight but formal bow.

"Aradin Teral will have more details for you, but since you and I have had the chance to meet more directly, I should like to reassure you that the Witches of Darkhana will be at your disposal for movement to and from the place of the Convocation, once we have firmly identified it and established the exact timing of the event.

"Since we cannot at this time guarantee exactly what sort of facilities will be available," Shon added, turning one hand over in a shrug, "my recommendation is that you pack and keep ready a bag with a few changes of clothes, some coinage for emergency funds, and a little bit of travel-ready food, just in case. Past records of previous Convocations have stated that entire retinues have traveled with the priesthoods of the various Patron Deities, along with baggage trains . . . but those were in the days when the great Portals worked, and everyone knew exactly what sort of hosting facilities the long-established Aian Empire had to offer. This time, it will be in the incipient kingdom of Nightfall, with who knows what level of amenities at hand."

"I understand—and I thank you for reassuring me of all of this," Saleria added politely. "I hadn't thought of the need to pack a traveling bag so soon, but it is a good idea."

"Just remember, we do not know exactly when the Convocation is set to resume," Shon cautioned her. "It could be three days from now, or three weeks, or three months. We only know that it will take place within roughly half a year. It is better to be ready than to be regretful."

"Of course. Do you have any messages for Witch Aradin Teral?" Saleria asked politely.

The other Guardian chuckled at that. His smile crinkling the corners of his eyes, he demurred, "Beyond saying 'hello,' I have no messages at this time, but I thank you for the courtesy. We do have other means to communicate directly, via our holy ways . . . but this neatly crafted scrying mirror of Guardian Kerric's would make things more convenient, if you would permit us to occasionally speak with our Brother Witch . . . ?"

"Of course," she agreed quickly. "Aradin has already offered to help me with certain local problems, which will greatly ease the troubles of my Guardianship if they can indeed be managed. I wouldn't hesitate to allow him to use this mirror to chat with you. It's the least I can do. With his . . . their . . . arrival, I feel as though I've been awakened to my own local problems, and that I finally have the power to do something about them. He—they—are most welcome, here in the Grove."

"Then I shall bid you good night with a happy heart . . . and head back to my bed, since it is very much the middle of the night here, and I am no longer a young man," Shon stated dryly. "It is a pleasure to meet you face to face, so to speak, but it is very late. May you sleep well, Guardian Saleria."

"And you, Guardian Shon . . . er, Guardian Shon Tastra," she corrected herself, wanting to be polite. "A good night to you and your Guide."

Nodding, Shon lifted his blue-and-black-sleeved hand to the frame of his mirror, ending the connection. Saleria stared as the blue background covered the mirror for a moment, then faded back into a reflection of herself and the rest of the Bower. Part of her was gratified to know Aradin Teral was exactly who and what he—they—said they were. Part of her wondered if the presence of all these Darkhanan witches scattered around the world was for the sake of the potential Netherhell invasion, and not just for the Convocation of the Gods being reinstated.

Part of her was tired, and hungry, and ready to call it a night. Leaving the mirror hanging in midair, Saleria picked her way out of the moss-lined swale of the Bower. The sunset glows in the west were almost completely gone, leaving her only with the glow of her staff and the faint hues of those locus-nodules for illumination.

Walking warily back to the sheltered courtyard by the entrance to the Keeper's house, Saleria began to realize just how creepy the Grove was at night. She had been wary before, but Aradin's revelation about the plant-bug mixtures earlier still unnerved her. Nothing actively leaped out at her, nothing tried to attack . . . but it felt like everything within the blue white glow of the crystal end of her staff was aware of her approach, her retreat, and her general presence. Leaves shifted on some of the plants, their broad surfaces swerving to follow her. Vines occasionally twitched. Little rustling sounds followed her, too, sounds which she couldn't pinpoint to a particular plant's movements.

Maybe it's worse that nothing is *leaping out at me*, Saleria thought, glancing behind her to see if she could spot the subtle lights of the Bower at the top of one modest rise in the path. *I'm constantly keyed up for an attack, which means I'll be over-stressed if one finally does happen.*

The lights were very faint from this distance, barely a quarter mile from the wickerwork dome. They weren't the only lights, though; where the overgrown roots and branches of the locus trees rambled among, over, and under the various other plants and paths, an occasional waxy nodule could be seen by its faint glow in the gathering darkness. But only from up close; the father away she got from a particular root or bough, the more likely it was to be obscured by other plants.

Glancing down the path toward the wall, Saleria frowned. Something had moved. Wary, she gripped her staff, peering through the gloom. The movement was subtle, seen more at the edges of her vision when she looked off the meandering course of the path. When she looked directly at them, the plants up ahead were standing still, but when she glanced to the side, they seemed to shift in her peripheral vision. Unnerved, Saleria readied herself for a fight.

It's not the walking marigolds. I can hear them rustling when they move. I cannot hear anything right now other than my own heartbeat, a bit of wind in the upper branches, and . . . footsteps? Frowning, she stopped moving and concentrated, looking off to the side to give her left ear a better chance to hear. Those *were* footsteps. When she glanced back toward the path . . . there was indeed movement, but not the sort expected.

It was a *light* source that moved, a soft-glowing ball cast in a distinctly greenish hue, not the expected bluish white. That was what made the plants seem to move even when they did not, the play of that leaf-colored light sliding over the various surfaces. Oddly though, none of those plants followed the mage-priest casting it, though the blue white glow of her staff continued to cause a subtle, unnerving stir in the foliage around her.

Saleria continued down the path toward Aradin. He looked unharmed, which relieved her, and the staff he carried was now dark, emptied of the energies used to refresh the Grove wards. Before she could speak, he called out to her softly.

"Saleria, can you cover the glow from your crystal, please?" he asked, nodding at the staff in her hands.

"My crystal?" Surprised, she eyed the blue white glow hers emitted . . . then quickly studied the plants around her, which were reacting to it but *not* to his green mage-light. Comprehension dawned. Pressing one hand to the polished, faceted surface, she focused on drawing energy out of the matrix until the glow dimmed. She didn't remove all of the energy, but did reduce it to the faintest of glows. Her skin tingled from the resumed energies flowing back into her sense of self, but it didn't otherwise affect her. ". . . Is that better?"

"Yes," he said. "Plants react to red light by growing more blossoms, and blue light by growing more leaves, but most cultivars tend to ignore green light. If you want to move around safely at night, I suggest casting a green mage-light, not anything blue, red, or white."

"Since white contains all colors, including blue or red," Saleria murmured, recalling her old magery lessons in optical illusion and illumination crafting. She looked around, pausing to listen, but there were no subtle movements, no rustlings. "No wonder I've never felt comfortable in the Grove after sundown; my pruning staff was the greatest source of light, and it's bluish white light, at that."

"All the attraction of a plant wanting to grow leaves and vines in that light, and the activity of an animal, able to see by it and move around at night," he agreed. "Thankfully, the path is fairly calm right now. Shall we return to your house?"

Saleria looked around at their green-lit surroundings, then at the Darkhanan Witch. At a man who had the knowledge she needed, and the willingness to help her when few others could or cared. Honesty prompted her to speak.

"Were you sent by my Gods, Aradin Teral?" she asked him. "Because for all the times I've privately complained about my task, you do seem to be the answer to my prayers. Or at least, you seem to know far more than I do about what is going on within the Grove."

He smiled but bowed his head, an oddly shy move. "If I am here by the will of any God or Goddess, I do not know. I do know I am drawn to help others—the habit of all these years in my unexpected holy calling, no doubt—but I find it even easier to offer you my assistance, because what you need help with dovetails with my secular calling. As I have said before, I am a Hortimancer," Aradin said, his smile broadening with a touch of pride. "Plants and their interactions with magic are my specialty."

"And I need all the plant-knowledgeable help I can get," Saleria admitted. "Right, then. Supper is served shortly after sundown.

Nannan will have it waiting for us—I told her you'd be dining with us tonight." She started moving down the path toward the wall and her home, then paused to flash him a teasing smile. "If you do good work, I'll even let you move into one of the guest rooms, and pay you in room and board."

He chuckled. "What, I'm not going to be paid in solid coin?"

"It's holy work, Holy Brother," Saleria reminded him, her tone mock-pious. She spread the fingers of her free hand, her gaze lifted toward the dark, half-clouded sky and the stars that were starting to show. "The Gods pay us in ways we cannot even begin to conceive."

A hastily lifted hand didn't quite hide the "—*horseshit*," he mock-coughed . . . but he did grin at her when he finished mock-clearing his throat.

She grinned back. "Yes, I do know it's a load of bollocks. That's what High Prelate Nestine told me when she said I was being assigned to apprentice the previous Keeper. I insisted on a high salary anyway . . . and I'm just as sick and tired of hearing it as you are. But I can afford to keep you in my employ, so long as you do not exaggerate your expenses."

"Room and board, and a modest stipend for supplies—most of which will be left here when my work is done—will cover my expenses nicely," he reassured her. "The rest can be negotiated."

SEVEN

"More spinach, Aradin?" Nannan asked. Or rather, pressed, since she was already holding out the bowl to him.

(*Ugh, not more of that sauce,*) Teral muttered in the back of the younger Witch's mind. (*I only get half of your sensations when I'm not in control, and even I think it's too vinegary to eat.*)

(*Agreed, but one must be tactful,*) Aradin thought back. Which amused him, since it was normally the elder of the two urging politeness and diplomatic caution. Smiling slightly, he demurred, "No, thank you; I appreciate the generosity, but I'd rather not overeat."

"Overeat?" Nannan scoffed, eyeing him. "You're nothing but a thin pole! Can you not afford an occasional haunch of meat in your travels?"

(*I think it's a good thing Priestess Saleria spends so much of her days on her feet, or she'd end up overstuffed on this woman's cooking,*) Teral observed dryly.

(*To be fair, everything has been quite good, except the sauce on the greens,*) Aradin pointed out. Aloud, he merely said, "I do have to walk back to the inn this evening. I'd rather not waddle."

"Hm. It's a good thing you're not staying *here*," the housekeeper asserted. She set the glazed pottery bowl on the polished wooden table with a *clack*. "It just wouldn't be proper!"

Ever since her nightmare this morning, Saleria hadn't felt like her normal self. Part of her wondered if it had been sent by Kata and Jinga as a pre-warning of Guardian Kerric's news about the Netherhell demons. It also felt like a wake-up call to her whole life. The normal smooth running of the Keeper's duties had been deeply disrupted today, but it made her feel better, not worse. Like the wake-up was needful, even necessary. But her housekeeper's attitude was threatening to sour that better-world feeling.

Sighing, Saleria put down her fork and cut off her housekeeper the moment the older woman drew in a breath to say more. "*Enough,* Nannan. The choice of who stays in the Keeper's house is up to the Keeper. Last I checked, that was me, not you. *If* I should decide it would better suit my needs to have Witch Aradin Teral stay with us, *then stay with us he shall.*

"I trust I have made myself clear." She did not make it a question.

Nannan opened her mouth, thought for a moment, then closed it and subsided. Satisfied, Saleria decided to turn the dinner conversation to work. Normally, she refrained, as Nannan grumbled that such things weren't appropriate at the dining table whenever Saleria tried to discuss various petitions with Daranen, but tonight, Saleria did not care.

"Now that we have some goals outlined—fixing the flaws in the Grove's containment of the rift-magics, undoing all the amalgamations of plants and animals, and investigating the sap pools— what materials or furnishings will you need installed in the Bower for your work?" she asked Aradin. "I was thinking perhaps you might want a tent, or a shelter of some sort. It's been hot and dry the last few days, but it might turn to rain without warning."

"I hadn't thought about the rain, but I think I'd like to examine the Bower structure itself, first," Aradin said, reaching for his water goblet. "There may already be some sort of weather-sheltering shielding on it, or a way to incorporate such spells into the existing structure. That would be the least intrusive solution to any weather problems."

"True. Will you need any tables?" she asked next. "I was thinking I should get some for my own use, and something for us to sit on, and perhaps a mirror stand—which reminds me, the call I received, it was a sort of group-scrying of several Guardians. One of them wished to say hello to you."

One brow lifting in surprise, Aradin blinked at her. Swallowing, he set down the glass and shrugged. "I can't think of who it could be."

"He was introduced to me as Witch Shon Tastra," Saleria explained.

Both brows raised at that. "Ah. Yes, I know who that is. He's one of our highest-ranked members, in fact. I hadn't realized your communication ability reached all the way to Darkhana. Teral says he met with Tastra shortly before returning to us."

"Teral says . . . ?" Nannan asked, looking mystified.

Saleria didn't bother to explain to the older woman. Nannan would learn as they went along. "I had no connection for that far away, but Guardian Kerric of the Tower does. He was the one to call the meeting. At the end of it, Guardian Shon Tastra wished to confirm the original reason why you came here, and to offer his thanks for my willingness to comply. He also recommended I pack a bag."

"Pack a bag?" This time, the question came from Daranen.

"Yes, for the Convocation," Saleria reminded him. Her scribe nodded at the realization.

"Of course, of course," Daranen muttered, following along since he had been privy to the earlier meeting.

"Pack a bag?" Nannan repeated, still mystified and frowning. "But you're the Keeper! Until you are replaced, you cannot leave the Grove unattended."

"I already have a potential replacement, Nannan," Saleria told her. She picked up her fork and scooped up a few sauce-drizzled leaves, but did not eat them immediately. Her housekeeper had that look in her eyes again. "Before you panic, it will only be a temporary journey. A visit to the location where the Convocation of Gods and Man will be reconvened. After it is over, I will return to my post. As for my going, I am the Keeper of the Grove; I am more than qualified to represent the concerns of our people, and *that* is all that matters—this subject is *not* open for debate. Nor are you to gossip about it."

"*Hmphf.*" From the frown still creasing the older woman's brow, it looked like Nannan was considering being extra cheerful and extra early in waking up her employer in the morning. The housekeeper had her ways of getting even.

Saleria didn't care for the attitude. That nightmare and Kerric's subsequent warnings had shaken her out of her complacencies with a vengeance today. "Don't even think it, Nannan. Your job is to run this household smoothly . . . which you do quite well, under normal circumstances," she allowed politely. "But all decisions regarding the Grove and its Keeping are mine and mine alone.

"Now, back to the topic. I think, if nothing else, we can take and enchant a piece of canvas for cover. It could also make a good projection wall for the scryings Guardian Kerric passed on to me," she stated. "I'd like you to observe and give your opinions along with my own. The more minds we have working on the problems at hand, the better off we'll be."

"What problems?" Daranen asked, looking between the Keeper and their Witch guest.

Saleria gave up trying to eat the rest of her greens. She loved the sauce Nannan made, but it worked best on fresh greens; once they started to go limp and soggy, she lost interest. Focusing on the conversation at hand, she explained. "This goes no further than this room, Nannan, Daranen . . . but one of my counterparts up in Shattered Aiar managed to capture a . . . a Seer-like scrying from some distance into the future. Depending upon the shifting, fickle ways of fate, we may or may *not* have a problem with Netherhell demons within the next year."

Nannan dropped her fork. Blue eyes wide, she stared at Saleria in shock. "N-Netherhell demons?"

"*If* we cannot figure out how to prevent their emergence. The important thing is that there are a good eighteen of the strongest and smartest mages around the world already working on the problem, myself included. If a solution can be found, we will find it. Which is why you shall *not panic*," she ordered.

*Hmphf*ing again, her face tight with hints of outrage and fear, Nannan rose and reached for the various food bowls. Daranen quickly snagged one of the last bread rolls before the basket was plucked out of reach.

Aradin waited until the housekeeper had taken herself and her burdens off to the kitchen down the hall. ". . . Was it necessary to tell her? Teral says she strikes him as the sort inclined to gossip."

"She can be discreet," Daranen told him. "She has to be; the Keeper's position has been endangered in the past by indiscreet staff. Saleria is no Seer, but she has some of the same level of fame. More, in many ways, for there can be two or three Seers alive at one time in an empire the size of Katan, but there is only ever one Keeper, and perhaps one apprentice."

"I think it might be best to remove temptation from her presence all the same," Aradin said. He didn't need Teral's mental nudgings to make his recommendations; they were simply wise. "The Netherhells are as real as the Afterlife, but considerably easier to access, since they do not require one to be dead. Gossip about a potential demonic invasion could be considered too alarming to keep silent. Perhaps if we retired to the study?"

Saleria knew he had a point. She shook her head. "I told her what little I did because she *does* need to know why your presence here is so important. On several levels. But you are right; she doesn't need to know the rest . . . and Daranen, at this point, your knowing of what are still mere possibilities would only trouble your tranquility and concentration. Whatever Aradin Teral and I have to discuss, we should probably do it in the Bower. Which means tomorrow morning—if you gentlemen will excuse me," she added just as Nannan came back, "I am in need of a bath and a good night's rest.

"Aradin, Teral, Daranen, I will see you all in the morning. Good night. And a good night to you as well, Nannan—I can draw my bath on my own for at least one night," she added, to prevent the older woman from having to choose between handling the supper dishes and preparing the tub. "I did it for many years before I came here. Have yourself an early evening's rest."

Aradin rose politely when Saleria did, and bowed to her. "Then I shall see myself out, and see you in the morning."

(*I can hear your sub-thoughts,*) Teral mused quietly. He sent his Host a fleeting, wistful smile. (*Alas, it is too early to offer to scrub her back. Perhaps later, though.*)

(*One can only hope,*) Aradin agreed, heading for the door. (*Let's see if the inn has a tub available for my own use.*)

* * *

Saleria did not want to get up. Her bed was comfortable, her body still tired, and she'd been enjoying a very delightful, if slightly bizarre, dream involving Aradin, whipped honey butter, sugared rose petals, and a waterfall made out of something thick and brown that looked like the spicy sauce Nannan slathered on meat when she grilled it. Alas, right on schedule, Nannan bustled into her bedroom, whipped away the covers, and smacked her on the rump. Just as the Keeper had suspected her housekeeper would.

"No mercy for you today, Keeper," Nannan stated sternly, ignoring Saleria's offended grunt. "I lay awake half the night, fearing I'd start dreaming about Netherdemons, and if I can't get my sleep, then *you* cannot. Up you get!"

Rolling over, Saleria stretched across the feather-stuffed mattress. Her nightshift had ridden up a bit, but at least the heat wasn't so strong this morning that she longed to be under the enspelled comforter again. A soft groan escaped, and her eyelids started to drift shut against the morning light. Hungry as she was, she was also still tired.

"Oh, no you don't!"

Saleria yelped as the older woman whapped her in the stomach with a pillow. "I'm up! I'm up!"

Climbing out of the bed, she gave her housekeeper a dirty look, but accepted the lounging robe without complaint. Now that she was upright, with a little adrenaline in her blood from that whap, she could think. *I'll have an interesting day, I think,* she decided, knuckling the sleep-sand from the corners of her eyes. *Getting Aradin Teral settled, figuring out what we can do about the various plants, working it all in around my schedule of prayers and patrols . . .*

Curiosity prompted her to ask, "Nannan . . . *did* you have any nightmares? If so, I am sorry."

"No," the older woman stated, her tone slightly sniffy. She shooed Saleria out of the bedchamber and toward the stairs. "But I wasted half the night worrying I would. Instead, I dreamed about getting into an argument with pickled turnips that looked like striped melons and talked like children. A very *odd* dream, but not all that frightening."

"I do love the way you pickle things," Saleria told her. She didn't mention her own dream. "Any chance there're pickled eggs for breakfast?"

Nannan snorted. "No, but Daranen went back to the inn with that man last night, and *he* certainly came home pickled. I'll not be surprised if your scribe cannot abide the scratch of his pen on the page today."

"He was probably enjoying the first new male company we've had in a while," Saleria pointed out. She felt a little envious; there used to be a time when, at the end of her daily duties as a deacon, even a prelate, she had been free to go off and have a drink at the end of the day. Just the one, and sipped slowly, but a drink with her friends. But that had been in a city halfway down the continent. Here, she didn't have the time or the energy.

Although I might, once we get going on sharing patrolling and energy-gathering duties. That would cut down on a lot of her work. Well, some of it. Aradin would no doubt want to stop and examine a lot of the plants during his patrols, and . . . she winced. *That means I'll still have a lot of work to do. I have to remember this is a long-term solution to the Grove's many problems, and* not *a quick one.*

Gentle Kata, Fierce Jinga, she thought in a brief prayer as she settled at the table to await her breakfast, *grant me the patience and the strength for the task of salvaging the mess that is the Grove, restoring it back into the glorious, safe, holy garden it rightfully should be.*

She didn't hear any reply, but as the Keeper of the Grove, Saleria knew her prayers were at least heard.

* * *

Aradin Teral arrived at the front door just as she finished her breakfast. Nannan made him wait in the front hall while Saleria dressed for the day, still not entirely happy with his presence in her otherwise neatly ordered world. Saleria wished the older woman would be more polite, but that would take time, she knew. The two clergy shared a mutual moment of eye-rolling before setting out for the morning's wall-clearing. Or as Aradin put it wryly, "I need to learn how to take over everything you do each day, for the time you're at the Convocation."

His words reminded her of the bag she had packed. Into it she had tucked a money belt, two changes of formal priestly gowns, two changes of Keeper-style pants and short-robes, dried meat, cheeses, and stasis-preserved fruit and bread, a stout cloak in case the weather turned bad, and a preliminary list of concerns she wanted to address to Kata and Jinga. It was a list she kept amending in her spare moments.

As the day progressed, she showed Aradin how she patrolled and cleared the paths, gathered energies from the locus trees, consulted with Daranen over the prayers to be said . . . and how she prayed in the heart of the Bower, kneeling on the mossy ground, glowing staff balanced in her hands. The rest of her tasks she felt he could handle, as any competent mage who could fight and cast would be able to manage that part. And he did manage, for most of it.

But prayer? To a God and Goddess he did not worship? That was where she wasn't sure he could do a proper job. How could a foreign priest with a foreign set of Patron Deities properly pray to, and connect with, the Katani God and Goddess?

But he was respectful while she prayed on the second day, and did not set up his alchemical tables or try to figure out the Bower structure. Instead, Aradin shadowed her every movement while they were in the Grove, asking an occasional question but mostly observing, copying, and attempting to get everything just right. He did a good job of it, too; by the end of the third day, Saleria felt he could have made a great apprentice, if it weren't for that ongoing worry about his ability to shape Katani prayers.

The ongoing worry of the Netherdemon visions was another concern. Each evening, they retreated to her study and used the whitewashed walls to project and view the images Guardian Kerric had captured. No concrete starting-point could be seen, but they took notes on everything they saw, of the types of demons, of the heroes who fought against them . . . and of the heavily robed and hooded humans who interacted with them, seemingly directing them.

It was a disturbing revelation, that people would actually consort with creatures from the Netherhells so willingly . . . and more disturbing that the demons would obey. But there wasn't much more either could contribute to what they saw, so far. As it was, Saleria herself believed that her own contributions as a Guardian would be slim until she could get the Grove under far better control, rather than merely maintaining the status quo.

On the morning of the fourth day, Aradin took off in one direction, Saleria the other, and they met at the far side of the Grove enclosure in half the time it took her to make her morning rounds. Taking the neglected back path to the Bower took away some of that spare time, but enough was left over that when they arrived—after rousting a nest of nasty root-snakes and a pathetic beehive-like thing which had tried to sting them with soft petals—Aradin started examining the natural wickerwork of the Bower dome.

Saleria pointed out the waxy nodes and mentioned that they had glowed in different pastel hues. Kneeling across from her,

Aradin knew within moments what they were supposed to be. He had seen similar effects in his Hortimancy classes. They weren't lanterns; the glow was merely a provident side effect of their intended effect: monitoring the flow and use of different kinds of magic.

"You see, they don't come on when dusk falls," Aradin told her in hushed, enthused tones as they knelt at the base of one of the bark-covered roots forming a main arch. "They don't, because they're *always* on; they're always active, always monitoring whatever powers are being used—that mirror floating over there, you said it came through the Fountainway? I'll bet you that had you been free from the need to concentrate and cushion its arrival that you would have seen the copper-hued ones, and maybe one or two others, lighting up with its arrival."

"The copper ones? So, do the colors indicate what they do?" Saleria asked him, reaching up to gently touch a copper-hued nodule. It felt more like crystal than wax, though the translucent look of it was more like the latter than the former. "Are they like the pools?"

"They should be connected, logically, but I'll need a special Hortimancy tool to discern their full function." He flashed her a smile. "That's why I've been shadowing you the last few days. I couldn't get to work even on the preliminaries without it, but it should be here by tomorrow. The previous days, I got a good look at the Grove overall and how it currently functions. Today, I have time to look around and set up my worktables. Tomorrow, I should be able to get to work on how it *should* function."

"*Here*, here?" Saleria asked, pointing at the ground between them. "Or . . . or somewhere that Teral can pick it up, like he picked up that chest, and those sugar cane seedlings?"

Aradin dipped his head, acknowledging her point. "Technically, it's in Darkhana, shipped from Fortuna. One of our fellow

Witch-priests will pass it to me tonight at the New Brother festival, and we'll bring it to Katan."

"New Brother festival?" she asked, once again feeling a bit ignorant of other lands.

"Every new and full of Brother Moon, we Witches gather in the Dark to meet and mingle, to discuss concerns and share news. Those who are ambassadors or envoys often use this time to pass along trade goods—like the sugar cane seedlings I bought," he told her. "They're to go to a specific cluster of Witches who work in the royal botanical gardens.

"It's supposed to be in the evening, but since this corner of the world experiences dusk several hours later than Darkhana does, either Teral will have to start without me, or I'll have to take the afternoon off," he told her. "Late afternoon. Can you handle the third locus tree and the Grove wall without me?"

His smile showed that he was teasing her. Saleria narrowed her eyes, but smiled back wryly. "*Maybe*," she teased in return. "I was going to offer to let you stay here tonight. I mean, in the Keeper's house."

The look of surprise on his face was expected, as was the pleasure, but the relief puzzled her. At least, until he said, "Thank you; that would relieve us of the worry that someone would break into our room at the inn and disturb our body while we're gone. It's a bit dangerous for both Host and Guide to be away from their shared body at the same time. Usually we ward the place we're in, but that takes away some of the energy we need for sustaining our visits in the Dark."

"I suppose it would be, particularly if they were out to kill you," Saleria murmured, not pleased by that thought. Not that she suspected anyone of wanting to kill the friendly, charming Witch kneeling at her side, but her imagination could easily supply such a scenario.

"Oh, there is that, but it's almost as bad if someone calls in a Healer, because they think we're in a coma of some sort," Aradin admitted. "Technically, the Hosts' bodies *are* in a coma, but meddling with the bodies can harm the link tying our spirits to our flesh. Most mages shield themselves against *harmful* magics, not helpful ones, and to shield against both is exhausting."

"Maybe I shouldn't offer you a room in the house," Saleria muttered, thinking about her housekeeper. At his puzzled look, she explained. "Every morning, I hate to get up, and Nannan bustles into my room and whips off the covers, and if I don't move quickly—which I usually don't, because I hate mornings—she smacks me on the buttocks with a hand or a pillow or whatever. And she *likes* me. I don't know what she'd do to you if she thought you had to get up at a specific time and found you lying in bed, unresponsive."

"Is she a mage?" Aradin asked.

"No," Saleria admitted. "Just a very good, if forward and, well, pushy, housekeeper. But then I do prefer to laze in bed each morning. I just cannot afford to do so, as the Keeper of the Grove."

"Then a simple ward on the door will do," he said. "Those who come to kill mages tend to come with magical abilities to aid them in doing so. As do Healers. We'll simply tell her that if I don't respond to three knockings on the door, I'm to be left alone. But that's only every two weeks or so, and I'm usually back by local dawn—earlier, since Darkhana experiences dawn before Katan does.

"Besides, once you feel confident that I can handle the morning rounds, you *can* lounge in bed," he said with a smile. At the questioning lift of her brows, he cocked one of his own at her. "You'll have an apprentice—me—who can do the morning rounds *for* you."

That . . . He . . . Wow, he's right . . . I can sleep in, Saleria thought with dawning wonder. It pinched into a frown in the next moment, accompanied by a rough sigh. "Except I'll have to get it through

Nannan's head that you actually *can* do morning rounds for me.
And that's assuming you're a morning person. I won't make you do
something you'd hate to do, otherwise. At the end of the day—or
the start of it, rather—tending the Grove is still *my* responsibility."

Aradin chuckled. "Teral isn't one, but I am. I *love* being out-
doors at dawn. The crisp chill in the air, the scent of dew on the
plants, the little trills of the birds waking up . . . and the colors of
sunrise, streaking the clouds and the sky in shades of peach and
gold and more? Glorious, all of it."

The way he looked at her, the warmth and enthusiasm in those
intriguing hazel eyes, the smile curving those lips, even the wisp
of blond hair that had escaped from its thong, all came together in
a very compelling package. Saleria found herself swaying forward
on instinct. She checked herself for a moment, then with a silent,
fear-dismissing, *Bollocks to that*, she finished leaning forward and
touched her mouth to his.

(*Well*, that *was unexpected*,) Teral observed in the back of his
mind.

(*Unexpected*, *but welcome*,) Aradin returned, his sub-thoughts
adding a mental hushing. Teral obediently fell silent. He didn't step
into the Dark, but he did give Aradin full control of the moment.
And Aradin gave it to Saleria, meeting her touch for touch but letting her take the lead. It was she who parted her lips first, and her
tongue that slid along his bottom lip. He matched her movements,
enjoying every moment.

It wasn't quite enough, though. Tipping his head, he deepened
the kiss. She sighed and leaned in closer. Somehow, somewhere in
there, they turned in the midst of their embrace until the kiss
finally ended with a soft, parting nibble. Sighing happily as he lay
next to her, Aradin looked up at the curving limbs of the Bower.
The moss was soft and springy under his head and back, and birds

twittered in the distance. The hue of the sky was a plain, mid-morning blue . . . but it felt like dawn to him all over again.

"Mmm," he sighed. "I could enjoy waking up to *that*, too."

Resting on her hip, skin still tingling from where his fingers had caressed, where his lips had brushed, Saleria chuckled at his quip. Just as her humor started to die down, a stray thought crossed her mind, and she choked on another peal of laughter, head tipping back. She caught the curious, inquisitive quirk of his brows when she glanced down again. Blotting a tear from the corner of one eye, she shrugged diffidently. "It's . . . hard to explain."

Glad they were within the Bower's protections, Aradin tucked his hands behind his head and shrugged. "Try me."

"Oh . . ." Searching for a place to begin, she gestured vaguely. "The other morning—I think the day you arrived—I had a grumpy thought when Nannan came in to wake me up and get me moving. I was wishing that one day she'd come in and be *silent* instead of so vocally firm and cheerful."

"Oh?" he prompted her, wondering why their kiss would make her think of that.

"Yes, well . . . I imagined, just now, her finding *you* in my bed, and was thinking *that* might actually shut her up for once, out of sheer indignation," Saleria said. She blushed and ducked her head. "Not exactly the nicest thing to think about doing—shocking her indignant, I mean. Not the you-being-in-my-bed bit. I, um . . . Oh!" Her blush faded and her eyes snapped wide. "Teral! Oh, I completely forgot . . . !"

(*And here it gets awkward,*) Teral muttered in the back of his mind.

(*Only if we let it,*) Aradin said. He repeated the words out loud, more or less. "It's only awkward if we let it be awkward. Yes, he was here, but he has nothing against it. You did enjoy it, yes?"

"Well, yes," Saleria said, since that was far too obvious to bother with a lie.

"As did I," the blond Witch asserted, before she could tack a *but . . .* onto her statement. "That's all he cares about—and he only cares about it because he is my friend." Shrugging to resettle his shoulders and spine, he said, "It's my body and my life, and *I* quite enjoyed it. Nothing will change that part, if we don't let it. Besides, you *can* request that he step into the Dark in the future, if that is what you truly want."

His matter-of-fact attitude was somewhat reassuring, but Saleria still felt a little odd about the situation. While kissing him, she had only been aware of Aradin, not Teral. It was only when that awareness came back to her that things had felt awkward. Unlike her previous worries, however, a new one had surfaced.

"What if *he* doesn't like being shut out?" Saleria found herself asking. "Is that honestly fair to him? I mean, yes, he's technically no longer alive, and it's not his body . . . but he *does* have *a* life of sorts. I guess . . ." She frowned and picked at some of the moss growing between them, trying to order her thoughts as well as her words. "It's not fair to expect the woman to have to deal with two men at once, one always constantly there and watching, but is it at all fair for the man and the woman to expect the watcher to have to leave, to . . . ah . . . never know intimacy, even if it's only sec-ondhand? Not that I'm *advocating* he, uh . . . I mean . . ."

(*Give me the body and I'll tell her myself,*) Teral offered.

(*I'm too comfortable to move,*) Aradin grumbled. He moderated his complaint with an extension of that thought. (*Besides, this is part and parcel of her complaint. Here—tell her much more directly.*) Unfold-ing one arm, he reached over and covered Saleria's fingers with his own. "Here. Let Teral tell you himself, directly."

"Directly?" Saleria asked.

(*Yes, directly,*) she heard the lighter-voiced, older Witch say in her mind. Gasping, she started to pull away, but Aradin tightened his grip, keeping her close physically. Teral, however, was the one to reassure her verbally. (*This is just a part of our holy magics—and no, it does not break the Laws of God and Man that state how the thoughts of mortals are our last bastion of privacy, and that there shall never be a spell to peer into the head of another living mortal.*)

"It . . . it's not?" she asked, blinking in confusion. "But I thought . . ."

"The Gods have decreed that no *living* mortal may read the mind of another *living* mortal," Aradin told her, gently squeezing her fingers. "But Guides are no longer alive, for all that I have given Teral a semblance of life."

(*If you think of it another way, there is no way that I* could *be a Guide, residing within my Host, if we could not share our thoughts,*) Teral added, silencing her next question. (*And I do not do this lightly, nor casually. It is holy magic, and as such, should not be profaned by carelessness or malice, or other ill intentions. I do this to reassure you directly, with no lies between us, that I* will *accept any request you make to have me step into the Dark whenever you wish to be intimate with my Host. It is* his *life, and no longer mine.*)

Aradin could hear what Teral was saying to her because Teral willed him to hear it. But Aradin could not share his thoughts with her, which left him with mere speech. "The choice is yours, Saleria. But I will be completely honest with you. Teral is now my closest friend . . . and like all closest friends, I'd be inclined to discuss any relationship I may enter into with him, to ask for advice, to offer a moment of humor, to seek sympathy over a misunderstanding or a mistake. I would try to refrain if you asked . . . but would you honestly refrain from discussing such details with your own best, closest friend?"

At his words, a face flashed into her thoughts, nut-brown and heart-shaped, with hazel eyes, tight dark curls, and flashing white teeth frequently bared in a smile. Saleria hadn't thought about Aslyn in weeks, but she did remember how close she and her fellow acolyte had been, back during their temple training. They still wrote to each other, with Daranen keeping Aslyn's letters separate from the constant stream of petitions so that Saleria could answer them in her spare time, rather than assume it was meant for some prayer.

Aslyn was now a full-fledged Priestess, not just a Deacon, but her assigned parish and chapel were far to the south. *And in her most recent letter, she* did *talk about the romance budding between her and one of the local landholders, and I wrote back to her with some comments and encouragements I felt I could add*, Saleria acknowledged. "I suppose that's fair. That you can talk to each other. But . . . watch?"

Both men consulted on a swift, subconscious level. Ideally, she would be a woman who could accept the presence of both Host and Guide as a constant in her life . . . but if they pressed that point now, she would resist automatically. The idea was too foreign, too strange; only time would allow her to observe, to think, and to come to a true, rather than a hasty, decision. Aradin sighed and sat up, drawing up his beige-clad knees. Resting his forearms on them, he tipped his head at the rest of their surroundings.

"As much as this debate could go on a bit longer—and should, at an appropriate time—you and I do have more work to do today. Such as figuring out where I can work within this dome so that it doesn't disrupt your tasks as the Keeper, but doesn't put me in an awkward spot." He nodded at the nearest moss-covered lump. "Having seen several of your Katani chapels and cathedrals, I can only presume those eight large lumps are moss-covered altars. Yes?"

Saleria blinked, looked around, then nodded. "Yes . . . yes, they are. I don't use them in my daily routine, and neither did Jonder. We just kneel in the center, face the direction that corresponds with the season—north for summer, west for autumn, and so forth—and pray. I guess that's why they've been covered over by moss. I mean, I knew they were altars, but I never bothered to strip away the moss. I guess I was thinking that the moss was just one more part of the Grove as a whole."

"Then there goes the idea of using some of them for my research needs. I don't think Holy Kata or Holy Jinga would mind if we cleared off the moss," he said dryly, "but it would probably be sacrilege to clutter their tops with beakers and retorts, and a mortar-and-pestle or three."

Saleria felt her cheeks grow warm. "I feel a touch of shame for letting things get to this state. All of it, really. The . . . the complacency, the blind obedience to habit and routine." She ducked her head. "I'm really not the best of Keepers."

Reaching over, Aradin tucked his finger under her chin, lifting her face so that he could gaze into those blue gray eyes. "Teral and I both disagree on that. You may not have seen or done anything about these problems in the past, but you *are* doing something about them now, and you're not letting the traditions, habits, and routines chain everything in place. If you were anything less than the best, you'd probably cling to tradition out of uncertainty or fear, but you're willing to embrace a different way. Teral says life is about change, after all."

"True," she admitted, taking some comfort in his words. She looked at him, her mouth twisting in a lopsided smile. "I feel like that old tale of the priestess being awakened with a kiss. I was asleep in the blindness of my duties, and you've woken me up."

"Then I shall continue to kiss you, to keep you awake," Aradin promised. Leaning in close, he pressed his lips to her cheek, then pulled back. "But we really do have work to do." Pushing to his feet, he offered her his hand, and when she stood at his side, squinted up toward the half-clouded sky. "There's the sun, so . . . that way is north, in this hemisphere—I kept getting all turned around the first few times I tried traveling below the Sun's Belt. I'm better at it these days, but there's a part of my brain that says the sun should travel through the *south* part of the sky, not the north . . . But since it does, and that way is north . . . then this southwestern corner here looks like it has a flat spot free of sap-pools, and it lies mostly out of your way, yes?"

Eyeing the spot he pointed to, Saleria gauged it in her mind against her daily routine, and shook her head. "That would do for me, but the southeastern spot is a bit more roomy. You just have to avoid that cream-dripping vine there, and it forms a sort of L-shaped area, see?"

Following her arm and finger, Aradin studied the subtly terraced area, and nodded. "That should work, yes. I may have to put up a screen to remind myself not to back up into the range of the drips, but it should do nicely. Moss off the altars first?"

"That moss may be saturated with sap below the topmost layers. We should use protective spells," she warned him.

He grinned in approval. "Now you're thinking like a Hortimancer. Our clothes are warded, but we should use gloves, too. I'll have Teral fetch out a couple pairs from my gardening supplies. Mine might be a little big for you, but better too big than too small."

Removing the moss from the first few of the eight altars led to removing it from around their bases. That in turn revealed a series of flagstone-and-pebble paths. Some of the stones were broad and mostly flat, if a bit worn by countless footfalls from the past; many more were tiny, naturally colored, laid in intricate designs: circles and arcs and diamonds and lines, all packed tightly into a sandy base that was as sap-soaked as Aradin had predicted.

The fumes released when they started stripping away the

masses of moss from the ground made both of them a little giddy, but an aeration charm helped avert the worst of the effects. Saleria had to stop every so often to attend to her regular duties, but that didn't stop Aradin from working hard. The worst trouble was figuring out a way to dispose of the moss.

Most of the magic could be sucked out by the crystal-topped pruning staves . . . but that filled them up more quickly and brightly than either mage expected. It also left a thick, sticky residue in the soft green tufts. Finally, for lack of a better solution, Aradin tried burning the stuff. With Saleria's permission, he used most of the stored energies to focus the fire and purify the fumes, burning it in a hot, bright sphere until nothing but white ash remained.

That did the trick. After a hearty lunch, and while Saleria focused on her prayer-petitions, Aradin focused on spell-raking up the moss from the underlying stones, draining the power with the spare staves, and searing the sap from the ground. More welled up as he worked, however, revealing the moss had somehow kept the stuff from seeping from the ground all the way to the topmost layers. It did prove his theory, though, that the sap-purified magic had soaked deeply into the ground over the last two hundred years.

(*Enough,*) Teral finally stated, when three altar platforms and paths toward the center proved to be on the edge of what Aradin could keep up with, containment-wise. (*Don't clear anything else. You need a break, and you need to go to the New Brother festival. I'll stay and work on this mess.*)

Carefully wiping the sweat from his face with his Witchcloak sleeve, since his Hortimancer gloves were stained despite their protective spells, Aradin gave in with a nod. (*It's not going as well as I'd hoped. We can wither the moss with the staves, but we need to come up with a way to burn off the sap faster than it wells up from the ground. Maybe a system of . . . of candles, of sorts . . . like an oil-lamp wick . . .*)

(*Enough!*) Teral softened the order with a mental chuckle, and a mental hand on his Host's shoulder. (*Give over the body, youngling, and get going. You're not the only one who can cure this problem; I do have a few ideas of my own. The sap that hasn't yet burned has simply pooled up around the sand-packed stones, but it isn't overflowing or going anywhere, so it isn't an immediate threat. Let me handle it, and get yourself to the festival.*)

Nodding again, Aradin turned to glance at Saleria. She was still resting on top of the—thankfully dry—moss at the center of the Bower, her hands resting palm-up on her crossed legs, the neatly penned petition papers laid out before her. Her voice had filled his ears with the steady, heartfelt recitations, invoking the holy names and aspects of Jinga and Kata which most closely aligned with each petitioned request. For all it was mental and emotional work, not physical, she had worked up a faint sheen of sweat from her fervent efforts.

He rested as he waited, leaning on the staff in his hands, until she came to an end with the current prayer. The moment she shifted forward to shift the papers into a stack to one side, he cleared his throat. Lifting her head, Saleria craned her neck, looking back over her shoulder at him. ". . . Yes?"

"I thought you should know that Teral's kicking me out. I'm off to the festival," he told her. "He'll keep working on the sap-soaked problem, but this is all we can clear for now." It wasn't the most coherent explanation he could have given, but from her nod, she seemed to understand. Nodding himself, he carefully set the staff on a thick, dry-topped patch of moss, then pulled the folds of his cloak down over hands and face, allowing it to envelop his body.

Releasing control of his body was much like releasing control of his balance. With a mental side step to avoid Teral as the older Witch moved forward, he fell back into the Doorway, turned, and strode into the Dark. Teral took over their shared flesh, reshaping it into his own, but Aradin did not stay to watch what happened next over his mentor's mental shoulder.

Unlike the sunlit warmth of the Grove, with its open skies, abundant greenery, and solid reality, the place between Life and the Afterlife was a cold, dark, echoing realm. Hard ground, barely seen in the gloom, scraped underfoot as he moved. A chilling mist shifted in the distance, rippling with hints of not-here and not-there. There was no clear light-source at this end of the Dark, though he could sense and half-see at the corners of his eyes the slender, silvery ribbon that bound him to his Doorway. The rest of the light illuminating his immediate vicinity came partly from Aradin himself, and partly from Brother and Sister Moons, a gift to Their long-vanished Elder Brother. It was just enough to see the barren ground, and a few lengths in any direction, but little more than that.

At least, right here, right outside his Door. Just like the wielding of magic, willpower was what gave him light, strength, and direction in the faceless, placeless Dark. Tightening his focus as he would have tightened a fist, Aradin concentrated, *willing* himself toward the Meeting Tree. Four, five, six swift steps into the mist brought him through the swirling wall and into a slightly brighter patch of moonlight . . . and into a place where he was no longer alone.

The light of Elder Brother Moon shone down on the Meeting Tree, one of the few places where Darkhan's light could shine anymore. It played down among the branches of the gnarled, graceful, flower-laden thing, each twig made out of metal, each blossom and leaf carved from precious stones. It sat in a large square planter carved from pale stone and ringed with redwood benches. The colors were dim but still discernible, jade and malachite leaves, mother-of-pearl petals, and little slivers of amber for the stamens and carpels. It also stood more than twice his height, which meant it rose up above the two dozen or so bodies gathered around its base, ensuring it remained visible and recognizable to all who used it as a waypoint in the directionless void of the Dark.

He had no idea who had first conjured this tree and its moonlit benches, nor how long ago, nor even what kept it here, a permanent fixture in a fixtureless place, but it was a most welcome sight. As were the smiles on the faces that turned to see who approached. Several of the men and women murmured his name, or simple greetings if they weren't quite sure of who he was. Each reached out with hands that ranged from younger and stronger than his to older and more wrinkled than Alaya's had been at her passing. He clasped them in turn with a stretch of his own, muttering a greeting here, a name there, enjoying the shock of living warmth against his skin in the intangible but still present chill of the void.

More approached as he settled into a spot near the edge of the group. Aradin turned to greet them, welcoming his brother and sister Witches. Each newcomer made the air warmer, the light a little brighter, until one of the eldest Sister Witches lifted both hands in the air, above her age-stooped back. "A place! A place! We need a place to meet and to worship! . . . Carradin Ruper, *you* choose the place!"

She asked it of one of the younger male Witches on the other side of the group. Aradin had arrived early enough to witness the night's selection. Rising a little on his toes, he could just see the younger man opening and closing his mouth in indecision, before the short-haired blond finally shrugged and said, "The Garden Lake?"

"The Garden Lake it is!" the eldest agreed, hands tightening into brief fists. Dropping her arms from overhead, Witch Brenna held them out to either side. Her voice was still strong, if a little roughened with her advanced age. It echoed over the crowd as two score and more approached, pressing near. "You know the rules; three stay to guide the rest, and the rest of us on our way!"

It had been a while since he last volunteered to wait and guide the rest, but Aradin didn't want to stay away from Teral, Saleria, or the Katani Holy Grove for long. Clasping hands with a middle-aged, dark-haired woman on his right, and a gray-bearded man on his left, he focused on the Garden Lake and followed the line of people as they snaked into the mists at the edge of the Meeting Tree space.

This garden was no twisted nightmare of a place—and he carefully kept the memories of the Grove locked down out of the way, to keep it safe. Within three, maybe four steps through the dark mists, he emerged with the rest on a long, sloping lawn bathed in silvery light. It led down to a vast lake that rippled with silvery streaks of moonlight—full moons, from both the larger Brother and the smaller Sister, despite it being the new of Brother Moon in the real world. Bushes lined the lawn, and benches provided resting places.

This was a vast area, larger than a village commons and filled with details as crisp as those found in real life, rather than blurred by uncertainty. They weren't the only ones there, though; other spirits, a handful of lost souls, had made their way to the lake. Once fully onto the lawn and with a good four or five emerged behind him, Aradin released the hands on either side. He studied the blurred images, the fading senses of "self" that had once been living people, and counted the heads of the Witches who moved toward them.

They don't need my help, he decided, as each lost spirit was flanked by a pair of his colleagues. This, too, was a task he had done before, though not recently. Witches were tasked with the guiding of the dead toward the Light, the Doorway into the Afterlife. Most of those who died found their own way, but a few strayed into the depths of the Dark, and a few got lost in their own thoughts, and a few, always a few, refused to believe they were dead. At least, at first. These stray souls were in good hands, though. *Time to turn my attention to—whup!*

A feminine chuckle distracted him from the arms catching his elbows and tugging him off toward the center of the grass. The voice that accompanied the hands on his right didn't come from a throat, though. (*Come, Aradin, youngling! Show these older ones how well we can still dance!*)

He didn't have to glance at her snub nose and her smiling eyes, nor see her long hair and graceful limbs, to know who had caught him. Josai of Glenna Josai, one of his earliest Witch-teachers. Josai was the Guide of the pair, and had lived to a ripe ninety-eight as Host and teacher, but her self-image was a mental projection of her body when it had been lithe and strong in her mid- to late-twenties; physically mature but still youthful and lithe.

The woman on Aradin's left, who laughed and pulled him along as well, was Glenna, the current Host. Her body in life was now in her mid-fifties, but like Josai, she thought of herself as younger, early twenties or thereabouts. Shorter, a bit plump but with strength and liveliness to match the bounce in her light brown curls, she tugged him into a line dance with her Guide, celebrating life and Afterlife with equal aplomb. Those Witches who had a talent for song-based magic held back from the gathering dancers, bringing forth instruments of will, of hand and of voice, filling the clearing with the sounds of fellowship and joy.

It felt good to dance, to sway and stomp, to twist and turn. He clapped his hands and sang along as several others joined, while still more lines of hand-clasped Witches emerged from the mists. He crossed places and skipped through the steps, grabbed hands and swung his partners around, not caring whether the arms he grasped belonged to man or woman, living or dead.

How long he danced, he could not have said, but Aradin finally spun free of the whirling masses, of the now hundreds of Witches moving in patterns old and new, continuing the cycle of worship and faith that had turned the tragedy of their God's unfortunate demise into a celebration of His continuing strength. Unfortunately, life moved on, and with it, all celebrations had to share space and time with tragedies, concerns, and the business of the living.

Saleria had told Aradin and Teral of the forescrying mirror and its future-visions of Netherdemon invasion. Spotting one of his fellow Hortimancers first, Aradin turned around, willing his coin-chest to appear in his arms, then approached the older man. Stefal smiled in greeting and shifted on the bench, giving Aradin room to set down the chest. "Ah, good; you brought payment! I got you the best deal I could, but diagnostic Artifacts don't come cheap. Four hundred twenty-three silver and seven copper pennies, please."

While Aradin counted out the funds, rounding it up to four hundred fifty as a courtesy, the other man rose, turned once, twice, then sat back down again with a neatly carved chest in his hands. He opened it, displaying the selection of crystal-tipped wands and the palm-sized sheet of glass with a hole along the top that the wands were meant to slot into. His brows rose at the sight of the fine quality. "Crystal? Not a marble slab?"

"This way does take a little bit of your own magic to power it every day, but you don't have to keep a sharpened grease-pencil tucked into the base, or go through the tedium of scrubbing it clean," Stefal told him. "We cribbed the design from the Artifacts used by the Master and staff of a place called the Tower, in Aiar."

"Guardian Kerric's Tower?" Aradin asked. At Stefal's surprised look, he nodded. "I've actually been in touch with him . . . and I have some concerns to bring to my fellow Witches tonight."

"About the Tower's Master?" Stefal asked.

Aradin shook his head. "About something he has seen in a sort of forescrying mirror he has."

"What concerns do you have?" The question came from a familiar voice off to his left. Walking with more strength in the Dark than she probably showed out in life, Witch Brenna lifted her chin. "What would you bring before tonight's synod, once the dancing and singing has ended?"

"Visions of an invasion from the Netherhells, Sister," Aradin stated, his tone respectful and his words grim. "We may praise Darkhan and Dark Ana that such things are few and far between . . . but the images suggest that somewhere out there, even as we speak, certain humans are making pacts with the demonic realms."

Her wrinkled face tightened into a stern mask. "Such things ended the life of our God, millennia ago. Are you *certain* of this Seer's vision?"

Someone else moved up on Aradin's other side, drawn by the ways of the Dark to join their conversation. Aradin handed over the coins to Stefal in exchange for his diagnostic wands while Guardian Witch Shon confirmed his words.

"I have been contacted as well. Those of highest rank already know, and a few who are in physical proximity to ourselves and our Fountain," the older man stated, meaning both himself and his Guide, Tastra, "but it was my intent to bring this before all of us at tonight's festival." He spared a brief, slight smile for Aradin. "I am pleased to see my younger Brother had the same idea. As one of my fellow Guardians has said, the more minds we have working on this task, the more likely we are to see a solution."

Brenna poked her thumb at Aradin. "How does he know what Guardians do or say?"

"I am assigned to Guardian Saleria of Katan, Keeper of the Holy Grove of Kata and Jinga," Aradin stated, giving his superior a polite bow. "The Dark has confirmed she will make an excellent representative at the Convocation of Gods and Man."

"Good. The sooner we get that task out of the way, the sooner we can pull our Brothers and Sisters back home," Brenna said briskly. "Our fellow Darkhanans are growing restless, not being able to call upon as many Witches for last rites as they normally can."

Shon tipped his graying head thoughtfully. "I'm not sure we *should* pull our brethren back to the kingdom, once the Convocation is over."

Brenna wasn't the only one to give him a sharp look; so did the two younger men. Aradin recovered first, realizing how his fellow Witches could be useful with the other problem on their hands. "Of course. If we *stay* in each of the kingdoms out there, those of us assigned to posts around the world, we can *observe* what is happening, and coordinate information swiftly among each other if we find anything that stinks of the Netherhells."

Shon nodded. "Guardian Kerric said that there were kingdoms, such as Garama on the west coast of Aiar, which have shown signs of being part of a demonic invasion, but which have no local Guardian to watch over its people and their doings. But Garama does have a Witch present, right now."

Dipping her head, Brenna relented her resistance to the idea. "That *does* make sense . . . and of all the clergy in the world, *we* are the ones with just cause to fight the blasphemous reach of the Netherhells."

"I agree, with one exception."

The newcomer made Stefal rise and all four of them bow politely. She looked young, with her blonde hair plaited and pinned around her head in marital braids—not a common sight among the other Witches of Darkhana, if not unknown—but she was far older than Brenna and Shon combined.

"High Witch Orana," Aradin murmured, dipping his gaze as well as his head. "You honor us."

She smiled wryly. "More like the Dark drew me over here. Niel is tending our body tonight—I do not see Teral; is he tending yours, Brother Aradin? Isn't it early in the day for where you're supposed to be?"

He nodded. "We've been working with Guardian Saleria to get her power-base cleaned up and prepared for use. I am not certain what use we will be with the Netherhell invasion at this time, but gaining full control of her, ah, version of a Fountain will ensure that we are not *un*prepared."

"A wise piece of battle planning. And Brother Shon's suggestion is most wise. Possibly even providential. The Witches of Darkhana who have scattered around the world to seek out true representatives of each Patron Deity are well-placed to observe and report. But most Witches are not strong enough to face demons alone. I should not need to remind each of you that the memories of the demonic ones are as long as our own, if not longer," the immortal Witch stated. "They know the Witches of Darkhana have *never* forgiven them for the death of our God."

Her words rippled outward, strong and resolute. The dancing came to an end as more and more of the rest turned to face them. The Garden Lake altered subtly, raising their portion of the lawn into a makeshift dais. Tucking his chest under his arm, Aradin shifted to one side, letting those with more seniority take center stage.

"Five thousand years ago, a demon queen of the Netherrealms tried to fake her way into the pantheon of our world's Patron Deities. She and her followers tried to slaughter our Gods and Goddesses at the Convocation in Fortuna . . . but we were vigilant . . . and almost completely successful at thwarting her plans." Raising her hands, Orana called out to her brother and sister Witches.

"Darkhan gave up His life so that His fellow Gods would live on! Dark Ana, High Priestess and beloved, gave up Her mortal life so that our God would stay ours, despite His demise.

"Every so often, the sinners and the fools of the world seek to make pacts with the demons, and seek to bring them into *our* realm for the vanity of fleeting power, fame, or glory—but this is *our* realm!" Lowering her hands, she clasped them lightly before her sternum, forefingers raised and pressed together. "And now we have a foresighted vision of some of them attempting such foolishness again? Yes, the Netherhells are well aware of how strongly we of Darkhana oppose their ambitions . . . but right now, it is highly doubtful that *they* know that *we* know they are coming.

"It is best if we *keep* it that way. For now . . . we will observe. We will continue to find representatives of the Gods and Goddesses so that the Convocation can be reconvened. We will gather support, and lend covert aid to those who are at this time free to act more openly . . . and we will watch for *any* sign of such foolish attempts in the near future." Parting her hands, she held one out to Guardian Shon. The other, she held out toward Aradin. "These two of our Brothers, Guardian-Witch Shon Tastra, and Witch Aradin Teral, are already tied into the efforts of the world's Guardians to seek out the source of these visions and stop the demons in their tracks.

"You will report to Shon and his Guide Tastra as your primary contact . . . and if you cannot find either of them, you will report to Aradin and his Guide Teral. Mark the names and faces of these Hosts; seek and get to know their Guides. For those of you who have stayed within Darkhana, take solace in the work you do in the stead of those who must wander. Say whatever you will here in the Dark, but speak not a word of this in Life—let the demons think we know nothing! Let them think they catch us off guard, even as we set our snares and our traps.

"This is *our* world, and we will *keep* it that way."

"Praise Dark Ana!" someone shouted. "Praise Darkhan!" someone else added. It was joined by a reverent, "For the world!" and an even louder, "For the *love* of the world!" The rest began chanting and singing, clasping hands and dancing as they swung back into their celebrations.

Serious plans would be laid later, but for now, the men and women, living Hosts and spirit Guides, needed something cheerful to do in the face of such disturbing news. The Dark was *not* the place to think of strong, unhappy thoughts. Not when a strong thought could become a force of will, and one's will literally created the reality of this strange place.

Orana moved up beside Aradin, her hand touching his shoulder. "Sorry to put you on the spot like that, Aradin Teral," she murmured, naming both him and his absent Guide. "But the Dark tells me you'll actually be more involved than Shon Tastra, in your own way."

Aradin accepted her warning with a slight nod. It often took him several moments of concentration, of focusing his thoughts and his will firmly enough to query the Dark and receive a response. He had only been a Witch for a little over a decade; Orana and her Guide Niel had been doing so since before the Shattering of Aiar, and no doubt could receive a response with a single, swift thought.

"I bow to your superior strategy, Sir Orana," he returned, referring to her status as an Arbran Knight of renown. She had been born and raised a Darkhanan, and selected to be a Host, but her Guide was not, and had never been, a Darkhanan Witch. Aradin knew many of the details of how the two had come to be paired, such as the curse that kept them alive and effectively immortal. Resurrecting the Convocation of Gods and Man was their path to ending that curse, and the task which all Witches had pledged to assist, including himself. "For the time being, I am but a simple

Hortimancer, striving to restore the Grove. My contact, the Guardian of the Grove, will be involved in some way. I will strive to be a liaison for the Guardians as well as for my fellow Witches."

She tipped her head for a long moment, thinking quietly, then gave him a wry smile. Squeezing his shoulder, Witch Orana said, "Please pass along my apologies to your Keeper friend for the Shattering of Aiar and the mangling of her Grove. Let her know the Dark approves of the two of you working to make amends for the centuries of neglect in that place. You in particular should be extra sincere when kneeling in the Holiest Garden of Jinga and Kata. Your prayers *will* be heard in such a holy place, and judged accordingly."

Okay . . . Bowing, Aradin excused himself from her presence. As much as he pitied and admired the other Witch, Orana Niel also unnerved him. Particularly at times like this. *I'd give up quite a lot to avoid being so God-touched as those two . . . yet she's just told me I'm more or less God-touched as well. Dark Ana, take pity on me and my Guide; all Teral ever wanted was to be an envoy and a world-traveling merchant, while all I've wanted is to be a successful Hortimancer.*

Of course, they already *were* what they wanted to be, both him and Teral; the problem was, those occupations now came with world-changing headaches attached. *Grove messes and Netherdemon invasions, and Goddess-blessed who-knows-what.* He lifted his gaze to the dark mists swirling far overhead in lieu of actual stars. *I hope at the very least You're being entertained by all of this,* he thought at his Patron Deities, and spared a thought for the Patrons of Katan as well. *I'd hate for all this craziness to pass unappreciated.*

EIGHT

"More spinach, Teral?" Nannan asked their "newest" guest, smiling at him. Almost simpering.

"Thank you, but no more, please. It's good," Teral temporized as politely as he could, "but the sauce is a bit tart for my foreign taste buds, I'm afraid." He softened his refusal with a slight smile, and Nannan set the bowl back down gently. She didn't thump it as she had for Aradin, but then she hadn't given the younger, blond priest such a coquettish pout, either.

Saleria didn't think Nannan understood *what* Teral was. From the way Nannan was reacting, the fact that Teral was a part of Aradin, physically, had gone right over the housekeeper's head. *No doubt she just fastened on to the half-truth that he's a fellow Darkhanan Witch-priest who is here accompanying Aradin on his visit . . . and completely ignored the part where they're technically two men in one shared body.*

Worse, she's flirting *with him.* Saleria winced when Nannan rested her chin on her fingers and leaned his way, her lashes fluttering briefly over her deep blue eyes. Saleria tried not to think about the love-quadrangle she had worried over earlier. For her own sanity, that was not an option, not if she herself was going to be playing courting games with Aradin. Which she wanted to do; she did not lie to herself about that. Aradin was fascinating, intelligent, learned, and kind. Not to mention helpful, handsome, funny . . .

Clearing her throat, she spoke up before her housekeeper could continue her flirtations. She knew her choice of topic would only encourage such things, but it had to be discussed. *At least, until Nannan realizes* what *Aradin-Teral is. Then the fecal matter will probably hit the aeration charm* . . .

"Teral, I believe you were listening when I discussed a change in living arrangements with your Host earlier, yes?" she asked. "If you like, I could assist you in moving your and Aradin's belongings to the Keeper's house after supper."

"Oh! I have just the room for you," Nannan agreed quickly, smiling at the gray-and-brown-haired priest. "It's the one right next to mine, with a lovely view of the neighbor's garden."

"Actually, I was thinking we could put Aradin Teral in the room next to mine," Saleria said dryly. "I figure that would be more convenient, since they will be my apprentices."

Nannan frowned at her briefly, then fluttered her free hand at her employer. "Oh, fine, you can put the young man next to you. *This* gentleman will be next to me . . . yes?"

"I'm afraid it doesn't work that way, milady," Teral stated, his tone quelling, but accompanied by a polite smile. "Where Aradin goes, I go. Where I go, Aradin goes."

"Nonsense!" Nannan dismissed. "You may be travel companions, but you aren't joined at the hip."

Teral slanted a look at his hostess. Saleria couldn't hear his voice in her mind, but she didn't have to; his expression spoke volumes. "*Nannan,*" she said firmly, forcing the older woman to glance her way. "They are more than just 'joined at the hip.' Teral is *dead*. He is a *ghost*. What you see is *Aradin's* body, shaped by holy magics to look like Teral's, but only in a *borrowed* sense. They *share* their body, and just the *one* body alone, which means they only need one bed."

"A . . . what?" Lifting her chin from her knuckles, Nannan stared back and forth between the two of them. Across the table from her, Daranen wisely kept quiet, but didn't let her dawning realization stop him from serving himself another helping of roast duck.

"A guh . . . ? *No,*" she denied, shaking her head. The housekeeper looked back at Teral and shook her head again, faster. "No, he can't be dead! Not in the holy house of the Grove Keeper! Kata and Jinga would *never* allow the dead to walk around! Your jest is not funny, young lady."

"She does not jest. I am quite dead," Teral informed her, cutting into his own meat with fork and knife. "My body was squished in half under a fallen tree, and in my last few minutes of life, I called upon *my* God and Goddess to transfer my spirit into the body of a young mage named Aradin, whom you have met. By holy magics I was able to join my spirit with his, rather than head straight for the Afterlife. It is the way of Darkhanan Witches to share the accumulated wisdom of the deceased Guide with the body and life of a younger Host."

"But . . . you're *real,*" Nannan asserted tentatively. She reached out, hesitated, then pushed on his forearm, felt the fabric of his beige-and-black sleeve. "You're clearly alive—and you clearly need to eat, and drink . . . right?"

"This is *Aradin's* body, not mine," he corrected her gently. "I am simply caring for it in his absence. His spirit has gone off to commune with our fellow Witches, and he has left me in charge for the time being. For the sake of alleviating an even worse state of confusion—since our personalities and behaviors are not the same—I have used holy magic to reshape his body into a semblance of what mine used to look like . . . but my own body has long since rotted and returned to the soil. I'd like to think it's been fertilizing some pretty flowers in the cemetery where it was buried. Pushing up daisies, as it were—I believe that's an expression they use here in Katan for the bodies of the deceased, yes?"

Biting her lip to quell the urge to laugh, Saleria nodded. Teral continued blithely, urbane and charming even as he ruined Nannan's grasp on her half-formed fantasies. The housekeeper's look of crumbling hope and dismay only grew as he spoke.

"This body is Aradin's. Mine has ceased to be. And I should say that Aradin's body may not like the vinegar-sauce you used on the greens, but I find the herb stuffing and the basting of the duck absolutely delicious. He'll be rather sorry he missed tasting this meal, I can tell you that."

"But . . . You . . . ?" Nannan stared at him, then looked to Saleria for help, her brow furrowed and her mouth turned down at the corners. "He . . . ?"

"Nannan, the ways of worshipping other Gods and Goddesses are perfectly valid, however strange they may be, even if they are rarely encountered outside their homelands," Saleria told her. "Aradin and Teral are two men sharing Aradin's body; they are both envoys of their people, and holy priest-mages of fairly high rank. We will treat them as honored guests while they stay with us, and you *will* treat them with respect. Aradin the Living Hortimancer and Teral the Deceased Guide are staying here to assist me as we finally strive to restore order and peace to the Grove. *That* task is far more important than any . . . any *flirtations* that may have been considered."

Like a lifeline, Nannan seized on that word. Arching her brows, she gave Saleria a disapproving look. "Oh, really? Isn't that why *you* wanted to place that younger man in the room next to your own? I do have eyes in my head, and I have seen how *flirtatious* the two of you have been at the other meals."

Teral chuckled at that, drawing her attention back to him. "True, but isn't life itself meant for the living to *enjoy*, milady, not just endure?" he challenged her. He nodded at Saleria. "Our kind hostess, the Keeper of the Grove and thus one of the holiest beings in your empire, is *also* a lovely young lady, quite alive, and quite worthy of seeking out all the joys thereof. Given she tends the very place where your Holy Jinga and Kata were wed, I would think she has every right to seek out a romantic union of her own—perhaps even as an imperative, to further her holy calling."

"That's true, I do," Saleria agreed, resting her chin on the back of her hand. Her pose was similar to Nannan's earlier one, but far more relaxed than flirtatious. She gave Teral a grateful smile, glad he had neatly cut the argumentative legs out from under her house-keeper's stance. "Not just any gentleman will do for me, of course, but I'll never know which partner is right for me unless I enter and trod the steps of the courtship dance."

"But . . . *you're* dead," Nannan asserted, glancing between the two before settling on the dark-haired Darkhanan again. "*You* can't have a romance with anyone . . ."

"I could, but only if my Host, Aradin, agreed to it. And only if the lady herself agreed to it . . . and only if *Aradin's* choice of romantic companion agreed to it." Holding up his hand, he fore-stalled another protest from the plump housekeeper. "Suffice to say, I am not concerned that the odds are so heavily stacked against such a thing from happening. I have had my share of romances while I lived in my own body . . . and I have lived through the romances of my own Guide, back when I was alive and was Host to a fellow Witch-priestess.

"It works when everyone involved agrees . . . but it is now Aradin's life, and Aradin's choice, first and foremost. *He*, I think, would far rather choose Saleria, who is close to his own age and engaged in work similar to his preferences," he concluded. "Romances work better when the partners are of a similar age."

"Not to mention, you've been rather rude to him all along, so I doubt he'd agree to let you have Teral borrow *his* body for you to flirt with," Saleria stated. That earned her a chiding look from the older Witch. Sighing, she refrained from rolling her eyes. "Pardon my bluntness, and forgive me for any offense."

Nannan sat back in her chair and frowned at the table. "This is all *very* strange," she muttered. "The dead should *stay* dead."

Daranen spoke, joining the conversation. "The Laws of God and Man state that the ways of *all* Deities, and by extension Their servants, Their priesthoods, shall be respected in every land, so long as those ways cause no harm to their neighbors or their surroundings. Foreign Gods and Goddesses need not be *worshipped* in someone else's land, but Their ways and servants are to be respected," the scribe clarified. "To do less than show common respect for a servant of the Dual One, Darkhan and Dark Ana, is to do less than show respect for a servant of the Married Gods, Kata and Jinga."

Saleria shrugged and spread her hands when Nannan glanced her way for support. "Daranen has it right. Even I learned that in my temple training, as part of our courses on how to behave as a holy emissary while traveling overseas. If it applies to a priest or priestess of Katan, then it applies in reverse to a priest, priestess, or Witch of Darkhana."

Caught between three such clearly united forces, Nannan scowled for a long moment, then sighed roughly and slumped against the carved wooden slats of her seat. "Well, it's still very strange. And very disappointing. And . . . and very strange!"

"You are of course free to feel that way, if you like," Teral allowed lightly. "It is simply a foreign way of service and worship, and does not cause any harm to the worship or the ways of Kata and Jinga, however strange our Darkhanan ways may appear. Now, to get back to the original topic . . . as you may have noticed, Holiness," he said, addressing Saleria once more, "neither I nor Aradin need help 'moving' our belongings. But I should return to the inn to close out our rental agreement.

"Milady Nannan," he added, turning back to the housekeeper, "do you think there might be a bit of that delicious apple cake left over from last night? And if there is, could you perhaps have a slice waiting for me when I return, with that spicy-sweet sauce? It'll be yet another treat my Host, Aradin, will have to miss out on, but I find I am enjoying most of your cooking, now that I am free to enjoy it directly rather than sensing it only secondhand."

The housekeeper blushed and smiled tentatively, not completely immune to his charm despite Teral's uncomfortable revelations. Saleria bit her lip again to keep from laughing. From what she had observed, Aradin had a different quality and style of charm, but both men were clearly used to smoothing their path diplomatically in their travels.

I can't blame Nannan for being re-captivated, she decided, listening to her housekeeper promising to save him a piece. The older woman didn't quite simper, but she wasn't quite as dismayed as before, either. *I do find Teral charming myself.*

"Good morning, Nannan!"

"*Aieee!*"

Wits scrambled by sleep, it took Saleria a few moments to process the noises that had awakened her. When she did, she realized her housekeeper was now berating their house guest for scaring the older woman. Dragging the spare pillow over her head, Saleria tried to ignore the argument in the corridor outside her door.

With the feather-stuffed cushion muffling some of the sounds, she couldn't hear any distinct words, but she could hear how cheerful Aradin sounded as he replied to Nannan's scolding. Teasing her, from the sound of it. An involuntary smile curved her lips, and she stretched under the covers, luxuriating in the thought that maybe, just maybe, she could sleep in.

Nannan's voice grew abruptly louder as she marched into the Keeper's bedroom, ". . . and you'll *never* be allowed to do anything of the sort, you—you *foreigner!*"

Oh, that does it! That was far too rude for her to ignore. Rolling over, Saleria flung her pillow at Nannan the moment she spotted the older woman. Shrieking and flinching as it hit her shoulder, Nannan clutched at her ample chest.

"Oh! Oh, how *dare* you?" she demanded, facing Saleria.

Pushing up onto her feet on the bed, Saleria towered over her housekeeper. She knew she looked ridiculous, with her hair in a tangled mess and her night-tunic barely covering her thighs, but she had had enough. "How dare *you*, Nannan of the family Bourain?" Saleria demanded. Two steps moved her to the edge of the bed, where she balanced and glared. "I *told* you to treat Aradin Teral as an honored guest in this house. Yet you have done nothing but insult and berate him—and for nothing more than giving you a polite greeting."

"But the man is a—" Nannan protested.

Saleria cut her off, jabbing her finger at the housekeeper. "*You* will attend the morning prayers in the cathedral today. You will say the Prayers of Penitence—*all eight of them*—and you will do it twice over. You will do one round of them as you apologize to Holy Kata for disturbing the tranquility of Her Keeper's house, and for failing to be hospitable to an honored guest. You will do the second round as you apologize to Holy Jinga for lacking a sense of humor, and a sense of grace under pressure.

"*You* are not the Grove Keeper," she added sternly. "You are the *house*keeper. You keep this house and its contents clean and tidy, you wash the linens, you make the beds, you cook excellent food, *and* you are supposed to make all visitors, guests, and residents feel welcome. *Most* of the time you do all these things well, but today, you have failed.

"Attend to your penance after breakfast," Saleria ordered the older woman, "and when you have come to accept that your actions have been rude and thus unacceptable behavior for the importance of your station, you may tender an apology to our holy guest. I will not have you lie to Aradin Teral before that point in time, but I hope that you will reflect on your poor behavior as you pray, and gain enlightenment as to what went wrong."

Nannan bowed her plaited head in subdued obedience. It wasn't often that Saleria used the "priestly voice of authority" on anyone, but she had trained on how to use it, and its sparing use made it all the more powerful in its impact. When she chose to exercise her authority as the Keeper of the Holy Grove, there were only four who outranked her: the King of Katan in all matters secular, the Arch Priest of Katan in all matters pertaining to the running of the Church of Katan . . . and Kata and Jinga Themselves in all matters religious. She still had to answer to others in terms of her budget, but then not even the King of Katan was above the headaches of fiscal meetings.

Stepping off the bed, Saleria softened her tone as she gently touched the older woman on the arm. "I know you've come to think of the three of us as a family, and yourself as the mother figure between you, me, and Daranen. I appreciate that you do feel protective of me, Nannan, and that you no doubt wish to guard what you think are my best interests. But in less than one week, I have awakened to the untenable *neglect* which the Grove has been subjected to all these years.

"And it is not just that I see the problem clearly now," she continued, trying to coax the habit-reluctant woman to her view. "It is that I now have a *solution* to the problem at hand, thanks to the understanding that Aradin Teral brings."

Sighing, Nannan mumbled under her breath, "But he's an *outlander*. How could he have the Grove's best interest at heart?"

She didn't bother with further coaxing. That wasn't going to sway the housekeeper's heart, or her emotional instincts. Only the most blunt truth would work, Saleria guessed. "Because he swore a mage-oath in front of me to do no harm to the Grove or its rightful Keepers while he is here. *That's* how both of us can trust him, Nannan."

Thankfully, the blond outlander lurking by her doorway did not object to Saleria's choice of reason. Not that it wasn't the truth, but it wasn't all of the truth. She trusted him as a fellow priest, too, and for other, half-formed reasons. Part of it came from talking with Guardian Shon Tastra, but part of it was just how well he and she were getting along.

"*Can* you be kind and polite to him from now on?" Saleria asked her housekeeper. Nannan sighed, but nodded. "Good. Go attend to breakfast for both of us, and remember to do your penance afterward. Since I'm now thoroughly awake," she added dryly, "I think I can get dressed and ready myself without any further prodding today."

Nodding, Nannan headed for the door. She slowed at the sight of Aradin, but dipped her head as he shifted out of her way. ". . . Sorry, milord."

"May your Gods bless you for your kindnesses," he returned politely.

Saleria lifted her brows at that, but didn't say a word until after

Nannan had vanished from view. Moving up to the door, she murmured under her breath, "It's a very good thing that woman never took Deacon Parella's classes on How to Insult People Politely."

"Hmm?" Aradin asked. Most of his attention was caught by the long, muscular legs revealed by the hem of her short sleeping tunic, but he managed to drag enough of it free to look up at her and ask a more coherent question. "What brought that up?"

She knew what had held his attention. It was obvious where his gaze had been, and the implied compliment warmed her skin. "Deacon Parella was one of my instructors at the temple. She taught us acolytes that a truly good insult sounds like a compliment," Saleria told him, striving to ignore her blush and stick to the topic at hand. "You just asked our God and Goddess to bless Nannan for her kindnesses . . . implying that the opposite should befall her for any *un*kind acts."

Mouth twisting in a rueful smile, he shook his head. "It was sincerely meant, though I do see your point. But Witches are strongly encouraged to let go of grudges; such things threaten to poison the relationship between Host and Guide. Teral says our task is to share the wisdom of accumulated lifetimes with any and all who need it. Holding a grudge would not be wise, and would definitely prevent sharing our knowledge with the 'any and all' part."

"A wise way to approach the matter," she agreed.

About to say more, she realized Aradin's gaze had drifted downward again. Down to the hemline of her night tunic. There were several responses to that gaze she could make. Had it been Daranen, she'd have muttered something about needing to get dressed and would have retreated. Had it been Deacon Shanno . . . *No, never. No way is that little twit ever getting a look at my legs*, she knew. *But Aradin . . . and Teral?* She had to include the older Witch, even if she couldn't see him. But mostly it was Aradin she could see studying her with those hazel eyes framed by those dark blond lashes. Aradin, whose masculine interest and appreciation warmed her self-confidence as a woman.

So she settled for a simple, pointed, and flirtation-laced, "See anything you like?"

Aradin flicked his gaze up to her face. "From this angle, yes," he admitted, giving her a slow smile. "But I'll need to see your legs from several other positions, too, to be absolutely sure."

Tipping her head back, she laughed. She hadn't even been awake a fraction of an hour yet, and already she had ridden a wild ride of emotions. From being annoyed at how she was awakened, to unhappy with Nannan's attitude, from feeling stern about seeing the insults stopped, to flattered amusement . . . the lattermost feeling was a definite improvement on her morning. She felt him lean close and lowered her chin in time to receive a kiss on her cheek . . . and an arm slipped around her waist.

Warm and male, fully dressed for the day, Aradin cuddled her close. It felt remarkably good to be cuddled in his arms, up against his side. Natural, in fact. Saleria gave in to the urge to snuggle close, enjoying the intimacy of his embrace.

"You are far too appealing like this," he murmured after several seconds. He kissed her brow and sighed. "Unfortunately, we have far too much work to do to dally in the mornings. You with your morning clearing rounds, I with my scanning wands, needing to take readings from all the plants and the wickerwork of the Bower. But one of these *evenings*, milady, I'm going to want to see your legs again, from several different angles . . . and quite possibly the rest of you, if you'll agree."

She sighed, reluctant to admit he was right, but knowing she needed to admit it. "Mornings are definitely out . . . but you're right. Evenings are a possibility."

He gave her a last squeeze and started to pull away, which

meant the kiss she aimed for his lips ended up on his chin instead. He stilled for a moment, lips curving in a slow, surprised, but warm smile. Giving her shoulders a little squeeze, he let her go. "I'll see you at the breakfast table."

Nodding, Saleria stepped back fully into her bedchamber and closed the door. Normally, she breakfasted in a lounging robe, but today she would get dressed first. Not because she felt the need to be fully clothed, but as a concession to Nannan's sense of propriety. In Katan, men and women could couple without stigma if they were responsible about contraceptive amulets and such, but not in the streets, and not at the table.

Contraceptive amulets. Bollocks, she thought, wincing. *I'll need to get an amulet, won't I? Because if I'm completely honest with myself . . . that comment about him wanting to see me and my legs in many other positions was rather appealing. As well as amusing.*

With a grin at that thought, she moved toward the dressing closet to find a fresh Keeper's uniform to don. It was rather nice being thought of as an attractive woman, and not just a priestess.

"Holy Saleria, at the Healer's?" Deacon Shanno called out. Wincing, Saleria turned to find the thin, blond priest clutching a hand over his chest. "I hope it's nothing serious!"

She finished shutting the door to the Groveham Healer-mage's shop and composed a quick, quelling reply. "It isn't serious, and even if it were, it wouldn't be your business. God and Goddess bless you for your kindnesses and courtesies, Deacon Shanno."

Saleria meant it as a parting comment, but he didn't let it end there. Instead, the young priest turned to join her as she strode down the street. "On the contrary: The health and well-being of the Grove Keeper is the business of every man and woman in

Groveham. Why, without you, who would we turn to in the advent of another perambulating peony attack, hmm?"

I'll lay odds he's just trying to suggest himself as a backup for that, she told herself. Out loud, she merely said, "Groveham will be fine. Shouldn't you be preparing for midday prayers?"

"Oh, I have time," the young man dismissed, flicking a hand. His mouth curved in a smug little smile. "Actually, I've just heard the juiciest news from the High Temple itself this morning."

"Oh?" Saleria asked, curious in spite of herself.

"Yes, it seems that, very soon, you won't be the *only* person talking directly with our Gods. Well, you and the Arch Priest," he dismissed. "*I* heard that the King and Council are working on getting the old Convocation of the Gods resurrected! I have an aunt who works closely with Lady Apista; you know, the Councillor for the Temples? And that it involves finding a special someone who can bridge the concerns of the Katani nation with our Patron Deities directly. The details are all a big secret, of course, but my aunt did say they were working hard on the problem."

Her first thought was that if it was truly "all a big secret" then Shanno shouldn't have known about any of it. Her second thought came with the dawning force of comprehension. *He has an aunt he talks with about state secrets—therefore a close aunt—who works with the Councillor for the Temples, a high-ranked priestess-politician. That must be why he was promoted to Deacon when he doesn't exactly inspire thoughts of maturity . . . and no doubt is why he keeps thinking so highly of himself. Of course he would, with nepotism on his side . . .*

Bollocks to that, she thought, giving him a polite nod as they parted company at one of the side streets. *It's a good thing he isn't on any apprenticeship list for the Keeper's position. I wouldn't trust him to keep silent on some of the more personal prayer requests, never mind huge secrets.*

That was another of the reasons why the Keeper did not inter-mingle publicly. That way all petitions were kept private, and thus respectful of the requests. It also meant she didn't have to say *no* to anyone in person. With written requests, a petitioner never had to face the sting of a rejection. There were certain things which, by the Laws of God and Man, she could not request Kata and Jinga to achieve through prayer. The destruction of other Gods, the deci-mation of an entire population, the death of a particular person . . . and other, subtler things.

Somehow, I don't think Shanno would hesitate to push magical power into a prayer for personal wealth and personal gain. Or to force a specific, named person to do something against their free will, such as fall in love with a petitioner. Or worse, with him, using the power of prayer for his personal gain. Though to be fair, he's not yet ready to settle on any one young lady, from what I've seen.

"Look, it's the Keeper!" someone called out as she passed the entrance to one of the town's four inns.

"Is that really her? She looks so young."

"We're not supposed to follow her—some nonsense or other about custom—but I heard that she . . ."

Saleria moved a little faster, looking neither right nor left. She let her feet carry her out of hearing range of the conversation. *Another problem Shanno has caused. He's too caught up in the prestige of being a priest to grasp that power comes with more obligations and responsibilities than privileges . . . and I am wasting too much of my time thinking about him.* Setting thoughts of the young deacon aside, she turned another corner and hurried back toward her home. Her midmorning break would soon be over, and she would have a pile of sorted petitions to pray over.

She reached the main street leading to the Keeper's House just in time to see Aradin coming from the direction of the market, and paused to await his approach. From the smile lighting up his face, he had been successful in gaining the centrifuge he wanted from the glazier, Remas. She didn't *see* it being carried anywhere, but now that she knew about his cloak, it was only a short guess for Saleria to realize where he had put it: into the Dark, where he wouldn't have to physically carry the awkwardly shaped metal stand or its carefully balanced, hand-blown flasks.

"Hello again, Saleria," he greeted her when he reached her side. They started walking together, matching strides fairly well without much effort. A couple children darted around them, hollering something about a game of tag. Aradin glanced at her. "Did you get whatever you were looking for?"

Saleria blushed a little. The anklet was hidden inside her boot, but she was aware of the smooth bit of carved stone resting against her skin with each step. She hadn't worn one in a while, and had just let the previous one expire before finally removing it at roughly the year-and-a-half mark, when such things tended to run out of magic. "Yes. I did. I trust you got what you wanted as well?"

He grinned. "Not *everything* I've wanted recently, but I did get the centrifuge, yes."

That was exactly the sort of flirting her housekeeper had been upset about. Saleria wasn't the least bit offended by it. Not when she was enjoying a level of attention she hadn't known since moving to Groveham. Acolytes were discouraged from forming any sort of long-term relationship, since that could interfere with their rather lengthy studies, but there had been a span of time where she, as first a deacon, then a fully-fledged priestess, had flirted occasionally with her fellow Katani. Even courted a little. But being the Keeper meant losing the time for such things.

Having Aradin Teral assist her with the Grove's needs meant there was actually a possibility of time for such things now. Flirtations. Courtship. Lovemaking. She felt her cheeks warm again and cleared her throat. "I, ah . . ." For a moment, her mind went blank, then she said the first thing she could think of. "I've been packing for the trip. Guardian Shon Tastra suggested it. I don't know what to expect, so I've been packing and repacking, and I'm not quite sure how much is enough, or too much, to take with me.

"I was wondering if I could get your advice tonight," she finished. "After the Grove has been tended, and everything is quiet."

"I've never packed for this sort of trip myself," he reminded her, avoiding the word Convocation since they were still in public. "I don't know what sort of help I'd be."

"Perhaps, but you've traveled farther than I have, and have served as an envoy to many lands," she said.

They passed a mother gently leading a toddler by one hand, the other holding an empty basket, no doubt on their way to the marketplace. One day, Saleria would be free of her duties and could contemplate having a child or two. For now, she could only look, long for a brief moment, and get back to the topic at hand.

"I know the Gods see us at all times, even when we're at our worst, but there will be representatives from . . . from hundreds of lands. I have no wish to let down the Empire by appearing less than my best. But neither do I care to haul around a full chest of clothes and accessories." She slanted her companion a pointed look. "Unlike *some* people, I have no ready access to a magical, infinite, portable storage room everywhere I go."

He grinned at her teasing, taking no offense. "How very true. I'd offer to hold on to your goods for you on this one . . . but I must remain behind by the very nature of the journey." They reached the front entrance of the Keeper's house. Aradin opened the door, but leaned close so he could murmur in her ear. "But if you do want my advice, whatever it's worth . . . I would be happy to visit you this evening. Your pack is in your bedchamber, is it not?"

That was definitely a flirtatious tone in his voice. And when it dipped deeper than usual on the word *bedchamber*, Saleria felt her body respond to the low baritone, almost bass, tones. Clearing her throat, she replied, "Yes. It is."

"I look forward to being invited inside." Again, his voice dipped, this time on the last word.

Blushing, Saleria hurried her steps a little to give herself some breathing room, since her skin now felt a little flushed, the air a little hot, despite the cooling charms stitched beneath the hems of her garments.

Behind her, unheard anywhere other than inside Aradin's head, Teral chuckled. (*I think she's a little rusty on her flirtations. She did start it, but . . .*)

Aradin smiled to himself. He nodded to Saleria when she excused herself to use the downstairs refreshing room, and decided to take advantage of the one up near his bedchamber. (*I think she's cute when she's flustered. But then I also think she's gorgeous when she's in her element, like she was this morning.*)

(*You sure that wasn't due to those legs of hers?*) Teral gently teased his Host.

(*That helped,*) Aradin admitted with aplomb. (*But seeing her in full priestly power . . . ? Magnificent.*)

(*Falling for her just a little?*) Teral asked.

(*Falling for her just a lot,*) Aradin confessed. Long accustomed to his Guide's constant presence, he took care of the needs of his body without hesitation. (*She's smart, she's funny, she's peaceful and wise, and she holds a position of great responsibility, even authority, yet she's down-to-earth and unpretentious.*)

(*Yes,*) Teral agreed. (*I suspect she'd be as wonderful a person if she were a mere temple cleaner. But even then, she'd probably be promoted to a place where her skills and leadership would be better utilized and appreciated.*)

Aradin moved to wash his hands at the sink. Unlike lever-operated spigots found elsewhere in the world, these Katani used cork-stuffed pipes. It was a bit odd, and one couldn't really control the volume of water, but at least there was a lever for controlling the heating spell. He noticed that today's flow didn't feel quite as warm as it had felt last night, even when he pushed it to the far left. He made a mental note to ask Saleria who attended to such spells in her home, herself, or some hired mage.

(*She said she was going to get some information from the, ah, Department of Prophecies on anything pertaining to the Grove, and why it has ended up this way. I hope she hears back from them soon,*) he stated. He corked the faucet shut, then frowned in thought. (*Teral, the prophecy mentioning the Convocation of Gods and Man, "The Synod Gone" . . . did any of that sound like it mentioned a Netherhell invasion to you?*)

(*Possibly. I'll fetch it out for you to study . . . in your copious free time,*) his Guide added as Aradin dried his hands. (*Try not to spend all night making love to her. Neither of you can afford to sleep in, in the morning.*)

(*You have great faith in my seductive abilities. I'm not planning on making it into her bed tonight. But I am hoping for at least a few more kisses,*) Aradin said. Exiting the room, he went downstairs to rejoin Saleria at the back door. (*Hand me the analyzer kit, will you?*)

(*Which wand would you like?*) Teral asked him, using the holy light which all of their kind could summon in the Dark to read the little instruction booklet that had come with the case. (*General-purpose sampler, or something more specific, like the power-flow tracer?*)

(*General-purpose sampler, I guess, until we get to the Bower. I'd like more samples of the plants and such on the path to the heart of the Grove, and particularly a sample of the* thettis-bug *vines. If I can figure out how the two plants and the insects are melded together, I might be able to figure out how to calm or even tame them. I won't hold my breath over being able to separate them back into their original three species, though.*)

(*That would probably be futile, yes. Let's see . . . you would want . . .*

the bronze and carnelian wand, I think. The kit says it's useful for discerning properties of plants and animals,) the older Witch decided.

Teral handed the tablet and the selected wand to his Host, who extracted them from his Witchcloak sleeve, only to tuck the tablet into the pouch hung on his belt. The orange-tipped wand, barely the size of a grease pencil, Aradin kept in his hand. Saleria wasn't yet at the back door, but she joined him within a few moments, carrying the satchel that held Daranen's neatly penned list of prayer petitions for the day. Slipping the strap for it over her head, she unlocked the back door and escorted Aradin outside, then opened up the shed to hand him one of the pruning staves.

"Mind if I take a cutting from that vine made from thettis, morning glory, and some sort of bug?" he asked her. "I'd like to study it in more detail, and compare it with my notes on what I've scanned elsewhere in the Grove this morning."

"Take what you need," Saleria said, gesturing for him to take the lead. "Just don't let it set down roots."

She didn't seem as cheerful as she had earlier. Aradin glanced back at her as he headed down the path that led to the Bower, noting the slight but discernible slump in her shoulders, the way her gaze aimed more often down than out and up. "Is something wrong?"

Saleria sighed, thinking of what Daranen had told her when she had fetched the day's work. "There's a special petition in among the rest. It's from a young boy who lost his parents. He's . . . not openly welcomed by his aunt and uncle-in-law. In fact, it sounds like they're openly resentful of the extra mouth to feed. He wants me to pray to Kata and Jinga to bring his parents back. It *could* be the complaining of a child who is exaggerating things, but it could also be the truth. Either way . . ."

"A moral dilemma," Aradin agreed. He returned most of his attention to the path, but being a fellow priest, he did know why she wasn't happy. "Attempting to pray for such things is forbidden by the Laws of God and Man, if I remember my lessons right."

"It is. A Healer can pray for divine aid when healing someone mortally wounded or freshly dead, attempting to revive them within moments of their demise, but those long departed?" She shook her head, then sighed roughly. "Nor can I pray for Kata and Jinga to change the minds of his next-family. We are given free will by the Gods, and it is the one gift They cannot, and will not, take back. *My* prayers are backed by magic. They can literally move . . . well, not mountains, but small hills have been known to shift. Little ones." She gestured with a hand down by her knee, and flashed him a rueful smile, her sense of humor tainted by her regret over the petition in her satchel.

He smiled back, enjoying the joke, since it leavened the otherwise somber conversation. "So what *can* you do?"

Something rustled in the bushes. Both froze, gripping their staves and looking all around for an attack. After a moment, an ambulatory marigold waddled into view. One of the bushes fought back, its branches gripping at the plant. The marigold smacked it with its leaves, flailing back and forth. Bits of greenery ripped off and drifted down before the marigold managed to free itself and continue on its way.

Saleria relaxed a little, though she wondered where the others had gone. Usually, they moved as a pack. They moved slower in pockets of sunshine, often stopping to set down roots and replenish themselves with nourishment from the soil. As she watched, the marigold hit just such a patch of mossy, sunlit ground, stopped, and wiggled its roots into the soil with a little shake.

"What can I do?" she asked, repeating his question. "I can pray that he finds himself in the tender care of people who love him for who he is, and encourage him for who he can be. I can pray that he finds help and mentors. That he has a good home to abide in, with food and clothes and a good education leading to a good career. I can pray that he finds friends who will help him, support him, and stand up beside him whenever he needs to stand up for himself, lending him their encouragement and their support as he grows up and becomes a man. If I set my prayers to target no one . . . then *that* will be allowed by the Laws of God and Man. The energy may be more diffuse when it acts, but it is free to encourage what is already potentially there.

"And who knows, maybe the diffused prayer will encourage his aunt and uncle-in-law to open their minds and soften their hearts. Maybe it will soothe his feelings of loss and pain so that he can see they do care about him; hopefully, they do, but if not, maybe it will do both. Or maybe it'll open the hearts of other kin to offer to take him in, where an extra mouth to feed won't be as much of a resented burden." She shrugged, mounting the next little hill.

Ah, there are the rest of the marigolds, she thought, watching them camped in another clearing . . . to the visible disgruntlement of some of the already established plants. There was a bit of leaf-slapping and branch-smacking as certain patches fought for the best sunlight, but otherwise they were relatively peaceful. Glancing at Aradin, she watched one of his sandy blond brows raise in that neat little trick of his, and smiled at his confusion. Personally, she found the marigolds' antics to be more amusing than annoying. As she had mentioned to him before, not everything in the Grove was outright dangerous.

Murmuring a harvesting spell, Aradin wafted some of the torn bits of foliage over to the path. Pulling out wide-mouthed sample jars, he sorted them with another spell and a tap of the carnelian-tipped wand in his hand, then scooped them into the glass containers, which went back into his sleeves. "I'll want to analyze these as well. I'll try to work quietly while you pray. If you finish with a little extra time to spare, you can help examine the Bower structure with the, ah . . . Teral says that one's the amethyst-tipped wand. The readings from that should help draw a map on the tablet of the various power conduits running through the trees. From there, we can better determine what spells were woven into the structure, but forgotten long ago by the various Keepers."

"Right. I think I should take that or a similar wand to the eastern locus tree, too, at midday," she offered. "Maybe if you and I use that air-walking spell of yours, and trace the paths of the branches and roots more directly?"

"That should work," he agreed, smiling briefly at her. "I could pull out some of the other wands, too, on the way, maybe get a few more samples. Particularly as we get closer to the tree, to see if a particular locus rift's energies have a greater impact closer to the source."

Saleria nodded. "I'm very grateful you're here to help with this, Aradin. Until the other night when Guardian Kerric called, I didn't even know that the waxy nodules on the underside of the Bower glowed. I was never here in the dark . . . yet I feel like I *was* lost in the dark, until you came."

"Sometimes it just works out that way. Teral says you shouldn't berate yourself for what happened in the past. Learn from mistakes and make amends when you finally notice the neglect. That's all any of us can do," Aradin relayed.

She nodded again. "It may take telling my brain that several more times before it sinks in, and I don't always succeed in believing it, but I do know that all I can do sometimes is move on."

NINE

Aradin's head snapped up in startled realization. He stared unseeing through the mesh of the Bower dome for a long moment, so startled, he couldn't even think a coherent thought at his Guide. Teral, equally shocked, stayed for a moment, then ducked into the Dark to ask it questions. Guessing which ones the older Witch intended to ask, Aradin focused on the outer world, leaving the inner one to his partner.

Turning, he spotted Saleria kneeling as usual in the center of the mossy ground. The midmorning prayers had been handled, a good lunch had been served by a contrite Nannan, and from the looks of the papers stacked in front of her, the Keeper of the Grove was almost done with the midafternoon lot.

Keeper, yes, but not fully its Guardian.

Aware she still had at least two more prayers to go, Aradin regathered his wits and turned back to the tablet resting on the worktable. A chime startled him into whipping around again just in time to see Saleria scowl and open her eyes. She glanced over at the mirror hanging in the air, little wisps of blonde hair floating around her head.

"I can get it," Aradin offered, seeing her tenuous hold on the magics she had raised, and nearly lost at the interruption.

At her curt nod, he hurried across the patchwork ground, sticking mostly to the moss and stepping over the sap-slick flagstones. Their earlier efforts to clear the greenery from the ground had simply let the overflowing sap slowly seep out and coat everything. If his flash of insight was correct, they would be able to stop that overflow in short order, but it would first require figuring out *how* to do what needed to be done.

Tapping the mirror, he activated it with a touch of will and his favorite activation word. "*Shauhan.*"

The silvered glass flickered blue, then resolved into the image of a brown-haired man. He wore a plain but fine-spun brown tunic fastened down the front with the cloth buttons favored by the eastern kingdoms of Shattered Aiar. It almost blended into the image of book-laden shelves at his back, but not quite. The stranger narrowed his gray eyes. "*You* are not the Guardian of the Grove. Who are you, and what are you doing with this mirror?"

"You must be Guardian Kerric Vo Mos of the Tower," Aradin stated quietly, making an educated guess. He kept his voice low and smooth, not wanting to disrupt his partner's concentration. "I am Aradin Teral, assistant to Keeper Saleria—Guardian Shon Tastra can confirm my assignment. Guardian Saleria is currently busy at the moment with her midafternoon prayers. If you need to speak with her directly, I would suggest rescrying in . . . a quarter hour?" He glanced over at Saleria, who nodded but didn't open her eyes. "Yes, in a quarter hour. Otherwise, if your query is simple, perhaps I might be able to handle it."

". . . I'll call back." A flick of Guardian Kerric's hand ended the link.

Aradin returned to his workbench. He rechecked the notes on the crystal tablet, waiting for Saleria to finish. Teral returned before she did.

(*Confirmed,*) his Guide said. (*The Keeper of the Grove is not fully attuned to all three rifts.*)

(*Why do I sense a hint of foreboding news in your tone?*) Aradin asked.

(*Because there is one,*) Teral returned grimly. (*The original Keeper, Patia, was strong enough to control and blend all three rifts at their full strength. None of us can do so. However . . . each of us is more than strong enough to control one of the rifts. Saleria, you . . . and me. And it would be a very good thing to attune each one of us to a specific locus tree, then blend our magics. But that draws up a host of other problems.*)

(*Such as our ongoing presence here, versus our duties to the Church back home,*) Aradin agreed. (*Teral, I can tell you right now that there is an entire lifetime's worth of Hortimancy work here in the Grove, and I feel very much compelled to stay and help fix it . . . but I am also a Witch of Darkhana. Not just you, but me. We would have to obtain permission to stay. Not just from the Church elders, but from our God and Goddess, and from the God and Goddess of this land.*)

Teral agreed. (*True. But we don't have to wait for the Convocation to do so.*)

(*I know we can petition Darkhan and Dark Ana directly, but we don't have that kind of connection with Jinga and Kata,*) Aradin pointed out.

(*No, but she does.*) Teral didn't have to nudge Aradin into glancing at their companion. Aradin was already staring at Saleria, if with a somewhat unfocused gaze.

Sharpening his attention, Aradin studied her. (*How do you . . . ? Oh! The prayer petitions!*)

Teral clasped him on the shoulder, soul to soul. Warmth flowed between the two men, until the older Guide patted and released him. (*I will go speak with our Patron Deities. You find pen and paper to write her a petition. And do hurry; it looks like she's down to her last sheet.*)

(*Last but one.*) Letting Teral step off into the Dark, Aradin tugged a sheet out of his notebook and, grasping his translation pendant for surety, carefully wrote his request on the page. He stepped away from the table and crouched in front of the quietly praying woman, waiting for her to finish.

This close to the Katani priestess, Aradin felt the magic of her efforts against his skin like a warm, prickly breeze. The moment she sighed and moved to set the sheet in her hands aside, opening her eyes, he placed his quickly written page before her, turned so she could easily read it. Saleria's brows rose, then drew down together . . . then rose again. She looked between him and the page, and recited what he had written.

"*Unto Most Noble Jinga and Most Gracious Kata, does the Darkhanan Witch Aradin Teral send greetings, honorings, and this most fervent request: Please grant Your permission, provided that Your Siblings Holy Darkhan and Holy Dark Ana agree, for Aradin Teral to be assigned permanently to Your Sacred Marital Grove as a Hortimancy assistant to Keeper Saleria, for the purpose of re-taming, healing, and rendering the Sacred Grove safe once more for Your many worshippers to visit and experience directly.*

"*Aradin Teral believes fervently that Your Sacred Grove should be restored to the peaceful, pastoral beauty it was renowned for before the Shattering of Aiar, and though he is oathbound into the service of Holy Darkhan and Holy Dark Ana, believes fervently that Their Siblings' Sacred Grove should be restored for the glory of Blessed Kata and Great Jinga,*" she continued, sneaking another look at him. "*Aradin and his Guide Teral are willing to dedicate time, effort, and many years to this task under Your Holy Keeper Saleria's guidance. If this is Your will . . .*

please make Your mark or marks upon this prayer request sheet so that all who view it may know that this is truly Your divine will.

"*If this is not favorable in Your Eyes, then let this page turn to ash, and Witch Aradin Teral will merely continue with his current assignments.*" Lowering the page, she looked at him.

Aradin pressed his palms together in the near-universal gesture of prayer, and asked, "Holy Sister, will you pray for the granting of my request?"

Wryly amused, a soft huff of a laugh escaped her. She stared past his shoulder for a few moments, considering the merits of his prayer petition, then shrugged. "As it is a prayer that would only bring glory and benefit to Kata, Jinga, and the people of the Empire . . . I will pray for your request. I cannot guarantee that it will be accepted, but I will pray."

"That is all one can ask," Aradin reassured her. Rising, he bowed. "I should get back to work—"

The mirror chimed again. Sighing, she pushed to her feet and moved over to it. "*Baol.*"

Guardian Kerric Vo Mos reappeared inside the silvery rectangle. "Ah, Guardian Saleria. I spoke with a gentleman a few minutes ago . . ."

"Witch Aradin Teral. He has my permission to answer the scrying mirror in my absence, accept messages, and make minor promises," Saleria stated. The mirror showed Kerric relaxing and nodding. Guardians tended to be protective over who had access not only to their own Fountains and so forth, but to their fellow Guardians' resources as well. "What can the Guardian of the Grove do for the Guardian of the Tower today?"

"We were wondering if you had on hand, or could get ahold of, any copies of Katani prophecies that might be pertinent to the Netherhell problem," Kerric said.

"Ah, sorry—I meant to go through mine and make copies for

you," Aradin told Saleria, joining her by the mirror. He nodded at the other Guardian as well. "But it's about as easy to enchant two copies as it is to make just one. You should have them within a couple days, if that's alright."

"That will be fine. I've asked the other Guardians to look for pertinent local Seer prophecies . . . and had a request from the Guardian in Mendham to send *her* copies of everything for the Great Library," Kerric added dryly. "I may be in love with a Mendhite of my own, but their national obsession with the written word can be a bit much at times."

"You're in love with a Mendhite?" Saleria asked, curious.

The smile that spread across Kerric's face looked a bit dopey, even mushy, for a moment before he returned to his normal businesslike demeanor. "Myal the Mendhite . . . whom you'd know about if you ever accepted my offer of a scrycasting contract. She's magnificent in action when she's running a gauntlet, intelligent when she's working behind the scenes . . . and for whatever Gods-blessed reason, she loves me just as much as I love her." He flashed Saleria a grin and a flick of his gaze toward the man at her side. "I hope the two of you get to know such a wonderful feeling. With whomever, of course."

Saleria blushed. Aradin coughed into his fist. Clearing his throat, he answered for both of them. "We'll, ah, keep that in mind. Actually, I was just thinking a little while ago that all our prophecies should be copied and distributed among all the Guardians. Particularly the ones that deal with multiple locations. A demonic invasion will cause ripples of change across many lands, not just one or two."

"Very true. The Tower will loan its magics toward the recopy-ing and distribution of all collated prophecies and other such information of interest," the curly-haired Guardian pledged, glancing off to the side and making a half-seen gesture. "I know

Tipa'thia would rather it was her doing all of this centralized paperwork, but the Tower has the centralized connections."

Saleria looked down at the prayer petition in her hands, looked up at the man at her side, then around at the Grove for a moment. She smiled softly. "On another note, Guardian . . . considering that I *might* finally have a solution to some local problems on my end . . . I *might* one day be able to take up that scrycasting offer of yours. If I actually do come to a point where I'll have the time and energy to spare to watch your Tower adventurers."

The Guardian of the Tower sat up at that. "You'd be interested in a scrycasting contract?"

"Not immediately . . . but with luck, I'll soon be able to stop running my own version of gauntlets and have the leisure to watch others navigating difficulties. Now, if that is all, Guardian, I still have one more prayer to complete today," she added politely. "We'll get those prophecy copies to you as soon as we can."

At his nod, she touched the mirror frame to end the call, then sighed. "I need to recontact the Department of Prophecies. They were supposed to gather up a collection of Convocation-related prophecies. I might as well ask them for Seer-foretold Netherhell invasion possibilities as well."

"We'll be a little late in the day's schedule, at this rate," Aradin warned her. "But his request is important."

She sighed. "I know. First I'll try to contact someone in the Department. If we have to wait, I can focus on your prayer request. Although I do wonder why you put in the bit about having Jinga and Kata mark this request sheet. Usually Their miracles are more subtle or widespread than that."

Aradin nodded, but gestured at the page. "It occurred to me that, with such a long-standing tradition of the true needs of your position going unmet or ignored, that it *would* likely take a Divine Decree to get your superiors to accept all the changes you and I would like to implement. It also addresses the very pertinent fact that I *am* a foreign priest, sworn to a different set of Patron Deities. I know there are sticklers who would object strongly to my presence, based on this fact alone, and that again it might require a Divine Decree to ensure I am permitted to stay here at your side, assisting in the restoration of the Grove."

"You have a point," she allowed. Glancing between him and the mirror, she fluttered her hand off in the direction of his worktables. "Well. Since you've pointed out you're not an officially approved presence just yet, go off over there and get back to work while I try to contact Councillor Thannig of the Department of Prophecies on this thing, if I can refocus it. We don't need them to see you here and be distracted by trivialities that will hopefully be settled by the end of the day."

Bowing politely in agreement, Aradin moved back to his table and his experiments on the flow and melding of three disparate sources of magic here in the Grove. Belatedly, he remembered he had not yet discussed the fact that each locus tree rift needed a Guardian attuned to it, but knew it could be handled later. *Such as tonight . . . when we're supposed to be discussing her packing needs for the Convocation, with all the temptations of being in her bedroom . . .*

Right. I'd better write myself a note to address it tomorrow, once we're back here in the Grove. Somehow, I think we'll be busy with other concerns tonight. One way or another.

Bᵧ the end of supper, Saleria could feel herself frowning. She managed to dredge up a smile of thanks at Nannan's choice for dessert tonight, a layering of different fruits, a drizzle of cream, and a light dusting of spices, but the frown came back even before she scraped up the last slice of juicy *toska*, sweetened by the pear from the other layers but still tart enough to make her mouth pucker.

It wasn't the naturally tangy-sour fruit that made her frown, though.

"Is something wrong?" Aradin finally asked, leaning close to murmur the question while Nannan took his and Daranen's dishes back to the kitchen.

She thought about it a moment, then nodded at the sheet of paper sitting next to her plate. "I haven't seen anything about the paper change yet. I *know* I put power into my prayer. And it's not an unreasonable request by any means. Not like . . . not like asking for a child's deceased parents to be brought back to life."

"Hm. Well, the answer isn't a flaming 'no,' either," Daranen pointed out. When both of the others looked at him, he shrugged and lifted his palms. "Jinga has been known to intervene when He doesn't want something to happen . . . and even Serene Kata has an occasional flare-up of temper."

"True," Saleria agreed, lifting her brows briefly. They came back down into a frown, making her aware of the tension building up in her muscles as they waited, and waited, and waited. She looked over at the Darkhanan to her left. "Hasn't Teral returned yet? You said he left when you presented this to me. He's been gone for several hours now."

"Time in the Dark doesn't always move at the same rate as time out here in Life," Aradin said.

"Maybe he got lost?" the middle-aged scribe offered. "The Dark *is* dark, after all. Otherwise they'd call it the Light, or something."

The blond Witch shook his head, letting his hair slide over his shoulders. "No. It'd be impossible for Teral to get lost. For one, he has many decades of experience traversing the Dark. For another, his soul is literally bound to my Doorway by an unbreakable strand of his very self. *Delayed*, yes. But lost, never. Not while we are bound together, and not while I live." He lifted his water glass, hesitated, then dipped his head. "Of course, if I were to die of a sudden shock, *then* his tether to my Doorway would snap. But he'd know it, and know to head for the Light, after reporting my death to the others in the Church . . . and probably not until after he'd gone looking for my soul, to steady it and prepare it for another Witch-acolyte to accept."

"I thought someone had to be on hand for that," Saleria said. "Like you were, for him."

"There's a small period of grace, a handful of days, where it's easy to bind a soul into a Doorway. The longer a soul wanders in the Dark, however, the more difficult it becomes for them to *find* a potential Host, enter their Doorway, and bind themselves in place," Aradin told them. "The longest case I know of would be Sir Niel, who wandered for almost a year and a half in the Dark before he found the Doorway of his Hostess, Orana."

"*Sir* Niel?" Daranen asked. "He wasn't a Witch?"

The emphasis her clerk put on that title made Saleria wonder what else she didn't know about the rest of the world. Aradin drank from his cup, set it down, and glanced between Saleria and her scribe.

"It's . . . a complicated story," he said. "It involves a deep, hidden betrayal, the framing of someone for a most brutal murder, and one of the deepest miscarriages of justice I have ever known or heard about. But the telling of it would easily take all night, and then some," he demurred, rising from his seat. Offering Saleria his hand, he added, "If I remember correctly, you requested my advice on what to pack for the Convocation once your work for the day was done, yes?"

Blushing, Saleria set down her spoon, scooted back her chair, and placed her hand in his. Covertly, she glanced at Daranen, only to see her scribe looking away, but not quite able to hide his smile. Her face warmed further, but at least he didn't seem to object to the idea of her and her guest heading off to her bedchamber. "Yes, I should like your advice on what to pack. I haven't traveled much in my career, while you have."

"Good night, you two," Daranen stated, picking up his wine cup to sip at the dregs. "Don't wear yourselves out by 'packing' all night long. You'll still have to work in the morning."

Aradin choked. Coughing, he tried not to grin too much. Leaning over, Saleria picked up her own water glass with her free hand and offered it to him. He accepted it, but cleared his throat and spoke before sipping. "Careful, milady . . . In *some* cultures, drinking from the same cup is the same as an offer, and acceptance, of marriage."

It was Daranen's turn to choke. Saleria blushed again. Before she could speak, however, Aradin sipped from the cup, cleared his throat again, and returned it to her with a slight bow.

"But then, it *also* requires a special drink to be held in the cup, and not just plain water. So you're safe from marriage." Keeping her other hand tucked in his, he tugged her gently away from the table as soon as she set the glass down. He waited until they were at the foot of the stairs to the upper floor, then lifted her fingers to his lips for a brief kiss. "That is, for now."

And I thought the ongoing frown was annoying, Saleria thought, following him up the steps. *I'm surprised my hair hasn't caught fire from the burning in my cheeks!* She didn't have to guide him to her bedroom; he went straight to the right doorway without prompting. He did, however, wait for her to step in front of him and open the door before following her inside.

Her bedchamber was just high enough that, in the daytime, she could see into the Grove over the top of its wall. She had plenty of windows, too—four pairs of sashes that could be swung outward, each one glazed with two dozen rectangular panes set in carefully leaded frames. But night had fallen while they ate their supper, leaving the pair with a greatly darkened view.

At night, only the two moons, the stars in the sky, the ward-stones on the wall, and little hints of those waxy, faintly glowing nodules could be seen through the gloom outside. There were lights in Groveham, lightglobes and oil lanterns and the like, but that was on the other side of the house; not much light reached the Grove itself, just whatever the stars and moons and the faintest traces of magic could provide.

The moment she rapped on the lightglobe by the door, even that much of a view vanished. It was replaced by awkward, if well-lit, reflections of the two of them entering her chamber. Saleria felt almost as disjointed as her gridwork-disrupted image did, as if there were several versions of herself competing for space in her room: The part of her that was the Keeper, knowing she had to get up before sunrise in the morning. The part of her that was a priestess, knowing she couldn't lead Aradin into expectations of a romantic encounter without at least some sincerity of affection from her heart. The part of her that honestly did want help in packing for what had to be the single most monumental religious moment in two hundred years, the chance to stand before not just her own Patron God and Goddess, but the Patron Deities of hundreds of nations around the world. The part that wanted to take him in her arms, and somehow get them to her bed without any awkwardness, or pauses, or . . .

Feeling awkward, she turned and backed up to the bed, with its feather-stuffed mattress shaken and patted and mounded until it was fluffy and high, and dropped onto its edge. Dented its perfection. Sat there feeling awkward, tired, and wanting without any getting.

"I have no idea how to do this . . ."

She didn't realize she had spoken until the words were already out, filling the quiet between them. In three steps, he was close enough to kneel at her white-clad feet. In two heartbeats, he had

her hands cradled in his. In one smile . . . lopsided and honest . . .
he warmed her heart.

"If you're talking about packing, I can help with that," Aradin
told her. He continued before she could correct him. "But if you're
talking about having a man at your bed, I have enough experience
to know *what* to do . . . but I also know it'll be different with you."

She considered his words, then eyed him warily. "Different,
because each woman is an unique individual when it comes to tumbling, and lovemaking, and all of that?"

Freeing one hand, he touched his finger to her lips. Content she
would stay silent, Aradin explained. "Different, because if I could
have stood before my God and Goddess—and before yours, too—
and said to Them, 'This is what I want with my life; this, and thus,
and so, and these are the things I have always longed for' . . . my
youthful visions of turning my predilection for working with
plants and my burgeoning magics into an outstanding, challenging
Hortimancy career . . .

"Things like my yearnings to explore the vast world, and my
longings for a wonderful place to settle down." He shifted his
hand, brushing the backs of his fingers lightly against the velvety-
soft skin of her cheek. "My dreams of a brilliant, willing partner to
work at my side and share my life . . . If I had gone to Them and
stood before them, and a hundred and more Gods besides . . . then
this is what They would have given me." Hazel gaze earnest, he
looked into her eyes and gave her the absolute truth. "I do not pray
every day like you do, conducting empowered pleas capable of
moving mountains, praying literally to make the world a better
place . . . but I have faith, absolute *faith*, that They will grant these
things to me, and grant similar things to you."

Touched deeply by his words, Saleria covered his hand with her
own, cradling it against her cheek. She turned her head to the side

for a brief kiss, then lowered their shared touch to her lap, where their other hands were still clasped. "Considering I know you didn't set out to *be* a priest originally, I am grateful you do feel a calling, now."

Aradin smiled, ducking his head a little. ". . . If I admit I'm a little surprised by the strength of it, will that count against me?"

She snorted, scoffing at the idea. "Considering I'm smart enough to realize your desire to serve as a priest is tied up with your desire to work as a Hortimancer, no, I'm not that surprised. You do so in a slightly different way than I, but we both still serve." Leaning close, she brushed her lips against his brow. "And that's why I'm falling for you. All of you."

Lifting his chin, he met her next forward sway lips to lips . . . and felt a jolt of sunshine within him, making him gasp. One strong enough that she gasped, too, from the touch of the Light carried in Teral's grasp. Swaying back onto his heels, Aradin struggled to retain his physical senses. It was difficult, for the bowl that his Guide carried was large, and over-full, and spilled with every breath, filled past the brim with a great big bowl of ". . . Yes!"

(*Yes, indeed,*) Teral whispered, sharing his revelation with both his Host and their hostess. He spilled some of the divine answer into Saleria's mind, sharing it in equal measure so that all three of them could manage what he had barely been able to carry home. (*Great Darkhan and His Beloved Dark Ana have agreed. We may stay and assist you, Keeper Saleria, with the restoration of the peaceful and safe sanctity of the Holy Grove of Katan . . . provided Jinga and Kata agree.*)

Aradin almost replied mentally, but knew Saleria would want to hear his own thoughts. He nodded and said aloud, "Yes, and I have faith They will agree, as I was explaining to Saleria just now." He smiled at the blonde woman seated on the edge of the bed before him. "I have absolute faith."

Saleria squeezed his hands. For the first time, it didn't feel weird for Teral to whisper into her mind. It didn't feel strange to know the older, deceased spirit was there inside this younger man's body. Aradin looked only a few years older than her, in his early thirties at most to her twenty-six years, and she knew the older Witch had been cut down in the latter half of his prime, but . . . it felt right for both of them to be there, in her bedchamber with her. Looking into those hazel eyes, fancying she saw hints of Teral's brown gaze amid the flecks of green, she smiled.

"I have faith, too, that *both* of you are destined to be here with me." Seeing Aradin smile again, lopsided and rueful, she cupped his cheek. "Mind you, I'm still not entirely sure about Teral actually watching everything, when we, ah . . . get around to using this bed. But he is a part of you, and I accept both of you for who you are, and who you've become so far."

". . . Saleria?" Daranen's voice echoed up the stairs. "Your Holiness!" Hurried footsteps and the swift creak of two floorboards preceded the scribe's appearance at her door, which still stood open. Daranen held the forgotten petition in his hand, his voice a little breathless. "Holiness, I have just witnessed a miracle," he said. Lifting the sheet of paper she had left on the dining table, he turned it to face her, to face both of them. "*All four* of Them signed it."

Along with the plain black ink which Aradin had penned onto the page, beneath the neatly scribed lines, yet somehow intertwined with the words, lay two images. The outermost one was a glowing, silver octagon edged with the eight tetragrams representing the Eight Altars of Kata and Jinga, each one inked in the eight holy colors of brown, red, orange, yellow, green, blue, indigo, and violet. In the center of the octagon lay a sigil unfamiliar to Saleria, of a doorway, just the posts, threshold, and lintel, marked in silvery white, and a small, glowing black disc cradled inside.

She looked at Aradin. "Is that the mark of your Patrons, in the center?"

He nodded, releasing her hands so he could rise. "Yes. The black circle is the long-lost Third Moon, representing Darkhan, which is carried inside the Light-filled Doorway of Dark Ana's soul."

"Well, holy or otherwise," Daranen said, nodding at the page, "what *I* want to know is how They got the color *black* to glow like that."

Aradin grinned and shrugged, spreading his hands. "They're Gods. Anything is possible when They have the faith of their followers to support it."

"Well, now it's *my* headache to figure out where to put this, without offending *four* Gods if I just try to stuff it into a records cupboard or something . . . But I'll bid you a formal welcome to the Grove, and to its service, Aradin Teral, holy Witch of Darkhana and Hortimancer of the Sacred Grove of Katan," Daranen told Aradin. He bowed and started to turn away, then gave both Aradin and Saleria a stern look. "Celebrate however you'd like, but remember, you *both* have to go to work tomorrow. And try not to be too loud. I may be three doors down, but the walls of this house aren't *that* thick."

"Considering you always stay up far later than I do, *and* have the freedom to get up later, you've no cause to complain," Saleria said somewhat tartly, feeling her cheeks warming once more. She softened her tone. "But we'll keep in mind that dawn comes early in the summer. Good night, Daranen, and sleep well when you get there."

"A good night to both of you, then," Daranen returned, and pulled the door shut as he retreated down the hall.

"That was tactful of him," Aradin murmured.

Unsure if he was trying to be sardonic or not, Saleria let it go. She still didn't quite know how to get the handsome outlander into her bed, but she did know how to get him into her baggage.

Namely, by crossing to it, carrying it back to the bed, and dumping out the contents.

"Right. Here is what I have. It's not a very big pack, more of a knapsack than a full pack, but I have a toiletry kit of soap and toweling cloth, a comb for my hair, a tunic for sleeping in, two sets of, um, undergarments," she said, pausing for a brief blush, "including socks and such, plus two formal priestly gowns, and two sets of Keeper's garb—those are the trousers, tunic, and vest-robe you usually see me wear.

"Oh, and a belt, and a pouch with some money in it, and this outer pocket on the knapsack has some seedcakes in it, made from several fruits and grains and carefully wrapped in a stasis-enchanted packet so they'll stay good for a long time." She gestured at the set, and shrugged. "Am I missing anything? I keep thinking of things I want to add, but they add bulk and weight . . ."

Aradin considered her words, consulting silently with Teral. The inner glow of their Patrons' answer had faded a bit, enough to think clearly. Both men gave her selection careful consideration, then sighed. "It's good, but you should add three more things. A knife, for eating or survival or whatever—you can add one of your distinctive staves if you must, but a knife is essential when traveling—a full waterskin for drinking . . . and a good weather-proof cloak, one big enough to use as a bedroll if needed."

"Oh, right, the cloak is over there. I figured that out already," she admitted. Saleria then frowned. "But I thought I was going straight to the Convocation and coming back via your Dark Portal trick."

"Ideally, yes," Aradin agreed. "But Teral and I both think you should be prepared for just about anything. We *believe* the Convocation will take place in a civilized place, but no one has seen it yet; we just know it has been foretold. Also, if you find you cannot stomach a return trip through the Dark, then you must be prepared for traveling until you can reach a mirror-Gate that can bring you back to Groveham. We can arrange to have more supplies sent across if there are still Witches around, but it's best to be prepared for the worst.

"Oh, and Teral would like to remind you that as a competent, trained mage, you can start your own fires, warm and cool your clothes, and even create warding spheres to hold off weather and such . . . but there may be a point where you cannot rely completely on your magic. A good knife, a stout cloak," Aradin told her, "and a waterskin to go with the food you've packed will be essential for just such a case. Teral says the knife doesn't have to be big, so it should fit inside the pack. The waterskin can be tied to the outside of the pack, and the cloak can be stashed next to it, so you can grab both when it's time to go."

She considered his words—their words, and their reasoning— and sighed. "I guess you're right. It would be better to be prepared than to find myself in need and have to do without. I thought about taking some jewelry, of doing my hair in some fancy way . . . but . . . They're Gods. They've seen me naked," Saleria said. "They've seen me when I've been red-eyed and runny-nosed with a bad cold, and trying to shape my prayers in the midst of a fit of sneezing—if I had more time to prepare, and could take proper baggage along, perhaps a few companions, then I'd go with more of the clothes and the means to represent the people of Katan the best I can in front of the others who will be there.

"I'm tempted to add an extra pack as it is . . . but there *is* that uncertainty in where and when the Convocation will be held. I don't want to be late for it, or burdened down by more than I can quickly grab and carry," she said, putting her feelings on the matter into words. "Far better for me to be *there*, and garbed in what They see me praying in every day, than for me to be absent on the most important day of my life." Saleria looked up at him, her expression earnest. "I may never be picked again for this task, but for this one time, I will do my absolute best for my people. I will *not* fail them."

Aradin wrapped his arms around her, tucking her against his chest. When she rested her cheek on his shoulder, he gently stroked her hair. It felt right to hold her in that moment, and right to say the words that came unbidden into his mind.

"I believe you," he murmured. "I believe *in* you, and I believe you will succeed. At anything you decide to do. Teral believes in you, too, you know," he added, cuddling her close. She felt right in his arms, a perfect partner for a too-brief, yet eternal moment of contentment. *Almost like hugging a mortal Goddess . . . with no blasphemy intended*, he thought quickly, averting any possible ill consequences.

(*And on* that *note, I shall retire to the Dark for a while,*) Teral muttered in the back of his mind. (*I won't deny I'd like to stay and enjoy the moment secondhand, as she's both quite lovable and quite lovely . . . but that, I think, isn't something she's prepared to understand.*)

(*No, she isn't,*) Aradin agreed. There were times when his Guide felt more like an extension of his own mind, a wiser, older, somewhat different version of himself, for all they were two distinct men. At times like those, it was easy to share every experience he had. But it wasn't fair to expect others to comprehend. There might be a few jests made, but there was no real rivalry between the two: The Host was the living half, with all the rights that entailed; the Guide was there merely to aid, to ensure that a lifetime's worth of wisdom was not lost to the Dark when that soul died. A lifetime, and more. (*Any advice on how to treat her, before you go?*)

(*Go slow. And focus more on the emotions than the sensations,*) the older Witch advised. (*It may sound cliché, but the two of you could make a great pairing from what I've seen . . . and since we're going to be here more or less permanently, it behooves you more to treat her with an equally permanent level of respect.*)

(*I already know how to suck eggs, Grandfather,*) Aradin retorted mildly, focusing more of his attention on the warmth and the softness of the woman snuggled in his arms than on their inner conversation. (*The Grove alone does not compel me to stay and explore this corner of the world. Being a Hortimancer for this place is a huge responsibility. This . . . might be a huge reward for all the good things I've done in life. If I don't muck it up. I'll see you in the morning.*)

(*Sweet dreams. Eventually. Oh, and I'll wager you a local silver coin that she's sensitive behind her knees.*)

(Go, *Teral,*) Aradin ordered. With a mental wave, his Guide disappeared, leaving him to hold Saleria in what felt like perfect contentment. *I could hold her like this forever, and I think she'd be happy to stay. I know I am, right here, right now.* It was a very good feeling.

It was an almost perfect contentment; she turned slightly after a few more moments and nuzzled her face against the underside of his jaw. That felt good, too, as did the nibbling of her lips along his chin. Aradin met those lips with his own; that made the sensations both different and better. The feel of her curves pressing against his muscles, the way she nibbled on his bottom lip, all of it was better than simply standing there, holding her.

Saleria wanted to touch him. She slid her hands under the edges of his black and tan outer robe, then stilled. Breaking their kiss, she started to speak. "Um, is he still—?"

"He's gone," Aradin reassured her. "Nipped off into the Dark to do whatever until dawn."

She relaxed a little, and slid her palms up his chest to his shoulders, easing back the folds of his Witchcloak. "Does he ever get jealous? Of not being able to . . . ?"

"It doesn't come up very often," Aradin had to admit. Shrug-

ging out of the robe, he draped it over the chair next to her bed as
he addressed her questions. "I think if he *never* got any physical
affection, either directly or secondhand in the back of my mind,
then it might become a problem. He may technically be dead, but
he also still has the chance to enjoy life in some part."

Following that line of thought, Saleria sighed. "And it would be
cruel to deny him the delights and comforts of life . . . Well, I can't
say I'm comfortable with it. Right now, at least. But . . . I'm not
vehemently opposed to it. He is handsome, you know—so are you,
in a different way."

Aradin grinned at her hasty amendment. "Be sure to give him
a hug and let him know, the next time he physically appears. Now,
since he is not here . . . care to tell me what you like about *my*
appearance?"

She blushed and cleared her throat, trying to find a good place
to start. "Well . . . I like your hair. It's soft, and healthy, and it
seems dark when you're in the shadows," she told him, lifting a
hand to one of his locks. "Yet it picks up all these lovely golden
highlights in the sun. I find myself anticipating each patch of sunlight we cross, when we're in the Grove."

"I see," Aradin murmured. Unbuckling his belt, he set it on the
black fabric of his cloak lining, then pulled his tunic over his head.
"What about my chest? Or my arms? Do you like them?"

Saleria started to speak, but found her wits distracted. Aradin
didn't have a muscular barrel of a chest, unlike his absent Guide,
but for all that he was lean, he was well-muscled. Having grown up
with a warrior for a father, having seen his fellow guardsmen—
who came in all body shapes, but were one and all fit men—she had
always enjoyed the various different ways a man could look and be
healthy. But as she sought for the words to admit she admired his
figure, she instead burst into laughter when he flexed his biceps . . .
and kissed the left one.

He grinned back at her, showing that he knew he looked silly. "See anything you like?"

That reminded her of her own pert question to him earlier. Regaining her breath, she smiled at him. "Aradin . . . you are lean and fit. I like that in a man." Moving close, she lifted her hands to his chest. Her palms slid over the warmth of his skin, enjoying the light dusting of hair coating it. Blond and faint, it was felt more than seen. It wasn't enough, though. Playfully, she leaned back, eyed his arms, then lifted her chin. "Flex them again, please? Something looked out of balance."

Obedient, he lifted his arms and bent them, making the biceps and triceps show. Satisfied, Saleria leaned over and kissed the right one.

"There," she said, straightening. "Now they're even again."

"Oh, no," Aradin argued lightly. He could still feel the imprint of her lips, and the tingling feel of the places her fingers had caressed. "Your kisses upon on my skin are not the same as my own, you know. They are vastly superior and far more potent. My left arm is feeling sorely underappreciated right now."

Mock-rolling her eyes, she leaned in and kissed that arm, too. Pulling back, she shrugged out of her over-vest. Saleria turned to pitch it at the clothes basket in the corner, and found Aradin's hands moving around her waist, seeking the buckle of her belt.

"What I like about your own hair is how soft and fine it is. Like sunshine spun from spiderwebs," he told her. He let her take the belt once he had it undone. Shifting his fingers to her locks, Aradin sifted them through the fine strands. "That is, if you're not upset at the comparison. Most people don't like spiders."

"So long as it's not trying to eat me, I don't mind," Saleria said. "Spiders and spiderwebs are all a part of nature, which means they're a part of any garden, including the Grove. Little ones are not the problem. It's the big, mutated ones that try to hunt me instead of something small and buglike—those are the ones I don't like."

"Then I'll make sure they never get in here," Aradin promised her. With her hair tugged gently out of the way, he brushed his mouth along the curve of her neck.

Shivering, Saleria enjoyed it for a few moments, tilting her head to give him more access. She couldn't stand like that forever, though. Stepping forward, she pulled her tunic over her head, baring her undercorset. The tunic went into the basket. A glance over her shoulder showed Aradin's hazel eyes following her every move, though he, too, had stepped back to give himself some room. As she watched, he pulled off his boots and set them on the cloak-draped chair, and followed it with his socks.

At her puzzled look, he smiled. "I'll fold the cloak over my things, and Teral will take them into the Dark and exchange them for fresh clothes in the morning. It's been a boon while traveling, storing everything in the Dark. No thief can steal what he or she cannot find, let alone reach."

"That is clever," Saleria agreed, bemused, "but what if they steal your cloak?"

"They cannot activate its powers, for only a Witch is attuned to the magics of a Witchcloak," he reassured her. Fingers unfastening the lacings of his trousers, he shed them, adding the garment to the pile on the chair. "So they cannot get into the Dark to steal any of our possessions."

"I can understand that part, but I meant, wouldn't that leave you more or less naked?" she pointed out, eyes sliding down his lean body to the loose undertrousers he still wore, dyed a faded shade of soft green.

"Most of us can cast a shadow-bubble spell, wrapping our bodies in enough darkness to be able to access the Dark, and we all store a change of clothes and supplies there," he reassured her.

Moving back to her, Aradin knelt at her feet and tapped one of her boots on the toe. Obediently, she lifted her foot, resting a hand on his shoulder for balance while he gently eased it off. "Or we can simply wait until nightfall, and fetch what we need then. Let me get your sock, too . . ."

She held still while he peeled it off, and nodded. "That's rather convenient. You make me wish I could use a similar arrangement when I travel to the Convocation." Switching feet, she let him remove the other set. "I think I might add a second gown. Summer-weight. And just put the belt—and the knife—on the outside of the . . . ohhh. Oh, Gods . . ."

Aradin grinned. For a woman who spent most of her days on her feet, he had privately suspected it was her feet, not her knees, that would be the most sensitive part of her body. He'd still have to investigate higher, of course, but for now, he just kept kneading her toes, leaving her heel braced on his thigh. "Like that, do you?"

"You . . . uhhh . . ." She could feel it all the way up her legs, up into their juncture and beyond. "Youhavenoidea," Saleria managed to blurt, if a bit breathlessly. She wobbled, though, not quite able to keep her balance when every little rub and caress threatened to liquefy her legs. "Careful!"

"Do you want me to stop?" He stroked gently along the arch, and firmly along the outer edge of her foot, then pulled his hands back toward her toes.

"Netherhells, no!" Saleria gasped. That felt so good, both sensual and sexual at the same time, a heady mix of sensations. "I just . . . bed. Need to lie . . . bed. On the bed."

Chuckling, he let go. At her pout, he patted her thigh and rose. "Pack up your bag, and I'll give you more, I promise."

"Both feet?" Saleria asked, considering his offer.

He grinned slowly. "All the way up your legs, if you like."

Whirling, Saleria grabbed her things on the bed and started

stuffing them into the shoulder pack. That provoked a laugh from her companion. Covering her hands with his own to stop her movements, Aradin pulled everything back out, then with quiet murmurs and little touches that combined demonstrations and caresses, he showed her how to fold, then roll up her clothes tightly to reduce the space they used.

Saleria had never considered such an ordinary sort of chore, like packing a travel bag, to have any potential for seduction before. It wasn't just how he handled her corset-vest, either, though the sight of such masculine hands stroking the gathered cups as he folded and tucked did make her long to feel that same gentle, deft touch on her breasts. It was everything else, too. The care he took in making sure her trousers wouldn't crease. The caress of his palm as he smoothed the sleeves of her formal gown.

Even the way he rolled up her socks and stuffed them into a pair of clean, nearly new ankle boots, adding them to fill the extra room that he had created in the pack, made her want those hands on her body instead. Inspired, Saleria let him finish the packing, applying her touches to him instead. While he folded in the sleeves of her spare summer-weight gown, she slid her fingers along his spine. When he rolled it up, she cupped his buttocks, enjoying the play of the muscles bunching and releasing under her touch.

Somehow, he got the extra gown in, too. It wasn't easy; Aradin had known this shared moment of packing could be a seduction, but it was supposed to be a seduction of *her*, not of them both. Not of him. Heat flooded his muscles everywhere she touched, tensing and releasing them, only to leave them with a slight shiver as the warmth of her fingers moved on. Standing there in just his under-trousers, no tunic or pants to hide his reactions, he carefully folded the flap of the pack, lifted it off the bed, and set it on the floor near his cloak.

She squeezed his rump when he straightened up. Cheeks

flushed with heat, he turned to face her . . . and found her hands sliding to cup the front of his hips. Losing some of his breath in a shudder, Aradin quickly covered her fingers with his own. "C-Careful," he stammered, feeling the blood in his veins rushing inward from his extremities to meet those beautiful, bold hands. "Or I won't be able to . . . concentrate . . . to massage your feet."

TEN

er fingers stilled. Saleria contemplated her choices. "Hmm. Playing with you, or getting a foot and leg massage. Playing with you . . ." Her fingers rippled briefly over his barely covered loins, testing the length and shape of him. The soft, deep sound that escaped his throat strayed somewhere between the ranges of a sigh and a groan. "Or a foot massage . . .

"Foot massage," she chose, and pulled her hands free.

Another soft groan escaped him, part disappointment and part acceptance at her choice. It morphed into a deep breath as she unlaced and shimmied out of her trousers. The fabric hit the floor, and he sighed, studying the limbs revealed. "Oh, milady, I cannot fault your choice after all. Days and months and years of walking the Grove has left you with *magnificent* legs."

She blushed with pleasure at the compliment, stepping out of her trousers, then stilled, frowning softly. "Wait a moment . . . didn't you call that thettis-vine hybrid 'magnificent,' too?"

I am heartily glad Teral is not *here to see* that *come back to bite me on the foot,* Aradin decided. He gave her a slow smile, and a quick-witted reply. "I am quite certain that you will be just as deadly to me as any hybrid vine, the moment you wrap those lovely legs around my body."

She gave him a blank look, not knowing what he meant.

". . . Forgive me. I forgot for a moment how far I am from home." Aradin held up his thumb and forefinger together a scant distance apart. "Darkhanans refer to sexual bliss as the 'little death,' because we believe it's a tiny little taste of the bliss found in the Afterlife. I am therefore hoping that your legs, when wrapped around me, will be *very* deadly indeed."

Caught off guard by his explanation, she laughed. Sagging from her mirth, Saleria backed up into the bed, then sat down. Her heart skipped a beat when Aradin stepped up to her, knelt, and took one of her feet in his hands. This time she was thinking of sexual bliss, and this time the sensations were stronger. Nerve endings on her feet somehow connected themselves up through her legs to her loins, up into her belly . . . even up to her breasts. It helped that he studied them, caught in their corset, making Saleria hyper-aware of his gaze, his touch, and her need.

With unsteady fingers, she plucked at the lacings holding the vest in place. His breath caught, his lips parting in anticipation. Loosening the garment, she pulled the laces free, then peeled it away. His fingers stopped somewhere near her heel while he stared. Wriggling her toes, she prodded him into kneading again. Sort of. Shifting her leg to the side, he kept his left hand working on her right foot, but leaned forward between her legs.

His tongue tasted the tip of one breast. Shivering, Saleria struggled to remember to breathe. Warm lips closed around her nipple, and a gentle suckling tugged little sparks all the way down through her body to her toes. Another swirl of his tongue accompanied the slow, rubbing thrust of his fingers between her toes. She gasped, but before she could clutch at his head for more, he pulled back, releasing her breast with a soft *pop*. Instead, she braced her hands behind her on the bed, waiting to see what he would do next.

Sitting back on his heels before her, Aradin focused on her right foot again, rubbing and kneading from toes to heel, from ankle to calf. An experimental tickle behind her knee proved Teral wrong; she twitched her muscles a little, as anyone would, but didn't squirm excessively. Stroking to soothe it, he picked up her left foot and began massaging it. When she licked her lips, he leaned forward, right hand working her foot, mouth moistening her other breast. This time, she cupped her fingers through his soft, sun-streaked hair. A soft moan escaped her, enjoying the play of tongue around nipple and fingertips between toes.

She had lost track of his left hand. It came into play soon enough, teasing her inner thighs. Two fingers slipped under the cuff of her undertrousers, teasing their way up to the curls sheltering her mound. Her legs twitched wider apart, almost pulling her foot out of his grasp. That removed his mouth from her breast. Aradin sat back to focus on her foot, bringing both hands back into play against her sole. Again, he stroked and rubbed from toes to heel, ankle to knee, but then he stopped.

She looked at him, licking lips gone dry from soft panting breaths. ". . . Yes?"

"If you want me to massage your thighs, and points farther up," he murmured, "you're going to have to remove a certain . . . impediment."

What? For a moment, her mind was blank. *Oh—undertrousers. Right.* Tugged impatiently at the strings . . . got them knotted. Frustrated, Saleria growled and struggled with them. Catching her hands, Aradin moved them to her sides, then plucked at the knot himself. At least he had the patience for it, though his show of restraint made her marvel. Particularly when he sat back and tackled his own drawstrings, because she could see his arousal straining at the fabric of his own undergarment. A moment later, the cloth dropped, pooling at his feet. Bared, his manhood bobbed a little above its curl-dusted sack, but otherwise pointed upward in cheerful salute, clearly happy to be so close to her.

The tapping of his thumbs against her hips distracted her from that intriguing view. With a bit of wriggling, she helped him remove her undertrousers. He finished it by lifting her ankles up into the air as he pulled off the garment, then kept them there, leaving her tipped onto her back on the soft, feather-stuffed bed. This time, his fingers were joined by his lips, tickling her with little kisses on each instep, and the flick of his tongue on her toes.

Saleria giggled, bit her lip, and squirmed. It wasn't that her feet were particularly ticklish, because they weren't, but the sensations did sear down through her legs, stirring her nerves all the way to her belly. With her legs held upright, her heels resting on one of his palms, she didn't see the goal of his other hand until it was too late. In a bold but light touch, Aradin stroked one finger through her netherfolds, stimulating her flesh.

Head thumping into the bedding, she gasped and arched her back. He did it a second time, lingering so that he could gently rub against that little nubbin of flesh. Saleria stiffened again, hands clutching at the bed. A third time made her cry out, a soft sound half-strangled because she was still half-mindful of the others elsewhere in the house.

Aradin teased her until she was squirming in his grip, until he had to rest her calves against his shoulders. Bringing his finger up to his mouth, he took a few moments to taste her dew. His own flesh, hard with longing, strained toward her body. Between her heady flavor and the feel of those glorious, magnificent legs, he was more than ready for her. Not knowing how flexible she was, he moved slowly, closing the gap between their loins while he kissed first one foot, then the other.

She didn't protest, and he didn't sense any great resistance until the tip of his manhood prodded her inner thighs. Then she sucked in a breath and blinked at him . . . then smiled and widened her legs. Quickly shifting his arms, Aradin hooked his elbows under her knees for support, stooped a little more, and slid his shaft along her folds. Warmth met his flesh, warmth and wetness. Head tipping back, he rocked against her flesh, enjoying the sensations of crisp curls, slick dew, and welcoming female.

Saleria shivered as much from the blissful expression on his face as from the deft stimulation of her body by his manhood. Her fingers released the bedcovers. Shifting them to her breasts, she cupped the curves, enjoying the way their flesh rubbed together. But when he didn't move on, she raised her brows. "Um . . . you do know that's supposed to slip inside me like a dagger in a sheath, right?"

Aradin grinned and lowered his gaze. "*Yes*, I do know," he teased back. "I even know which 'sheath' to use. But I'd rather liken it to exploring and enjoying the garden outside a fine house. I'll knock on the door and enter your home when I'm good and ready."

His analogy made her laugh at the absurdity of it—though he was a Hortimancer—and that was when the tip of him slipped into her "doorway" and prodded on his next slow stroke. Breath catching, she strained for more contact, but the Darkhanan merely grinned and teased her. She tried reaching for him with her hands, but he was out of range; next, she tried curling her legs, but couldn't tug him more than an inch closer.

Her stern look was accompanied by a flexing of her calves, not quite thumping him in the back. "Get inside, Aradin, before I decide you *aren't* allowed in!"

"Yes, milady," he complied, grinning. He pressed in deeper than the mere inch he had teased. "But it's such a lovely garden outside. I shall have to remember to explore it in more detail, later."

He felt so good, pressing inside, slowly filling her, that she could only manage a distracted mutter. "You do that. Later . . ."

She felt so good, enveloping his straining flesh, Aradin wanted to make a quip about what a lovely "home" she had, but it was difficult to think when he could feel each of his heartbeats pulsing against her slick, hot walls. So all he replied as he leaned in, as he pressed in, was a soft-murmured, "Yes, later . . ."

Guiding her legs around his hips, he braced first one arm, then the other, on the soft-stuffed bed. A few more inches allowed their mouths to meet, her lips parting beneath his. Her fingers stroked through his hair, holding his head close before sliding down to cup his shoulders. Resting there for a moment, fully embedded in her body, groin to groin, Aradin wanted to tell her that he loved her. Darkhanan wisdom, however, advocated that such things be considered outside the heat of passion and desire as well as within the moment, that they be examined, and spoken only when one was in a calm frame of mind. Only then would it be considered true.

He thought it might be, but filled his lips with the taste of her chin, her throat, of the sweat beginning to sheen even her collarbone. Filled his senses with the smell of her, of faint hints of soap, flowers, feminine musk, and sweat. Filled his mind with the softness of her breasts, the heat of her sheath, and the flex of her muscles as she wrapped her arms around him and brought his mouth back to her own.

Saleria enjoyed that, particularly combined with the slow, deep thrusts of his body into hers. She enjoyed it enough that she stroked her fingers through his soft locks, then tugged on the fine strands, wanting more. That made him grunt and hold still. She tugged again and whispered, "Faster. Please."

He was trying to go slowly for her sake. Trying to keep ahold of his passion for her. But when she tugged again, tipping his head to the side and nipping at the muscles of his throat, Aradin complied. The first few thrusts he gave her were deeper, stronger, but not faster. Not in this position. Pausing a moment, he pushed upright, caught and lifted her legs up to his shoulders again, then bucked into her, hot and fast. Her startled cry made him pause, but the whimpering moan that followed let him know it was alright. It also warned him she might get loud.

"*Silunudormo*," he muttered, and kissed her left foot. She shivered, so he licked her instep, holding himself still. That made her twitch, so he did more of it, until she was squirming and breathing hard, and *then* he flexed his hips, thrusting into her with rapid strokes.

Unwound by the dual attack, Saleria cried out. Hands once again digging into the bedding, clutching at the blankets, she tried to hold on while his hips slapped into hers in a strange sort of sexual applause. An odd urge to giggle rose at that stray thought, but was then whisked away under the lightning strokes of pleasure connecting her groin to the toes he suckled. Her climax began with her right foot, and ended somewhere well after he grabbed the left and laved it with his tongue, too.

His began somewhere in the midst of hers. Glad he had cast a soundproofing charm on the room, Aradin let himself go, pounding hard, pouring into her in waves of release. He almost lost his footing as he sagged, but found the strength to stand and brace himself against the edge of the bed. With her lying before him, body flushed with passion, all he wanted to do was collapse next to her. But that would leave them with their legs off the bed. And if he moved her right away, well, there was the bane of all post-bliss lovers to deal with . . . not to mention his favorite dessert.

Sagging to his knees, he parted her thighs, inhaled their combined musk, and started lapping. Her breath hitched and her hands quickly moved to his head, clutching at his hair.

"Wh-what are you doing?" Saleria asked, startled. She had never known a lover to want a taste *after* lovemaking, only before.

Several possible answers ran through his mind. That he was cleaning her personally rather than finding a toweling cloth. That he wanted a post-copulative snack. That he couldn't get enough of her. But he smiled when the right answer came to him, and paused just long enough to give it to her.

"You had me so hot and sweaty with all that exercise deep in your house," he murmured, "I just had to step back outside to admire your garden up close while I cooled down."

Her laughter was about as loud and hearty as her final cries of passion had been. And as lusty, when he resumed his tasting of their combined desire. He knew they had to get some sleep soon . . . but not just yet.

She drooled in her sleep. Not a lot, just a little, and possibly it wasn't a common every-night thing, but Aradin watched the damp spot on her pillow for a full minute before deciding he not only did not mind, he thought it was cute. A touch of mortal normalcy in an otherwise dedicated, holy life. Not that such things were easy to see in the dim gray light of predawn, but Aradin was used to peering into the Dark. Mortal night held few secrets by comparison.

As much as part of him longed to lie there all day and just watch her sleep, the rest of the Witch wanted to be up and about, to seize the dawn and thus the day. Not wanting to disturb her slumber, he eased from the bed, then realized he had no clean clothes yet. Not because Teral hadn't returned—his Guide had slipped into his Doorway at some point while the younger man slept—but because he hadn't flipped the edges of his Witchcloak over his clothes.

(*Noticed that, did you?*) Teral offered dryly.

(*Hush, you,*) Aradin returned without rancor. He folded the cloak over the pile of clothing and waited. (*I—we—had a glorious time last night, and I am in far too good a mood, post-bliss, to be teased.*)

(*Well, we have only one change of clean clothes left. All of mine and most of yours are dirty. Since I'm not sure if that housekeeper of hers would be willing to scrub our things gently, we should visit the laundering shop you spotted on our way into the town. And I am glad the two of you had a good time,*) his Guide finished. (*So . . . did I win the bet?*)

(*Feet, not knees. Not ticklish, but sexually responsive all the same,*) Aradin informed him. The dimly lit lump of tan fabric shifted. At a mental nod from his Guide, he unfolded the cloak and started pulling on his clothes for the day . . . formal court clothes, crafted from fine silk and velvet in the Darkhanan style, with silver buttons and ribbon trim in flattering shades of green and brown. (*You weren't kidding about this being our last clean outfit, were you?*)

(*No, I wasn't. I apologize for losing track of how many clean clothes were left,*) Teral added.

(*It's partly my own fault, too,*) the younger Witch said. Both men looked through Aradin's eyes as Saleria mumbled and shifted on the bed, snuggling into the warm spot Aradin had left. She didn't wake, just relaxed into a deeper level of sleep. (*But can you fault me for the source of my distraction?*)

Teral chuckled. (*Considering she's the source of my own as well, plus we've all three been distracted by the situation with the Grove . . . no, I cannot fault you. Oh—speaking of situations, Orana Niel are on their way. They will reach the site of the Convocation within the week. How long it'll take to get things moving after that point . . . only the Threefold God of Fortuna knows.*)

(*Then we'd better get working on the task of taming the Grove as hard and fast as possible.*) Donning his Witchcloak over his formal clothes, Aradin slipped out of her bedchamber and made his way downstairs. He found Nannan in the kitchen, adding more wood chips to the hearth fire under the soapstone cooking slab to ensure a good bed of coals. This time, at least, she heard him coming.

The look she slanted him was still a little grudging, but not as bad as before. "Good morning, milord."

"Good morning, milady Nannan." He parted the folds of his Witchcloak, showing her his court finery. "I seem to be out of regular clothing. Would you have time and the willingness to do my laundry today?"

"Laundry is done once a week in this household, since I don't have any fancy spells for helping with the cleaning, and you've missed it by two days. Lavender down on the end of Baking Street, near the southwest corner of Groveham, does laundry every day," Nannan informed him. "She's not a strong mage like Her Holiness is, but she has enough to aid in the scrubbing and drying. If you want something clean to wear tomorrow, you'll need to visit her today, or just re-wear whatever you've got—I'd think that, mucking around in a garden, you'd be willing to re-wear whatever was dirty."

"Much like Saleria's Order, my own insists on being clean and neat as frequently as possible," Aradin said. "Do you know when this Lavender opens her shop?"

"She'll be open for customers at sixth hour, which is almost an hour after dawn this time of year," Nannan gauged. "If you want to be helpful, you can grab a broom and sweep the floors or something, since I doubt you could cook."

"I do know how to cook, though I am not familiar with how to prepare the local foods." A thought crossed his mind. "Saleria has mentioned she prefers sleeping in. Since I have been accepted into her service by both her Gods and mine, why don't we *let* her sleep in? I'll grab one of the staves and make the rounds of the walls, and you can take your time preparing breakfast for all of us."

She frowned at that, but sighed after a moment. "Fine. Though if I hadn't seen the holy symbols myself on the page Daranen showed me last night, I'd not have allowed it. And I'll blame *you* for it," she added, poking him in the chest, "if the Grove goes wild while it's in your care instead of hers."

Rubbing the bruise she had left, Aradin raised one brow at her. "I should think all four Patron Deities would make you wait in line if I should fail to tend the Grove, milady . . . though They might just appoint you Their taskmistress for my punishment. I assure you that if I have any say in the matter, the Grove will be tended well, its dangers contained, and its inhabitants carefully restored to its long-lost glory."

Nannan eyed him a long moment, then flipped her hand at the hallway. "Go on. Out the back door with you. If you get eaten by a carnivorous flower, though, it'll be what you deserve for not being smart and fast enough to avoid being devoured."

". . . And a glorious good morning to you, too, milady," Aradin replied, bowing himself out of the kitchen.

(*A wise man knows when to retreat, hm?*) Teral teased.

(*Quite. I have no idea what I've done to get on her bad side,*) Aradin sighed.

(*I suspect she instinctively knows you're a huge distraction for her employer. She fears change and the familiar order of her daily routines being upset,*) the elder Witch observed. (*She fears, too, I think, being supplanted in Saleria's affections. A woman does not need a mother figure nearly as much when she has a husband to be her life-partner.*)

(*That could be,*) the younger Witch allowed, opening the back door to the Grove. He closed it behind him and paused for a moment, inhaling the cool, damp air of pre-morning. (*Or maybe it's just because she didn't pick me out for the household. She does seem to like being in charge.*)

Teral chuckled. (*That could be. Depending on when Daranen gets the morning's correspondence sorted, we may be able to visit the laundress right after breakfast. Then the three of us could work on fixing the Grove for the rest of the morning in a solid block of time.*)

(*If not . . . then we'll just take a break midway to stretch our legs into town.*) Opening the shed door, he grasped one of the staves, found the triggering rune to light up the cutting spell, and readied himself for the hike. (*Now help me concentrate. Given the past few mornings' weirdness, I don't know what we'll be facing, and I'd rather not have to pay for repairwork to my court clothes.*)

(*I'm still in yesterday's clothes,*) Teral reminded him. (*And they're relatively clean; I wouldn't mind wearing them today for a bit more. Would you rather risk them than your velvets?*)

Aradin paused a moment, then shrugged, leaned the staff against the shed, and slipped into the folds of their Witchcloak. (*Take the body then, until it's time to head into town.*)

Saleria woke slowly, gradually. The scent of egg-dipped toast perfumed the air. Along with hints of spiced meat minced with fruit, it lured her out of one of the best slumbers of her adult life. Inhaling deeply, she stretched and tensed every muscle, then let them all relax on a deep sigh. She almost drifted back to sleep, too, save for the nagging feeling that something was wrong.

It was too bright in her bedroom. Too bright . . . *Daylight! Jinga's Sweet Ass!* Bolting upright, heart pounding, she looked at her windows, where the pink linen curtains couldn't keep out the bright morning sunshine glowing through their thin weave. *I'm late for the Grove!*

She twisted to get out of the bed . . . and felt her muscles protest. Sore with exertion, she blinked, remembered, and blushed. *Last night . . . oh wow. Three times for me, twice for him . . . Oh wow . . .*

Cheeks hot with her blush, she tried to piece together why she was still in her bed after the sun had risen . . . and realized what must have happened. *He must have told Nannan . . . Uh, not to wake me, not that we . . . He must be doing the morning rounds—oh, did I tell him not to touch the collection crystal to the fissure? I don't think I did!*

Climbing out of the covers, she hurried over to the windows. Pushing back one of the curtains, she squinted and raised an arm to block out the glow of the sun. Not that she could see him, of course, but while her eyes were narrowed, she looked for the Grove's flow of magics. It was a relief to see everything looked normal from here. Such things were always easier to see when one squinted, though she didn't know why. Even her teachers at the temple had just said that was the way magic worked.

Then again, they're more or less the same group of people who said there is only ever one Keeper of the Grove at a time. Well, that's just fine, Saleria decided. *Whatever happens, I'll still be the Keeper and the Guardian. But I am definitely hiring more people to work under me. As soon as I can figure out how to work that into my budget.*

One person's needs, her stipend could cover. She wasn't really using much of the money she earned as the Keeper right now, though she would eventually need it when she had to retire. Possibly, it could cover a second person, though that would cut into her retirement funds. *But I could easily use five or six mages with gardening experience, if not outright Hortimancers . . .*

Blessed Kata, I actually have the time to think *in the morning?* Saleria blinked and turned away from the window. *I do! I have time to think . . . Waking up isn't quite so tedious or awful if I'm allowed to sleep in, is it?* She owed Aradin Teral for this kindness, though she wasn't quite sure how she could repay it. *Heh, I owe him for whatever he managed to do to Nannan to get her to agree to let me sleep in . . .*

From the smells wafting through the cracks around her door,

breakfast wasn't far off. Donning her unused night tunic, she wrapped her dressing robe around it and headed downstairs just in time to meet Nannan at the bottom of the steps.

"There you are," her housekeeper said. "I was just about to wake you, since Daranen has already come down for breakfast." She frowned at Saleria. "I'm not sure it was wise, but I agreed to let you sleep in while that man took your morning walk around the Grove wall. I *hope* I haven't made a grievous mistake."

Saleria smiled; her mood was too good for anything less, given her leisurely start to the day. "I'm sure he'll be just fine. I think—"

The back door at the far end of the hall opened. Saleria gave up what she had meant to say, instead hurrying down the last few steps so she could see what condition her new partner was in. To her surprise, the man stepping into the house had the tall, broad-shouldered, dark-haired visage of Teral, not the slightly shorter, leaner, blond Aradin. She smiled at him all the same.

"Good morning, Teral. And good morning to your Host, too," she added politely, guessing that either Aradin was somewhere inside the older man, watching and listening, or that he would return shortly. Oddly enough, the scent of mint wafted into the hall, mixing with the spiced fruit sausage and the egg-toast Nannan had made. "How did the morning round go?"

"Some sort of horned, rabbity thing with willow leaves instead of fur," he recited, counting off on his fingers, "a swarm of bees acting rather agitated in what turned out to be a patch of rage-inducing bleeding hearts, a new species of ambulatory orchid-beetles, and a rather aggressively friendly cross between a fern and a mint plant. Either that, or it was attempting to copulate with me. For our sanity's sake," the older Witch muttered, "Aradin and I have agreed to think of it as just being aggressively friendly, and not amatory."

"Did you drain the northern locus? I forgot to tell you, don't touch the crystal to the rift," Saleria added, moving down the hall toward the entrance to the dining hall. The closer she got to him, the stronger the scent of mint became. The stains were subtle, but she thought she could see hints of green along the beige outer layer of his overrobe. "Do you need Nannan to wash your Witchcloak?"

"Yes, I drained it carefully; no, we've agreed to go see the laundress in town, since we have far too much laundry at the moment to burden your kind housekeeper with it; and no, you didn't tell either of us, but Aradin did watch you do it, advised me on the care you took, and thus we avoided it adroitly. The Witchcloak is supposed to be self-cleaning, but sometimes it does require a little scrubbing. We'll have the laundress look at it, too. If you'll excuse me, miladies," Teral added politely, lifting callused hands that showed a few signs of scratch marks, "I also tangled with some sort of rose hybrid while clearing the outer path, and will need to wash up before breakfast."

Giving both women a slight bow, he turned to the right, not the left, and ducked into the downstairs refreshing room. Behind Saleria, Nannan sighed. Curious, she turned and lifted her brows at her housekeeper.

"He's so handsome . . . but it's so weird, that he's technically dead," Nannan confessed. She flipped a hand and shook her head. "I'm not sure I could stand getting involved with him, when he's also . . ."

"Also what? Also Aradin? Also dead? Also not . . ." She cut herself off before she could say, *Also not interested in you?* It would not have been kind, however true, as far as she knew. Saleria shook it off. "You know, you can look at him all you like, and become friends with him—with Teral—but try to understand that in doing so, you must accept and become friends with Aradin, too . . . because wherever Teral goes, whatever Teral does or sees, Aradin is right there watching it all. I suggest you start trying to be friends with *both* sides of the Darkhanan, since he is going to be here for quite some time, praise Kata and Jinga . . . and Darkhan and Dark Ana."

"I do realize that, now," Nannan grumbled. "I'm not happy, but I realize it." She fluttered her hands at Saleria. "Off to breakfast with you before your scribe eats it all—I'll bring you some freshly grilled egg-toast, if nothing else."

"Thank you, Nannan," Saleria told her, heading for the dining room.

Aradin had forgotten about his note to himself from the previous night. It was a good thing he had written it down, too. Expanding the crystal tablet until it was the size of a large chalkboard—almost as big as the bed they had slept in together—he showed Saleria what his samplings of the aether and the plants of the Grove had revealed to him yesterday. With the additional samples taken during his morning walk, three patterns emerged clearly, one per locus tree.

"As you can see here, the energies build up and ripple around the triangle—you always drain the north locus tree, the east one, and the south one in that order, right? So the energy always has a dip in it that is traveling sunwise around the garden . . . and that means the energy always has a peak as well, just before you drain one of its contributors," he explained.

"Just one problem with that. The direction you're gesturing is *counter*-sunwise," Saleria said, tapping the sketched map of the Grove with its three giant trees coming together in the Bower at the center, and line-sketches for the paths and other major terrain features. "The sun actually travels the *other* way across the northern part of the sky. You tell me it moves sunwise, and I think it'll move like *this*, not that."

Aradin frowned at her as she demonstrated, frowned at the tablet map, then squinted up at the sky. He sighed roughly. "Well, forgive me for being born north of the Sun's Belt, where the sun travels across the *south* half of the sky. Clocks were invented in ancient Aiar, and they all go around the same way wherever you are in the world, so we'll call it *clockwise*, yes?"

"Thank you," she allowed. "That'll be far less confusing for me to remember. So this wave of magical energy traveling clockwise through the Grove, that's what's causing the mutations?"

"Some of it, yes. Some of it comes from the sap saturating the ground. Now, the good news is, I think we can tap into the magical sap, transmute and cleanse it alchemically, and burn it off. It does require the construction of Permanent magics, but we can at least get started with some temporary usage—you always have prayer petitions for rain or drought or such, right?"

"Yes, but those come in cycles that are unpredictable," she told him. Saleria gestured at the mossy spot where she usually prayed, in the center of the Bower. "If we build a Permanent magic, it will constantly be raining in the deserts of northern Katan, and dry as dust along the southwestern hills."

"You're thinking of a Katani faucet, which is plugged by a cork. Unplug it, and you cannot control the flow of water through the pipe," Aradin said. "I'm thinking of a spell-controlled lever that opens and shuts from a trickle to a gush and back, depending upon the incoming need. We could use spells to control which regions get what they need in what quantity needed, based on the number of petitions for that area. That's a long-term plan of course, but for now . . . maybe just build a radiant crystal to bless the land of Katan with good health? Teral tells me that's a common use of Fountain energies, and it's quite clear the Grove's foliage is quite healthy and abundant. Warped, but abundant."

"Well, I certainly don't want to go warping the farmlands

around Groveham, let alone the rest of the nation," Saleria stated, hands going to her hips. She flipped one at the tablet map. "If I wanted that, I'd not renew the wards on the Grove walls each night. How can we stop *that* effect from happening?"

"That's where my note to myself comes in," he told her. "See, the Bower acts as a focusing effect for the untamed energies of the Fountain-rifts in each locus tree. You call yourself the Guardian of the Grove . . . but according to what Teral remembers of what his Guide Alaya said about her Guide's Guide, who served the Witch Guardian, you're not actually *in* control of any of the rifts, because you're not *attuned* to them. You access all the energy from here in the Bower, and only collect it at each locus tree."

Saleria blinked a couple times, distracted by trying to figure out the relationship string he used. She figured it out after a few seconds by placing Teral as Aradin's "father" and Teral's own Guide when he was a living Host as Aradin's "grandmother" . . . which placed the Guide's Guide as Aradin's great-great-grandparent. Then the rest of what he had said caught up with her. "I'm . . . what? *Not* in control?"

"You're not attuned. You cannot tap into it directly," Aradin explained to her. "The Bower is attuned to all three rifts, and you are attuned to the Bower, but not to any of the rifts. Unfortunately, while the magic from any one locus tree rift could be handled by a reasonably strong mage such as one of the three of us, all three at once would be too strong for any single mage I personally know of, and would be a challenge even for our greatest Witch pairing."

"So what's the point?" Saleria asked him. "If I am attuned to the Bower, why should I worry about the locus rifts?"

"Control. Direct control of the energies, and their overflow spill. See, all these limbs and tree roots converge to form the Bower, yes? But they're not the whole of each locus tree. *These* branches and roots are end-points that build up in energies," Aradin showed her, tapping the crystal map, which started lighting up at key points around the Grove. "Much of it flows back toward the trunk and either spills into the hollow where the rift is, requiring it to be collected, or it gets siphoned into the Bower, where it collects and condenses as sap.

"But *some* of it pushes through the bark and the leaves, causing local eddies in the overall wave of energy. Possibly through some damage to the tree, leaking magic as a wound would leak blood, or leaking sap, or both sap and magic, since it does get converted."

"I see—*that* is where the mutations take place, in the convergence of the greater wave and the little eddies. A drop of magic-imbued sap lands on a foraging insect, which eats a plant soaked in ground-sap, and the next thing you know, we have a crossover between a buttercup flower and a stag beetle, yes?" she asked.

Aradin nodded. "Add in the wave being at its crest, or perhaps at its trough in certain circumstances, and you have just enough energy to push a mutation. Particularly if the affected target gets hit more than once over the span of a week or so. But we can take control of these energies—*if* we take control of the rifts."

"'We'?" Saleria asked, lifting her brows. She wished she could arch just one to convey her skepticism, but that was the best she could do. "Aren't you geased by your oathbinding not to take over the energies of the Grove?"

"Teral and I did not swear that in our oath," Aradin reminded her. "We are oathbound not to *steal* the energies of the Grove, but doing so *with* your permission as Keeper is not stealing them."

He had her there. Choosing to be amused by his law-sayer's cleverness rather than annoyed, she shook it off. "Right, then. I always wondered why I couldn't do much more than I've already been doing—and not just because of my busy schedule. I've sometimes had a little free time to experiment, but I never made any progress on improving things."

"Yes . . . The drawback to the Bower's design is that it is easy to attune to, easy enough that even a medium-powered mage could tap into some of its energies," Aradin warned her. "If I've configured these power flow spells right, the lower-strength the mage and the less energy they tap into, the more of the concentrated sap will be produced. The stronger the mage, the more energy is used, the less the sap flows.

"If you can attune to at least one of the rifts, that will reduce the sap-flow. If I can attune as well, that will reduce it significantly, since between your prayers here in the Bower and our efforts to restore the Grove, we should be able to use up most of what the three rifts produce . . . and if Teral can attune separately to the third one, then we will be able to not only control the excess energies, we will be able to burn off the sap saturating the ground, restore the Grove section by section, and craft Permanent magics to continue to harvest and use up the energies spilling into the aether."

Saleria considered his words. She wasn't so sure about the Permanent magics, since that was not an area of expertise for her; she had never been interested in Artifact construction, and not very good at it. Barely good enough to pass the required basic classes, in fact. As she pondered the problem, her gaze fell upon his workbenches, narrow tables hauled in from the town and set up between two of the no-longer-moss-covered altars near the southeast corner. The middle table was bare, but the left held a collection of beakers, flasks, and other implements of the Alchemist's trade, and cutting and pruning tools on the right table.

Between her and those tables were three pools, each with a vine or two hanging low enough to cross her vision with their verdant, sap-oozing tendrils. The combination reminded her of something he had said. "I think . . . I think it would be more useful to use the saps as they actually are. To use them to make concentrated potions.

I barely passed my Artifact construction classes, but I wasn't bad at alchemy. I'm rusty, and probably nowhere up to your level of expertise, but I could make a good assistant. I do like the idea of using *un*warped energies to encourage the health and vitality of the surrounding land, but as you yourself said, force-feeding a plant too much magic isn't healthy for it, so we'll need to do other things with all these excess energies as well.

"So we *should* bottle the various saps and experiment to find ways to make use of them . . . and sell them so that I can pay you a decent salary for all your hard work, plus hire a handful more of other Hortimancers and Alchemists—oathbind them to work for the Keeper and the best interest of the Grove and Katan, or something, but that shouldn't be too difficult to arrange," she dismissed. "I've heard any number of excuses over the last three years about why I couldn't get a second helper, and the budget has been one of the biggest ones.

"If we make the Grove pay for itself, they'll have no fiscal objections to make. And with that petition request of yours, approved and prayed over by me, and signed by both sets of Gods, they'll have no other ground to stand upon for any of the other changes I'll want to make." Staring off at the worktable, she nodded firmly at the thought. "That's what we'll do. That's what feels right."

"Then that's what we'll do," Aradin agreed. "You're in charge."

"Even if you and Teral manage to each attune to a rift, outpowering me two-to-one?" Saleria asked.

"You're still in charge," he reassured her. "It's your Grove. We'll make recommendations, but the ultimate decision is yours." He watched her brow slowly furrow into a frown. "What's wrong?"

She sighed, striving to explain it. "I'm not sure, but . . . I guess I'm not used to the whole *not* having to fight for control over what I want to do with the Grove. I think that's why I sort of fell asleep, as it were. Fell into the dull-witted acceptance of my traditional routine." Rubbing at her brow, she tried to shake it off. Honesty prompted her to add, "I'm rather grateful you woke me up to my own rights, even if it's going to cause both of us a lot of work— speaking of work, I need to get to work on those prayers. Did you want to keep working on this, and see if we can attune me to at least one of the rifts? Or were you going to go handle your laundry first?"

"I'd rather go handle my laundry. We should also consult with the other Guardians via your new mirror," Aradin added. "Teral says he got the impression from the memories passed down to him that it helps to have a clue on what to do before you try. To be frank, the Grove will still be here tomorrow, but both of us would like clean changes of clothing to greet the new day."

"Take a bath while you're at it," Saleria teased lightly, tapping him on his chest. "Teral worked up a bit of a sweat from the look of him this morning. I'll be fine on my own while you're gone . . . and I can cut you the slack, my new, official apprentice, because *you* let me sleep in this morning."

Stepping close to him, she looped one arm up behind his neck, tugged his head down into range, and kissed him in thanks. It wasn't their first kiss of the day; they had done so earlier while picking up their staves at the back shed. But it was a nice way to part company. Aradin enjoyed it for a few moments, then hugged her and stepped back.

"Not much more of that, or I might be tempted to profane the Sacred Grove with the sight of our naked hides rolling around on all this moss," he muttered.

"It's a marriage Grove; I sincerely doubt They'd mind. The real problem is that we do have work to get done, and only so many hours of daylight in which to do it," Saleria returned dryly, but let him go. Plans or no plans, there were still plenty of prayer petitions to attend to today.

* * *

" ♦ ♦ ♦ **A**nything should happen to her, of course, but if something should, then *I* would be the next Keeper. It's only logical."

Aradin stopped in his tracks. He had gathered his spell-cleaned and -dried laundry, paid the bill, tucked the packet back into the Dark for Teral to deal with, and started back toward Saleria's home, content with his errand and eager to get back to work. But those words were rather out of place, given what he knew of the Keeper's life.

Twisting, he searched through the plaza for the source of the voice, knowing it had to be nearby. No one was within several lengths of him, however, puzzling the Darkhanan. At least until the same voice, a light tenor, chuckled and replied to an unheard question.

"Well, of *course* they'd choose me. You have to admit the Prelate is getting on in years, and tending the Grove is very much a young man's job."

It came from the tavern, or rather, from an open window in the tavern wall just a few paces away. Aradin could hear the clinking of glasses and cutlery, the murmurs of half a dozen conversations, and a feminine voice fawning over the speaker. Her words weren't nearly as important as that speaker's, though.

(*That sounds like vain boasting to me,*) Teral stated. (*Or possibly a potential troublemaker.*)

(*Then we should check it out,*) Aradin decided. He tried to peer inside discreetly. The sun wasn't quite at the best angle, but he got a glimpse of a young man with golden hair several shades lighter than his own. At just that moment, the other male lifted a water glass to his lips and looked out the window. Their eyes met.

(*We've been spotted. Confront, or leave?*) Teral asked him.

Aradin decided quickly. (*Confront.*) Stepping up to the opening, he folded his arms on the sill, grateful the tavern owner had chosen to swing back the windowpanes to take advantage of the warm yet comfortable weather. "I don't believe we've met."

Swallowing, the younger man set down his drink with a charming smile. "Well, you do have the look of a stranger to Groveham, milord." He gestured gracefully toward himself. "I am Shanno of the family Lorwethen, Deacon to the Cathedral of Groveham. And you are . . . ?"

"Aradin Teral, Witch-Envoy of the Darkhanan nation . . . and current guest of Her Holiness, the Keeper of the Grove. I couldn't help but overhear your claim that you are next in line as a potential Keeper," he added. Elbows braced on the windowsill, fingers laced together, he eyed the younger man. "It's strange, but not once has she mentioned this idea to me."

His comment received a smirk. "Well, she'd hardly mention internal religious structure to an outlander," Shanno dismissed, chuckling a little. "I'm not surprised you didn't know."

"Considering we *have* been discussing religious structure, and the Keeper's job in particular, I'm certain she would have mentioned it," Aradin stated. (*I can't tell if he's just arrogant or an actual troublemaker. What's your opinion of the little snot?*)

(*That he's an arrogant little snot,*) Teral agreed as both of them watched the deacon's smug expression falter. (*But not a deliberate troublemaker, I think. I'd guess he's just trying to inflate his status in the eyes of the two lovely ladies to either side.*)

Aradin honestly hadn't noticed the ladies, one a brunette, the other a dark blonde. They were lovely enough, he supposed, but he'd rather have looked at Saleria. Out loud, he stated, "Whether or not your claim is true, there are two things that should be considered carefully. If it *is* true, and it is such a secret, then would Her Holiness honestly care to have it discussed by someone supposedly trustworthy enough to hold the position, and discussed so openly and casually that a virtual stranger could overhear it out here on the street?

"And if it *isn't* true . . . have you paused to consider what trouble such false rumors could cause the Keeper, whom I presume you respect?" he asked. "The higher a priest's rank, the more discretion is expected of him. The higher a priest *wishes* to rise in rank, the same must be expected from him. With that in mind, perhaps you should find something else with which to impress these lovely young ladies—I'm sure you have many excellent qualities," Aradin added diplomatically. "You are, after all, a fellow priest, and that alone should be recommendation enough for your good character, yes?"

He aimed a smile at the blonde and the brunette on either side of the deacon. They smiled back at him, trading amused, flattered looks with each other. The deacon, Shanno, gave Aradin a look somewhere between hard and sullen. It shifted to thoughtful after a moment.

"Funny," he said, eyeing Aradin, "but I hadn't heard of anyone staying with the Keeper."

"Well, I've just been assigned to Groveham, which means I'll be here for a long while . . . so I suppose you'll have plenty of time to get to know me," Aradin offered, giving all three of them a smile. "If you'll excuse me, milord, miladies, I need to get back to helping the Keeper now that my errands are done. Have a good day."

(*Not too badly done,*) Teral observed. (*You no doubt tweaked his pride, but you gave him a few options to save face along the way.*)

(*Well, I have had a few years' practice with diplomacy,*) Aradin thought back. (*He probably bears some watching, though; a young man with ambitions like that—and I'm certain Saleria would have mentioned him being next in line—is someone who might put the wrong foot forward at the least opportune time.*)

(*Possibly yes, possibly no. We'll wait and see how he takes your set-down,*)

Teral offered. (*With luck, he's a good young man who'll gain a little wisdom from it.*)

Aradin chuckled, turning right to head down a side street that connected to the avenue ending in the Keeper's house. (*Optimist.*)

(*Mage,*) Teral corrected. (*Our thoughts literally shape the world, so why not think happy ones?*)

(*Optimist,*) Aradin concluded, teasing his Guide.

ELEVEN

Touring the Grove while in charge of one third of its energies was a new experience for Saleria. A mostly pleasant experience, since when she walked through it with Aradin Teral, the plants and animals actually behaved around them. Unnaturally so, which was ironic, considering nothing about the denizens of the Grove was natural anymore. But the thettis-vine did not attack them, though it had regrown since the last time it had been trimmed; the ambulatory marigolds swerved around them rather than just blundering forward blindly; and they were able to actually catch a not-rabbit for examination without it trying to bite anyone.

Saleria figured it out within an hour of Teral attuning himself to the last of the rifts, when they had retreated to the Bower to conduct more experiments. "We finally belong here."

"Hm?" the Guide asked, still in control of their shared body. He was the one examining the not-rabbit on the middle table, since he knew more of diagnostic spells than either Aradin or her. "We finally belong here?"

"We're no longer foreigners in the Grove. Our energies match the magics that have soaked into every living being within the Grove walls," Saleria told him, standing at the left table, the one with the flasks and jars. "It just came to me. That's why we've had a peaceful day, relatively speaking. That's why most of the plants and animals are getting along, rather than trying to tear each other to leafy shreds."

"That . . . makes sense," Teral replied thoughtfully. "Hold on . . . Aradin's going into the Dark to ask a few questions for us. . . ."

"Of course," she said.

Her own task, the daily petitions, had gone quickly. Used to gauging how much power to push into each prayer, Saleria had discovered it took only a fraction of what she had done before. More of her concentration was required since the energies were now concentrated, but less power while applying it. That freed up more of her time to work as an assistant in turn to the two men. Her current task was the tedious chore of gently grinding up plant matter in a mortar and pestle and staining sheets of absorbent paper with the liquefied remains, so that the spells Aradin had scribed upon them would sort the various components into their individual categories: toxic to humans, not toxic, alkaline, acidic, nutritional, medicinal, and more.

From there, they would be tested on other spell-scribed papers, breaking down their components further into categories of usefulness. Enchanting the papers alone had taken Aradin and Teral two whole days. Tedious work, and boring enough to allow her mind to wander freely. It wandered now to this morning, and the surprise early round of lovemaking in her bed.

Rather than being woken up with the light of dawn filtering through her curtains and the yank of the covers being stolen by her housekeeper, she had awakened in the dim gray light of still-barely-night on her back, with Aradin buried deep under the covers. With his mouth buried between her legs. Just thinking about it, about those lips and that tongue, and the stroking of his fingers up into her depths, questing for that dear-Gods-in-Heaven spot . . .

"Blushing cheeks, far-off gaze . . . idle fingers on the pestle," Teral teased her, his voice dipping almost as low as Aradin's could get. "Did he do something this morning that you liked? Or is it just a general memory?"

She blushed and resumed grinding the current batch of leaves, trimmed from a tree that might be useful as a new kind of cold medicine, given the two plants that had been its magically con-joined parents. "This morning." She debated a long moment, then asked, "Teral, do you . . . strongly miss physical intimacy?"

"Now that's a loaded question," he murmured, stroking the antlered rabbit-thing before lifting it off the worktable an arm's-length from hers. He carried it to the edge of the Bower. Releasing it, the Darkhanan Guide came back to her table, not to the one he had been using for his examination. He leaned his hip against the stout wood, watching her work. "For a man, the *physical* urge is very real, a literal pressure for release. It doesn't *harm* a man not to achieve release—no matter what capricious young lads may try to tell a young lady to get into her bed—but there is always that urge. It diminishes as one gets older, of course, but it is always there.

"From what I learned while sharing my body with my Guide, Alaya, women don't have the same pressure, as it were. Urges, oh yes," he agreed. "A woman seems to have a lot more *capacity* for pleasure than a man. I was privileged to learn these things from her as we shared her form, even if it was my body while making love with friends and dear companions. Of course, our tastes var-ied; I still prefer making love to a woman as a man over making love to a man as a woman, naturally. And it's very different while wearing Aradin's body than when I wear my own . . ."

At her wide-eyed look, Teral leaned close and murmured in her ear.

"He might get mad at me for telling you this weakness, but if you take your feet and gently stroke his manhood with them, he'll be delirious with pleasure. I myself am more of a breasts-to-manhood type. That really gets *my* blood flowing," the older Witch added candidly, straightening back up. He smiled at her, enjoying her flustered blush. "So I suppose the answer to your question is yes, I do miss physical intimacy. But it *is* Aradin's life, not mine.

"And as lovely and charming and wonderful as I find you, too," Teral added, lifting a hand to brush back a wayward curl of her hair, gently tucking it behind her ear, "it is still his life, not mine. I knew it would be, long before I ever met Aradin and became the Guide to his Host. And I knew it long before I became Host to Alaya as my Guide. This is the way life is, as a Witch. Of course, given how strongly the young man is falling for you, this means that *you* have more say in what happens in any 'physical intimacy' than I do."

She considered his words for several seconds, until the leaves were a well-ground paste, then reached for the purified rainwater to dilute it into a liquid for the testing sheets. "Kata and Jinga have declared that . . . male-and-male pairings, and female-and-female pairings, are just as acceptable as male-and-female pairings. But it's still just two people. Three and more are . . . Well, they're not *directly* discouraged by scripture, but it is considered implicit, since we only have a God and a Goddess in marriage, not . . . well, a God and a God and a Goddess."

"I wouldn't build a long-lasting relationship like that unless all three were equals and equally amenable," Teral agreed, shifting to lean back against the table again, giving her a bit of room. "They say that a triangle is the most stable form of structure . . . but it is only for a physical structure. Two people manage a relationship much more easily than three. There are some lands where they manage three or more in a relationship, but they are rare. However, for a bit of physical fun, if all are agreeable . . . it can be quite pleasurable."

"I'll presume you speak in general, since there's no way for the two of *you* to ever be in two places at once," Saleria said. A corner of her mind did wonder what it would be like to be with two men at once, but she wasn't about to share Aradin—who already carried Teral more or less everywhere he went—with a third man in the equation. That would be more than unfair to Teral.

"Not exactly," Teral said. "It is possible, if rare, for there to be two of us at once."

"You mean, in the Dark?" Saleria asked, dubious. "I wouldn't think anyone would want to make love in a place where the dead roam."

"No, I meant in life, in two separate bodies." At her sharp look, he folded his arms across his chest and rubbed at his gray-streaked beard. "It's not often discussed with outsiders, but there *is* a way for a Host and a Guide to manifest in two separate bodies. We call it the wedding-gift of the Moons, for in the light of both Brother and Sister Moon—reflected via mirror or spell onto both sides of a Host's body—the Host and Guide can separate physically.

"It is doubly exhausting for the Host, and isn't done casually . . . but the power of temporary separation was granted unto our Goddess, Dark Ana, so that She could enjoy the delights of being husband and wife with Her beloved Darkhan. Most of the time They are the Dual One, two Gods in one form . . . but sometimes They are the Dual Ones, and we rejoice whenever They appear side by side," he said.

She blushed at the thought, then paled at the implication . . . then blushed again. *In the light of the Moons . . . say in the Grove . . . with just Aradin and Teral, and me . . . oh my.*

Clearing her throat, she muttered, "I wouldn't think you'd, ah . . . That is . . ." Gathering her wits, Saleria asked, "Teral, *why* did you tell me this? Why not earlier than now, I mean?"

"Because before, you were not open to the idea. Now, you don't seem to object to my presence anymore," he stated. "And because if things keep progressing as they have between my Host and you . . . well, Aradin's a bit of a romantic deep down inside. He's been thinking vague thoughts about you and him restoring the Grove well enough that the very first new wedding to take place within its walls would be yours and his. And vague thoughts of raising children, should you be amenable.

"You see, in this place, with you," Teral said, gesturing with one hand at the Bower, the Grove, and her, "he has all of the great loves in his life combined. The man is besotted with the idea of spending the rest of his life here, working on this place, the ulti-mate Hortimancer's dream task . . . and with you in particular. The more he helps you with the Grove, the less likely you are to 'burn out,' as you once said all Keepers do, within an average of ten years—I think you will find that the rift now tied to you will make all the magic you have been marshaling and expending that much easier to manage. You will be able to last for scores of years as one of its Guardians. So will he. And so will I, as his Guide."

"Yes, I've already noticed the boost to my powers, though now I'm worried about accidentally sneezing while walking through the Grove, leaking a burst of magic, and creating some new blend of species," she agreed dryly. "So you're telling me this, about how you and Aradin can become two separate men, because . . . ?"

"It is an option, nothing more," Teral stated, refolding his arms.

She couldn't quite believe him. She was ignorant of other lands and customs, not naive. "With *no* personal agenda, or ulterior motive?"

Leaning over, he gave her a direct look. "So long as you keep *Aradin* sexually satisfied, *I* will feel no physical pressure while I'm in control of our shared flesh. And so long as you do not *hate* me . . . if you can, in fact, feel and express some level of kindness and caring toward me . . . then my *emotional* needs will be met. That, above everything else, will satisfy me." His brown gaze softened. "*Do* you feel some small affection for me?"

It was a wistful question. Despite the gray streaking his dark hair and his beard, Saleria could see for a moment the younger man he had once been. On impulse, she rose up onto her toes and kissed his cheek. "I feel a *lot* of affection for you, Teral. As much as you are technically two separate men . . . you are a package deal, and you are very much a part of what makes Aradin the man he is today. And I do care for you *as* you, yourself. As Teral."

Unfolding his arms, he wrapped them around her, embracing the young woman. She returned it, gripping his ribs with a snuggle of her cheek against his collarbone. Teral rested his own on the top of her head, enjoying the soft strength of her body. That was when he felt Aradin return from the Dark.

(*What the . . . Teral, is there something I should know?*) Aradin asked, his mental tone amused by the situation in which he found his Guide and the woman he loved.

(*Hush, or you'll embarrass the woman. I explained and reassured a few things for her, then asked if she has any emotional affection for me. She stated that she does care for me, and I hugged her for it,*) his Guide calmly stated. (*And I am quite enjoying this hug, thank you for asking.*)

Rather than take offense—or worse, feel jealous—Aradin instead laughed. (*Marvelous! I'm glad she's taking to you so well. I suppose you'll want the body for a little bit longer?*)

(*Yes, please,*) Teral decided after only a brief moment of thought. (*She smells wonderful, feminine without being overpoweringly flowery, and she feels . . . !* You *know how she feels in our arms. So, yes, please.*)

(*No worries. But eventually I'll want to explain what I found out about reverting all these magical mistakes.*) Aradin let his inner laughter fade. (*I'm afraid there's not much we* can *do to separate the animals from the plants . . . and that over seventy-five percent of whatever's in the Grove in this day and age is too dangerous to let loose on the rest of the world. On the bright side, somewhere between thirty-five and forty percent of it will be useful. Particularly the saps, when added to potion bases. We just have to be extremely careful about not letting certain plants out of our control.*)

(*I'll let her know in a few moments,*) Teral stated.

Saleria was the one to break the hug. Inhaling deeply, she let go of her breath and the Guide. "Thank you. I think I needed that."

"Oh, it was my pleasure. I haven't had a good long hug in quite some time. By the way, Aradin is back," he told her. "And before you ask, he approves of me hugging you. Now, the rest of his news isn't quite so happy. If you both like, I'll hand the body back over to him now."

Saleria nodded—then bounced up on her toes and kissed his other cheek. "That's so you remember I do care, even when you're not in charge of the body. Now bring Aradin and his lips back, please, so I can kiss him and them properly."

He chuckled and started pulling the Witchcloak into place. "Impertinence, milady. I'll have him give you a swat on the rump for me, once we've swapped."

Saleria waited for her turn in the discussion of prophecies among all the Guardians on her Bower mirror. The sharp-nosed, face-shrouded Alonnen was talking. She glanced briefly at her lover, who was gently decanting some sort of sap-infused potion into a set of jars, but didn't call out to him. He had his task this afternoon, and she had hers.

At least she had the time for this discussion, rather than having to hurry everyone along so she could work on draining the eastern locus tree post-lunch. Now that she was the actual Guardian of the eastern rift, she could drain it from within the Bower directly, a very neat convenience. Which left her waiting for her turn to speak.

". . . But that's just it. 'When the floodgates open' *could* refer to something on my end of things, but I can't say even to the lot of you what it is. A lot of these prophecies so far point toward this corner of the world, either Arbra or Fortuna or Mekhana or its neighbors, but none of them peg it exact," Alonnen concluded, cap-covered, scarf-wound head waggling in a visual shrug. With even his eyes obscured by those green-tinted lenses he wore, he looked more like a puppet from a children's show than a man.

"Guardian Saleria," Kerric stated, turning to her. It was an interesting visual effect because his chair actually swiveled one way and the view of a book-lined wall behind him swerved the other, as if he really were surrounded by a circular library. "You said you finally sorted through the copies you received from the Katani Department of Prophecies? What have you to share with us?"

"Well, I did share the earlier one, from Seer Haupanea from two hundred years ago," she stated. "Now, I know you all don't think the verses, '*Gone, all gone, the synod gone, brought back by exiled might; By second try, the fiends must die, uncovered by the blight*' have much to do with a potential Netherhell invasion. But 'fiend' often refers to the denizens of those blighted dimensions, and that Nightfall Isle—founded by an exiled group of brothers—is trying to reconvene the Convocation of the Gods."

"We'd know more about it if Guardian Dominor weren't so distracted by Serina's pregnancy," Guardian Ilaiea snorted.

Saleria wondered what the pale-haired woman had against the as-yet-unmet Guardian Serina. She had to let it go, however. "As I was about to say, Guardian Ilaiea, I have here *another* prophecy by the same Seer, Haupanea, which seems to speak much more directly of the events in question . . . and Seers have been known to make several prophecies about one really big event, or a related series of events.

"*This* one I actually thought would be important for all of us to hear," she added, selecting the scroll from the table she had moved near the mirror. "Because the *title* of it is 'Song of the Guardians of Destiny.'" That got her their respectful, quiet attention. Nodding to herself, Saleria unrolled the scroll. "Here is the full prophecy:

> "*When serpent crept into their hall:*
> *Danger waits for all who board,*
> *Trying to steal that hidden tone.*
> *Painted Lady saves the lord;*
> *Tower's master's not alone.*

> "*Calm the magics caught in thrall:*
> *Put your faith in strangers' pleas,*
> *Keeper, Witch, and treasure trove;*
> *Ride the wave to calm the trees,*
> *Servant saves the sacred Grove.*"

"So it mentions Kerric's Tower and your Grove," Ilaiea scoffed, interrupting her at only the second verse. "So it's coming true. Tell us something new."

"I am *trying* to, Guardian," Saleria stated sternly. "There are eight verses in all . . . and the *third* verse is when things start getting hairy:

"Cult's awareness, it shall rise:
Hidden people, gather now;
Fight the demons, fight your doubt.
Gearman's strength shall then endow,
When Guild's defender casts them out.

"Synod gathers, tell them lies:
Efforts gathered in your pride
Lost beneath the granite face.
Painted Lord, stand by her side;
Repentance is the Temple's grace."

She paused and gave the others a pointed look.

Pelai, still sitting in for Guardian Tipa'thia of Mendhi, sat forward, her tattooed brow pinching in a frown. "Synod gathers, tell them lies? And a verse about a Painted Lord? If the synod referred to is the same one that means the Convocation of Gods and Man . . . then does that mean something will happen at the Convocation to set this all off? Or . . . well, it *could* refer to the Mendhi Temple of the Painted Warriors. Our most formal gatherings are called synods."

"I don't know," Saleria stated, shrugging. "There are four more verses to go."

"The part about Gearmen makes me think of what we've discussed of Mekhanan *engineers,*" Alonnen mused. "And it's very clear that the demons are involved somehow . . . which does not make me happy."

"Nor I," Sir Vedell stated. "Arbra has borne the brunt of far too many *normal* attacks by the Mekhanans. I do not like the idea of throwing demons into the mix."

"What are the rest of the verses?" Guardian Sheren, the eldest female in the group, demanded. "Can we please get back to that? Go on, Guardian Saleria. We're listening. Or we *should* be."

> *"Brave the dangers once again:*
> *Quarrels lost to time's own pace*
> *Set aside in danger's face.*
> *Save your state; go make your choice*
> *When Dragon bows unto the Voice."*

"Dragon?" Ilaiea interjected. She was hushed by five of the fifteen Guardians attending this meeting. Saleria squared her shoulders and kept reading doggedly.

> *"Sybaritic good shall reign:*
> *Island city, all alone*
> *Set your leader on his throne*
> *Virtue's knowledge gives the most,*
> *Aiding sanctions by the Host."*

"That is *definitely* Senod-Gra," Keleseth, Guardian of that city, muttered. She gestured for Saleria to continue before anyone could hush her, too.

> *"Faith shall now be mended whole:*
> *Soothing songs kept beasts at bay*
> *But sorrow's song led King astray.*
> *Demon's songs shall bring out worse*
> *Until the Harper ends your curse."*

Saleria paused, but no one interrupted, so she gave the final lines.

"Save the world is Guardians' goal:
Groom's mistake and bride's setback
Aids the foe in its attack.
Save the day is Jinx's task,
Hidden in the royal Masque.

". . . And that's it. All eight verses," she concluded. "Eight Guardians, eight verses. Lines speaking about demons more than once, and how it's the task of the Guardians of the world to save it."

"Well, the first verse has already happened," Guardian Kerric asserted before anyone else could speak. "The serpent was the mage—technically mages—who tried to steal the power of my Fountain. First the mage who also tried to take over Sheren's and Rydan's Guardianships, Xenos or something, then that fellow Torven, who betrayed the trust expected of my Maintenance staff. And the Painted Lady in question is my own beloved, Myal . . . so there's the link to the other verses from the Synod Gone prophecy, the romantic aspects of it as it were."

"And I can definitely confirm the second verse is about *my* Guardianship," Saleria added. "I am the Keeper of the Grove, I am being helped by Witch Aradin Teral, there is a wave of magic that needs to be calmed . . . whatever role we are to play in all of this, part of it comes from the Grove calming down."

Mother Naima chuckled. "Guardian Serina would no doubt say that's a sign her project to calm the world's aether for the reinstigation of the old Portals is coming true . . . since that's what she wants you to do anyway. Calm the magics of your Fountain, and you should be able to recreate the old Portals across the length and breadth of Katan. *If* I've followed her lectures on the subject aright."

Aradin abandoned his project, hurrying over to her side. "—Excuse me for interrupting," he called out, moving into the mirror's viewing range. "But from what Guardian Saleria, my Guide, and I have been able to figure out, it's going to take a few years to get the energies of the Grove quelled to *that* level of stability. Portal magics are *nothing* to muck around with. A Gate, you can push through a small patch of the aether, but a Portal requires far more stability.

"Don't expect to step from here to Fortuna in the span of a heartbeat within the next three to four years. In fact, don't expect to step from far northern to far southern Katan within the next three to four years," he finished dryly. "But we will work on it, yes."

The abbess chuckled. "That's all she can rightfully expect, that you'll work on it—and I'll tell her so if she starts getting frenetic about it. I . . . hold on a moment."

She shifted away from the mirror, face craning past its edge. Aradin, seeing he wasn't needed, gave Saleria a reassuring touch on her back and moved off to resume his work once more. A moment later, the middle-aged woman with the white wimple and head veil leaned back into full view of her mirror, her expression a delighted smile.

"Well, now, Natua be praised! Serina's actually in labor this time, and not just false pains. I should have enough time to wrap this up, but hopefully it won't go on too much longer. I'll want to be on hand for the traditional Natallian blessing of the newborn. So let's not take forever parsing out who gets which verse to study and dissect, hm?"

"Study and dissect?" Sir Vedell asked her.

"Well, yes, of course," Naima said. "If those of us who think the verse refers to our own purview study it in depth, we can look for specific local instances which match the prophecy. That will free up the rest to study the prophecy as a whole, looking for larger patterns, or for anything pointing it at some other place or person instead. It's a good way to divide the labor."

"I concur," Kerric said. "That was my own thought."

"Well, the next one would probably be my purview," Alonnen stated. "I'm the Guardian tasked with keeping an eye on the Mekhanans, and 'Gearman' and 'Guild' both reek of Mekhanan society."

"I suppose Tipa'thia and I will have to keep an eye on the fourth verse," Pelai said. "It could mean any Painted 'Lord' anywhere around the world—any male Painted Warrior—but combined with the words 'synod' and 'Temple,' which is where Tipa'thia's Guardianship resides, it should mean something will happen in Mendhi. Also possibly 'beneath the granite face' or whatever the verse said."

Saleria nodded, since that was the correct wording for that line. She looked at the middle-aged woman with the pale platinum hair. "Guardian Ilaiea, you questioned the line about dragons?"

"It . . . well . . ." For a moment, the normally self-possessed woman looked a little flustered, before she gathered her dignity and her authority. "The Draconan Empire *might* have something to do with it, but they haven't had any real dragon-sightings in hundreds of years. The Moonlands, however, have dragons aplenty, but we've been separated from the rest of the world by the will of the Gods Themselves."

Guardian Koro spoke. Like Alonnen, he had once again hidden most of his dark hair behind a deeply cowled hood, and his eyes behind deep blue viewing lenses. "Somehow, I doubt the mighty Draconan Empire—the 'Dragon' of the southern hemisphere— would ever deign to *bow* to anyone."

"The power of the Singer of the Moonlands is *not* to be mocked," Ilaiea retorted. "We are the Voice of the Moons, and wield power beyond your comprehension."

"*Guardians*, please," Kerric interjected, his expression calm but his tone conveying a hint of impatient eye-rolling. "We are all on the *same* side. We do not need to play 'my Guardianship is more powerful than yours' . . . because if we judge solely by the size of the power-flows we handle, Guardian Saleria has *all* of us beat, as she commands the powers of *three* singularities at once."

Saleria blushed at the mention of her power, and cleared her throat. She wished she could be like Aradin and return to some other task, but she had to stay here and be a good Guardian for the sake of the world.

"Sybaritic good, island city, and Host all refer to Senod-Gra," Keleseth reconfirmed. Second eldest of the Guardians, not quite as old-looking as Sheren but still quite gray-haired herself, she nodded firmly. "That would be my Guardianship, and I can tell you that while I'll allow quite a lot to happen in the City of Delights, demon-worship is *not* one of them. I'll keep a very vigilant eye on what's happening out here."

"It does say 'Host' and not 'Hostess,'" Guardian Miguel stated, speaking up for the first time since greeting everyone at the start of the meeting. "Perhaps it refers to your successor?"

Keleseth opened her mouth to argue, but Guardian Sheren got there first. "Oh give it up, Kel. You know you've been looking at possibly retiring in the next few years. I'd *be* retired myself, if I had a successor I could count on. Guardian Dominor's promised me that his younger brother Koranen and my apprentice Danau can somehow combine their abilities to make up for Danau's deficits, but I won't rely on that until I've seen it for myself, and tested it for a good year solid—I suggest you start casting around for a good male successor for your own needs, and follow the prophecy."

"I already have a perfectly good *female* successor," Keleseth replied.

"But if you follow the prophecy exactly, we have a chance of success," Guardian Koro reminded her. "That means picking a male successor, not female."

"If that is true, do *you*, Guardian Koro, really think the Dragon

Empire will bow to the Voice of the Moonlands?" Guardian Ilaiea asked him archly. "Since you seem to be on their side."

Saleria couldn't be sure, given the hood and the tinted lenses, but she thought she saw Guardian Koro narrow his eyes at the older woman. Guardian Kerric cleared his throat firmly. "Gentle-ladies, gentlemen, we are getting off topic . . ."

"I'll keep an eye on the verse that mentions the Dragon," was all Koro said to that. "It may not be within my jurisdiction, but I do know something of the Draconan Empire, being a sort of . . . neighbor . . . to the Five Lands."

"As will I, since it involves a Voice of the Gods," Ilaiea stated primly. "And I can think of no better than myself, or my daughter. We are, after all, the Singers."

"That's just fine, but that leaves us with two verses I personally cannot place," Guardian Sir Vedell told the others, capturing their attention. "Something about harpers and something about jinxes, a king being led astray, and a royal mask or disguise of some sort. Does anyone know what any of that means?"

The others shook their heads, save for Kerric. The Guardian of the Tower flicked his hand out in a vague gesture. "Possibly the seventh stanza refers to the old Fountain of Garama. If I remember correctly, Garama has a sect of quasi-priest-mages called Harpers, and that *would* tie into the Synod Gone prophecy, which speaks of the line, '*By eight who are kin, by six familiar, one runaway, one unknown.*' If we take the '*eight who are kin*' to mean Guardians Dominor, Rydan, and their six brothers, then that leaves six of *us* who have been able to identify our verses, plus a 'runaway' and an 'unknown' Guardian."

"About the only advantage we have," Pelai stated, "is that those last two verses are indeed last. Two have come true so far . . . but if I recall correctly, Guardian Kerric, your verse took place almost half a year ago. Guardian Saleria's is only just now coming true.

We do have some time, still, before knowing who the unknown and runaway Guardians need to be becomes important to the prophecies."

"Some time, yes," Kerric agreed, "but just because there have been a couple turnings of Brother and even Sister Moon between my situation and Saleria's is no guarantee it will take another six months between hers and Alonnen's, since he's the closest Guardian to Mekhana and that verse. In fact, it could be another six months from now, or it could be only six days. But you are right, in that those two verses appear to be at the end of the chain of events leading up to the lot of us hopefully thwarting a Netherhell invasion.

"Guardian Saleria, do you have copies made of both prophecies in question?" he asked her, turning back to the Keeper.

"Yes. My scribe spell-copied a good dozen prophecies onto these scrolls," she said, lifting the one in her hand. "It starts with the 'Guardians of Destiny,' since that one speaks the clearest of the problem, then moving on to the Synod Gone, one that seems to speak of Senod-Gra and demons, and a few others of lesser importance. The Guardians one is the most significant, so Daranen put it at the top. I can pass them through the Fountainway to you, Guardian Kerric, for distribution."

"If you would send them now, I'll make sure they get rerouted. Is everyone ready to receive a copy of these Katani prophecies?" Kerric asked.

Saleria watched the miniature scrying windows flanking either side of Kerric's face. When all nodded, she murmured a levitation spell, lifting one scroll after the other up into the air, then muttered a second spell to open up the Bower Fountainways. With a tumble of the rods and a flutter of the ends of the silk ribbons tying each scroll shut, they vanished into the Fountainway, headed for Kerric's hands.

She had already received five similar prophecy-laden scrolls from the others, as each Guardian had come prepared to share their findings. Mother Naima looked eager to be off soon, to witness the birth of Guardian Serina's children. Saleria had no such convenient excuse to get back to work, just the more tedious task of helping prepare potion ingredients for Aradin. *Although if I brought some sort of stool or chair to the Bower to sit on, maybe it wouldn't be quite so tedious,* she thought, listening to Kerric redistribute her offerings. *I could sit and sort ingredients while I listened to the others talk. Yes, I think I'll do that.*

The Bower was rapidly filling with tables, storage chests, various bits of alchemical gear, and more. The moss had been trimmed well back from several paths, and the intermingled saps saturating the ground had been collected into barrels for storage until it could be separated and purified or burned somehow. A stray corner of her mind, bored with the mirror-scryed meeting, wondered just how different the place would look in another month, if it had only taken a single turning of Brother Moon to change things as much as they had . . . and only in the Bower, so far. The entire span of the Grove awaited their efforts.

Listening with half her attention to what Guardian Marton was reporting from the prophecy archives of Fortuna—which wasn't much more than what they already knew—she wondered if she dared sneak off-mirror long enough to grab a mortar and pestle to grind something while she listened. Anything to help keep her normally active body busy, however important and interesting the discussions at hand might be.

(*Wake up, both of you!*)

Guhh . . . whah? Wits swimming in a fog of deep sleep interrupted, Aradin became aware of himself and his surroundings. He had been sleeping in his favorite position, wrapped around Saleria from behind. The moment he identified the warm curves in his arm, the shapely naked bottom pressed against his equally naked groin, he instinctively cuddled closer. Nudged her with his loins, hoping it was early enough for . . .

(*Oh for the love of the Light*—wake UP!)

Both of them jolted, Aradin with wide eyes and Saleria with a gasped, "T-Teral?"

(*Yes, and I apologize for coming back so early in the morning without warning, but it is time.*)

"It's time?" she asked. "Time for wha—*oh!*"

Aradin, struggling more with his body's reaction to hers than to Teral's words, found the source of his interest elbowing him accidentally in her awkward wriggle to get out of the bed. "What the . . . ?"

"Convocation! It's time!" she clarified.

His eyes snapped open. Then squinched shut as she rapped the lightglobe by her bed, flooding the night-dark room with light. He grunted as his eyes smarted, waiting for them to adjust to the abrupt glow.

(*Both of you need to hurry. The people of Nightfall are going to have all the petitions timed in the order of each priest's arrival, so they want Katan's representative to show up quickly, as a diplomatic courtesy from their rival, Nightfall. I have to go tap the rest of my fellow Guides in the contact-chain, but I won't be long.*)

"Right, right . . ."

Sliding out of the bed, Aradin squinted against the rapping of another lightglobe and followed Saleria into the dressing room. Now that they were more or less stationed here in Groveham permanently, and Nannan was able to do his laundry along with the rest—he and Teral had scrounged up and enchanted some tools to help that task go more easily for the non-mage housekeeper—he was keeping half of his things in Saleria's dressing room. Their dressing room.

"Teral says they want you to arrive among the first, since the order of petitions heard will be in the order the priests arrive. As a courtesy from Nightfall to Katan, since they're stealing your nation's chance at reconvening it, as well as gaining their independence in the act." He reached for a clean set of undertrousers.

She nodded, barely keeping her balance as she struggled into her own undergarments. "More power to them—oh! Prelate Lanneraun! I'm scheduled to go visit him today for lunch to discuss the upcoming Autumn Festival, one of my eight public appearances. And I thought of something: Aradin Teral, I give you both permission as officially appointed assistants to the Keeper of the Grove to use its powers in any way you best see fit while I am gone, in the understanding that you shall hide nothing from me when I return. I almost forgot about your oath-binding, but now you should be free to use the Grove energies to defend it against any possibility. I just need to find some paper and a pen and an inkpot for a note to the Prelate . . ."

"I'll pray to all four Gods that it won't ever have to come to that. And I can go visit Prelate Lanneraun for you," Aradin reminded her, touching her arm in brief reassurance before pulling on a pair of trousers. "We don't need to waste time with a letter. If nothing else, I can always tell him to postpone making the arrangements until your return."

"Aradin, we don't know how long this Convocation will take. The ancient records spoke of it lasting up to a month! If I am gone more than a month, the whole festival would have to be postponed, and *that's* not going to happen," she reminded him. "Not here in Groveham, the town right next to the Sacred Grove."

"Then as your assistant, simply appoint me to stand in your

stead," he offered. "Or better yet, ask that other Guardian, uhh . . . Dominor, if there's a way to transmit a mirror-scrying of the Convocation on that mirror Guardian Kerric gave you, and we'll make *that* the focal point of the festival. Or even a captured recording if you come back early, like what we've been viewing of the Nether-hell invasions."

Her brows rose. "That is actually a very good idea. I'll talk with Guardian Dominor as soon as I can, since he has one of Kerric's mirrors, too. He did say yesterday that he and Guar . . . er, ex-Guardian Serina had returned to Nightfall, now that the nun-lady, Mother Naima, was back in control of Koral-tai. Something about crafting spells to make it safe to move their newborn twins."

Aradin nudged her hands, which had paused midway through donning her pink-edged white tunic. "Keep putting on your clothes, woman."

Nodding, she continued donning them. He did as well, shrugging into a tunic and slipping his feet into a pair of house-sandals. Picking up the belt, which now held a leather scroll case filled with a list of Katan's needs which Daranen had compiled for them, as well as the knife and the pouch added earlier, he helped buckle it around her waist while she adjusted the fit of her overvest. He handed her the backpack next, then helped swirl the cloak into place over it all.

"It's a good thing my clothes are spell-stitched for comfort," she muttered, "or I'd sweat to death before I even arrived."

(*I'm back,*) Teral announced, returning to his Host's Doorway. (*Good, she's ready—not that Witchcloak, the big one! The one they specially made for priest-transport.*)

(*Right, sorry,*) Aradin shifted his hand from the robe that had the tan outer lining to a more voluminous, all-black robe. Shrugging into it, he turned to Saleria, cupped her face in his hands, and kissed her. Not a very long kiss, but a heartfelt one. Pulling back a little, he rested his forehead against hers. "Put your trust in Teral and the other Witches; we are all bound to help you in this trip. If you absolutely cannot return through the Dark a second time, it will be alright. You have the money for both ship passage and mirror-Gatings, once you reach the mainland. Just send word back through our fellow Witches to Teral, is all I ask."

"Yes, Groveham does have a mirror-Gate station," Saleria agreed, distracted with worry. "Should I get something to eat before I go? I don't know if they'll have food."

"That's what the travel cakes are for," he reminded her. "But you should be fine. Besides, some people feel the urge to vomit after traveling through the Dark, so, ah, best if you don't have anything in there."

(*Ready?*) Teral asked both of them, since Aradin was still touching the Keeper.

They both nodded, and Aradin kissed Saleria one last, quick time before releasing her. Shrugging the hood of his cloak up over his head, he opened wide the deep black edges and swept them around her. "Grab my body with yours," he directed, "and be ready to have it shift into Teral's. The moment it does, he will pull you through my Doorway into the Dark. Do *not* be afraid . . . though you may feel uncomfortable."

"I'm not afraid," Saleria promised him—both of them. She wrapped her arms around his chest and Aradin wrapped the folds of his Witchcloak around them both, sealing out the light from the enchanted white globe resting in a bracket near the dressing room door. "I love you both."

"*Oh, sure*, now *you mention it*," Teral quipped dryly with both voice and mind, as much to distract her from the sudden shifting of the flesh under her arms as to simply comment about it. Wrapping his arms around her, he pulled her from the comfortable land of the living to the breathless, gloomy chill of the Dark. "*Keep your thoughts firmly on me, if not on our destination.*"

She wanted to say, *Considering I have no clue where we're going . . .* , but she carefully blanked that out of her mind. She also wanted to breathe, but didn't know how, in this horrible, uncanny place. Aradin and Teral hadn't said so directly, but she had the feeling that thoughts became reality here in the Dark. So instead of dwelling on either fact, she visualized as strongly as any prayer that Teral would take them to exactly where they needed to be in just three easy steps—and sure enough, in just three steps, they were in a strange, dimly lit place by a tree.

The ground around the odd-looking tree was crowded with the bodies of black-robed men and women moving back and forth. It wasn't easy, walking with her arms wrapped around Teral's chest, but they managed. She had been warned not to let go, for without a Witch's holy powers to shelter her, the Dark could quickly become a very confusing and dangerous place. The last thing the Keeper of the Grove needed was to get physically lost between Life and the Afterlife.

"Priest coming through!" Teral called out, escorting her into the midst. The sea of faces—since the dark robes were hard to see in the gloom—parted before them, until they came to a tallish, black-haired man with astounding, vivid blue eyes. "Saleria, this is Guide Niel, who will take you through to Host Orana's Doorway. Niel, this is *Guardian* Saleria," the gray-bearded man told the clean-shaven one. "Make sure she gets anything she needs while she's in Nightfall."

"Within the constraints of time and duty, she will have priority in our attention," Niel promised. He touched Saleria's shoulder, gripping it for a moment before sliding his arm around her. "Shift your grasp to me, and be ready to be holding my Host. It will be safe to let go when you see the light of day."

She nodded and wrapped her arms around his muscular chest, squeezing her eyes shut as the other Witches helped pull the folds of his cloak around the two of them. A shuffling step back and to the side, and the hard male chest morphed into a softer feminine one. A moment later, light bloomed around her, air rushed in to meet her . . . and nausea welled up inside of her.

With a nudge from the Witch, Saleria let go and staggered free, trying not to heave. Hands caught her, holding her more or less steady while she fought a battle between casting up the lack of food in her stomach and the desperate need for air. A brief retch escaped her, but nothing actually emerged, sparing everyone that embarrassment.

"Easy, you're okay now," a female voice soothed her. It took a few seconds for the urge to stop, and a few more beyond that for her to be able to focus her eyes. When she did so, she found herself in a stone corridor lined with an astonishing number of images carved into the solid granite walls. So solid, she couldn't see any seams, so it was a set of walls that either had been magically grown or had been carved out of a mountain. Probably the latter, since magically it was far easier to part and rend stone than grow it seamlessly whole. At least it gave her something to focus her mind upon.

For a moment, all she could think of was the line from the Guardians of Destiny poem, *Lost beneath the granite face*, but then her gaze focused on the woman holding her by the shoulders. A little shorter than Saleria, the other woman looked to be about the same age, mid-twenties, clad in similarly cut, dark green trousers, but with a matching dark linen corset over her pale green tunic. Strawberry blonde hair and aquamarine eyes met her curious gaze.

"Feeling better?" the woman asked. Saleria nodded. "Good. Priestess Ora," the woman stated, looking over Saleria's shoulder, "a little warning about how they might react in coming through your Dark-place would have been in order. Thankfully, she didn't actually puke anything up on me." A squeeze of Saleria's arm, and the redhead released her, facing her again. "Now then . . . I am incipient Queen Kelly of Nightfall, and you're the second of a long line of priests who are about to descend upon us all, when we're not the least bit ready for you . . . but we're going to try to be. May I have your name, your nation, and the name or names of your Patronage?"

"Ahh . . . I am Guardian Saleria, Keeper of the Sacred Grove of Katan, and my Patrons are Kata and Jinga," she said, mind reeling with the thought that she had dry-retched over the boots of this high-ranked woman. "Ah, no offense with my stomach, and . . . sorry."

The incipient queen chuckled and patted her on the shoulder. "No offense taken—Ora, you might want to go back to the amphitheater hall and just wait while people start coming through, rather than having to pull them out of that cloak of yours in the middle of a corridor. I'll send someone down to help you . . . Priestess Saleria, Rora already took the priest of Fortuna off to get him some rooms, so I guess you're stuck with either following me around, or heading back into the amphitheater with Witch Ora, there, to wait until we can get some actual servants down here—we've had a bit of an emergency, making it imperative that we start the Convocation unexpectedly early, you see."

She didn't see, but Saleria nodded anyway. It wasn't her place to worry over something she didn't know anything about yet. But that did bring up the request she had promised to make. "Oh—I need to see Guardian Dominor. Do you know who he is, and where I can find him?"

The oddly dressed queen chuckled. "Go with Priestess Ora, there; she'll take you back to the amphitheater. As for Dominor, he's busy unlocking the great doors between the amphitheater and the Fountain Hall. They're only to be used by the Gods, of course;

the rest of us mere mortals have been instructed to take the long way around—it seems he's picked up at least a couple bad habits from Rydan since taking over the Guardianship of this place. Don't worry, priestess; he'll be along shortly to start getting ready for everything. If nothing else, you'll see him when the Convocation begins."

"I really should see him beforehand. I promised I would ask if he could figure out a way to pass along a scrying of the Convocation to Guardian Kerric, of the Tower," Saleria said. "I figured everyone around the world will want to see a recording of what happens here, and as it's Guardian Dominor's Fountain . . ."

Queen Kelly blinked her blue eyes twice, then shrugged. "I suppose it makes sense you'd have some magical way of doing that." Before Saleria could ask why she phrased it so oddly, the other woman lifted her wrist and tapped a strange bracelet on it. "I'll call him and have him meet you in the amphitheater. If you'll go with Orana?"

Turning, Saleria found herself face to face with a woman in a voluminous black Witchcloak, with green eyes and a braided coronet of hair just a little more golden than her own. The Witch smiled at her, eyes dipping down briefly over Saleria's cloaked body and back in an assessing look. "So you're the priestess our Brother Witch has fallen in love with?"

"If you mean Aradin Teral, then yes. Guardian Saleria, Keeper of the Sacred Grove of Katan," Saleria introduced herself.

"Sir Orana Niel, Darkhanan Witch, High Priestess, and twofold Knight of Arbra . . . it's a long story," the other woman stated. She gestured behind her. "If we walk this way, it won't take long to get back to the amphitheater. You may call me Ora if you like. While my strongest instinct is to help Queen Kelly organize everything her people will need for this Convocation, I have just been reminded a second time that I will be pretty much useless for anything but bringing two hundred forty-six more clergy through my Doorway."

Saleria gestured as well. "Lead on. So long as I get to attend the Convocation of Gods and Man, you can put me wherever you wish."

Orana chuckled. "Tempting. Actually, given how both you and Priest Etrechim—the representative from Fortuna—came through first . . . if you could stay by me and comfort the rest of the priests coming out of the Dark, that would be very useful. At least, until we get more helpers down here."

"Alright," Saleria agreed. Ducking into an alcove, the pair stepped into a vast, vaulted chamber lined with hundreds of benches arrayed in curved rows on one side of the hall and hundreds of thronelike stone chairs on the other half. There were two others here: a middle-aged man with gray-salted black hair, and a young-ish woman with plain ash-brown hair. "If anyone actually retches on me, I'll deal with it, but I reserve the right to go change clothes before you're allowed to start the Convocation. Just for dignity's sake. I know the Gods have seen every moment of my life, even at my worst, but this *is* a formal occasion."

The other woman chuckled again, heading for the center of the amphitheater. "I think you'll be a good match for Aradin Teral." At Saleria's questioning look, the Witch-priestess smiled at her. "I've become rather good at judging a person's character over the years."

"So you think I'll be good for him?" Saleria asked. She guessed that, being a fellow Witch, this woman and her Guide must have been talking with Aradin and Teral all along. The name sounded familiar.

"I think he'll be good for you. Ah, here we are. Lady Rora, Priest Etrechim of Fortuna, this is Priestess Saleria of Katan."

The somewhat elderly man smiled and bowed. *"Vershu'da, Clergy Saleria. Natuska gar shuden ona faishoudo sbesidin."*

"Uhh . . . beg your pardon?" Saleria asked, confused by his words.

"Oh, right. I speak via Ultra Tongue, which translates everything I say so that both of you can understand, and allows me to understand each of you," Ora explained. "But that does not guarantee that either of you can understand each other. Etrechim simply greeted you, and said he is honored to share this momentous occasion with such a lovely representative as you."

The other woman, Lady Rora, nodded. "Several of us on the Isle of Nightfall have drunk the Ultra Tongue potion, and we'd all be happy to translate in between carrying out our duties."

"I see." Saleria looked at the priest, whose wrinkled face showed an equal level of comprehension. She bowed to him. "Please extend my greetings to the Clergy of Fortuna, and tell him that I am honored to be sharing this moment with him as well."

"She greets you in turn, Holiness," Rora translated, though it felt odd to Saleria that she could understand every word of the other woman's efforts, "and is equally honored to be sharing this moment with you as well."

". . . I think I need to get a dose of this 'Ultra Tongue' translation potion as well," Saleria said. "Is it expensive?"

"It can be, depending . . . Ah, excuse me," the blonde Witch murmured, stepping back from all three. She tugged at the folds of her black robe. "It is time to bring across another holy voice of some far-flung nation."

Saleria quickly shed her cloak and backpack onto a nearby bench, readying herself to catch whoever would stagger out next. "Translations can wait; comforting those who cross the Dark cannot."

"*Gar taknim lostock ona sbesido*," Etrechim stated, looking ready to assist as well.

The black-robed Witch swirled and disgorged another male,

shaken and pale. He fell into Saleria's arms and trembled, breath hitching in a near-sob.

"There, there," she soothed, grateful she was a strong woman. She patted him on the back and hoped he understood her tone, if not necessarily her words. "You'll feel better in a few moments, I promise . . ."

TWELVE

Guardian Dominor, she had met before. With those nice blue eyes, and that long, dark brown hair, he was an attractive Katani male. She might have been far more interested in Aradin, or even Teral, but Saleria could acknowledge he made a handsome figure in his formal dark blue velvets.

His wife, Serina, on the other hand, was a shock. Tall, thin, and pale-haired, for a moment Saleria mistook her for Guardian Ilaiea. A much more pleasant-looking, younger, smiling version of Ilaiea, with none of the usual superior airs showing.

Her shock showed in a sagging mouth and a double blink. The ex-Guardian of Koral-tai quirked her brows at Saleria, then at her husband. "Do I have baby spit-up on my shoulder or something?"

"I—no, forgive me," Saleria said, blushing. This stately woman was too young to be the middle-aged Guardian Ilaiea. "For a moment, I mistook you for someone else."

Dominor looked between the two of them, then snapped his fingers, pointing at his wife. "Your mother!"

"My what?" Serina asked.

At the same time Saleria said, "—Her what?"

"Her mother," Dominor explained to Saleria. "Ilaiea Avadan, Guardian of the Moonlands. You met her via Guardian Kerric's mirrors, remember?"

"*She's* your mother?" Saleria asked, turning to his wife. At the other woman's wince, Saleria quickly switched her surprise to a look of understanding. "You have my sympathies."

The amber-eyed woman blinked . . . then tossed back her head with a laugh. That woke up the baby snuggled to her chest in a simple cloth sling with a disgruntled, "*Meh!*"

"Whoops," Serina said, and quickly started humming, rocking the infant in her arms. The other half of their twins, cradled in a similar way to Dominor's chest, only yawned sleepily. Speaking more gently, the ex-Guardian addressed Saleria, though she kept her eyes on her child. "I do thank you for your sympathies. Mother isn't the best person in the world to get along with, and it got even worse when I became a Guardian, a near-equal to her. *I* wasn't born with the mark of the Singer, after all."

"The what of the what?" Even without needing a translation amulet or potion for this conversation, Saleria was still a bit lost. "Look, I just wanted to chat with you, Guardian Dominor, about sending one of those scrycastings to the Tower for Guardian Kerric to record and distribute. I thought it would be wise to make something that could be copied and replayed all around the world. This *is* the first Convocation of Man and God in roughly two hundred years. What transpires here should be made available for everyone to witness."

"You have a point, though given *how* the Gateway to Heaven gets opened, I'm not sure if a scrycasting is even possible," Dominor stated. "But a recording, that we can do. Let's get Serina settled near the front, then I'll take you over to the Fountain Hall and we'll contact Kerric. That is, if we have the time."

Saleria glanced around the Convocation hall, counting heads. "There are only fifty, maybe sixty people gathered so far, and it's been at least half an hour . . . so I think we have time, yes. And since this Convocation is related to the Netherhells problem via Prophecy—"

Dominor winced, holding up his hands as he tried to shush Saleria. His wife narrowed her amber-gold eyes. "A what of the what is related to the *what*? Dominor, dear, is there something you haven't been *telling* me?"

Within the span of one second, he switched from a hunched wince of regret to a square-shouldered, head-high stance. Staring down over the inch or so that separated him from his tall wife, the Guardian of Nightfall gave her a quelling look. "I did not tell you that the Convocation is related to the Netherhell forescryings you've been examining because you have been working on something *far* more important in the last month. The safe birth of our children, and the resolution of the Natallian/Mandarite mageborn imbalance."

"Now that they have been born," Serina stated, not in the least bit quelled, "*when* were you going to tell me? Or Mother Naima, for that matter?"

"After a full turning of Sister Moon. You heard Mariel," her husband cautioned her. "The first three months of our twins' lives are crucial to their good health, and that requires their mother to be well-rested."

Saleria decided that, as *she* had spilled the news, she had to make up for it. "He is right, in that you don't need to focus on it just yet. At the current rate the prophecies are unfolding, we still have several months to go before things get anywhere close to a head. Of the pattern-of-eight in at least two of the prophecies involved, we're still only up to the second verse, and that after at least five or so months since the first one's conditions were met."

The ex-Guardian drew in a breath to protest, but the sleepy wriggling of the infant slung across her chest distracted her. She let it out, argument abandoned. Mostly. "Fine. I'll agree that Galea and Timoran need most of my attention right now. But I *do* want copies of all these pertinent Convocation prophecies—and no arguing, *dear*. I have quite a lot of experience at extracting information from such things mathemagically."

"Mathemagically?" Saleria asked her, wondering what that had to do with the words of the Gods as transmitted through Their Seers.

Serina smiled. "I'm an Arithmancer. Graduated in the top of my classes when I studied in the kingdom of Guchere."

Saleria had no idea where that was. Once again, she was feeling her ignorance of non-Katani matters, and resolved to find a map of all these far-flung places.

"A really good one," Dominor agreed, giving his pale-haired wife a fond look. "I'm not bad myself, but Serina is a master-class mathemagician."

"Ah. I never really did all that well at mathemagics. I am a mage-priestess, but that doesn't really qualify as a specialization, per se. I do know a really good Hortimancer," she added. "But that brings me back to my idea about the scrycasting mirrors. While we're talking with Guardian Kerric, Guardian Dominor, I can ask him if he can send over a copy of the prophecy scrolls for your wife, if you like."

"I'll do that myself," he stated. "Or I'll never hear the end of it. Let's get to the Fountainway before something else crops up."

Trailing behind, Saleria followed the pair down the hall where

they had met, around a corner, and into a large, oval chamber filled
with columns . . . and a shimmering, pulsing sphere that spewed
colorful ribbons in all directions. The look of them, the feel of the
energies wafting against her inner senses, was familiar. It took her
a few moments to realize the ribbons were streams of differenti-
ated magic, much like the sap-dripping vines of the Bower. But
where those fed pools on the moss- and cobblestone-lined ground,
these vanished into sculpted pipe mouths.

Dominor did not lead them to the shining spark-in-a-bubble
that was the Nightfall Fountain, however. For one, there were subtle shimmering walls in the way, protective wards that would prevent anyone unauthorized from getting close. Saleria knew the
commands for similar wards for the Grove, but rarely used them,
as they required a great deal of energy to invoke prior to attunement. For another, that wasn't the reason why they were here.

Instead, the Guardian of the local Fountain led them to a mirror hung on one of the artfully carved walls, set in the center of
bas-relief knotwork carved by some mathemagically precise hand.
Used to the chaotic natural lines of the Grove, Saleria couldn't
help but admire all the formal symmetry and smoothness, the
timeless stillness of all the images she had seen carved so far.

"*Anan!*"

The spellword, backed by a faint but still tangible pulse of
power from the tall, dark mage, pulled her attention back to the
mirror. Shaped out of the same materials for the frame and hung
sideways just like her own back in the Bower, it quickly resolved
into the familiar sight of the curly-haired Master of the Tower. He
only glanced their way briefly, however.

"Ah, Guardian Dominor—please hold just a few moments,
I'm almost done here—" The screen turned a soothing shade of
blue for a long moment. Just when Saleria was ready to sigh with

impatience, the image of Kerric Vo Mos returned. He smiled at them—then widened his eyes. "Guardian Saleria? With Guardians Dominor and Serina?"

"Yes. We're about to start the Convocation of Gods and Man," Dominor stated. He paused briefly when Kerric blinked and stared, and dipped his head in acknowledgment of the occasion. "And Guardian Saleria—who is here to represent the Empire of Katan—suggested we make a scrycast recording of the event. It was suggested to maybe try a live mirror-scrying, but given how the Convocation is opened, I'm not sure if that's even possible. But you said you could capture mirror images for later viewing, so—"

"Yes, yes!" Kerric stated, recovering from his shock in a hurry. He twisted in his seat, or rather twisted it, making the bookshelves turn behind him. "Topside Control, I need five—no, six—recording crystals up here on the double! Pack an instruction manual with them, in the Katani tongue. They're really easy to use," he added to Dominor, his wife, and the Katani priestess as he turned back to them. "Just stick them to a wall with a good viewing angle of the whole chamber, activate them with the spellwords from the book, and they'll do the rest. Normally we'd charge for this sort of thing, but this one's on the Tower."

"This one's on the what?" Serina asked, frowning. "The Convocation is taking place *here*, not there."

"I meant, everything those crystals record will be offered in free distribution to all kingdoms with access to Tower scrycasts," he explained. "Normally all scrycastings come at a cost, because the Tower has a lot of expenses behind the scenes, but this is too important to the whole world."

Saleria smiled at him, pleased he wasn't interested in making gold off such a momentous event. "You are a credit to your Guardianship, Master Kerric."

"Call me a Guardian for this," Kerric muttered. "The Master

of the Tower side of me will have to figure out how to juggle expenses for the rebroadcastings, and I'm not looking forward to that. Oh—don't worry about editing anything on the crystals. I'll have the Tower scrycasting mages review it for good angles, audio augmentation spells, and cutting out any unwanted or sensitive information. Here, let me dig up a contract for that; we sometimes record and recast scryings of important events for certain clients . . . such as Senod-Gra . . . ah, here come the crystals. Put a couple up high, so they get a bird's eye view of things, and put the others just over head-height, so that they won't have their viewpoints blocked by too many bodies in the way."

Saleria thought about it, and nodded. "I think I see your point. I've climbed some of the trees in the Grove, and seen different views of the Sacred Garden. It changes everything . . . If you like, Guardian Dominor, I can place them around the amphitheater."

His attention had shifted to his Fountain, but he nodded. "Since it was your idea, I'll entrust it to your hands. No crystals are to be activated in here, though, and none directly across from the giant doors. I don't want anyone seeing the exact layout of our Fountain."

"Understood."

The reply came from both Kerric and Saleria, who exchanged a quick look. Kerric dipped his head. "That'll definitely be on the list of things to get blocked out of the scrycastings; you have my word as a fellow Guardian."

Dominor moved off to catch the incoming objects. Idly turning to watch him, Saleria noticed that one of the copper-colored ribbons was ruffled. It was the same hue as the sap-pool for communications back at the Bower. Mindful of the sleeping infant, she nudged Serina. "Um . . . is that ribbon-thing supposed to be doing that?"

Just as Serina turned to look in the direction of her finger, Saleria saw the ribbon roil with the slightly distorted, strident tones of a familiar voice. "*Guardian Dominor! Whoever you're chatting with, get off the mirror and get my daughter!*"

"Oh, Moons," Serina muttered. "*Mother.*"

The one word clearly summed up her entire feeling on the matter. Or rather, the tone behind it. Saleria silently touched her arm, giving Serina some sympathy. Her own family loved her, and she loved them, but not every novice in the training temple had come from such a pleasant background. Sighing roughly, the tall, pale-haired woman strode toward the ribbon. Saleria, torn between her curiosity and the need to stay by Kerric, felt relieved when the Guardian of the Tower spoke.

"And . . . that should be it. You should have everything you need now. Those crystals can record up to twenty days' worth apiece, so long as they're not tampered with, and provided there's enough light to read a book by," he informed Saleria. "If it grows dark, that'll use up the spellpower imbued into them."

"I'll let Guardian Dominor know," Saleria reassured him.

He flashed her a brief smile and flicked his hand, ending the mirror-call. Faced with her own, ordinary reflection, Saleria ignored it and peered into the silvered glass, trying to see what Serina was doing beyond her shoulder. The Arithmancer seemed to be muttering to herself and tugging on her long pale braid with her free hand, then she stuck her fingers in the coppery mist-ribbon.

"*Yes*, Mother?" she asked tartly.

Saleria quickly raised her voice. "The mirror's free!"

Serina nodded. "The mirror's free, Mother. Would you like to make this a civilized call, or just rant via the Fontways directly?"

"*I have had a very trying day with a very serious shock, child. Do not sass your mother. I'll be on the mirror in a moment.*"

The Keeper of the Grove watched the ex-Guardian of Koraltai roll her eyes, turn around, and trudge back to the mirror . . .

which chimed when she was not quite halfway there. Serina flipped her hand at their guest. Saleria reached out to it, activating the surface. "*Baol*."

It responded to the intent shaping the magic behind her choice of word, even though it was a different one than Guardian Dominor had used. The older version of Serina appeared on the screen, her lips compressed into a thin line and her lightly tanned face a bit mottled from an indignant flush. She drew in a breath to make some comment . . . then stopped, squinted at Saleria, and quirked her brows. ". . . Guardian Saleria? What are you doing on this mirror? I know I connected the scrycasting correctly—Serina! What is this Guardian doing on this mirror?"

"Don't answer that," Serina muttered under her breath. Raising her voice to a conversation level, she dredged up a smile for her parent. "Greetings, Mother. How are you doing today?"

"Terrible!" Ilaiea snapped, scowling. "Do you know what your niece *did*?"

"Which niece, Mother?" Serina asked patiently. "At last count, I had five of them."

"Reina, Ranora's daughter?" Ilaiea clarified impatiently.

"Since I haven't chatted with her directly in almost five years, and since you've rarely mentioned her when you and I chat . . . no, Mother. Do enlighten me," the ex-Guardian told the Moonlands Guardian. "What did she do?"

"She has the *eyes* of the *Singer*!"

Once again, Saleria felt incredibly ignorant of other lands, because the Arithmancer's bored expression changed in an instant to a shocked look. Eyes wide, she blinked at her mother. "*Reina* has the eyes of the Singer?"

"Yes! Today was her channeling day, when her magics were to have been given to the . . ." Ilaiea trailed off, her gaze sliding to Saleria's face, then to Dominor's, who was moving up behind the two women, joining them. "Never mind that. Priest Soren was doing it—we were all in attendance, all the extended family—and just as he raised the sacred stone to her forehead, the normal brown of her eyes drained completely away!

"And worse, when I tried to dispel any illusion, not only did they *not* change back, Soren couldn't even touch the Sacred Stone to her hand, never mind her forehead!" Ilaiea looked upset at that thought. Clueless, Saleria waited to see what else might be revealed of their foreign ways. "It's like the child has somehow found a spell or a source of magic more powerful than the Gods Themselves! She defies the very bloodline of the Inoma with those eyes. She is my *sister's* child—and I'll remind you that *your* younger sister, Kayla, is still very much alive and well, so it's not like the impertinent girl is some sort of post-tragedy replacement."

Nope, Saleria thought. *I have not a single clue what they're talking about.*

Serina studied her golden-eyed mother with her normal, round-pupil, honey-amber eyes, then sighed heavily as if making up her mind. "Don't fret, Mother. I am quite certain that it is *not* some sort of act of defiance. Reina is a lovely child—or she was when I last visited five years ago—and I cannot think her temperament has changed that much in the interim. But if it makes you feel better, I shall make sure to ask Brother Moon and Sister Moon directly as to whether or not this is a genuine Mark of the Singer."

Ilaiea arched one light blonde brow. "*You*, ask the Gods Themselves? Since when did *you* take up a holy calling, child? Last you mentioned, you were still playing with numbers."

Serina smiled. It was a tight expression, evoking yet another wave of sympathy from the Katani priestess at her side, for Saleria did *not* like Ilaiea. The priestess had to respect the older woman as a fellow Guardian, and even trust her to do her job well, but Saleria did not like her.

From the way her hands clasped and clenched behind the small of her back, tugging on the end of her long, pale braid, it was clear Serina didn't particularly like her mother, either. "Unlike you, I am not confined to any one land . . . or any one role, Mother. A few days ago, I became a mother myself. A few years ago, I became a Guardian. And in just a few hours, maybe even a few bare minutes . . . I will become a personal witness to the restoration of the Convocation of Gods and Man."

Ilaiea looked like she had swallowed a small, live fish, one that was was wriggling on its way down. Saleria carefully bit her tongue behind closed lips, not wanting to laugh at this inopportune moment. Serina wasn't through, after all.

"During said Convocation, I will politely and respectfully ask Brother and Sister Moons, holy siblings and Patron Deities of the Moonlands, as to whether or not Reina's Mark of the Singer is a true Mark. I will do so on your behalf, with the priest or priestess being collected from the Moonlands as we speak being a second witness to this momentous event . . . and then I or he or she will get back to you eventually . . . because I don't think we'll be able to use the Fountainway to communicate with anyone for who knows how many days the Convocation will last. According to the old scrolls I read, this could take up to a month. In the meantime, it would be best if you treated Reina as if this *were* the will of the Moons . . . for They will be watching her, if she is indeed a new Singer."

She smiled at her mother, and snapped her fingers. The mirror link stayed active. Belatedly, Saleria muttered her power-word for ending such things, and the image of Ilaiea on a plain blue background vanished, replaced with a reflection of the three of them and the shimmering, pastel energies of the Fountain in the background.

"Well," Dominor muttered, "*that* was a bit different. Is she always that unpleasant? Because every time I've chatted with her . . ."

"*The* Inoma of the Moonlands? Arch mage and sovereign queen and who knows what else rolled into one?" Serina replied tersely. "I'd be more likely to die of shock if she were ever *not* arrogant. The desire to actually learn and use my magic instead of having it bound into our nation's many protections wasn't the only thing that drove me out of the safety and secrecy of the Moonlands."

A deep breath, and she let it go. Literally and visibly, for she had started tugging on her long plait. Releasing it, she took another breath and let that go, too.

"But I am in a wonderful nation with a magnificent husband, two adorable little melons who are no longer making me feel bloated and cranky . . . just sleepless and cranky . . . and I don't have to deal with her if I don't want to."

Saleria started to say something, then reviewed what it was and changed it around. "I was about to say I wish you could've had a more caring mother like mine . . . but if yours hadn't driven you out of your homeland, then you wouldn't have gained a wonderful husband and your lovely twins. So I hope you take it in the spirit it was meant, and not a wish to ruin what you now have."

Serina smiled wryly. "I do understand, thank you."

"I guess in the end it turned out for the best. Didn't it, my love?" Dominor asked his wife.

"Yes, my swaybacked donkey." Serina said it fondly, as if the words were a form of endearment. Guardian Dominor grinned and kissed her briefly. The box in his hands and the infants slung in front of both their chests got in the way for anything more than that.

Saleria held up her hands. "I'll take that, if you like."

"Yes, please. And thank you, Saleria," Dominor added, handing her the heavy chest. "It's good to know we have friends in Katan—

we may seem lighthearted at the moment, but the reason *why* we're reconvening the Convocation so quickly is because Duke Finneg, the Councillor for Conflict Resolution, has kidnapped Kelly's blood-bound sister, Hope, and done something to hide her from all scrying eyes. He's joined forces with a group of Mendhites who want to steal away the ability to create the Convocation from us, including a fight up in Nightfall Castle shortly before you and the others started to arrive. But with the aid of the Gods on our side, we should be able to find and rescue Morganen's lady . . . but I fear with the political might of Katan arrayed against us, it may indeed take an act of the Gods."

She didn't know who Morganen was, but that wasn't important. It was the dangers and threats his family had just gone through that made her frown in confusion. She looked around the Fountain hall, then back at him. "All these troubles besieging you, yet you trust me—a near-stranger and a Katani, associated by default with the Councillor for Conflict Resolution—here in the heart of your Bower? This close to your Fountain?"

"Of course we do," Serina answered for him. "You're a Guardian. You know that the world itself must be your first concern, because of the great power at your beck and call, and the great responsibility your Font demands of you. National boundaries don't even come into it."

"Plus, you're a priest. Even Lady Apista, the Councillor for the Temples, knew to do the right thing when we demanded a sacred bell so we could declare our independence," Dominor stated. He gestured for them to head toward the corridor. "Now, trusted or otherwise, we do need to get back into the amphitheater. Even with the newly recruited servants trickling in, we'll still be needed to help welcome and make comfortable all the other holy representatives."

His comment about doing the right thing made Saleria smile

wryly, remembering something Aradin had told her. "Not every priest or priestess would be so altruistic, Guardian. The first pick for coming here as the holy representative of Katan was actually rather anti-Nightfall, according to Witch Aradin Teral—oh, and speaking of them, I hope to get my hands on a recording of the Convocation for them to watch, as well as for the people of Groveham and its surroundings."

"Groveham?" Serina asked her.

It felt good to know something that someone else—a foreigner—did not. "Groveham is the town attached to the Sacred Wedding Grove, where Holy Kata and Blessed Jinga were wed, uniting Katan into an empire many centuries ago. I am the Keeper of the Grove as well as its Guardian. There is a Prelate—a sort of mid-ranked priest—who tends to their daily spiritual needs, but I am still a member of the community. My work is a bit more broad in its scope, for I tend to the daily stream of petitions from all over the empire. You specialize in mathemagics," she allowed, "but I specialize in prayer."

"Which makes you a *very* apt choice as a holy representative for this," Serina agreed. The infant in her chest sling started to wake up again, making little grunting noises. The blonde Arithmancer sighed. "Oh, Moons . . . I know that sound. That's the sound Galea makes when she's starving. Timoran will follow her lead, too, if I don't get them settled for a snack . . ."

"Then let's get you seated," Dominor told his wife. "Saleria will tend to the crystals, I'll tend to the incoming priests, and you'll tend to our children."

With the arrival of the last priest, a bound and gagged fellow from the kingdom of Mekhana who arrived in an alarming condition she couldn't quite catch the reason for, since he was quickly taken to a bench on the far side of the front row from the seat she had claimed, the Convocation was called to order. The incipient Queen Kelly wasn't the most divinely inspired public speaker Saleria had ever heard, but she wasn't too bad, either. At least the red-headed woman spoke with enough volume and clear diction to be heard by the roughly three hundred or so people gathered in the chamber.

The moment the Gateway of Heaven opened, Saleria knew it was the real thing. She had felt this pulse of pure, clean ... magic wasn't the right word for it, and energy wasn't, and even light and warmth only circled around the sensation, rather than described it. The touch of the Divine, the holiness of pure holy. Difficult to describe in words, because it was felt with the soul and the heart.

She felt a tiny scrap of it every time she sent off a perfect prayer. Not perfect in its wording, but perfect in its intent and its goodness. Like releasing one of those dandelion tufts into a gentle, warm wind and watching it rise to dance in the blessing of the sunshine before being whisked off to parts unknown. Of course, the first God summoned through the Gateway was not her God or Goddess, but the Threefold God, Fate. Even Saleria, ignorant as she was about many outlander things, knew of the Weaver of Time, the oldest acknowledged and continually worshipped God of the world.

Staring at Fate as They walked toward Their indicated seat, old-young-middle-aged, male-female-neither, was like looking at a blurred ray of sunshine. A quick glance at Etrechim's face showed tears trickling down his cheeks, his gaze fastened on his ever-changing God, his lips parted on a breathless, beatific smile. For a brief moment, she wondered if she would look like that, too.

Then They were called, summoned by the strong, respectful voice of the incipient queen. "I summon Jinga and Kata, Boisterous

God and Beloved Goddess of Katan, Patrons of the Four Seasons of Life!"

The coruscating shades of light streaming through the great arched door between the amphitheater and the Fountain Hall rippled, and They stepped through. The mere sunbeam of Fate quadrupled, filling Saleria's world. She did not notice Kelly bidding Them to take a seat, nor did she hear the names of the next few Patron Deities. All she could see was dark-skinned Jinga, His full lips parted in a grin that made His brown eyes twinkle, and the serene, closed-lipped smile of the pale, blonde, blue-eyed Kata.

They came clad in the finely embroidered clothes and adult faces of Their summer aspects. Spring was the Lover and the Maiden, the youthful aspects; autumn the Father and Mother of the harvesttime, the providers for Their people. Winter, of course, was reserved for the Crone and the Guide, filled with the wisdom of the elderly. Summer, however, was the time of the Lord and the Lady, sometimes called the strong Warrior and the benevolent Guardian. Saleria was relieved to see Jinga clad in the silks of the Lord, rather than the leathers of the Warrior; had there been any doubt as to whether or not They approved of this incipient kingdom restarting the Convocation, that one key difference was all the proof *she* needed.

(*Of course We come in peace,*) she heard a male voice whisper in her mind. Not Teral's, not Aradin's, not any voice she had ever heard, but definitely a voice she knew well. (*Though I wouldn't put it that way to yonder queen,*) Jinga added, His voice filling her heart with the sound of His mirth. (*She'd laugh for reasons far too difficult to explain.*)

"Oh, Jinga . . ." The name of her Patron Deities escaped her on a sigh. She could feel the tears welling up in her eyes as she looked upon Them. They had chosen a pair of granite thrones set close together, and clasped Their hands with a fond look for each other. "Oh, Kata."

(*You've done very well by Our people all these years, Keeper of the Grove,*) she heard her Goddess reply, those bluer-than-blue eyes turning her way. (*As you yourself have put it, you were asleep until just this last little while. Awakened by the kiss of awareness. Do not fret over the regrets of the past, and do not worry over the choices of your present. Just be mindful that the path of your future should be constantly double-checked to make sure you are still headed in a rightful direction.*)

(*Kiss of awareness, My Sacred Ass,*) Jinga snorted in Saleria's mind. Such blunt speech was so very much the way the Katani people imagined Him to speak, it made her want to laugh. He slipped her a wink across the many lengths between her seat and His. (*More like a hundred kisses of love. And caresses, and . . .*)

(*Shhh,*) Kata whispered back, sounding both quelling and mirthful at the same time. (*This is supposed to be a solemn occasion.*)

(*A joyous occasion,*) Jinga corrected Her.

Listening to Them, Saleria wanted to laugh and cry, sing and shout. *These* were the God and Goddess she had been raised to believe in. The God and Goddess whose divine touch she had felt while singing one day. The benevolent, joyous Patron Deities of Katan, boisterous and serene, protective and encouraging . . . everything. Everything she had ever believed.

It was a good thing she had all the time it took for Queen Kelly to summon forth the many other Gods and Goddesses of the world. All Saleria could do, all she wanted to do for that first long while, was bask in the glory of her Patrons. It felt like . . . well, it felt like being wrapped up in the snuggliest, cuddliest warm hug of her parents' arms, and she didn't want it to end.

Eventually, of course, she had to address the concerns of her people. But for a long while, wrapped in that spiritual embrace, she was able to just be. That, and being connected directly to Their thoughts, she took the time to ask a few questions about the Grove.

So . . . the Grove . . . it's okay for me to make all the changes I've been making? She tried to think the thoughts as clearly as she could.

(*Of course. You are the Keeper of the Grove. It is your task to decide how to tend its grounds,*) Kata told her.

But all this time, just one Keeper, no support staff . . . ? She couldn't help her confusion and its plaintive question.

(*Prophecy.*)

The one-word answer came from Jinga, His tone sober. Most of the time, the Katani people thought of him as the passion-filled, boisterous God, always ready to celebrate life at the drop of an excuse . . . but there were times when He was the stern and serious Warrior, protector of the people. He didn't say outright, but Saleria got the feeling that there was a definite purpose behind the non-sense all past Keepers had been forced to put up with until now. It was equally clear They were not going to discuss it, however.

So . . . I have Your official blessing to demand a bigger staff for the Grove? she wanted to clarify.

Kata smiled at her, as warm as sunshine, if the sun could shine from the inside out rather than merely against her skin. (*Of course. You are now the chief Guardian of the Grove, as well as its Keeper . . . but We will discuss its needs later.*)

(*For now, you may relax and just be yourself,*) Jinga told her. He flicked His gaze to the side, toward the unseen source of all those shimmering rays pouring in through the Fountain Hall door. (*Things will get a little . . . interesting . . . as soon as the Naming of Names is done, and this Convocation fully begins.*)

Interesting wasn't the word for it. Saleria preferred jaw-dropping when she thought about it later, because that was exactly what it was.

Certainly, she was a touch afraid at first. Even with the Lord and the Lady aspects of her Deities on hand to protect her—and she knew They would protect her—it was still unnerving to watch the scene that unfolded the moment the last God was Named.

Stepping through the Gateway of Heaven, Mekha looked half-dead, with one arm clinging to his shoulder via some sort of Artifact-mechanism dotted with gears and crystals and who knew what else . . . and He did not resize Himself to fit in the thrones allotted for the various Deities. He in fact challenged the entire existence of the Convocation, and the presence of the very woman who had brought all of the priests and priestesses here through her Doorway.

Within moments, the plan their red-headed hostess had outlined for the orderly progression of all these priestly petitions before the Gods was thrown out the nearest window. Accusations of power-stealing flew back and forth between the Patron of Engineering and the blonde Witch-priestess. It was like watching children throwing a ball back and forth between themselves, save that this ball had spikes on it.

The moment Mekha lifted His massive arm to strike down the defiant blonde Witch was the moment Queen Kelly made Saleria's jaw drop. Bounding up to stride between the two of them, the incipient queen proved she had more bravery than anyone Saleria had ever heard of, not only demanding that both quarrelers sit down, but threatening to *spank* the God of Engineering—the *God* of Engineering!

Saleria did not know all the details behind what she was hearing, but the priest who had arrived bound and gagged as the last to arrive was the priest for the God Mekha, the Patron of Engineering, the supposed God for the kingdom of Mekhana . . . and the tale that priest told, when it was his turn to speak, was a chilling one, corroborating the accusations that had been flying across the chamber between Mekha and the Witch-priestess Orana Niel.

Saleria couldn't help it; when she heard how Mekha had been *stealing* the powers of His worshippers literally for centuries, she leaned back in revulsion from the Thing that dared call itself a God. She wasn't the only holy representative appalled, either. Anathema! This, what they were all hearing, went against *everything* she had ever heard of about the covenants of trust implicit and inherent between a Deity and the people He or She patroned!

It was Fate's question that pulled her out of her disgust.

"Arbiter, you have reached your verdict?"

The arbiter in question was the queen of Nightfall. Something in the way the Threefold God spoke those words sharpened all of Saleria's senses. A quick peek around showed she wasn't the only one blinking and focusing. *This is something important . . .*

(*Yes,*) she heard both Kata and Jinga whisper to her, Their voices curling around her thoughts in unison. Sitting up straighter, she paid close attention.

The strawberry blonde incipient queen cleared her throat, looking a little nervous, or perhaps unnerved. But she didn't hesitate more than a moment. "Ah, yes, Holiness. I have heard and seen enough to make a judgment. Mekha is *not* a Patron Deity," Kelly stated. "Not by its definition. He does *not* care for the people He claims are His. We have heard how a member of His own clergy serves more out of fear than of love, and we have seen Him ignore that cleric. He steals His subjects' powers like Broger of Devries tried to steal the powers of his relatives."

Once again, Saleria had no clue who that was. She hoped that, at some point in this Convocation, she would get to hear at least some of the rest of this story, which seemed to have spanned more than two centuries, and had apparently caused the destruction of the last Convocation of Gods and Man, and the subsequent Shattering of Aiar that had torn the once mighty empire into shredded little kingdoms on the continent to the north . . . and who knows what else. But for now, she had to sit in puzzled silence, a bemused spectator of the resolution of a long history she did not yet know.

"There is an old saying from my world in regard to certain belief systems," the queen of Nightfall continued.

On my world? She's an outworlder? She's the outworlder on throne? A subtle hush from Kata made her quell her thoughts.

"'As above, so below,'" Kelly recited. "And it meant that Heaven and Earth should be aligned in how they behave. Mortals are encouraged to behave in good ways. In turn, Heaven is supposed to be the ultimate definition and repository of good. But in this world, that saying works both ways. As below, so above. What we *believe*, You *become*," she stressed, looking at the Gods before her. "Broger and his son Barol both died as a consequence of their crimes, the attempt to steal the powers of others for their own use and purpose."

Gods—more anathema! Magic was inherent in people; most had only a little, some had more, and a rare few had a lot, but that was just what a person was handed in life, and you had to deal with your lot, just as you had to deal with a snub nose or a pointy one, red hair or brown, long legs or short ones. She hushed herself before Kata or Jinga could, fingers clinging to the edge of her bench as she waited to hear more.

"They killed or intended to kill others, and they died for their murderous crimes." Squaring her shoulders, Kelly pronounced her judgment as Arbiter of the Convocation. "Thus it is only fitting that Mekha suffer the same fate. He is *not* a Patron Deity . . ."

She felt it. Saleria *felt* all the Gods and Goddesses in the chamber wrapping Their will around the God of Engineering, stifling His powers.

". . . and he is not a God." Kelly stated grimly. "He is nothing more than a magically enhanced, murderous thief. A bully, beating up whomever he can find for the magical equivalent of lunch money."

A bully indeed, Saleria silently agreed. Then blinked, mind reeling, as Kelly continued. Their hostess outlined how Mekha should be stripped of all power, and that energy purified and given back to the people of Mekhana, who had suffered most under His rule, because He . . . or rather, he . . . was *not* a living being? Her jaw dropped again. It was true that Saleria didn't think that Kata and Jinga needed to eat, breathe, or sleep like mere mortals, but . . . to not consider a God a being? Yes, They were manifestations of the group will and belief of Their worshippers, but . . .

. . . It was done. As she watched, each of the Gods and Goddesses raised one hand. Mekha, diminished in stature and eminence by the Arbiter's words, by her mortal judgment . . . dissolved and faded. Leaving Saleria with the echo of Kelly's last words tumbling through her mind.

They'll have a rough time figuring out what to do with themselves, and who or what to worship next, but at least they'll finally be free to try . . . ? Oh Gods, those poor Mekhanans . . . The horror of what they must have endured all this while struck her. Raised in the Katani Empire, where the strongest of mages often took up positions of power in the government, and where any young girl or boy could dream of developing enough magical power in puberty to one day contend for the throne of the empire and be its sovereign king or queen . . . It was unspeakable, what those poor Mekhanans must have endured, living in fear of their so-called God finding out some of them had magic and sucking it out of them, just to selfishly keep himself alive.

She could feel Jinga's arms enfolding her soul, lending comfort to her in her distress. (*It's alright . . . They will find their way soon enough.*)

(*You have your own thoughts to gather,*) Kata added. (*For you will soon have your chance to speak the will and the wishes of Katan. Not only* to Us—*who have heard them every single day, prayed to Us by you and the other Keepers—but to all the Gods of this world. Make sure your requests are* worthy *ones. You will have a lot of power to back any changes you would have Us make, if We agree they are worth being made.*)

(*Don't think you have to present them right away, either,*) Jinga added, as their hostess strove to come up with a suitable symbol for the Convocation. (*We will be here for several days, and you may make requests of Us at any point in time. This Convocation . . . will not be the most organized of sessions,*) He added, a touch of amusement coloring His thoughts. (*But it will continue to be interesting.*)

I've no doubt, she thought back at Him, a bit dazed still at having seen a God stripped of power and dissolved back into the aether. A moment later, she sharpened her focus on what was being done and said outside of her head. . . . *Chocolate? What exactly is this "chocolate" thing Queen Kelly mentions?*

This time, it was Kata who chuckled. (*Did you not hear her? She claims it's the food of the Gods!*)

. . . *Right.*

Etrechim was not the most eloquent of speakers. It was clear he was a true priest of his people, for he spoke passionately before his Patron and the other Gods, but he wasn't very organized, he hadn't really brought anything written down to help him stay on track, and it was clear he was still overwhelmed by being in the presence of his Deity.

Slightly more accustomed to at least praying to her Deities, if not always to receiving a direct reply, Saleria wasn't entirely overwhelmed. Still a bit in awe, but not overwhelmed. In fact, she discreetly slipped out of her seat to go find one of the hastily assembled servants at the back of the now crowded room. Her request for writing materials to augment the original notes she had made was greeted with a nod and a murmur that the man would do his best to find and fetch her something.

As she returned to the Convocation hall, she crossed paths with a light-brown-haired man, his eyes as aqua-blue as Kelly's, but with the look of Guardian Dominor about his face. She turned to watch him go, wondering if he was one of Dominor's apparent plethora of brothers, but the young man had his attention on a woman retreating from the hall. Hoping she would have time to meet Dominor's kin later, she resumed her seat.

Two minutes later, the servant in the sunset-clad tabard made his way over to her, crouching a little to try not to disrupt the view of the others watching Etrechim continue his somewhat rambling recital. She accepted the inkpot, quill, and blank sheet of paper he handed her, and wrote down, *Suggest to Queen Kelly the next Convocation of Gods and Man starts with more time to accustom everyone to their Deities, or at least have them come a lot more prepared for their allotted time.*

Only then did it occur to her that she was *understanding* Etrechim's long-winded, rambling speech.

(*Of course you're understanding it,*) Kata whispered in her mind. (*The Convocation of Gods and Man would be nigh-useless as a way to bring the world together in peace and understanding every four years if you* couldn't *understand each other the moment the Gateway of Heaven was opened. But it only works in proximity to the Gateway of Heaven.*)

(*Keep in mind that, once the Gateway is shut, you'll have to go back to either babbling at each other without comprehension, or you'll have to actually learn each other's languages, by rote memorization, spell, or potion,*) Jinga cautioned her. (*Now organize your thoughts, Daughter of Katan.*)

She had that much warning before the Fortunai priest ceased his speeches with a trio of heartfelt bows and thanks to his God, and a sweeping bow to all the Deities. That allowed Queen Kelly to step up and speak.

"Um, Nauvea," she said, addressing the least powerful of the Goddesses gathered in the chamber. "If I may petition you very quickly on behalf of my sister?"

"*She is ready. Do not delay your own duties*," the young Goddess in the white dress with the white flower in Her hair stated, smiling.

"Right . . . the next person . . ." Kelly consulted a pad of paper. Saleria was already in motion, leaving the quill, inkpot, and paper behind, but fetching out the scroll Daranen had prepared for this moment. "That would be Priestess Saleria of Katan," the newly confirmed Queen of Nightfall asserted. "Speak your piece, worship the, ah, Father Kata and Jinga as you see fit—"

The Father what? Saleria blinked at the other woman in shock. Only the chuckling of Kata Herself in the back of her mind saved her from being affronted by such mangled near-blasphemy.

(*Be gentle and gracious,*) Kata encouraged her, as Kelly pushed her pad of notes onto Guardian Dominor, muttering something about queenly business elsewhere. (*She's in the middle of rescuing her blood-bound sister from the "bad guys" as we speak. It has the woman a little flustered, as it would fluster anyone.*)

Right, Saleria thought back at Her and Him. *Gracious it is. I can do gracious—if things are as bad as Dominor hinted, please, lend Your aid to helping these kind people*, she prayed, moving to the center of the hall. *They* have *reconvened the Convocation of Gods and Man . . . and . . .* bollocks *to this. I'm saying this* out loud, she asserted mentally. And got a chuckle from Jinga.

"Unto Holy Kata, Maiden and Mother, Lady and Crone, and unto Holy Jinga, Lover and Father, Lord and Guide, Patrons of the Four Aspects of Life and of the Empire of Katan . . . thank You for watching over and blessing Your people all these many years," she stated in preamble. "Before I read from the list of Your people's greatest concerns that have been assembled over these last two hundred years, I would like to take this moment to greet all the

Gods of the world, and to ask that You continue to shower blessings upon Queen Kelly, her family, her friends, her citizens, and all
those who have ever showed them kindness in the path they have
taken to reach this day."

Though her words were not one of the carefully crafted prayer-
speeches Daranen usually developed for her, she spoke them with
the same heartfelt conviction she gave to any petition for the sake
of Katan. Several of the Gods and Goddesses dipped Their heads
slightly in acknowledgment of her request, encouraging her to
continue.

"I know that there have been some concerns as to whether or
not Katan as a nation should even acknowledge this newly founded
kingdom—"

(*Empire*,) Jinga corrected her.

"—Empire, sorry," she apologized, heeding His correction
without thinking. "But literally being the person the vast majority
of the Empire sends its concerns to, concerns which they wish You
to address, I can safely state that the vast majority of Katani harbor
no feelings or wishes of ill will toward these Nightfallers . . .
despite whatever our government may have complained about. So
on behalf of the *people* of Katan, I thank You for your support of
our Convocation's host-nation."

"*Well-spoken*," Fate praised her. The Threefold Deity had apparently been selected to speak for all the rest when a group response
was required.

She bowed politely to Them in Their ever-changing Aspects,
then returned her attention to the scroll in her hands. If she looked
too long at Kata and Jinga Themselves, she might start to babble
like Etrechim. It was important for the people of Katan to be represented well, however, so she unbound the rods and unrolled the
first portion.

"Hear then, O Gods, the concerns of the people of Katan as

they may have touched not only the citizens of the Empire, but those of other lands as well . . ."

Prelate Lanneraun was a riot when away from the sanctity of his cathedral and its eight altars, very much resembling his Patron Deity, Jinga. He was almost as old as that priest had been back in the Westraven Chapel, Prelate Tomaso, and had a plethora of amusing, even outright hilarious tales regarding his job as the chief Groveham priest, most of which centered around various hilarious incidents involving all the weddings he had officiated over the years. Aradin found himself laughing so hard that at more than one point he had to wipe tears from his eyes, particularly over the story about the hunter whose pet ferrets had somehow gotten loose and gone on a rampage through the wedding banquet set up on a table in one of the Groveham cathedral's side halls.

". . . And of course by then, there was absolutely no way anyone was going to eat *anything* at any of those tables. That is, until the huntsman's *dogs* broke loose, chased down the ferrets, and started *licking* them! Not to mention all the platters smeared with food!"

Aradin howled in amusement, clutching at his stomach because it hurt so much from all the effort. Lanneraun waited politely while he recovered most of his breath, but neither Aradin nor Teral—who was equally breathless with laughter, for all the Guide technically didn't breathe—completely trusted him. The wrinkled seams of Lanneraun's face creased even further as he delivered the final punch line, his dark brown eyes twinkling with merriment.

"*That*, my dear boy, was when the *bride* looked at the mess and said, 'Well, I guess I'll just have to thank Sweet Kata for ensuring I'll never need to clean another plate again!'"

He dissolved, helpless with laughter. The Groveham prelate grinned at him, enjoying his breathless mirth. Aradin finally managed to get one full breath, then a second . . . before starting to laugh again. A knock at the door was followed by the panel opening, and a familiar blond head poking itself inside.

"Whatever in the Names of the Gods is going *on* in here?" he heard Deacon Shanno ask without preamble or leave to enter.

The appearance of the arrogant young man quelled some of Aradin's merriment, though not quite all of it. He didn't like the younger man, and didn't trust him, but Aradin was grateful for the respite. Squirming to sit more upright, he focused on regaining his breath, stomach muscles sore from their workout.

Lanneraun lifted one of his age-gnarled hands, gesturing between them. "Deacon Shanno, I would like you to meet Witch-Envoy Aradin Teral, of Darkhana. Witch Aradin here is the equivalent of a prelate in rank, if not a high priest."

"Actually, I'm a lot closer to a high priest, if I have the various Katani rankings right . . . deacon, priest, prelate, high priest, and then your holy leader . . . right?" Aradin asked, and received a nod. He managed a smile in Shanno's direction. "And we have met, if only briefly. I am glad to see you again, Deacon. Your mentor here has a marvelous sense of humor."

"So I heard," the young man stated dryly, folding his arms. "Prelate, what is this outlander doing here?"

Lanneraun lifted his age-thinned brows, their color long since turned white above his brown eyes. "*Manners*, Deacon Shanno. Witch-priest Aradin has been assigned here by the Gods Themselves as an assistant to Keeper Saleria. Even if he weren't assigned to Groveham, he should still have your respect as a holy guest."

Shanno compressed his lips into a thin line. He gave Aradin only the slightest tip of his head . . . then narrowed his blue eyes. "Wait . . . as an *assistant* to Keeper Saleria? On whose authority?"

"On the authority of the Gods," Aradin said, glancing at the younger man from under his lashes. It was clear from the faint sneer on the deacon's lips that he didn't quite believe the Witch. "Both my own God and Goddess, Darkhan and Dark Ana, and your God and Goddess, Jinga and Kata, approved of my assignment to assist Keeper Saleria in the management and reclamation of the Sacred Grove."

"You?" Shanno asked, flipping a hand at Aradin. "A *foreigner?*"

"Yes. Me. A foreigner." Aradin wasn't surprised by his disbelief, or his disdain. The younger man had struck him as a bit arrogant.

"Actually, Aradin Teral here is a highly trained Hortimancer," Lanneraun stated, supporting Aradin. "He certainly knows his herbology—at the very least his Aian teas. He was able to discern purely by taste the region where the brew I served him was grown, and the spices I like to add."

Shanno narrowed his blue eyes. "I'll bet he is. Well. Gods bless you, foreigner. If you'll excuse me, I must tend to my duties."

(*Oh, for the ability to skulk off in a different body,*) Teral sighed in the back of Aradin's mind. (*I don't quite trust that youth where we are concerned.*)

(*I don't think he can really do all that much to us,*) Aradin dismissed. (*We have the blessing of the Katani Gods, after all.*)

"Deacon Shanno is young. A bit arrogant, but hopefully some sense will be knocked into him," the prelate dismissed.

(*Isn't saying that tugging on the shirt-tail of our divine neighbor, Fate?*) Teral asked Aradin.

(*Fine. If it happens, I'll try to be ready for whatever "it" is,*) he sighed.

"Now, where were we?" Lanneraun asked rhetorically. "Ah, yes, the huntsman's wedding . . ."

Aradin quickly held up one hand, the other going to his still-sore stomach muscles. He chuckled lightly, but even that much was motivation to quit. "Please, have mercy, Brother Prelate; I don't think my stomach can take much more mirth. That, and it's past midafternoon. I'll need to hurry to make my pre-dusk rounds. With Her Holiness at the Convocation, maintaining the safety of the Grove is up to me in her absence."

"Ah, well . . . it's so nice to have an appreciative audience who hasn't heard my tales before. But I do understand the call of one's duty. May Kata and Jinga bless you in your tending of the Grove, Brother Aradin," Lanneraun stated, rising to his feet with a little effort; but only a little.

Rising as well, Aradin clasped hands with him. "I do look forward to hearing the rest of your tales another day. Gods bless you, too. I'll go let myself out."

Nodding, Lanneraun waved him off, moving from his visiting chairs to the seat behind his desk. Aradin turned left as he exited the room. There was a side door he could use that would avoid the main sanctuary, one that would get him closer to the Keeper's home by a full city block. As he passed the next door, he could hear Deacon Shanno speaking.

"What do you mean, she's *busy*? I need to speak to Lady Apista immediately!" the deacon asserted.

An unfamiliar voice spoke in an apologetic tone, but by that point Aradin was well past the doorway and couldn't hear the exact words. Mindful of the passing time, he hurried out the side door. Between Aradin and Teral, the two of them could control and use up the flow of two thirds of the Grove's rift-energies without having to visit each locus tree. But with Saleria absent, her rift's magic would have to be gathered and used up the old-fashioned way, which meant walking the outer wall to empower its wards.

THIRTEEN

her quarters for the Convocation were sparse, little more than
a stone platform and a pallet for the bed, two blankets, a
heating rune, a modest table for a nightstand, and a shorter version
that could serve as a stool. It didn't even have a door, just a curtain
made out of a tapestry with some hastily stitched runes along the
edge for privacy. The sunset-liveried servant who brought her to
the chamber apologized profusely for the lack of amenities, showed
her how to operate the crystalline strips of the ceiling for lighting
and the metal rune set into one of the walls for heating, and promised everything would be vastly superior at the next Convocation.

The woman showed her the refreshing room, which would
have to be shared between her quarters and three others—at least
it had a wooden door for true privacy, plus a bathing tub as well as
the usual facilities—and the stack of strange, loop-covered fabric
that made up the Nightfall version of toweling cloths, then left
Saleria to find some rest for the night. The room wasn't bare-walled;

it had been carved in a forest motif, with suncrystals grown in such a way that they formed softly glowing clouds overhead when the control-rune by the door was set for daylight, and became tiny pinpoints of stars when she touched the rune for turning them off.

It was just enough light to see her way out to the corridor, which was lit a little brighter by softly glowing moons set at intervals among the overhead stars. Whoever had grown the crystals had possessed an artisan's touch. Setting the suncrystals in her bed-chamber to be nothing but stars for eight hours, Saleria stripped down to a tunic and undershorts for sleeping clothes. It felt like she was camping in a silhouetted forest, or perhaps in the Grove as it should have been. A comforting thought.

The suncrystals brightening eight hours later woke her from her slumber. Grumbling to herself over how hard the pallets were in the novices' hall, Saleria slapped her pillow over her head. Voices in the corridor added to the thought she was back in the training temple, until she heard someone laughing and calling out in a for-eign language. Eyes popping open, she pulled the pillow from her head and looked around the room.

Convocation! Not *the old teaching temple . . . All the Gods and God-desses are here!* Scrambling out of bed, she snatched up her back-pack, wrapped a blanket around herself for decency, and hurried to the refreshing room. And had to wait a few minutes until a priestess in an odd red-and-orange-streaked gown came out. The dark-skinned woman smiled at her, bowed with a hand over her chest, and swept the other at the room she had just vacated.

"Thank you so much! Gods bless you," Saleria told her, slipping inside.

"*Ongi etorria,*" the woman replied.

Saleria had no idea what that meant, other than that it sounded friendly. Shutting the door, she breathed in the warm, moist air and hurried to make sure there was still enough heat in the spell for the faucets. Plenty of heat, actually. She made a fast bath, grateful to see someone had brought in linen toweling cloths of the kind she was used to, plus jars of soft soap. Trying one of the nubbly cloths spoiled her for the plain-woven ones, though. There was just one clean towel available, with the rest tossed into a laundry bin.

When she emerged, freshly dressed in a proper priest's gown with her hair braided back out of the way, she met a tabard-clad woman pushing a hovering sled covered in bins and cleaning supplies. The woman greeted her in heavily accented Katani and slipped into the refreshing room to tend to it. Returning to her room, Saleria found a pair of men and a second woman inside, all servants. The men were unbinding a feather-stuffed mattress to lay on top of the stripped bed, while the woman was sweeping the floor. A stack of sheets and nicer-quality blankets than the previous ones waited on the stool, and a chest sat next to it, the lid opened to reveal colorful layers of fabric.

"I'll take that, milady," the woman stated, setting aside her broom so she could relieve Saleria of the wool blanket. "Everyone has been donating something for the comfort of all the holy representatives at the Convocation. Your quarters are being made more comfortable by the generosity of the family Michan. Bobran of Michan, his husband Severth, and their two adopted sons, Goffer and Farathan."

"Ah—his husband?" Saleria asked, blinking.

"Yes, husband, because the government of Nightfall doesn't care what genders are paired in marriage," the woman told her. "So long as we're all productive citizens and good people, we are welcome here." She eyed the Keeper of the Grove. "You don't have a problem with that, do you, Priestess of Katan?"

"Well, no. No," she stated more firmly. "Kata and Jinga have said that same-gender marriages are acceptable. I was just a little surprised, is all. Please let the family Michan know how much I appreciate their generosity, and their warm welcome. May all the Gods bless them for their kindnesses, including the Patrons of Katan."

The servant smiled warmly at her. "I will be happy to let them know that, Holiness. Oh, you should have a door within the next two days. We can craft them from wood easily enough, but the latching mechanisms take a little more time. Your name will be written on a card on the door so that you can recognize it, along with your nation, and the symbols for Kata and Jinga, the eight altar tetragrams."

Bemused, Saleria thanked her, tucked her pack under the night-stand table, and took herself out into the maze of corridors. She got lost twice, the second time thanks to muddled directions from one of the servants, but eventually found her way back to the familiar territory near the amphitheater. One of the chambers had been set aside as a great banqueting hall, with tables and benches for din-ing, and more tables without benches laden with different kinds of food. Some of it hot, some of it cold, some of it fresh, some of it preserved . . . most of it was familiar, though there were a few unfamiliar items. One in particular, a strange dish filled with pale strips of some sort of boiled flour-paste and slathered in a creamy cheese sauce dotted with shrimp, proved quite tasty.

No sooner had she settled at one of the dining tables than a familiar black-robed figure stopped next to her, turned, and sat with her back to the table. "Good morning, Keeper of the Grove," Witch Orana said, smiling at Saleria over her shoulder. "And how are you faring on this second day of the Convocation?"

"Oh, fine, thank you. Ah . . . are you really over two hundred years old?" Saleria asked, saying the first thing that flew into her head.

Ora nodded. "When you're cursed—under false accusations—by the mages of Fortuna, it takes the will of the Gods to overturn it . . . but for reasons known only unto Them, They have chosen to keep my Guide and me alive for the full thousand years of our so-called punishment. I did manage to barter a lack of aging out of them, but it's a very long story. How about your story? How is the Grove doing?"

"I left Aradin and . . . I left Aradin Teral in charge of it, and I have confidence they'll keep it well," Saleria told the Witch, correcting herself. "Part of me wants to go home and tell my people all I have seen, and said, and received in reply. But a larger part of me knows my duty is to stay here and continue to witness the Convocation. If anyone were to have a concern regarding Katan, or its citizens, or even our Gods, then it is my duty to remain on hand."

"Well, if you have any messages for him, Niel and I now have the time to deliver them. Or if you need something from home," Orana said helpfully. "The laundry services are working now, though I'm told they're still gathering enough baskets for collecting it. I suspect in three days this place will be ruthlessly organized. I quite approve of how well everything is pulling together, despite its suddenness."

"Yes, I'm rather impressed by the changes between yesterday and today," Saleria admitted. "I look forward to seeing what will be here by the end of our stay."

"I think I should go have a word with His Holiness of the Moonlands," Orana murmured. "It would be an appropriate act of kindness for his nation to lend the ingredients for enough Ultra Tongue for each nation's representative to have a drink. Don't you think?"

Ultra Tongue . . . Ultra . . . oh, the translation potion! Saleria nodded. "That would be wonderful. Someone spoke to me this morning, a woman in bright red and orange robes, but I couldn't understand a word of it other than her tone, and I'm sure she felt the same about the greeting I gave her."

"I'll see to it, then. Oh, Guardian Dominor wanted to let you know that the Fountainways are blocked by the Gateway of Heaven. He's tried everything he could think of to connect with the others, but all he gets is interference from the sheer energy involved," Orana told her.

"Well, that makes the kind offers to transport goods and messages from you and your fellow Witches all the more important, doesn't it?" Saleria pointed out.

"True," Ora chuckled. "Have a good breakfast. I'm actually off to bed, myself. I've been up all night listening to the ongoing petitions. Even at roughly an hour to the priest, it's still going to take a bit of time to get through all of them. Dominor told me you were going to be recording all of it in scrying crystals. Niel and I look forward to seeing it all . . . but for now, we are very tired."

"Sleep well—Dark Ana watch over you," Saleria added. From the smile the other priestess gave her, it seemed to be the right thing to say. *One of these days*, she thought, watching the black-robed, blonde-braided woman move off, *I will learn the full of her story. But for now, if I don't eat, my food will grow cold. It may be freely given by these Nightfallers, but it shouldn't be wasted.*

Folding her hands together, Saleria gathered her thoughts and her energies, and carefully reworded her normal breakfast prayer. *Gods of all nations, please share the blessing of this food with not only myself, but with the bounteous lands that produced it, the skillful hands that plucked and prepared it, and may the energy it gives me as I eat it this morning in turn permit me to give my energies back to the world at large today . . .*

Being a morning person, Aradin chose to walk the Grove wall before breakfast, rather than after. Despite the fact that two thirds of the magic was now controlled rather than rolling around the place from locus tree to locus tree in slow, mutation-inducing surges, it still had to go somewhere. Aradin and Teral could use the power from the northern and southern tree-rifts to begin making changes to the warped plants and animals, turning them docile and obedient, but not the eastern one.

The power of Saleria's locus tree was nowhere near as wild as it had been. It was not, however, under the Witch's control, either Host or Guide. That meant the eastern stretch of the wall and the side-paths nearest the middle tree had to be tended warily as well as carefully. Aradin considered it an invigorating, appetite-building task.

Breakfast, however, did not await him in the Keeper's house when he returned. Instead, teal-clad men seized Aradin the moment he entered through the back door, clasped metal cuffs around both of his wrists with ominous *clack*s, and dragged him to the Keeper's study . . . where a rather smug-looking Deacon Shanno, seated in Saleria's chair, was staring down a red-faced Daranen.

"And I'm *telling* you that parchment was signed by all *four* Gods!" the scribe growled. He thumped his fist on the desk. "You have *no* right to interfere with what the Gods in Their infinite wisdom have decreed!"

"So you *say*," Shanno drawled, picking up the paper with its glowing runes. He tensed his muscles, attempting to tear it. It didn't budge. His smug look faded a little, and he tensed and tried again. A third time, and he crumpled up the paper, tossing it on the desk in disgust. "Cheap theatrics! Some sort of anti-tampering spell, no doubt."

(*I don't like the looks of this,*) Teral told him, as both Guide and Host watched the paper uncrumple itself, smoothing out as flat as if it had never been creased.

(*Go tell Saleria what that blond brat is trying to do,*) Aradin ordered. (*I'll be fine on my own. They don't dare harm me, in case it is the truth. I'll be demanding a Truth Stone to swear it, too.*)

(*You do that, but be careful. I'll have her bring up the matter with Kata and Jinga directly, if I have to.*) A step back, and Teral vanished from his Host's Doorway.

"You cannot tear what the Gods have signed, Deacon," Aradin stated calmly. "And it *is* signed by the Gods Kata, Jinga, Darkhan, and Dark Ana. Bring me a Truth Stone, and I will prove my declaration true."

Shanno sneered at that. "The words of a foreigner are near-useless!"

"A Truth Stone is a Truth Stone," Aradin countered. "Or a Truth Wand, for that matter. I know they exist in Katan."

"You can swear all you like that the Gods signed this . . . thing," Shanno retorted, flicking a finger at the sheet. "Unless the Gods Themselves swear it, then for all we know, *you* have been tricked or deluded into believing it was Their hand, when it was in reality crafted by that power-thieving braggart who now tries to call himself our king!"

Aradin had no clue what he was talking about, though he had a fairly shrewd idea for why. "Deacon Shanno, your hunger for power has caused you to suffer from delusions. I come here at the will of *my* Gods, with no falsehood or pretense, to be the assistant to Keeper Saleria. *Her* Gods, *your* Gods, have accepted my presence."

"Well, if that's so, then why don't we just ask the Keeper herself?" Shanno offered mock-reasonably. He made a show of looking around the room, then shrugged. "Oh dear, it seems she's nowhere to be found. For all we know, *you* are the unwitting, unknowing distraction manipulated into coming to Groveham by hidden strings so that the rebels of the so-called kingdom of Nightfall could kidnap Her Holiness."

Aradin blinked. The younger man's logic was convoluted, absurd . . . and very, very hard to disprove via Truth Stone. "You are delusional, Shanno of the family Lorwethen. There's no other word for it in your language. Delusional," he repeated. He looked at the guards holding him, clad in the imperial blue-green uniform of Katan. "I'll bet he wouldn't even take Keeper Saleria's word once she returns that I am here with her permission as Keeper of the Grove."

"So you say," the stern-faced guard on his left said. He lifted his square chin at Shanno. "And *he* says otherwise. Given that the rebellious Nightfallers have overthrown the true King of Katan . . . I find myself disinclined to believe the word of *any* foreigner right now."

"Then fetch me a Truth Stone, or a trusted equivalent," Aradin said, staring over Shanno's head. "I have the right under the Laws of God and Man to be questioned by spell. If my words are true, then *I* am innocent of any wrongdoing, and must be set free."

"*I* think we should wait for the questioning until Holy Keeper Saleria has returned from . . . well, wherever," Shanno offered lightly, flicking one hand vaguely. "That way we can question all parties involved."

"I told you, she went to the Convocation of Gods and Man, to stand as the holy representative of the Katani people before your God Jinga and your Goddess Kata," Aradin repeated patiently. "They have roughly two hundred and fifty priests and priestesses representing the three hundred–plus Gods and Goddesses of all the nations in the world. It may take her a couple of *weeks* to return."

"So you are deliberately obstructing justice?" the guard on his right asked.

"No!" The situation was getting ridiculous. "I am willing to abide by the Laws of God and Man, which grant me the right to speak the truth and have it gauged by true spell. Either bring forth your Truth Stone and present your accusations in a *lawful* manner, or let me go."

"Sounds to me like he's resisting arrest," Shanno drawled.

"I am not!" Now he wished Teral were still with him, so he could alert his Guide to this new twist.

"What is your name?" the guard on the right asked him.

"Aradin. Why?" he asked

The guard on the left clamped his hand around the Witch's throat. Aradin struggled, alarmed, but it was too late; not only did both guards tighten their grip, but the left one spoke. "*Voche Aradin obstrum obstarum!*"

Magic washed over him from that grasping hand, first up into his head, then down into the rest of his body—where it quickly drained to the rune-etched cuffs on his hands. Still, enough remained that when Aradin tried to protest, nothing but the hiss of his own breath escaped. *Some sort of silencing spell? And that little blond turd is looking twice as smug now.* He glared at the deacon. *I wonder how much you bribed these guards . . . and how badly your own Patron Deities will punish you for giving false witness, False Priest!*

Daranen started arguing, equally shocked, but the middle-aged scribe was merely shoved aside while the two guards hauled Aradin out of the Keeper's house. Without his breakfast, and without any way to continue to protest his innocence aloud. Wisely, Aradin did not resist. There was a loophole in his capture; the spell said *Aradin*, but not *Aradin Teral*. Wherever they were taking him, so long as he was allowed to keep his Witchcloak with him, or could at least wait for the darkness of night, he could fix everything.

All it would take was a bit of patience . . . when he didn't want to be patient. Being a priest hadn't been his first choice for his life's calling, but he had learned that praying sometimes actually helped. *Darkhan, Dark Ana . . . Kata and Jinga, it doesn't hurt to pray to You, either. You all know the truth. May this idiot get what he deserves, without anyone else being harmed.*

He knew it wasn't the most gracious prayer in the world. Of course, he could have argued that he had just cause, but if there was one thing he had learned from watching Saleria pray, a true spirit put as much power as any rift-spilled magic could. Part of her power came from the purity of her intent. Marched up the street between the two guards, Aradin sighed and strove to do better.

At least the cell they gave him was clean. Aradin had stayed in far worse places trying to pass themselves off as inns. While he wasn't completely sure the pallet was free of fleas, the walls and floor were stone, the high, barred window had glazed panes that let in just enough light to have read by if he'd had a book with him, and the facilities were quite civilized, with a porcelain flush-bowl and a small sink behind a chest-high privacy screen. Katani-style corked faucet, of course, but one couldn't have everything. There was even a small wooden cup for drinking, rather than anything crude like a bucket of stale, possibly scummy water.

The only thing missing was a fourth stone wall. His was one of half a dozen cells, each with one wall of stout, rune-chased bars to keep in the criminals of Groveham. Currently, he was the only prisoner, set in one of the middle chambers. With a cell on either end and the remaining four facing the far wall, there was nothing between him and the two guards lounging at their table but those bars and a few body-lengths.

Clean, but boring. After four hours, he rapped on the bars until he had the attention of the guard who had spell-silenced him, and brought his fingers to his mouth, miming eating. Then he rubbed his stomach and gestured at his mouth again.

"What's that?" the imperial guard mocked, lifting a hand to his ear. "I can't hear you! You're going to have to speak up." He chuckled.

Aradin planted his hands on his hips and gave the guard his best stern priest's glare. It worked. Grumbling, the guard flipped his hand.

"Fine. I was just having some fun. I'll get you a bucket of pig-slops."

Aradin folded his arms, glaring from under his brows. Though mind-to-mind speech was forbidden between two living mortals, he thought as hard as he could, *Try it, and you will be chastised by Kata Herself, even if I have to go all the way to the Convocation in person to fetch Her!*

That, too, worked. At least, the glare did. Defensively, the guard backed up toward the door. "Fine. But don't expect the bread to be fresh. And you'll be lucky to get scrapings out of the roasting pan. You're a prisoner, foreigner, not an honored guest."

Aradin arched a brow at that, but obviously said nothing. Moving over to the cot, he sat down on it to await his meal. As annoying as she could be, he knew he was going to miss Nannan's cooking right after the guard returned with something for him to eat.

Teral slipped into his Doorway. He paused on the threshold, taking a few moments to absorb Aradin's new surroundings, then sighed and settled into place behind his Host. (*You're not going to like Their reply.*)

(*I'm not?*) Aradin asked, both brows lifting. (*Have They refused to prove Their word is true?*)

(*Sort of,*) his Guide hedged. (*Orana spoke with Kata on our behalf, since she was in the amphitheater, and Saleria was apparently elsewhere, probably having lunch given the time of day on that side of the continent. Kata said, and I quote, "The young man in question needs a lesson in humility if he is ever to become a true priest. Let him ride the wave a bit before you save the day." Orana didn't know what She meant by that, but I think I can guess.*)

So could Aradin. He winced and sat back on the narrow cot, resting against the stone wall. (*Oh, that's going to be unpleasant.*)

(*Exactly. Without either of us on hand to shunt all the energies, the Grove is going to go wild in just a matter of days,*) Teral said.

(*Yes. And to add insult to injury, I'm going to have to sit here like a good little prisoner and eat jailer's slops.*) Aradin knew he was complaining about a very trivial matter, when the Grove running wild was anything but trivial. He couldn't help it, though. He'd missed breakfast after having gone on a vigorous hike, manipulating magics and taming wild plants along the way.

(*You know . . . she didn't say we had to stay locked up,*) Teral mused. If he'd had control of their body, Aradin knew from his tone he would have been scratching his bearded chin thoughtfully.

He also could guess from long association with the other Witch what was going through his Guide's mind. (*. . . You're right, She didn't. And Jinga has a reputation for being occasionally mischievous.*)

(*And perhaps we could speed things up by ensuring the "wave" in question was a truly wild one?*) his Guide offered.

Aradin grinned. One of the other two guards glanced his way. He smothered the urge to smile, affecting a sober expression while he waited for his food. (*We'll still have to wait until nightfall. Our spare robe is hanging up in Saleria's dressing room. Think we can make the Witchcloak transfer to it?*)

(*After nightfall, yes. We both know exactly where it is, after all. But until you can get those anti-magic cuffs off, you won't be able to leave, let alone manifest, once you go into the Dark,*) Teral warned him. (*They will anchor you there. Only when they're safely bagged in silk will we have a chance of getting them out again.*)

(*Well, then you'd better go round up a Host or a Guide in the Dark who knows how to pick locks, and who has a spare shielding sack on hand,*) Aradin told him. (*If you're lucky, you won't return until after I've choked down whatever gets scraped out of the prison's dirtiest pots.*)

(*Oh, it won't be that bad, surely,*) Teral dismissed.

(*And who was it who warned which one of us about speaking rashly, hmm?*) Aradin countered.

(*Fine. Consider it your punishment for tweaking the nose of the*

Threefold God,) Teral retorted, and ducked into the Dark. He left Aradin smiling, though, for all it would most likely be true.

The food was divine. Miracles had been wrought since just that morning. Saleria felt guilty for enjoying all the fruits and vegetables and even fish and meats, when she knew how hard Nannan cooked for her. But she did enjoy it.

The Keeper of the Grove could not remember a more exotic feast in her life, though she felt sorry for Witch Orana, who had been pressed into delivering bushels and baskets and stasis chests of food from various nations around the world via the Dark. The more that word spread about the Convocation of Gods and Man being restored, the more people from all over the world wanted to donate to it, to touch it in some way and be a part of this momentous occasion.

"Excuse me, but are you Priestess Saleria of Katan?" a middle-aged woman asked, interrupting Saleria's next bite of the latest version of *pasta*, a dish she had learned came from a land called Guchere.

Setting down her fork, Saleria nodded. "Yes, I am. How may I help you?"

"I've a message from Priestess Orana Niel," the brunette in the sunset tabard stated, and handed over a rolled up piece of paper. An oddly rolled up piece, for it had been pinched at alternating angles, which made it look something like a cross between a bit of honeycomb and a chewed-up stick. At the Keeper's odd stare, the servant gestured at it. "She explained to me that this is the easiest way to conceal a message without using a spell, because she said once it's been rolled up and pinched, you can't get it to roll up perfectly a second time. You can see I haven't peeked at it, milady."

"Yes, I can see that. I just didn't know *why* it had been rolled up like this," Saleria told her, taking the scroll from the Convocation servant. She peeled open a layer and a half, then tried to rewrap it . . . and failed. "How clever . . . It really can't be rewrapped, can it?"

The older woman grinned. "I've been delivering those half the day, now. Everyone's been amazed by the trick of it. Have a good supper, milady."

"And you, when you get to it," Saleria replied, more of her attention on unscrolling the sheet of paper. The message, when she got to it, made her eyes widen. Neatly penned in Katani lettering, its content was alarming.

Aradin Teral has been harassed by someone named Deacon Shanno. They are now under arrest, if unharmed. Goddess Kata in Her wisdom has decided to let things stand for now. She said this would teach "the young man" a lesson in humility, and something about "ride the wave," whatever that means.

Yours, Orana Niel.

Dear Kata! Saleria thought, alarmed. *Aradin, arrested? And to be taught a lesson in humility?*

A voice laughed inside her head. Not Jinga's, but Kata's. Normally serene, the Goddess chuckled in Saleria's mind. (*Not the Witch, Keeper, but the deacon-child, who in his arrogance does not understand what he attempts to wield. Here, let Us show you . . .*)

Blinking, Saleria swayed and clutched at the dining table, anchoring her sense of balance as the world shifted. She knew she was still seated in the dining hall somewhere under the mountains of Nightfall Isle, but her sense of sight and sound showed a completely different scene, of leaving her body behind to fly high over a broad island, then a vast span of water, chasing the sun like a spell-flung skylark.

Her mind relaxing into Kata's control, Saleria blinked as the width of Katan itself streaked rapidly past, until she alighted on a curving, interwoven branch of the Bower itself, in a spot which allowed her to peer down at a familiar blond man.

Deacon Shanno, oblivious of the bird's-eye view which Saleria now had of him, picked up a flask from one of Aradin's tables, sniffed at the contents, made a face, and set it back down again. "Poncy fellow. Smells like a perfume shop in half these bottles. The other half like a child that's been rolling in the grass . . .

"I think I shall have to get rid of all of this," he decided, fluttering his hands at the collection of tables interspersed between sap pools and altars. "Cluttering up a holy sanctuary with alchemical equipment? Blasphemy!" Shanno asserted. Then he cleared his throat and tried again, this time with less volume, but a deeper tone. "*Blasphemy*." He attempted it a third time, testing out yet another way of emphasizing it. "*Blas*phemy . . . blasphe*mous*. Hm. I'll have to work on that."

He turned in place, squinting up at the vines as they slowly oozed and dripped around him. Saleria almost held her breath, for he looked like he was about to step backward into a pale amethyst sap-pool which Aradin had identified as concentrated fecundity—in other words, perfect for lust potions, conception potions, and even contraception potions, if treated just right alchemically. Unfortunately, he noticed it before anything could happen. Shanno gave the puddle a bemused look, then stepped away.

"No, no, this is all wrong! Why would the seat of power be *dripping* with . . . goo?" Shanno muttered in disgust.

Tentatively, he reached out to touch a sap-slick vine, the one which Aradin Teral had used to show how it caused a sugarcane plant to grow faster than natural. Nothing happened, other than that he got the slightly sticky stuff on his fingers. Stooping, Shanno scrubbed it off on a bit of moss. From the way he immediately straightened and moved on, Saleria assumed he did not see the moss quiver, then thicken.

"This should be a true garden, filled with flowers, and trees, and bowers . . . ew, is that a bug?" He peered out between two of the interwoven, rough-barked roots forming the edge of the Bower's dome, and made a face. "Far too nature-filled for my tastes. But still, I'll have the prestige of tending it while the Keeper is away . . ."

Oh, Kata, Saleria thought in disgust. *I think I've seen enough . . .*

Apparently not, for her literal bird's-eye view followed Shanno out of the Bower and down the paths. Sunset was only an hour or so away. By this point in time, all three of them—herself and Aradin Teral—would be channeling power directly from the Bower to the Grove walls. That slowed the sap-dripping as well as ensuring that the heart of each locus tree would not overfill and thus overflow with untapped magics. But it was clear Shanno had no clue what to do. He hadn't even grabbed a pruning staff from the shed just inside the Grove.

Sure enough, something lunged out of the bushes, slapping at his ankles. Shanno shrieked when the thettis-vine attacked, stumbling back. By pure miracle, the thorns only snagged his white priest-robes. Yanking his hem free, he hopped back out of range of a second lash, his blue eyes wide.

"U-Unnatural place," he stammered. Then muttered to himself, snapping his fingers. A faint shimmer bubbled around him in a protective ward. ". . . There. That should do it. I'll come back and burn you out, see if I don't!" he warned the bush. A blush stained his cheeks. "Listen to me; I'm talking to myself! Unnatural place. I'll take great pleasure in casting several fire spells on that patch tomorrow morning. But *you* can wait until morning. I'm off to have myself a nice supper, and a bit of dessert for a job well done . . ."

Nothing else attacked him, which was a pity. Saleria watched him disappear into the Keeper's house, where he received nothing but tight-lipped, dark glares from Nannan. From the unlit state of the kitchen, she would apparently rather let herself and Daranen starve than fix the deacon anything. Shanno gave her an arch look, the kind that said he would be back, and marched out of the house.

The skylark's view swooped into the streets after him, but rather than following the deacon all the way to the cathedral, it detoured to the guard hall. Settling much like a bird on the sill of a glazed window, Saleria had a few moments to peer inside past the bars. She caught sight of a familiar, beloved dark blond head, of a well-known hand dipping a chunk of bread into a bowl of something unidentifiable, an unfamiliar bit of metal wrapped around Aradin's wrist . . . and then the skylark took off, winging its way back to her body with breathless speed.

(*Give it two more days, Keeper,*) Kata advised her. (*Then you may join your Witch-lover if you wish . . . though only briefly. You are needed to stand witness here as well as there.*)

Saleria landed with a swaying jolt in her body, no longer a mental bird lofted by her Patron. She felt a feather-soft touch, as if Kata had brushed Her lips against Saleria's brow, then nothing more. Alone with her thoughts, Saleria wondered if she should do anything about what she had seen. Not go to Aradin immediately—not against her Goddess' advice—but if she should tell anyone what was happening. Hunger distracted her.

Her food was still warm, though not quite hot. Digging into her meal, she nibbled on some exotic reddish carrot-thing cooked into a sweet dish with bits of spice-dusted fruit. A yellow nubbly something that had been pickled and chilled hit her palate next. It reminded her of Aradin and Teral politely declining some of Nannan's vinegar-based sauces . . . and that in turn reminded her that the Keeper of Katan wasn't the only member of the priesthood involved.

I shall have to seek out the Witch-priest representing the people of

Darkhana, she decided, dipping a bit of fresh-baked bread into the spicy-sweet dish's sauce. *Darkhan and Dark Ana would no doubt like a say in how Their priest has been treated by a deacon of my own Order* . . . Lifting the bit of bread to her mouth, she hesitated. *Oh. Oh, right . . . Poor Aradin. Who knows what he's dipping his bread into at this very moment? Kata, Jinga, make sure he's fed something healthy, at the very least! Or I shall have to have* very *cross words with the Guard Captain of Groveham.*

While the night shift guards quietly played some sort of card game in the glow of a modestly rapped lightglobe, Aradin meticulously draped the folds of his Witchcloak over every inch of his body. Tugging the deeply cowled hood over his head, he fitted his wrists into the oversized sleeves, wriggled just a bit to make sure even the cuffs overlapped . . . and relaxed into his own Doorway. Teral took his place, anchoring their shared body in reality.

Glenna awaited him, as did her Guide, Josai. Glenna smiled and wiggled the strange implement in her hand. "Bet you didn't know I could pick a lock . . ."

"You'd win that bet," Aradin told her. He held up his wrists. "Anti-magic cuffs, wrongfully applied. The instigator will get his comeuppance shortly, if Teral and I have anything to do with assisting it along . . . and of course we will."

The other Witch chuckled, then started poking and prodding at the cuffs. "Good thing these are more or less nullified by the Dark . . . ah, there we go. Simple enough mechanism. A twist, a push, another twist . . . huzzah!"

Josai swooped under Aradin's wrist and caught the falling cuff in a quilted satchel before it could land on the not-ground of the Dark. She hovered, waited, and caught the second one as well. Pulling the drawstring tight, she wrapped the ends around the throat of the bag, knotted them, and held it out to Aradin with a bow.

"Thank you, ladies," he praised both women. "Since I've only been borrowing them, I'll make sure to return these to their proper owner. When everything has been cleared up, of course."

"Just don't touch those nasty things while you're in the Dark," Josai reminded him tartly. "Or you'll be stuck in here again until someone can separate you."

"You also owe us both a dance, next turning of Brother Moon," Glenna added. "Be careful when cloak-swapping."

"I will," he promised. Bag in hand, Aradin turned to his right, took three steps, and arrived back at his Doorway. (*Ready to go?*) he asked Teral, stepping just far enough back to be out of the way, yet close enough to still hear.

(*More than ready; this hard pallet is not good for my back.*) Drawing in a deep breath to brace their body, Teral sank through the Doorway. Silently, the Witchcloak sank downward onto the cell cot. Unless the cloak remained exactly where it was, unnoticed and untouched, they would not be able to return to it.

Aradin kept his fingers on his Doorway while Teral pulled their flesh through. One short step, two—with their free hands clasped, the fingers of his other hand brushed the frame of the other, fuller Witchcloak, still hanging in Saleria's dressing room. Then, with Teral to anchor him, he released the other cloak and pulled himself into the new opening. Thankfully, the room was dark, for the deep hood was how the cloak had been hung on its peg. A gentle tug released it from the wooden projection, allowing him to step away from the wall and cast about for the lightglobe.

Which should be . . . two steps to the left, about head-height . . . there. His fingers bumped into it, summoning a gentle glow. Once he had enough light to see by, Aradin set the bag with the cuffs on an empty patch of shelving. He made his way to the refreshing room, freshened up, rapped off all the lights, and worked his way down-stairs. The moment his foot touched the ground floor, a board squeaked beneath it.

"—Back again, are you, you little snot? By the Gods, I think *not!*"

Aradin jumped back, tripped on the bottom step, and landed on his backside with a grunt. "Nannan!" he gasped. Or tried to. All that came out was a strangled wheeze. (*Dammit—the spell's still choking me from speaking?*)

He flipped the cloak folds over his body and quickly swapped places with Teral—who hastily threw up an arm to block the smacking of whatever it was the housekeeper had in her hands. A broom, from the rustling thump of it.

"Enough, woman!" Teral ordered, grasping the shaft and wres-tling it to a standstill. "This is *Teral*, not that little snot, as you so aptly named him."

"T-Teral? Oh, Gods!" Dropping her end of the broom, the housekeeper tried to cuddle him in apology. The Darkhanan Guide put up with it for a few moments, then pushed her off. Gen-tly, but firmly.

"Enough. Now is not the time nor place," he added. "I take it the little snot isn't here?"

"No—and I'll thank you to put a stop to this nonsense! I would've stopped him before, if the guards hadn't been here ear-lier. And I would have come up directly, if I hadn't been, erm, indisposed," she mumbled, blushing. "You know, in the refreshing room for a bit."

Teral held up one hand, determined to regain some dignity. "Please, nothing more need be said of the matter. I'll value the bruises you have given me as a sign of your devotion to your mis-tress' household, but there's no need to demonstrate more of your combat prowess. Your broom, milady."

Blushing again, she took back her makeshift weapon. "So . . . what will you be doing now?"

"I shall be preparing the Grove for Deacon Shanno's visit on the morrow. If he wants to handle the Grove, I say let him try . . . as in, try it at its worst."

Nannan blanched a little and clutched her broom close. "You . . . you're going to unleash it on the town?"

He hadn't considered going that far. "Er, well . . ."

A masculine chuckle startled the Witch. Not just Teral, but Aradin as well, for it came from neither of them. A deep, laughing male voice whispered in their minds. (*Now,* bring no lasting harm to anyone else . . . but prove beyond a doubt that the "little snot" has not what it takes to handle the responsibility of My Wedding-Grove.)

(*Ah, certainly, Lord Jinga,*) Aradin managed to reply. (*Certainly. We'd better get going—would You be willing to arrange our safe return to the prison cell, unnoticed?*) he asked daringly.

(*It would help further the illusion that Shanno is free to do as he pleases,*) Teral added.

The deep chuckle they heard was the only answer they received, for Jinga did not speak again.

(*Wait—my voice . . . ?*) Aradin asked. Nothing. Sighing mentally, he prodded his Guide. (*Well, get on with it. Even with only one of us able to speak, I can still cast whatever spells I've made an instinctual habit, so I'm not completely useless . . . but you'll still have to do most of the work.*)

(*Not* unless we *can distill a counter-potion from the communications sap, which we should be able to do quickly enough,*) Teral told him. Out loud, he said to Nannan, "It's best you don't know what I'll be planning, so you can claim on a Truth Stone you don't know what I'm up to or where I've gone."

If Aradin had been in charge of their shared body, he would have smacked his forehead. (*Of course! With magic that concentrated, it'd be like a modified Ultra Tongue brew! Not that I know how to brew one, but I* do *know the potion variety that allows you to learn another language permanently, and it does so by using an enchanted talisman. If I dunk all of the translation amulets we've collected over the years . . .)*

(First we have to get to the Bower,) Teral reminded him. *(The wards were not refreshed tonight . . . and given our charming visitor, I don't think we should do anything to restrengthen them just yet.)*

(Between you and me, we can keep the worst of the Grove's amalgamations from running free. We'll have to keep an eye out for whatever Saleria would've been here to control, though. Some *things can be let through to Groveham's streets,)* Aradin said. *(But as much as that little snot needs to learn a lesson in humility, the rest of the city doesn't need to have their homes invaded by walking clumps of clawed, thorny skunkweed.)*

Teral nodded and dusted himself off, heading for the back door. *(Right. We'll grab a pole from the pruning shed for our own safety's sake, and maybe to siphon and redirect some of tonight's wave of magic— amplifying it carefully—and then return to the Dark to see if we have been given a window of opportunity to return to the cell before the morning slops come round.)*

(Come now, it wasn't horribly bad. Those drippings were rather tasty, and there were a few scraps of beef in the bowl, plus a few vegetables,) Aradin joked. *(A bit mushy from being overcooked, but not too bad all the same.)*

"Teral?" Nannan's voice arrested the Guide. He turned in time to see her holding out a small bucket covered with a kerchief tucked into the top. "A bit of bread, some cheese, and smoked sausage slices, in case they didn't feed you . . . well . . . Aradin right, when they hauled him away. I didn't have time to actually cook anything. I'm sorry."

He smiled at her and accepted the luncheon pail. "We both thank you for your kindness. Rest assured, this will be quite enough. Aradin wasn't starved, though we've both had much better. Sleep well, Nannan. We'll make sure the house is well-warded before beginning the night's mischief."

"You'd better," she half-threatened. "Or I'll use my broom to smack you and that young Aradin, too."

FOURTEEN

(Would you like to see again?)

Saleria blinked, losing track of the conversation. Serina, Dominor, and Guardian Daemon of Pasha—who had accompanied his sister, the priestess selected to represent their nation's Patrons—continued discussing the feasibility of reopening the old cross-continental Portals, which had been vastly superior to the modest mirror-Gate systems used now. The Grove was a part of that network, since the untamed energies of its three rifts were causing a great deal of disturbance in the aether across Katan . . . but when that voice spoke, she listened.

. . . *Jinga?* she asked, and received the God's chuckle. *Is something happening in the Grove?*

The chuckle became a full-on laugh, and she found herself swept up in a warmth and darkness utterly unlike the chilling breathlessness of the Dark. This time when she landed, she seemed to be in the body of a rabbit or other small animal, for her view was low to the ground and half-sheltered by the leaves of a bush.

A strange sound reached her ears. It resolved into the voice of a young man yelling, of heavy, frantic running, and the crackling of branches breaking and being shoved aside. As Saleria watched, Deacon Shanno stumbled into view, twisting and swiping at some sort of dark green vine that had wrapped itself around his head like the tendrils of a cuttlefish. His fine white robes were stained with mud and greenery, leaves were plastered to his skin—leech leaves, she realized with a touch of alarm—and he didn't see the low rock in his way.

Tumbling to the ground with a yelp, he struggled with the cuttlefish-vine. The fall seemed to have stunned it, for its grip relaxed enough for the disheveled deacon to yank it off. Furious, he grabbed it by its tentacle-tendrils and bashed it against the rock several times, then flung it away. Shanno sat there panting for a few moments, then winced and started picking the leech-leaves off his skin.

"How could she make this look so easy . . . ? No, no," he corrected himself. "The Keeper was *not* doing her job. Well, I'm not defeated yet! By Jinga, I swear you'll learn to obey me! I'll burn you all to the ground, if I have to!"

Saleria lifted both of her brows at that. *Ah . . . Jinga? I really should intervene. Warped and mutated though they may be, the plants and animals of the Grove don't all deserve to die.*

(*Hush, My child,*) Jinga chided her, enveloping her in darkness once again. (*He is salvageable, if he can learn humility. That, and I have a bet with Darkhan going.*)

She came back to herself with a rush . . . and dropped her head into her palms. *Oh, Jinga . . . Your sense of humor is unlike any other I know . . .*

(You should speak with the priest-Exarch Melulose Filomen-Amon, who worships Tifrang, God of Mischief.)

There's a God of Mischief? She lifted her head, blinking. *And people worship Him? As their sole Patron?*

(Yep.)

With that, she was alone again in her mind. Vaguely, she heard Serina asking if she was alright, and managed a weak nod. *Maybe I don't want that Ultra Tongue potion Orana promised to get; I'm not sure I'd want to understand a culture that worships a God of Mischief.*

She refocused her attention on the conversation the others were having. Guardian Daemon was speaking now.

"... And *I* cannot do anything about the mid-latitude aether disturbances until the missing Guardian of Garama's Fountain shows up. As much as it pains me, you're going to have to leave Aiar out of your equations, Serina."

"But if I don't expand our efforts into Aiar, then I *have* to get Senod-Gra fixed!" the Arithmancer complained, tugging on her long, pale blonde braid. "*You* know what Keleseth is like."

"Then the solution to your problem is to *wait*, young lady," Daemon told her. "The prophecies are slowly coming true, which means the Garama problem will probably fix itself on its own. However, I should point out that Portals to various places in this world in theory can be seized and used to create Portals to other universes. Which includes the Netherhells."

Serina rolled her eyes in exasperation. "Not if you shield them correctly! Honestly, am I the only one who reads all the pre-Shattering texts anymore?"

"You're probably the only one with time, interest, and access to a library old enough, love," Dominor told his wife. The ornate bracelet on his wrist chimed, startling Saleria. He winced. "Right. Time to go relieve Queen Kelly of her duties for the evening shift.

I am very glad Rora volunteered to be the nighttime coordinator for the Convocation."

Kissing his wife, he headed for the door. Not every room had them; some were stone instead of wood like this one. Not every room had furniture, though someone had scrounged up a set of benches and two chairs for this room. But no one could say the location for the new Convocation lacked enough rooms for it. Serina sighed, watching him go, then glanced down at her napping twins. Today, they were cuddled together in a floating, spell-rocked cradle.

Guardian Daemon eyed them, too. The wistful look in his blue eyes made Saleria wonder why such a handsome, commanding man hadn't found a wife yet. Or even a husband, if such were the ways of his homeland. She ventured a question. "Do you like children, Guardian Daemon?"

"I do, though it's hard to juggle being the Guardian and having a private life. I can't wait until my sister Daria can speak to Pashon and Pashana about this stupid civil war tearing our country apart. The only bright side is that it's winter, which means the fighting has slowed . . . if not the jockeying for power," he muttered. "As much as I'd like to help you with your project, Serina, that, too, must be quelled and settled first, much like the aether. There are times when I could smack my cousins."

"I hope the Gods can bring a solution to your nation's problem," Saleria offered. "The only turmoil I have to face at the moment involves ambulatory blackberries, and a young deacon in need of a lesson regarding his unwarranted hubris."

"Sounds fascinating," Serina said, giving her slumbering son one last gentle caress. "We've gone on and on about my problems. Let's hear about yours—you said the rift-Fonts in your Grove actually get concentrated down into a sort of sap?"

"A concentrated sap? You mean, as in a magic-infused sap?"

Daemon asked her. "That's very odd-sounding, but I'd imagine it might be useful in various potions."

"That's what Aradin thought," Saleria agreed. "Witch Aradin Teral; I think you've seen him on Kerric's mirror-links? He's a Hortimancer, so he deals more with the base ingredients than the end result, but he has some interesting ideas on what the original Keeper who created the Bower might've had in mind for the sap."

"If you need help, I offer my services; I originally trained in Alchemy, though these days I have my hands full trying to keep the civil war from boiling over. With luck, my Gods will give me a solution to the problem so I can recapture all that wasted time with something I actually enjoy doing." Daemon frowned for a moment, then sighed and shook it off. "But back to the sap. If there's any chance I could get my hands on some samples of it, I could do some testing for you, maybe some experimentation, see if it's actually viable as a potion ingredient."

"Yes, it would be good to get a second trustworthy opinion," she said, trying not to think too much about the amusing-yet-sad image of Deacon Shanno stumbling through her unprotected Grove. "I'm not an Alchemist or a Hortimancer myself, but here's what Aradin told me about the Bower's sap varieties, and from what he's already tried, something of how they could be turned into potion bases . . ."

Aradin heard her coming. Though the exact words were muffled up until the point the stout wooden door was unlocked and pulled open, the stern alto scolding which the accompanying guardsman was receiving made the Witch grin to himself. Nannan in full fury was a force to be reckoned with, if one was constrained by laws regarding the safety and well-being of law-abiding citizens.

"—knows what you've been feeding the poor boy! I will *not* fail in my duties to the Holy Keeper's household by letting *you* poison him just because that daft deacon *says* he's guilty! And I *will* have that boy given a fair trial by Truth Stone, even if I have to drag Duke Finneg himself, Councillor for Conflict Resolution, all the way here from the capital!"

Levering himself up on one elbow, Aradin watched the pair stop by the guards' table, halted by the hand her escort raised.

"Technically, that would be the job of either Lord Stotten, Councillor for the Law, or Lord Gregus, Councillor for Foreign Affairs, as he is a foreigner," the guardsman stated. He wasn't one of the ones that had grabbed the Darkhanan, and didn't seem the kind to perpetuate a cruel misjustice. Then again, all Aradin had to go on was how the other man's tone lay somewhere between firm and weary.

"I don't care if he's one of my baked salmon and cheese pies!" she retorted. "Locking him up when he's only been doing Her Holiness' orders is the *real* crime here. Now open up that door so I can serve him a *real* supper," Nannan ordered, pointing her finger briefly at the bars serving as the fourth wall of Aradin's temporary home, before poking it into the teal-clad guardsman's chest. "None of that slop I wouldn't feed to a pig!"

His eyes narrowed, but he sighed heavily and gestured at the table. "Let me examine the contents of your 'supper pail' and I will see if it is safe to pass to the prisoner."

"You can examine it, but you haven't earned the right to eat it," Nannan bartered stoutly.

Amused, Aradin rubbed his chin. The housekeeper made a show of fussing and slapping the guard's hands when he tried poking and prodding, chiding him for, ". . . not knowing where those fingers have been lately!" and in general making up for all the aggravation she had given Aradin in their earlier weeks. Mainly because she was giving it to his jailers.

Finally, with an exasperated sigh, the guardsman led her to the cell. Curtly ordering Aradin to stay back, he allowed Nannan to step inside. She sniffed, wrinkled her nose, and brought the bucket over to him, muttering about nasty fingerprints in her good food.

It was good food, too; she actually remembered he didn't like pickled flavors nearly as much as Saleria did, for the seasonings were sweet and spicy rather than sweet and sour. Just thinking about the absent Keeper made Aradin wish the Convocation were over, so that she could take everyone to task for imprisoning him. He didn't have much time to mope, however. Nannan had more than delivering dinner on her mind, and she gave a piece of it to everyone within hearing range.

Today, that included four guards, Aradin, herself, and an older man who had drunk himself into disorderly conduct and had been hauled here to sleep it off, before working it off with some sort of compulsory service in the morning. Picking garbage off the streets, from the sound of it.

"Well. That fool, Deacon Shanno, seems to think he can handle the wildest beasts of the Grove, but let me tell you, he was in very sorry straits when he came in through the gate earlier! Torn and scratched and bleeding and covered in leaves and stains. Let me tell you, he looked like he'd been in a fight with a cross between a blackberry bush and a cat, and come out the lesser for it." She shook her head. "I have no idea what all that boy thinks he can manage, but the Grove is *not* one of them—if there weren't stout wardings etched into the very stones of the Keeper's house, why, I'd be afraid for my life, and I've been telling everyone exactly so, all afternoon long!"

Wait, why would she . . . ? Ohhh, clever girl, Aradin thought to himself. He merely nodded and used the spoon she had brought to dig into the first dish, vegetables and greens that had been cooked, chilled, then drizzled in honey and mustard for flavor. The stout stone walls of the city prison kept out most of the day's heat, but it was still warm down here, and the chilled dish tasted good.

Teral picked up on his meaning. (*Clever, indeed. She's also probably spreading word that Shanno cannot manage the Grove, along with word of the Convocation and the Keeper's presence at it, and our presence here, and how we're meant to tend the Grove at Saleria's expressed wishes. If we let the Grove mutations crawl over the walls . . . they'll wreak havoc in the city, and throw all sympathy for Shanno's self-professed declarations of competency right out the nearest window.*)

(*If we let the mutations crawl over the wall, the town will be in danger,*) Aradin reminded his Guide, frowning. Out loud, he pitched his voice just loud enough to carry to the guards outside the cell without seeming too obvious about it. "What about the wards on the Grove wall? Is he tending to those? Has he been pruning back the more volatile plants?"

Nannan snorted. "I doubt it. More like *they* have been trying to prune *him*. Aradin—as a Hortimancer—how much danger is Groveham in?"

"With Keeper Saleria gone off to represent Katan at the Convocation of Gods and Man, and myself as the only other person authorized, powerful enough, and knowledgeable about what the Grove mutations can do . . ." He dropped his already low voice into a grim bass warning. "It will *not* be good, Nannan. And though I am *here* in Groveham, as you can see they have locked me up. I am helpless to stop the coming wave of unmanaged, untamed mutations."

"*Wait* a moment . . . how can you talk? I thought we slapped a silencing spell on you!" one of the guards exclaimed. He pushed to his feet and stalked over to Aradin's cell, glaring at the Witch through the bars.

"Obviously, the will of the Gods allows me to speak," Aradin retorted dryly. He returned to addressing the housekeeper, knowing the other guards were listening. "The Grove is *nothing* to mess with. I don't know what this young deacon thinks he can do to control and contain it, when he hasn't even spent a single hour following Keeper Saleria around, never mind the month-plus it took me to train under her—and I, a mage-priest of twice his experience."

From the way Nannan was now smiling at him, her back thankfully to the guards, he had chosen right to play along. Though "play" wasn't the right word for it, since Aradin meant every word.

"Now, do not make his mistake. Do not go into the Grove yourself, and if you see anything untoward around the house, either run for the guard so they can fetch me to deal with it, or lock yourself inside, behind the many wards laid on that place," he cautioned her.

"At least I *have* a safe haven from the beast-bushes," Nannan told him. "What about the rest of the city?"

"If you know any mages, even those with only a little bit of power, have them go from house to house warding all the doors and windows. That won't stop the beast-bushes from roaming the streets, but it should give the people a safe place to hide. I'd fix the problem more directly, but all I can do is extend my apologies for anyone who comes to harm over this mess," Aradin sighed, shrugging expressively. "I have been cast into prison simply because a certain, foolish young man envies my position and covets what he thinks are its privileges, without comprehending its many duties, responsibilities, and pains in the posterior. Deacon Shanno's presumption and arrogance will cause this city to suffer. *Not* anything I would do . . . since what I *was* doing was everything needed to keep this city safe."

"Well, I'll at least try to make sure the food is far better than the accommodations. Eat up before it goes bad," she directed him. "When you're done, just hand the pail to the guards. I'll come collect it in the morning when I bring you a hot breakfast—you can let me out now, milords, now that I'm satisfied the man won't starve, or die of food poisoning."

"Oh, come now," the lead guard protested, moving up to the section of bars that formed the cell door. "What we serve wouldn't kill a fly. But what makes you think we'll let you bring in a hot breakfast for the prisoner?"

Nannan gave him a pointed look. "And just what sort of reaction do you think the *Keeper* will have, when Her Holiness finds out you've thrown her duly appointed, Gods-blessed assistant in prison for *doing his job*?" She *tsk*ed and shook her head. "I'd hate to be in your shoes, when the wrath of Heaven comes down on your heads."

"So you say," one of the other guards stated, lifting his chin. Aradin recognized him as the second man to put him in the anti-magic cuffs. "But *you're* just the housekeeper. You don't have your finger on the pulse of the Department of Temples."

Nannan exited the cell and gave the other speaker a sniffy look. "*You* don't *live* with Her Holiness day in and day out. *You* don't commune with the Gods on a daily basis like Her Holiness does . . . and like she *did* when she asked Them if Holy Brother Aradin had Their approval to work with her. Which is why *you* aren't getting a hot breakfast cooked by *me*."

And with that, she flounced out. Aradin was a little bemused by the sight of a somewhat plump, middle-aged woman stalking out with a huffy look and a bounce to her step, but Teral was outright amused.

(*Be very, very glad I find Saleria more appealing than Nannan,*) he told his Host, chuckling. (*That almost endeared her to me.*)

(*The food's endearing her to me,*) Aradin replied, spreading out the layers of carefully stacked plates tucked into the metal bucket. (*Roast beef cold cuts, four kinds of cheeses, that salad we both like of greens with that tasty honey sauce, a dish with chicken and fruit mixed with nuts . . . ah, Gods bless the woman. She's included one of her* cinnin *cakes at the bottom!*)

Grinning like a little boy receiving presents on his birthing-day, Aradin bit into the broad, flat roll. Unlike the ones found in his homeland, where the sweet added to the spice was found as an icing drizzled over the top, Nannan had figured out some way of injecting a thickened cream filling into the spice-infused, round, bready disks.

Teral sighed in the back of his mind. (*I'd chide you for not being a man and eating your vegetables first . . . but even I would eat her* cinnin *cakes above all else. Eat up, then rest. Tonight, we sneak back through the Keeper's house to the Grove and augment the wave of beasts that little snot must face.*)

(*You really like her nickname for him, don't you?*) Aradin asked.

Teral snorted mentally. (*He is one! If he were my son, I'd turn him over and blister his backside.*)

It wasn't often that Aradin got to turn the tables on his Guide and give sage advice. (*Now, Teral, you must remember he is young, and Youth Equals Stupid. At least, until the bludgeoning of a personal learning experience has been applied to a young man's head. Sometimes thoroughly applied, first.*)

(*I look forward to witnessing it,*) his Guide replied. (*Eat your vegetables. We'll need our strength.*)

Nannan brought the Witch a hot breakfast as promised, and for lunch, and for supper. She kept this up for two full days . . . then didn't appear with his anticipated lunch. Instead, Aradin Teral could hear even through the glazed windows the shouts of alarm and the cries for the guard. Something about strangling vines and tumbling weeds.

The guards didn't know what to make of it. He could make an

educated guess as to what was happening, of course, but he didn't speak up about it.

Lying on the narrow cot, hands tucked under his head, Aradin listened to them debating the matter in hushed tones. Should they hold to the requests which the young deacon had given them, or should they interrogate Aradin under a Truth Stone? Not every word was clear enough to hear despite the way he strained, even held his breath occasionally, but the Darkhanan still got the impression that Shanno had held some secret over the captain of the Groveham city guard, demanding certain concessions of the older man.

The current shift of jailers didn't know what that secret was, but it did impress them that the deacon would know some secret that would make their stern captain eager to obey. They finally ended their debate by deciding to just sit tight and wait. All three of them waited, Aradin and the two men in their leather armor and teal-colored tabards . . . until the ground started shaking with a rhythmic thudding.

The noise was accompanied by panicked shouts and screams of fear from somewhere outside. Levering himself off the cot, Aradin moved over to the window, stood on the tips of his toes, and peered out through the bars. He didn't see anything other than the multistoried wood and plaster building across from him for several long moments—then something grayish-brown, leafy, and bizarre strode past with an odd creaking sound between each *thump, thump, thump,* shaking the walls and the floor. An even louder sound escaped whatever-it-was, somewhere between a creak and a groan.

A rather wooden creaking, he belatedly realized. (*That extra magic we poured into the aether circling the Grove, all these nights?*) he reminded Teral. (*I think it just bore unexpected fruit.*)

(*Fruit, hell,*) Teral countered as something crashed and crumbled in the distance, accompanied by more frantic screaming. (*I think it bore an entire tree!*)

Sure enough, the huge thing came back. From this angle, Aradin could actually see partway up its tree-trunk legs. From the bits of long, slender leaves on the ends of drooping branches, he guessed it to be some member of the willow family, but the bark was thick, rugged, and much more auburn in hue than a proper willow gray. If he had to place the other parent tree, he would have guessed a redwood or some other conifer. (*I hope this didn't break off from one of the locus tree groupings.*)

(*That would be bad,*) Teral agreed grimly. (*I think we overdid it a little.*)

"—I've got it!" he heard Shanno shouting somewhere out of sight. The youth came closer, though Aradin still couldn't quite see. "*Ignifa shoudis!*"

Hissing noises sliced through the air, along with a faint glow of golden-orange light off to the left, and a *whoompf* sound that ended in a rising, groaning creak, the sound of a treeman screaming. Aradin wished for a stool, or that the cot could be pulled away from the wall, but it was firmly secured. Teral was a little taller and might have had more luck in his own body, but he didn't want to risk the guards knowing he could swap faces. All he could do was listen to Shanno cast a few more spells, hear the crackling and snapping of more than just moving tree limbs, and see the glow of increasing flames reflecting off the building across the street.

"There, that should do it," he heard Shanno proclaim in a grim, satisfied tone. Except there wasn't any crashing reminiscent of a tree hitting the ground, just the snapping of flames . . . and the creaking of limbs. The deacon's voice cracked in a yelp, followed by a bashing that shook the ground, but was too gentle to be the tree falling down. Sure enough, the deacon yelled, "*Why* won't you fall *down?*"

The treeman groan-roared and smashed again. Someone else screamed, "—My house! My shop! Fire! *FIRE!!* Somebody *help me!*"

"Everything—everything's under control!" Shanno called out. "Everything . . . Someone get a water mage out here!—Damn you, tree, why don't you *die*? All those stupid bush-beasts did!"

(*Because a tree is far larger than a fireball spell,*) Teral answered the deacon, his words heard only in Aradin's head.

(*And because it's covered in conifer bark, which is very thick and insulative,*) Aradin agreed, remembering his Hortimancy lessons. (*The exteriors of such trees might get scorched and the leaves burned off, but the core of the tree will continue to live, if it's large enough.*)

"Dammit—*hudorjen hudorsomm!*"

A long, heavy splashing noise was joined by a massive hissing. Moments later, a great cloud of steam and smoke billowed past his prison window. Faintly through the cracks around the edges of the glass-paned, iron-barred barrier, Aradin could smell burnt pine pitch. Shanno shouted his water-summoning spell again, splashing more liquid on the unseen battleground. The treeman thumped off into the distance, its flames hopefully extinguished.

Aradin could hear it evoking more panicked screams, and an occasional crash from its limbs swinging against whatever got in its way, or displeased it, or for whatever reason a treeman might rampage through a town, then it faded into the distance. He relaxed back onto his heels and sighed. (*No, this is not good for poor Groveham . . .*)

"What was out there?" one of the guards called out to him. "What did you see?"

Pushing away from the wall, Aradin crossed to the bars and braced one hand on the rune-chased metal. "What did I see? I *saw* very little from the window . . . but I could guess most of it from what I heard."

"So what did you *hear*?" the teal-clad man rephrased impatiently.

"I heard the warped amalgamation of an utterly untamed,

uncontrolled Grove-tree transformed into a living, moving, angry treeman, rampaging through the streets of your city, because I am locked up in here and am unable to do my assigned job as the Keeper's assistant. I *heard*," he continued tersely, cutting off the guard as the other man opened his mouth to speak, "Deacon Shanno utterly *failing* to destroy that treeman, and in fact, only enraging it further, into bashing into a house and setting it ablaze. I *heard* Shanno attempting to put the fire out . . . and the sounds of the tree-man moving on, continuing its rampage through town unstopped.

"I *heard* your fellow Groveham citizens crying out for help as their homes were damaged and set ablaze . . . and I *see* you sitting there, complicit in the deacon's arrogant stupidity, compounding the damages hour by hour of a situation already out of your combined control." He flicked his gaze over the gaping guardsman, then over at his equally slack-mouthed companion. "Tell the good deacon that when he is ready to admit he *cannot* handle the Grove, I will step in and bring it back into line.

"But tell him to hurry. The longer the Grove runs unchecked, the harder it will be even for a powerful mage-priest such as myself, or even the Keeper, to contain what he has let loose upon this town . . . and the surrounding countryside . . . and its neighboring lands, and their neighbors."

Returning to his cot, Aradin stretched out on it, wondering how much more of Shanno's madness the people of Groveham could take, and trying to let go of his mounting anger over the whole mess.

(*I swear, if I didn't trust Orana to bring back the true word of the local Goddess in this matter, I'd be doing a lot more than just "ride the wave to save the trees."*)

(*Actually, it's "ride the wave to* calm *the trees,"*) Teral corrected him. (*But if the little snot does get his head out of his rectum, you and I had best be prepared to counter all the madness out there.*)

(*It shouldn't be too difficult for most of it,*) Aradin sighed, thinking of the things he and Teral and Saleria had learned over the last few weeks. About the magic of the Grove, how it had gone wild, how it affected the denizens of the Sacred Garden, and how that magic was still tied to the three distinct resonances of each locus-tree's rift. (*Between you and me, we should be able to control two thirds of anything that comes of there.*)

(*Unless it's one of the two-rift mutations, or an exceptionally rare one-rift variety. If it's one of Saleria's, we'll have half or little chance at controlling it via our attunement to its rift-energies.*)

(*Oh, thank you. You're such a warm and shiny ray of positive thinking,*) Aradin mocked.

(*I'm dead. I'm allowed to be gloomy from time to time. Though I prefer the term "pragmatic,"*) Teral replied. (*Besides, normally you mock me for being optimistic.*)

(*True.*)

The people of Groveham didn't wait for the next day. Within an hour of the treeman's badly thwarted rampage, they flocked to the entrances of the guard hall and shouted for answers, for assistance, and for Aradin's release. Finally, the captain of the guard, the same mage-warrior who had silenced Aradin's voice, stalked into the basement and snatched the keys from one of the two men on duty.

"Damned citizens . . . damned deacon . . . Damned Department of Temples," he muttered, approaching the door. "Get out here, foreigner. You're being given *one* shot at proving you can tame the Grove. Nobody else in this town is strong enough as a mage, not even me."

Aradin uncurled himself from the cell cot, grateful he had chosen to use the facilities a few moments ago and didn't have to stop for that now. The *not even me* made him look closer at the other man.

Soot smeared his armor, and blood stained his tabard, a slightly fancier version than the other guards' covering. Some of it seemed to be the captain's own, for he had a fresh pink scar on his chin, the kind that said someone had applied some Healer's magic to seal it, though not quite enough to render it completely smooth. Another session or two might heal it scarlessly, if he had the time to spare for that.

"I've also heard how you broke my silencing spell *somehow*, so you're bound to be incredibly powerful. *If* you are what you say you are, then you will put that power to work protecting Groveham and restoring the Grove to a contained menace rather than a rampant one," the captain added, unlocking the door. He didn't swing the barred grille open yet, though, choosing to instead fix Aradin with a hard look. "Fail, and I will kill you myself. I can kill *men* far easier than those giant walking trees."

"I am the Gods-appointed assistant to Her Holiness Saleria, Keeper of the Sacred Grove. I am everything I have said, and more," Aradin said calmly.

The guard swung the door open. "Hold out your hands, so I can remove the anti-magic cuffs."

Aradin stepped through, then reached into one deep sleeve and pulled out the pink silk bag Josai had given him, unwinding the cords wrapped around its neck.

"I have stayed a guest of that cell for only one reason. I respect the word passed to me by Kata Herself that Deacon Shanno has needed a lesson in humility. If you have a problem with the disasters that have plagued Groveham, blame *him* for his arrogant choices, and the consequences therein. It was *his* choice to interrupt my solemn duties, weakening and ruining the protections woven by the Keepers of the Grove for the last two centuries . . . and *your* choice to assist him in making all of this happen."

As the guard blinked at his cold words, Aradin upended the bag. Belatedly, the captain tried to catch them, but the cuffs tumbled free of his grasp and clattered onto the neatly swept flagstones of the prison floor. Stuffing the bag back into his sleeve, Aradin flashed the other man a brief smile and strode for the door leading upstairs.

"After all, had I 'resisted' my arrest, it would have been the first actual act of law-breaking on *my* part."

(*Easy,*) Teral cautioned him. (*Not a word more. Don't overplay it.*)

(*I know how I'm playing this,*) Aradin said. He heard the captain tossing the cuffs on the table downstairs, and the guard's boots on the stairs catching up, but didn't stop. (*I'm going to exercise my authority as Saleria's assistant—or rather, according to prophecy, her Servant—and then hand over all the aftermath details to her, since she knows more about what would be an acceptable punishment than either of us.*)

(*Let me send word to one of the others to be on standby to fetch her,*) Teral offered. (*If we have giant treemen stomping around, who knows what else might have been created, or escaped.*)

(*Agreed. Don't be gone long,*) Aradin cautioned him, for time in the Dark sometimes flowed oddly compared to the living world.

(*Three steps, and I'm there; three steps, and I'm back,*) Teral promised, slipping out of his Host's Doorway.

Aradin headed for the street. Most of the townsfolk, trying to crowd their way into the courtroom on the ground floor, ignored him. The merchant who had sold him all those glass flasks, however, recognized him. "Hey . . . Hey! That's Aradin." Denisor pushed his way through the crowd. "Yes, it *is* him—this is the man Nannan says was handpicked by the Keeper to cover for her while she's at the Convocation!"

Quickening his steps, Aradin made it out onto the street before the tide of citizens overwhelmed him. They spilled out after him, calling out for his help—then skidded to a stop, eyes wide. He didn't even have to ask why; the creaking of wood behind him and the sobbing breaths of an utterly exhausted young man met his ears the moment the crowd fell quiet. *Teral, I need you!*

No reply. Spinning on his heel, Aradin flung up one arm, invoking a mage-shield. The treeman wasn't attacking the Darkhanan. Instead, the massive willow-pine had cornered a shaking, crying Shanno in the damp rubble below the house that must have been smashed and scorched earlier. The willow-pine creature, only vaguely man-shaped because it had two trunk-legs, poked at the faltering bubble protecting Shanno from its touch, and poked again. It didn't have an actual head, nor any real suggestion of a face, but the way its upper branches were tilted made it look like it was tipping its head in contemplation of what to do with its tormentor.

It curled up several willow branches at the end of one of its upper limbs into a knotted tangle of a fist, and lifted it high, preparing to smash down on that rubbery bubble.

Aradin firmed his will and reached for the resonances of the rift he had attuned to, pushing magic and mind into a single command. "Stop!"

The tree swung its canopy-head his way. It contemplated him for a few moments, then turned back to its target. Aradin bit back a curse—and felt Teral reaching his Doorway.

(*Get under the cloak! I have her with me!*) his Guide ordered. The treeman lifted its limb high once more.

(*Give me your power first!*) Aradin snapped back, and pulled on Teral's own magics, on his attunement. "*Stop!*"

The tree stopped. Its lesser twigs and leaves swayed, making Shanno shudder, but the thickest sections of the treeman ceased moving. Gasps escaped the watching townsfolk behind him, and a few cheers broke out. Aradin didn't pause; he knew Saleria was utterly untrained to keep herself alive and breathing while in the Dark, a trick only the strongest Darkhanan Witches could manage for long with their physical, real-world bodies. Spirit form was one thing, but flesh was entirely another.

Flicking up the hood of his Witchcloak, Aradin hunkered down, wishing it was the bigger, all-black cloak back at the Keeper's house. He did the best he could, however, whispering one of the spells all Darkhanan Witches had to master. "*Sonoxo mortori.*"

Darkness spilled out of his cloak, shoving aside the daylight. With his back to the happy townsfolk of Groveham, Aradin stepped back once, twice . . . and caught Saleria as she stumbled free, gasping for breath. A mutter dismissed the darkness, leaving her swaying in his grip, clad in the better of her two priest-gowns. She still had a half-eaten chicken-leg in her hand, and blinked owlishly at the streets, the frozen tree-thing looming over the sobbing deacon, and the gaping, crushed hole in the building behind the huddled blond youth.

". . . What in the Netherhells have you *done to my town*?" she demanded, her voice cutting through the happy noises behind her. She started toward Shanno, then checked her stride, looked at the drumstick in her grip, sighed roughly, and tossed it to the side of the street. "Interrupting my dinner, *ruining* my town—what is *this* thing?"

Shanno didn't answer. He was still a huddled ball of misery. Aradin moved up to join her, answering in the deacon's stead. "I think it used to be a willow. And a redwood. And possibly a fox, or maybe a ferret. It doesn't seem to have the fearfulness of a rabbit, at any rate."

"I don't care what it is. You, back to the Grove!" Saleria ordered, pushing some of her will behind her words. This close to the Grove, she was once again within reach of the rift to which she had been attuned.

Aradin and Teral backed her wordlessly, pushing their own energies behind her command. The treeman creaked, shifted, and started walking. Mindful of the fact it might just keep walking around the Grove if it didn't have a purpose, Aradin ordered firmly, "Find a sunny spot inside the Grove, and plant yourself."

"You heard what he said," Saleria added, confirming his command. The tree relaxed its knotted branches, letting them brush the walls of the buildings it passed or trail on the ground with little scraping sounds interspersed between the *thud, thud, thud* of its makeshift feet. It turned a corner, some of its higher branches visible over the tops of the city's roofs, and kept going toward the Grove.

As much as she wanted to yell at the blotchy-faced, huddled figure of the young deacon, to rail at him for allowing Groveham to be so badly harmed, with who knew what damage to buildings, and injuries to people . . . she refrained. Drawing a deep breath, she let it out slowly, then did it again in the meditation techniques for calmness which all novices were taught. In fact, she began the ritual prayer-chant for such things, moving closer to Shanno as she spoke.

"I call upon Kata, Goddess most serene, to calm my troubled mind and soothe my ire-filled soul," she recited, her eyes on the disheveled younger priest. "I call upon Jinga, God of inner strength, to teach me to let go of my anger, rather than hold on and let it tear me asunder."

Shanno's face, tear-streaked and blotchy from crying, came into view as he slowly uncurled. Licking his lips, he moved them near-silently, echoing her words. Reciting the meditation ritual with her helped ease most of his trembling when she continued.

"I call upon Kata, most benevolent, ever-wise, to remind myself that most troubles are fleeting and thus not worth fretting over. I call upon Jinga . . . I *call* upon Jinga . . . ?" she prompted him, stopping just a length or so away.

"I . . . I c-call upon Jinga . . . to help me admit my weaknesses . . . to strengthen my character . . . I'm *s-sorry*! I'm so sorry!" he sniveled, wiping his dirty sleeve across his face. Some of the dark stains and red patches remained, for they were bruises, not soot or shame-stirred blood. "I didn't know—I'm so sorry I did this to Groveham!"

"Well, now you *do* know what the Grove is capable of, Shanno," Saleria said, studying the upset young man. She might not have been the best priestess in the world at that moment herself, either, for she couldn't feel any real sympathy for him. Every single bad choice leading straight to this situation had been a free-willed choice made by him in spite of her many warnings. "Now, having seen it firsthand, do you think you have the power as a mage to command and control it?"

The deacon shook his head rapidly, his hair sliding across his shoulders. A twig with a few willow-style leaves had tangled in the light gold locks at some point, proving he had narrowly escaped several attacks. "N-No. I don't . . . I won't *ever* have that m-much power. I c-couldn't even . . ."

He gestured lamely at the destruction, shifting to sit on the lightly charred, cracked, plaster-covered boards that had once been part of an upper story wall. Saleria folded her arms lightly across her chest. "And now that you *know* this . . . what do you plan to do about the results of your misjudgment?"

She nodded pointedly at the rubble under his backside, then lifted her chin at the hole in the building overhead, and tipped her head toward the rest of the town and the other signs of treeman-wrought wreckage.

Sniffing hard, Shanno looked around, then hung his head. "I . . . I'll use my magic to . . . to help fix everything. Everything I can. But . . . there's beasts and things and bushes, and a second one of . . . of those trees . . . *please*, help save the city! I'm so sorry, Holiness, I didn't mean to cause any harm! I—I just thought . . ."

"Next time, when someone tells you what your limitations are, give careful consideration to whether or not there are actual limits to what you can do, Shanno," Saleria told him. "Because every single mortal in the whole of this world has areas where we are weak. I myself am incredibly ignorant of foreign lands and foreign ways, but I am not ashamed to admit it. And I will never cook as well as my housekeeper, Nannan. But it does not pain me to admit that, either.

"My strength as the Keeper of the Grove may seem enviable, and something worth grasping . . . but you have not seen the thorns lurking on the branches you would grab. Well, now you have," she allowed, then firmed her tone. "And now you will get up and *shield* all these people, Deacon, with what magic you *do* have. Go inside, *stay* inside," she ordered, "and wait for Aradin, Teral, and me to corral and contain all the creatures your weaknesses have let loose."

Nodding, he pushed wearily to his feet, staggered a little on some of the crumbled bits of wall, then limped toward the guard hall.

Saleria watched him go, then moved closer to the very welcome face of her assistant and lover. Under her breath, she asked, "You know more about what's been going on than I, so . . . how are we going to do this?"

"I know only parts of it," he returned in a murmur of his own. Gesturing along the path the treeman had taken, he started walking with her toward the Grove and her home. "Teral has an idea, now that he's seen all three of us controlling that thing with our attunement."

"I'd like to hear it, Teral," Saleria stated, looking straight at Aradin. It was a subtle courtesy she had seen some of the others at the Convocation giving to Orana Niel.

Aradin almost handed his body over to his Guide, but checked himself. Now was not the time to be swapping consciousnesses, not when Teral had far more experience at watching for danger out of the corners of his Host's eyes than he himself did. "Teral says most Guardians work in conjunction with their Fountain, at their Fountain, to cover the area affected by its magics. That it's easier to start from that strongest position. And that . . . ah . . . yes, and that it's possible to set up scrying spells to track down anything carrying the taste of the Grove's locus-rifts."

Saleria nodded, reasoning it through. "Yes, that makes sense. Since most of the magic has been confined within its walls all this time, the stuff that reeks of the Grove outside those walls should be easy to find."

"It may take time, but if we sweep around the Grove and the outlying land in the same direction the aether circles, we should be able to use the crest of the wave to augment our own efforts—that's my own suggestion," he added.

She smiled slightly, skirting another patch of rubble. "Considering you didn't preface it with 'Teral says,' I figured as much."

He smiled back, and caught her hand. "I've missed you. How much longer will the Convocation take?"

"Another week or so—is that an azalea bush? With little snake heads for flowers?" Saleria asked, taken aback at the raggedly spherical bush-thing slowly moving up the street. It did so by shifting its serpent-heads to make itself sort of tumble and roll this way and that.

"I . . . really can't say," Aradin replied cautiously, unsure he wanted to get close enough to tell. "The real question is, with, what, forty heads? With forty heads . . . what does it eat, and with what part does it excrete?"

Caught off guard by the oddball question, she chuckled and leaned into him, letting their shoulders bump as they walked. "I've missed you terribly, too, Aradin. Both of you, Teral. I can only stay a day or so; the Nightfallers want me to be on hand to represent

Katan when the, ah, priest of the Independence of Mandare—
some rude, woman-hating kingdom somewhere to the east—has
his chance to speak with his God."

"Oh?" Aradin asked. "I've heard of the Mandarites, and they're
just southeast of Darkhana by a few weeks of sailing. But Katan is
its own continent, with no other neighbors other than Nightfall.
What have they to do with you?"

"It seems they've tried to invade and claim Katani and Night-
faller territories for their own without either of our nations' permission, and Queen Kelly wants me to help lay out some strict ground
rules for their future behavior. Particularly if they ever want to get
near the Convocation again." She shrugged, then stopped, watching
the snake-bush thing warily. "I think it's spotted us. Let's tell it to
head back, and anything else in our path, shall we?"

"Right. *Back to the Grove*," Aradin and Teral ordered the mutation, putting rift-power behind their combined will. The serpent-
azalea hesitated, fumbled a bit, then got itself lurching into
movement the other way.

"*Go on*," Saleria urged with voice and will, making it lurch-
tumble a little faster. She swung their clasped hands a little. "I'm
not going to be able to stay longer than a day . . . but at least I do
mean a full day. Hopefully this won't take that long to clean up.
The Grove-escapees, I mean. I, um, won't be able to stay long
enough to help put Groveham back together. I have to head back for
the Mandarite thing."

She wrinkled her nose at the other signs of fighting and fire-
damage.

Aradin squeezed her fingers. "I know what you meant. We have
about an hour until sunset, locally, but we don't need daylight to
track magical energies. The first thing we need to do is walk the
wall and repair it, since somehow I doubt that treeman used the
door to your house."

"He was certainly almost tall enough to just *step* over the wall. Or she, or whatever it was," Saleria agreed. She shook it off, and squeezed his hand lightly. "Kata and Jinga gave me visions of you and the deacon over the last few days. You in that cell, Nannan bringing you your first real meal . . . Some of what Shanno suffered was funny, but this . . . *This* isn't funny. I honestly don't know what to do. About assigning penance, or punishment, or whatever. Restitution I guess is the best word."

Glad he didn't have to explain what had happened to him to keep him from stopping Shanno, Aradin gave her some of the ideas he'd been mulling over during his daylight incarcerations. "Fine everyone involved. Hit them in their income. Shanno, the captain of the guard he somehow blackmailed into helping imprison me, the other guards . . . take some of their wages and share it out to all the people whose homes were damaged. Make them labor by hand and by spell to restore what was ruined in these last few days."

She mulled that over, then nodded. "That's a good idea. It forces them to live with the ongoing troubles they have caused, days and months and years of consequences, because they didn't take a few extra minutes to really *think* through in advance what would honestly happen if they made the wrong choices. I'll have to consult with Prelate Lanneraun, and then with the Department of Temples, though. I may be the highest-ranked cleric here in Groveham, but I'm not Shanno's superior, never mind the prelate's."

Aradin winced in memory, touching his stomach. At her concerned glance, he brushed off her worries. "Oh, it's nothing. I'm just remembering how much Lanneraun made my stomach hurt with all the laughing I did."

"Oh, Gods . . . he didn't tell you the weasels in the wedding cake story, did he?" Saleria asked with a wince, instantly sympathetic when he nodded. She touched her own stomach. "I was sore for a full week after he told me that one—I'm sorry I forgot to warn you about that old man's wicked sense of humor. And yes, I know they're technically ferrets, but 'weasels' sounds better."

"Yes, it does," he agreed. "By the way, Teral says the serpent-bush is slowing down. He thinks it may need another command."

"Or maybe it's just getting tired because it's an azalea bush with snake heads instead of flowers," she countered. "But I guess we can give it a magical push to keep it moving—I will be so heartily glad when we get the Grove tamed and returned to *normal*. Or as close to it as we can. A year from now, five years, or fifty . . ."

"We'll get it done," he promised her.

FIFTEEN

With the wards on the wall unpowered, two chunks of the stone barrier had been damaged enough to let plenty of bush-beasts through. There were two other treemen wandering around, too; one had headed northeast into the hills away from Groveham, and the other southeast into farmland. Saleria paused at the house to have Daranen dig through the Keepers' archives in the basement of her home to look for instructions on how to repair the wardings, and focused on that aspect of the work for several hours. She had to unward and unlock the main gates to allow all the scattered mutations to return safely to the Grove, but at least that way they wouldn't undo all the repairs she had to make.

Aradin headed into the Bower to start reining in the ever-circling energies of the Grove with Teral's help. Since all that power had to go somewhere, they used the excess magic to start identifying, tagging, and compelling anything within four days' walk with the resonance-signatures of their two locus trees to return to the Grove, find a place to plant themselves, and rest. When Saleria joined them—laden with a basket of food picked up from Nannan, filled with good energy-boosting vegetables and stamina-boosting meats and cheeses—most of the bush-beast mutations were on their way back. Adding her locus-rift's powers to the mix made the resulting combination of spells look like it was going to catch everything that had escaped over the last couple of days.

By that time, it was near dawn, the air cool but promising the heat of another late-summer day. Aradin sighed and leaned against one of his tables, the one the basket was still on. He plucked out a handful of nuts and raisins from one of the wide-mouthed bowls the housekeeper had packed, and looked around the Bower. The soft pastel nodules embedded in the roots and branches forming the Bower dome were no longer static lights; some shone brightly, linked to the spells the three of them had woven. The rest pulsed slowly with the flow of energies being managed, forming a rippling, soft rainbow over their heads.

Somewhere out there to the east, he could hear the creak-and-thump of one of the treemen returning and looking for a place to take root and rest, as commanded. The eastern sky above the hills had turned from star-strewn black to a dusky shade of dark blue, and a few of the local birds were starting to twitter. Tired though he was, he took a few moments to chew and contemplate.

Saleria moved up beside him and leaned back against the table, too. Sidling close, she sighed and leaned against him, letting her temple rest on his shoulder. "A lot of work . . . but a good night's work. Yes?"

He nodded, swallowed, and offered her the last few nuts and raisins in his hand. Gently grasping his fingers, she pulled them open and nibbled the treats directly from his skin, then pressed a kiss to the center of his palm.

Aradin smiled softly and closed his fingers around the lingering imprint of her lips. He tucked his arm around her and rested the side of his head on the top of hers. "An interesting week, I'd say. I'm glad Nannan told you no one was killed in the rampage. I'd hate to have that on my conscience. And your permission to 'do anything it takes' also helped . . . even if it was a bit backward, saving the Grove by wreaking havoc with it."

"Blame that one on Shanno, because you were saving it from him." She shook her head slightly, not enough to dislodge their comfortable side by side cuddle. "Enough of him . . . You know, Kata and Jinga approve of you. In the Grove, and in my life."

No fool, Aradin knew what that meant. As devout as she was, having Their approval would mean everything to her in regard to a relationship with him. He breathed deeply again, enjoying the lightening shade of the eastern sky. It was on its way from dark to medium blue now, picking up hints of green in anticipation of the pale yellow of sunrise. His favorite time of morning.

By chance, his gaze fell on the now nearly circular, bed-sized patch of thick, green moss at the very center of the Bower. The sap residue had been successfully cleansed from the Bower cobblestones, though there was still more than enough to cause problems out in the rest of the Grove if one touched the soil with a bare hand. But that patch of moss had been left alone because it made for a very thick, comfortable cushion for his beloved to kneel upon and pray each day.

No doubt she would want to pray upon its cushioning surface at least once before leaving Groveham for the Convocation . . . but his mind thought of another use for the bed-thick material. "Saleria, my love . . ."

"Yes, Aradin Teral?" she replied, letting him—them—know she fully accepted Teral's presence. If there was one thing she had learned about relationships while at the Convocation, it was that her God and Goddess did not object to these two men sharing her life at the same time.

"I'm speaking for just myself, Aradin, right now," he corrected her. "What say I send Teral off into the Dark, so we can honor the Wedding of Kata and Jinga right here in the Bower, hm? Or would that be blasphemous, making love in here?"

She grinned. "It would actually *not* be blasphemous. Before the Grove turned into a hazard, the previous Keepers had the right to shoo everyone out of here by nightfall . . . but nothing prevented the Keepers themselves from coming back in at night to do just that. But . . . you don't have to send Teral away."

Both Host and Guide stilled. Aradin blinked, not quite daring to breathe. Teral hesitated, then reached through the physical contact Aradin had with Saleria. (*Are you absolutely sure, my dear?*)

"Yes. You can stay and watch. And, erm, enjoy. Secondhand," she amended, a little nervous with her choice even knowing it was the right one to make. Twisting a little at his side, she looked up at Aradin. "You see, I love Aradin deeply . . . but I've also come to love you. I've come to understand just how close your lives are intertwined. And I honestly accept that . . . and in accepting it, I accept you. Except I'm still a bit nervous about having you here, so let's just have Aradin take and keep the lead this first time, hmm?"

Aradin could feel Teral's sub-thought urge to kiss her. Acceding to her wishes, he leaned in and did it himself . . . but opened up his thoughts and sub-thoughts to his Guide so the older Witch could experience everything freely. The soft warmth of her lips, the slight hint of raisins and almonds in their taste, and the feel of her curves as she shifted to press her body against his . . . (*Glorious,*) Teral breathed into both their minds. (*Beautiful, and glorious . . . and even a bit "magnificent."*)

Reminded of Aradin's comparison of her legs to the thettis-vine mutation, Saleria broke the kiss with a chuckle. She stepped back from Aradin, moving toward the moss-covered ground. "Come here, both of you," she told the man in front of her, "and help me recreate the wedding nights of both our Gods and Goddesses."

Host and Guide stilled. Teral recovered first, since he wasn't confused by her double-meaning. (*I, ah, told her about the wedding-gift of the Moons to our God and Goddess . . . but I don't think she meant it that way.*)

(*I didn't think so, either.*) Out loud, Aradin cautiously stated, "As lovely as that suggestion is . . . first of all, you said you wanted only *me* to make love with you this time, and just let Teral watch. And second of all, both Brother and Sister Moon have to be up in the sky. You can only have one of me right now, even if that was your intent."

Saleria blushed bright red at his blunt reminders. "I, er . . . that is . . ." She cleared her throat. "Ahh . . . one little step at a time, alright? I'm not sure . . . I'm, um . . . oh, bollocks," Saleria muttered, still blushing. "Maybe—*maybe*—one day, but right now . . ."

"You're not sure at this point if you could," Aradin finished for her, pushing away from the table to join her. Catching her hand, he continued on toward the mossy sward at the heart of the Bower. "Don't worry; neither of us are offended, either way. In fact, we both consider it an honor that you're willing to let Teral enjoy the moment secondhand. But as it is *my* moment . . . my deepest wish is for *you* to enjoy this moment."

Allowing herself to be tugged in his wake, Saleria stopped with him at the edge of the ragged circle and started removing her clothes. To her surprise, he didn't shrug out of his Witchcloak; instead, he pulled the folds around his body, hiding his clothes for as long as it took her to unfasten her priestly gown and pull it over her head. Once clear, she glanced his way again, expecting him to begin disrobing.

Instead, he let the front edges of the Witchcloak drape open to either side, revealing his now nude, lean frame. Saleria pouted, gown half-folded in her hands. "That's not fair. You can get dressed and undressed in the Dark, too?"

"With Teral's assistance, yes," Aradin admitted, flashing her a smile. "He just hasn't been around to help put my clothes away until now."

She pout-scowled. "*Definitely* not fair."

Grinning, he gently took her robe from her and stuffed it up the broad, black-lined interior of one sleeve. It started pulling itself in on its own accord at about the halfway point, or rather, under his unseen Guide's touch. He took the other garments she removed, too; her underthings, socks, even her boots, then removed the Witchcloak once they were stored and neatly folded it. Setting it on the cobblestone path circling the prayer-moss, the Darkhanan Witch gently tugged her into his arms and kissed her forehead.

"As many drawbacks as there may be to sharing one's life with another soul, there are some nice advantages to compensate," he admitted, holding her close. "It's not the life I originally envisioned for myself . . . but it has led me here to you."

"And the Grove," Saleria agreed.

"And *you*," Aradin asserted, hugging her. "I can find a gardening job anywhere in the world. Easier ones, for sure. But you are unique and special, Saleria, and I . . ."

(*Not easy to say the words, is it?*) Teral sympathized privately.

(*I can* think *them just fine, as you well know*,) he muttered mentally. (*I just don't want to mess this up when I ask her to be my wife.*)

Teral snorted. (*Tell her, then show her, and you'll be fine.*)

"I love you," Saleria said.

Aradin blinked, staring at Saleria. She hugged him and repeated herself.

"I love you, Aradin. I love Teral in there, too. And I want enough of this Grove fixed fast enough that we can be the first mortal marriage celebrated in here," she added, pulling back just enough to poke a finger into his naked chest, "so cleaning it up had better not take fifty years."

"Yes, my love," he agreed, gently catching her hand. He drew her finger to his lips, kissing it. "I—we—love you deeply, too. And it would be our joy to be your husband for as long as we all shall live, if that is your desire."

She smiled and ducked her head. Placing her hand against his chest, she felt his heart beating, and felt her own respond. Saleria looked up into his hazel eyes. "That is my desire, yes." For a moment, she hesitated, then gathered her courage, leaned in close, and murmured into his ear, "Teral tells me you like it when a woman rubs you . . . there . . . with her feet."

The twitch of his manhood against her thigh was all the proof she needed. She didn't need the sound of Aradin's soft groan, or his muttered, "That dead rat traitor . . . !"

Chuckling, she tickled his chest and stepped back, up onto the mossy ground. "Is he really a traitor, Aradin, when it's something you want to receive, and something I want to give?"

He groaned again, because she had a point, and because her willingness made his whole body ache.

"I just . . . don't know how to do it, is all," Saleria admitted sheepishly. "I've never done that before with a gentleman."

Moving away reluctantly, Aradin lowered himself to the ground, then patted his crossed legs. "We can get to that later, since it's usually easiest done when both people are sitting in chairs or something. Come here, love, and sit on me. I want to kiss you thoroughly."

Saleria stepped onto the moss, but did not straddle his lap. Instead, she balanced herself carefully on one foot and gently placed the other on his thigh. Checking his expressions to see if she was getting this right, she wiggled her toes. The movement inadvertently inched her closer to his groin.

Breath hitching, Aradin bit his bottom lip. Fire, delicious, impassioned fire, seared his nerves with each tiny shift of her foot incrementally closer to his loins. His manhood had been ready ever since seeing her naked—and always halfway ready any time he was in her presence, as if he were a full decade younger—but this had him jutting up proudly, blatantly.

She slid her foot along his thigh, caressing his skin and the soft hairs on it, but her balance wasn't perfect. Seeing her wobble, Aradin held up his hands. Saleria accepted them with a grateful smile, then went back to concentrating on stimulating his body with her foot.

(*You know,*) Teral stated, startling both of them, (*this would be considerably easier with your air-walking spell, so she could just sit on a floating bit of mist and play with you that way.*)

Saleria blushed bright red. Aradin grinned . . . then lost it, mouth agape, when she spoke.

"Well, if you'll kindly *cast* it, Teral, I can do just that, rather than wobble around like an idiot. Hand him control for a moment, love," she ordered.

It took him a few seconds to remember how to breathe. Licking his lips, Aradin snapped his fingers, conjuring a little puff of mist. It expanded into a vague armchair-shaped cloud. "I can cast it myself, you know."

"Well, I insist the two of you teach me it at our earliest convenience," she stated, checking her position versus the mist before settling into the makeshift seat.

A little flick of Aradin's fingers wafted it up against the backs of her knees and then some, bringing her feet very much into range of his groin. In fact, as soon as she was seated, he grasped her ankles, settled her soles on his hip bones, then stretched out on his back. Sighing happily, he tucked his hands behind his head.

Distracted by the way his muscles flexed and moved on his lean, fit frame, Saleria caught the arch of one of his eyebrows—a trick she still couldn't figure out how to do—and realized she was neglecting her side of things. With the mist-chair supporting her weight, she was free to slide her feet everywhere. Up onto his belly, where his stomach muscles tensed with a laugh, down onto his thighs, where he spread them apart slightly, giving her access to trail her toes along their insides. When she gently nudged his bollocks, he gasped and arched his back, fingers digging into the thick moss.

Saleria played with him for a little bit, circling around the base of his shaft, then finally tipped her feet and slid her soles up along the warm, silken flesh jutting up from his groin. For her part, this was just a thing of curiosity, of different textures and the fascinating ways he reacted. But oh, how he reacted! Liquid seeped from the flushed-red tip, and the whole shaft throbbed and jumped when she gently caressed it with her soles.

Soft groans became louder ones, which mutated into helpless whimpers. Finally, his hands flew from clutching at the moss to clutching the tops of her feet. Cupping them around his shaft, he helped guide her up and down, up and down, his hips flexing in counterpoint. Face flushed, skin glistening with sweat, mouth open and eyelids strained shut, he looked beautiful to her.

That was the word for it: beautiful. Men were normally handsome, but lost in his passion, Aradin was beautiful. What had started out as a simple act of wanting to pleasure her lover, and which had become an act of curiosity along the way, morphed now into an act of pleasure for her, too. It excited her to see and hear him so needy, so urgent. Saleria found herself speaking aloud, encouraging him.

"Yes, love, yesss . . . Find your release with me—enjoy my feet! You feel so hot and good against my toes," she told him. "It's making me tingle all over; I can't imagine how good it must feel for you . . . yessss. More—more! Harder!" she added as he bucked upward. "More! Give me your love!"

He tried to say her name, but it emerged incompletely in a cross between a yell and a hiss. Pushing up between her clasped feet, he came. It felt glorious, and so satisfying—the first time in well over a year that any woman had been willing to fondle him this way. The other ways were good, even great, but this . . . this was a special treat. One made all the more special because it was a beautiful, precious gift from the woman he loved.

Sated and smiling, he relaxed into the moss and blinked sleepily up at the pastel-lit wickerwork of the Bower dome. His fingers stroked her ankles, then patted and released her feet in silent thanks. While she chuckled and dug her toes into the moss, wiping part of the mess he had made onto the green tufts, he focused on enjoying the afterglow while he stared upward. Beyond the brown-barked, blossom-dotted tangle, the sky had brightened to the vivid medium blue found on morning glory flowers.

Wait . . . blossoms? He blinked and stared upward in confusion. (*Teral, am I imagining this, or . . . ?*)

(*No, I see them, too.*) Teral started to say more, but Saleria rose from the mist-chair, her attention clearly still on Aradin's body and not on the odd change in the dome overhead.

"Well, that was a lot more fun than I thought it'd be," she purred, dropping onto all fours to straddle his hips and lower her head to his. Kissing him gently, she nibbled on his bottom lip, then deepened it for a moment. Ending it, she smiled at him. "I think we can do that again sometime."

"Mm, yes," he growled, twining his fingers in her soft, golden hair. Bower blossom questions could wait. Pulling her close, he kissed her thoroughly.

Teral took brief control of one hand, dismissing the mist-chair with a snap, then gave the limb back to Aradin, who rolled onto his side. Guiding Saleria onto her back, the younger Witch stroked his other hand down her body. He followed his hand with his mouth, nipping and kissing, licking and loving every inch he caressed.

Some of the areas he went to were ones he chose to please; others were suggestions murmured by his Guide. From her breathy moans and the fingers stroking and tugging through his sandy blond locks, both had a good idea of what the Keeper of the Grove found pleasing. Aradin didn't stop until he had reached her feet, praising her generous loving and repaying it with a bit of foot-worship, kissing and kneading and stroking until she trembled and clutched at the moss.

Her thighs parted enticingly when he finally set her feet down, settling them to either side with her knees bent. Enjoying the sight, Aradin started to rock forward to worship her inner folds, but hesitated. Aside from his steady breaths and her uneven ones, beneath the twittering of birds and chirruping of insects waking up and greeting the rising dawn, there was one more sound. The intermittent *plip*s and *plop*s of sap-droplets falling into their collection pools.

Saleria frowned in confusion when he pushed back from her, rising to his feet. ". . . Aradin?"

"Stay right there," he cautioned her. "Don't move." Casting around, he hurried over to a worktable with his alchemical supplies. One of them was a jar of clean glass rods, with smooth, impermeable surfaces perfect for stirring ingredients without fear of contamination.

Selecting one, he picked his way across the Bower to one particular vine, one with a clear, faintly amethyst sap. Touching the end of the rod to one of its droplets, he gently coated the very tip with a small bead. He carried it back to her, and found her still with her knees up and thighs parted, but with her gaze fixed on the canopy of the Bower dome.

"There are flowers up there," Saleria stated quietly, frowning in confusion. "Not many, but there have *never* been flowers on the Bower itself. Well . . . not since the Shattering. Daranen says he's run across occasional mentions of the gazebo-dome being covered in blooms, but I don't remember the details. Do you think it's because we've reconvened the Convocation of the Gods?"

"I think that's a question you will have to pose to Them when you return," Aradin told her, dropping to his knees between her feet. Sliding his hand up her shin to her knee, then down to rub her inner thigh, he recaptured her attention. He lifted the stirring rod, displaying the tiny drop of sap on its tip. "Do you know what this is?"

Saleria started to shake her head, then blinked and blushed, feeling his fingers shifting to the crux of her thighs. Breathless, she felt him gently part her folds, exposing the little pleasure-bud they concealed. A moment later, her blue gray eyes widened in comprehension. He grinned at her, leaning forward, and she held up a hand, trying to forestall him. "That's . . . no. No, Aradin. That'd be too much. Don't—ahhh . . . *Bollocks*!"

Grinning, he touched the droplet to her flesh. The temperature of the liquid was the first sensation, a tingling coolness that was more akin to chewing a sprig of mint than sucking on a chip of ice. She felt the hard, smooth-rounded end sliding over and around her nubbin, felt the tingling liquid soaking into her skin. Felt every nerve prickling to life with icy heat. Dimly, she heard him murmuring once more for her to stay right there, but she couldn't have moved anyway.

It was rather like descriptions she had heard of poison-leaf, the oils of which caused an itchy rash which scratching only made worse. Panting, she clung to the moss, knees carefully splayed apart, convinced that if she touched her throbbing flesh or even just pressed her thighs together, the passion rising in her would burn and burn and burn until she had rubbed herself raw in frenetic need.

The sweet, loving bastard returned, knelt once more between her thighs . . . and this time slid the droplet-tipped rod up *into* her. She convulsed with pleasure, nails digging deep into the thick greenery. That only made it worse, for her hips snapped, wanting more sensation, more thrusting and filling and pleasure from the too-slender, too-hard glass shaft. Aradin had to press down on her belly to hold her still while he worked the rod in and out a few times. Worse, he turned it, coating her in pleasure internally.

"B-Bastard! Bastard, bollocks, b-buhhh!" She couldn't think of any other b-words to call him or to curse with; her body was melting, turned into liquefied fire by that second drop. She was a burning sap-pool of flesh and need.

Withdrawing the rod, Aradin rose and carried it back to the jar, muttering a strong cleaning spell twice to be sure it was safe. He didn't want to just toss it aside and risk the brittle glass breaking, not when his intent was to make love to her thoroughly. Once it was tucked back into the jar, he returned to find her legs fluttering open and shut, her hips twitching and rolling. Crouching, he crawled over her—and found her legs snapping up and around him, ensnaring him as fast as that thettis-vine.

With a hard twist, Saleria rolled him onto his back. Settling over him, she growled and nipped at his chest, his collarbone, his chin, until her loins were snuggly settled against his. She rocked against him, nestling his re-hardening shaft among her potion-doused folds. The sound of his breath catching pleased her, but it wasn't enough. Reaching between them, she grasped his shaft and teased the head into her opening . . . then sat up, sinking down onto him.

That scratched the sap-itch. She hummed softly in pleasure, in brief satisfaction, then rocked up and dropped again. And again, and again and again, until she had to toss her hair to get it to stop clinging to her sweating face, until he had to cup and guide her hips for fear of losing his place. Back behind her ears in that spot where she heard the voices of Kata and Jinga, where she heard Teral's, she could hear the Guide groaning in pleasure. She heard Aradin's, too, with her outer ears, and grinned.

"Thought you could . . . mmm . . . infuse *me* with pure lust . . . without consequences?" she panted, struggling to think.

Aradin grinned and pulled her down, pinning her on him. "I was planning on it! But first . . . oh, Goddess . . . I was going to . . . to . . ."

It was hard to think. Saleria leaned over him, palms braced on his chest. "You were going to . . . ?"

He looked straight into her eyes. "Lick you."

His tongue darted across his lips. Saleria shuddered, undone by the blunt promise in his words, in his gaze. Flinging her head back, she rode him through the waves of her bliss, rode him through his, and let the aftershocks carry both of them onward, around and around.

Overhead, every vine and branch and bark-covered root in the Bower burst into bloom, the translucent blossoms so thick, their petals could have blocked out the rising light of the sun, if they hadn't glowed like fragments of stained glass.

They slept as hard as they had made love. The first to wake, Saleria breathed deep, stretched languidly, and rolled onto her back.

Opening her eyes, she found the Bower dome still covered in blossoms, blotting out half the sunlight and not really giving her a clue as to the time of day, other than somewhere vaguely in the vicinity of late morning, midday, or early afternoon.

A moment later, a blonde head swayed into view. Startled, Saleria stilled and blinked. Her first impulse was to cover herself, to demand who the intruder was and how they got past the wards. Her second thought came on the heels of realization. The *who* was Kata, and She was quite capable of getting past a mere mortal's shields.

Kata smiled down at her, an impish sort of look one might expect to see more on the paintings and sculptures meant to represent Jinga, not Her. (*Good afternoon, My dear.*)

My Goddess . . . Oh bollocks, I'm naked in front of my Goddess. She started to wince, then opened her eyes in a panic, glancing at the man at her side. *Aradin is naked in front of my Goddess!*

Laughter filled her head, sounding like perfectly tuned bamboo wind chimes. (*Did you not say that We see you even when you're sick in bed? Don't be silly, Keeper. I have manifested not to ogle your bodies . . . though he is a nice one, isn't he?*) Kata observed on a smug, feminine aside. (*. . . But rather to let you know what We have done to the Grove. When you return to the Arithmancer, let her know the aether in western Katan will be calm and still by the end of this Convocation.*

(*For your safety and for Groveham's sake, My Husband and I have rounded up all the stray mutations, and separated those with components that were too dangerous to keep, yet too dangerous to let loose. The rest . . . They have either been restored to pure specimens, or will have usefulness in the days and years and centuries to come. But what that use is . . . that is* your *task, the three and four and more of you to come. And you will still have to tidy the paths and catalogue what's left before you should let people in without an alert escort,*) Kata told her. Or rather, told both of them.

Aradin mumbled something, pawed at his face, wiped some of the sleep-sand from the inner corner of one eye, and squinted up at Her. His voice was deeper than usual when he formed coherent words. "*Thank* you. Your intervention is deeply appreciated, and Teral and I truly appreciate the shortening of our task. But, umm . . . Why is the Bower covered with flowers?"

Kata spoke out loud, lips curved in Her beatific, serene smile. "*What, that? Oh, that always happens whenever a Keeper makes love with her or his true love in here. It's a side effect from when Jinga and I . . .*"

"I don't need to know, honest," Saleria quickly interjected. Naked and sated from lovemaking and rest, she twisted onto her side and held up her hands. "I'm overwhelmed enough by the mortal version. I don't need to envy the godly kind."

Jinga's boisterous laugh filled the Bower. He came striding into view through the eastern path, one of Saleria's crystal-topped pruning staves resting on His shoulder. The end of it glowed red, and in its light, every flower within reach grew visibly larger. "*No worries, Keeper. When you join with the right person for the right reasons, it is always special. Not necessarily as intense every time, but special.*"

He offered His hand to Saleria, who accepted without hesitation. It was warm and strong, like clasping solidified sunlight for all that it seemed to be an ordinary brown hand. There was no fear in her, no worry; she had His approval, and that was all she needed.

The moment she stood, she could feel her body covered in soft fabric. A glance down showed it surpassed her best Keeper's garb. The tunic and trews were pure white edged with a rainbow of flowers stitched along the edges of the sleeves, hemlines, and neck in appliquéd silk. Her overrobe had long sleeves instead of the sleeveless vest version she was accustomed to wearing, and when she released Jinga's hand to finger the collar, she discovered the slight weight behind her shoulders was nothing less than a deep hood.

A glance at Aradin showed him being helped to his feet by Kata . . . and a ripple of black that flowed down over his body. It, too, was covered in silk flowers at all the hems. The plain black edges of the neck-to-toe opening did not have flowers, but the cowled hood did. Amusingly enough, the clothes beneath the mostly black cloak echoed hers in cut and flower, save that the main color was also black, where hers was white.

Bemused, she looked at her Patrons. With Their approval of not only her work as Keeper, but of her choices in life, she was not afraid. In fact, she dared to tease the Boisterous God a little. "Does my cloak come with access to the Dark as well? Instant clothing changes and all?"

"No; that would require you being dedicated to Our divine companions, and We will not part with our best Keeper in centuries," Kata told her. *"These robes—yours and his—are for the Keepers of the Grove to wear, not for Witchly needs. Aradin Teral's has a Witchcloak lining stitched into his, but it will be removed by Us when it is time for both of you to retire."*

"You both will be able to prune or wither, bloom or transport any plant within the Grove with just a thought and a touch while you wear these sacred robes," Jinga told her. He paused, then shrugged His shoulders. *"That, and on any patch of soil you tread, you'll leave a trail of tiny flowers in your wake. You might find it annoying after a while, so I suggest taking it off when you're not being official."*

"They have been crafted to mark Our favor upon you, and to ensure no one can doubt that We approve of your joint continued management of Our Grove," Kata stated, giving Her mate a quelling look. He accepted it graciously.

"You still have some serious work ahead of you before you can safely reopen the Grove to anyone else," Jinga warned both of them. He shrugged and spread His hand expressively. *"Things like the bleeding*

hearts, which must be contained and studied before any varieties can be cultivated, or even encountered by the unwary or unprepared. But the treemen have been restored to mere trees, and things like the snake-bush and the thettis-vine are no longer a concern."

"When you are ready to open the gates and once again celebrate marriages in Our Grove, do invite Us to your own wedding," Kata told them. She took Aradin's hands in Hers and kissed his cheek, then did the same to Saleria.

"We'll be the first ones to wed in here," Aradin promised Her. "And You'll be the first ones to know the date, right after we do."

Jinga chuckled and wrapped an arm around the Darkhanan's shoulders, squeezing him. *"Fate already let us know."* His other arm wrapped around Saleria for an equal hug. *"Now get to work. You have only three hours to eat your luncheon, gather your supplies, and inform the people of Groveham that everything is once again safely under your control."*

"And . . . Shanno?" Saleria asked, wondering what They would have to say about that.

"We only grant miracles when they are needed," Kata chided her gently. *"The rest, We leave in your hands. That's why it's called free will."*

Releasing the pair, Jinga held out His hand to His Mate. Kata accepted it, the pair stepped into a shaft of sunlight peering down through the blossoms shrouding most of the Bower . . . and vanished.

Saleria stared at the empty air, her heart as light as that sunbeam. It took her a few moments to realize she still had a thousand questions, about the new condition of the Grove, how long it would take them to render it safe for visitors, about the Netherhell invasion, and so much more. But They were gone. ". . . *Bollocks* to that."

"Bollocks to what?" Aradin asked, bemused by her expletive.

"We've just had our task lightened by your Patron Deities, and you're upset?"

She flipped her hand at the shaft of light. "They left before I could ask all the rest of the questions I've been wanting to ask! A load of bollocks, sneaking off like that . . ."

He chuckled at that, and wrapped his black-clad arms around her from behind. Kissing her temple, Aradin murmured, "Never change, Saleria. Remain the brilliant, blunt, beautiful inside-and-out woman that I love."

(*What he said*,) Teral agreed in the backs of both of their minds. (*Though I do wonder what They meant by "gather your supplies" . . . ?*)

Saleria blinked, her mind blank for a moment. Until her gaze settled on one of the nearby vines, its sap trickling slowly down around the flowers dotting its length. "Oh! Right. Guardian Daemon. He wanted some samples of the sap to analyze. He actually trained as an Alchemist—not so much a Hortimancer, but he says he knows his potions, salves, and brews."

Aradin looked around the Bower and slowly started nodding. "Yes . . . Yes, I think I can see which ones he'd want to experiment with right away. It'll probably use up every flask with a stopper I bought from the merchant here in town, and we'll need a large chest with some cloth for padding . . . that is, if you're not afraid of helping carry it through the Dark."

She shook her head, nuzzling her cheek against his. "It can be a very unsettling place . . . but with the two of you, knowing you, trusting you, working with you at my side . . . I'm not afraid, Aradin."

"You're not?" he asked, pleased by her acceptance of the odder aspects of his conjoined life.

"Not even with the threat of the Netherhells looming up ahead . . . and the annoying knowledge that They aren't going to help us so long as we have the power to help ourselves," she muttered, covering his arms with her hands. A contented sigh escaped her. Unlike in her dream of several weeks ago, she wasn't going to be forever bound in chains of duties and vines to an ever-worsening problem. "Nope. I'm not afraid."

Song of the Guardians of Destiny

When serpent crept into their hall:
Danger waits for all who board,
Trying to steal that hidden tone.
Painted Lady saves the lord;
Tower's master's not alone.

Calm the magics caught in thrall:
Put your faith in strangers' pleas,
Keeper, Witch, and treasure trove;
Ride the wave to calm the trees,
Servant saves the sacred Grove.

Cult's awareness, it shall rise:
Hidden people, gather now;
Fight the demons, fight your doubt.
Gearman's strength shall then endow,
When Guild's defender casts them out.

Synod gathers, tell them lies:
Efforts gathered in your pride
Lost beneath the granite face.
Painted Lord, stand by her side;
Repentance is the Temple's grace.

Brave the dangers once again:
Quarrels lost to time's own pace
Set aside in danger's face.
Save your state; go make your choice
When Dragon bows unto the Voice.

Sybaritic good shall reign:
Island city, all alone
Set your leader on his throne
Virtue's knowledge gives the most,
Aiding sanctions by the Host.

Faith shall now be mended whole:
Soothing songs kept beasts at bay
But sorrow's song led King astray.
Demon's songs shall bring out worse
Until the Harper ends your curse.

Save the world is Guardians' goal:
Groom's mistake and bride's setback
Aids the foe in its attack.
Save the day is Jinx's task,
Hidden in the royal Masque.

—BY SEER HAUPANEA